ANYONE SO HEROIC

Callista approached the tall man who'd saved them. His back was to her, and she realized the shirt taut across his barn-wide shoulders wasn't cavalry issue. And the revolvers that rode low on his hips rested in quick-draw holsters.

"Thank you for routing the Apaches, sir. Where are the remainder of your colleagues?" she asked.

He turned with disconcerting swiftness, radiating such fierceness that it made her heart lurch against her ribs. His face was all harsh angles and planes, his skin tanned by the wind and sun.

But it was his eyes that stopped her in her tracks. They were the color of steel beaten into swords—and just as hard. Callista swallowed a gasp as he gave her a sharp blow of a look that stripped away her clothes and saw all the way to her soul. A look that seared her and made her want to run for her life.

Steel-hard eyes, she thought. *Steel-hard man.*

**Winner of the National
Readers' Choice Award
for *ARIZONA RENEGADE***

Other AVON ROMANCES

Coming Soon

And Don't Miss These
ROMANTIC TREASURES
from Avon Books

Avon Books are available at special quantity discounts for bulk purchases for sales promotions, premiums, fund raising or educational use. Special books, or book excerpts, can also be created to fit specific needs.

For information, please call or write:
**Special Markets Department, HarperCollins Publishers, Inc.,
10 East 53rd Street, New York, NY 10022-5299.**
Telephone: (212) 207-7528. Fax: (212) 207-7222.

KIT DEE

BRIT'S LADY

AVON BOOKS ▨ NEW YORK

This is a work of fiction. Names, characters, places, and incidents either are the product of the author's imagination or are used fictitiously. Any resemblance to actual events, locales, organizations, or persons, living or dead, is entirely coincidental and beyond the intent of either the author or the publisher.

AVON BOOKS, INC.
An Imprint of HarperCollins*Publishers*
10 East 53rd Street
New York, New York 10022-5299

Copyright © 2000 by Melitta K. Dee
Inside cover author photo by Image Bureau
Published by arrangement with the author
Library of Congress Catalog Card Number: 99-96439
ISBN: 0-380-80693-2
www.harpercollins.com

All rights reserved, which includes the right to reproduce this book or portions thereof in any form whatsoever except as provided by the U.S. Copyright Law. For information address Avon Books, Inc.

First Avon Books Printing: March 2000

AVON TRADEMARK REG. U.S. PAT. OFF. AND IN OTHER COUNTRIES, MARCA REGIS-TRADA, HECHO EN U.S.A.

Printed in the U.S.A.

WCD 10 9 8 7 6 5 4 3 2 1

If you purchased this book without a cover, you should be aware that this book is stolen property. It was reported as "unsold and destroyed" to the publisher, and neither the author nor the publisher has received any payment for this "stripped book."

To Delmar Kolb,
the first artist in our family.
A great uncle, a wonderful friend,
and a dog person, too.

Chapter 1

⌒◯◯⌒

Friday, March 23, 1883

Dispatch to the *Times/Tribune* Newspapers

I alighted from the train in New Mexico Territory with great trepidation. Here I must leave this most civilized mode of travel and go west by horse and carriage.

The officers of Fort Grande and their ladies welcomed me with a sumptuous dinner in a magnificent two-story hacienda. Afterward, I retreated to my quarters to prepare for the rest of my journey.

Tomorrow I leave for Fort Bowie, Arizona Territory. As I will be traveling through Apache country, I will have a military escort for protection. I venture forth into this vast wilderness of desert and mountains with excitement and uneasiness. What will the coming weeks bring?

Until next time, this is Callista Warwick.

"Don't worry, Miss Warwick, I'm saving bullets for you and your mother," Lieutenant Caruso yelled as he dived behind the boulders where Callista hid. Crouching beside her, he levered his rifle open and began to reload.

1

"What are you talking about?" Callista Regina Warwick frowned at the brown-haired, younger man. "My mother and I can't shoot." She rested her white-gloved hand on his arm. "Go ahead and use them."

He grimaced. "No, they're—" Another shot boomed through the canyon. He hunched over the rifle he had steadied on the breastwork of boulders. As if unwilling to face her, he muttered, "They're in case the Apaches overrun us."

"Overrun us? What . . . ?" Suddenly she realized what he was telling her: the bullets were for Mamere and her. "Oh, no!" She slumped down against the boulders as the canyon and soldiers spun around her in a kaleidoscope of sand and army blue.

"Here, Miss Warwick, are you going to faint?" His rifle clattered to the ground as he grabbed her shoulders. "You're white as a sheet."

The hammering of her heart was so loud that he sounded as if he were far away, talking down a long tunnel. She shook her head, afraid that if she opened her mouth, she would scream.

Get hold of yourself! "I won't faint," she gasped through tight lips. She waved him away, pretending a strength she didn't have. Without the support of the boulders, she would have collapsed in a boneless heap. She pressed her hand to her bosom, as if that would slow her galloping heart.

He nodded, then braced his rifle on the boulders and took careful aim at the Apaches high on the opposite slope. Callista clamped her hands over her ears, but even so, she recoiled as the gun's roar rumbled through her. The sulfur smell of gunpowder filled her nostrils and left a foul taste in her mouth.

She peered down the line of soldiers crouched behind boulders, at her mother, to see if she was all right. They'd become separated as they ran for cover.

Everyone was pinned down behind the boulders at the base of the canyon wall. Bright green mesquite trees grew among the rocks, providing feathery shade. On the other side of the narrow canyon a tiny stream gurgled through the rocks, its path marked by sycamores stretching white, winter-naked branches toward the deep blue sky.

Rifles boomed on both sides of her, startling her. The booms echoed and reechoed between the canyon's rocky white walls. Slowly they died away.

Leaving a waiting silence.

A green-winged dragonfly hovered over the stream, its hum carrying clearly in the stillness.

"H-how are we doing?"

Lieutenant Caruso glanced up at the sun. "If we can hold them off until nightfall, we've got a good chance. Apaches don't like to fight at night."

She followed his gaze. "But it's only midmorning—there are hours until sunset."

"But we've got an advantage. Notice how few shots they're firing? It means they're low on bullets."

"But we're trapped here."

They had just come around a landslide that partially blocked the canyon when the Apaches had opened fire. She and Mamere were in the open carriage Mamere preferred, and the lieutenant and sergeant had swept them to safety amidst the boulders.

"Can't you send someone for help?"

Lieutenant Caruso shook his head. "He'd be out in the open, and the Apaches would pick him off before he could get away. We're safe as long as we stay behind the boulders."

The minutes passed, long as hours, silent as a grave. Even though it was only March, the heat built up between the canyon walls until it felt like a summer day. Callista plucked at her serviceable brown-cotton traveling dress. It had been crisp with starch when she put it on that morning, but now the starch seemed to have melted out of it. Out of her, too, she thought, pulling out her handkerchief and dabbing at the moisture beading her forehead.

Minute by minute, she waited. A bee buzzed past her and nosed into the yellow flowers growing from a cleft in the boulder. Beauty amidst death? Were they all going to die in this barren canyon?

How had it come to this? When she'd attended Miss Porter's Academy for Young Ladies, she'd studied the classics in their original Greek and Latin. She'd learned needle arts and deportment, so important to a lady. She'd even attended gymkhanas where she competed—in a ladylike way, of course—in horsemanship and archery. Nothing had prepared her for this fiercely wild land of rugged mountains and mesas.

Her hands were ice-cold within her gloves, and she clasped them tightly in her lap, telling herself to remain calm. *As if she could!*

She sniffed experimentally as woodsmoke drifted past. What was burning? The wagon! With her books and Mamere's special mattress! The things they would use to bring civilization to their temporary home in Arizona.

Leaping up, she peered over the boulders. Orange flames licked at the side of the freight wagon and gray smoke swirled around their possessions.

"Get down!" Lieutenant Caruso yelled, grabbing her arm and yanking her down behind the boulder as guns boomed. One of the troopers farther down the line gasped and stood up, then tumbled forward, into the open.

"Don't move, man," the lieutenant yelled. "The Apaches won't waste bullets if they think you're dead."

Yet he was saving two bullets for her and her mother. The cry of a hunting eagle knifed through the canyon like the wail of dying woman. Its shadow passed over her as it sailed on the wind high above. Was this how her life would end? Would the last thing she saw be Lieutenant Caruso's revolver as he pointed it at her?

The eagle shrieked again. Just as the last echo died away, a volley of gunfire broke the stillness. But none of the troopers around her were firing. Where—?

"Look! On the ridge above the Apaches!" a soldier shouted as he pointed.

The troopers surged to their feet and began to cheer.

A man in cavalry blue led the charge, sending his huge red horse bounding down the slope. He grasped the reins in his teeth and held a revolver in each hand.

"Hurray!" Callista cheered along with the men. The cavalry had arrived—they were saved!

Turning to meet this new menace, the Apaches scrambled over boulders, trying to get a clear shot at him. The soldiers around her rained bullets on the newly exposed Apaches, sending them scurrying back among the rocks.

His horse was dodging so violently around boulders that Callista knew the stranger couldn't aim with any accuracy, but he still fired at the Apaches who popped up from behind rocks shooting at him. Dust and gun smoke swirled around him, blurring his outline and making him seem larger than life.

Suddenly realizing she was shouting like a crazy woman, Callista clamped her hand over her mouth and glanced around to see if anyone had noticed her unladylike behavior. She didn't want to do anything that would embarrass Papa at his new command.

"Stay down!" Lieutenant Caruso yelled. "The Apaches will make a run for it, and they'll come this way."

"How do you know?"

"They don't want to get trapped in this canyon, so they'll head for the open desert." He rested his rifle on a boulder as he took aim.

Callista crouched, but watched through a notch between boulders. She heard the blood-curdling cries of the Apaches before she saw them. They lay flat on their horses, firing at the soldiers as they galloped past. The clouds of dust churned up by their ponies' hooves were so thick she couldn't see how many there were. The troopers ran to their horses, mounted, and raced after them.

Callista listened as the clatter of hooves on gravel gradually faded away, then she sprinted along the low wall of boulders to where her mother sat, her eyes closed, her hands clasped tightly in her lap, her lips moving in silent words. "Mamere, are you all right?" she asked, kneeling at her side and clasping her hands in Callista's.

"Are the savages gone?" Her mother's eyes flew open, and she squeezed Callista's fingers. Her eyes were red-rimmed.

"Yes. Mamere, did you see that man charging down the slope with his guns blazing?"

"I saw no such thing. Really, Callista dear, you sound like you're writing another of your dispatches. Is our conveyance ready?"

"There hasn't been time to right it yet. You stay here, and I'll see to it. I'll be right back."

Callista emerged from the boulders. Russ Caruso was all the way across the canyon. Much closer was a tall man in dark blue. His back was to her, and he was speaking to the wounded man, who was leaning against a boulder.

Walking up behind him, she realized that the shirt stretched taut across his barn-wide shoulders wasn't cavalry-blue. And the revolvers that rode low on his slim hips rested in quick-draw holsters.

"How are you, trooper?" His red stallion pranced at this side, tugging at the reins he held loosely.

"Weren't nothing but a scratch, sir. I'll be fine."

"Good. We'll have you taken care of in no time." His deep, gravelly voice vibrated across her skin like the wind ahead of a thunderstorm, and she shivered with a strange uneasiness.

Quelling the odd feeling, she walked up behind him. "Thank you for leading that charge and routing the Apaches. Where are the remainder of your colleagues, sir?"

He whirled with disconcerting swiftness. He radiated such fierceness that it gave her goose bumps and made her heart lurch against her ribs. His face was all harsh angles and planes, his skin weathered by wind and sun, the lower half darkened with beard stubble.

But it was his eyes that stopped her in her tracks. They were the color of steel beaten into swords—and just as hard and sharp. She swallowed a gasp as he gave her a sharp blow of a look that stripped away her clothes and saw all the way to her soul. A look that seared her and made her want to run for her life.

Steel-hard eyes, she thought. *Steel-hard man.*

* * *

The feminine voice coming from behind Britton Chance was husky as a dance-hall girl's. Surprised, he whirled.

"Judas Priest!" he muttered, giving her an up-and-down inspection. She didn't match her voice at all. Not in any way, for she was tall and decidedly thin. Her hair was the rich golden yellow of ripe corn, but that was all he could tell, because she'd skimmed it back into such a tight prissy knot, it was a wonder she could blink.

Her high-necked brown dress, which was suitable for a convent, crackled with enough starch to stand by itself. And she wore white gloves!

He shook his head, not believing what he was seeing. What did she think, that she was parading down New York's streets? He'd seen other women who were unprepared for the harsh reality of Arizona, but she and her white gloves were easy winners for the most out of place.

A single golden lock had dared come loose from her knot during the Apache attack. It curled over her shoulder so softly that he wanted to feel it and see if it was as silky as it looked.

"Well, sir?" Her eyes were a soft lavender that reminded him of lilacs, and he drew a quick breath, surprised by the color—and her direct gaze. "Your cohorts?"

"My cohorts?" Brit rubbed his hand over the five-day-old stubble blackening his jaw. Good Lord, did she think he led a bunch of men who went around rescuing people from the Apaches?

"The colleagues with whom you peregrinate." The breeze stirred the loose curl over her cheek, and she captured the offending strand and smoothed it back into her prissy knot.

"Peregrinate?" Lordy, she sure did like big words. "Do you perhaps mean, travel, ma'am?"

Her chin went up. "If you choose to employ that appellation."

He nearly laughed at her uppity tone. "There aren't any cohorts, lady. Just me."

Turning away, he stalked toward the smoldering wagon.

"Wait." She fluttered along beside him like an angry brown wren, half-running to keep up with his long strides. "But—" She glanced at the slope he'd come down. "You descended that incline in a solitary manner?"

"Give the lady a cigar," Brit muttered. He walked around the scorched wagon, studying its contents. Trunks, a burnt chair, a charred mattress.

He kicked the rim of a broken wheel propping up one corner and it collapsed, dropping the back end of the wagon into the sand. A cloud of ashes swirled up, carrying the stench of burned feathers.

"My father is Marsden Warwick the Fourth, the new commander at Fort Bowie," Miss Starch said crisply, "and that's his furniture you just dropped into the dust."

Brit stiffened at the mention of Warwick. Miss Starch was Warwick's daughter? Why hadn't General Crook warned him Warwick had a daughter?

"The fourth, eh?" Did she think that would impress him? "The fourth is going to have to make do with burnt wood, not furniture."

Russ Caruso hurried up. "Miss Warwick, this is Britton Chance," he said, saluting Brit automatically. "He used to be Lieutenant Chance, Chief of Scouts."

She scanned him with a coolly dismissive look. "In what army?"

How could such a sexy voice sound so damned icy? Brit flicked two fingers against his battered, sweat-stained Stetson in a deliberately negligent salute.

"I am no longer in the one that fights Apaches for people like you, Miss Warwick the Fourth." Anger flashed in her eyes, but he didn't give a damn. Not when she was Warwick's daughter.

"How are things at the ranch?" Russ Caruso asked quickly, before she could reply.

"Lots of work to do. I'm glad to be out of the army." He watched Miss Warwick out of the corner of his eye. She was staring past him at the wagon. What the hell was she looking at?

"Fire burns up, doesn't it?" she asked.

He turned, following her gaze. "Yes. Why?"

"The burning arrow landed high on the side, and fire burns up. That means—" Brushing past him, she pulled off her gloves and stuffed them in her skirt pocket. Ignoring the wisps of smoke still curling up, she reached over the tailgate and tugged at a blackened wood panel covering the contents. "The boxes underneath this panel might be all right."

"So?" Oh, for God's sake—she was worried about her damn clothes.

She pulled at the panel, but couldn't lift it out of the wagon. "Would one of you remove this wood so I can examine my books?"

"Books!"

She turned slowly and tilted her head as she gave him an I-dare-you-to-object look. "Yes, books."

I should have known better, Brit thought grimly, as he lifted the panel and swung it off the wagon. Why would a woman wear a dress as ugly as hers if she had prettier ones?

She leaned over the wagon side and peered at the scorched wooden crates. "My book boxes are on the bottom, because they're so heavy. Can we get them out, so I can open them?" She shoved the top crate, trying to move it.

"There could still be hot embers in there." He set the panel down where it would be out of the way.

"I am well aware that embers could remain, and am being suitably cautious to avoid—" She snatched her hand back and sucked her forefinger.

"Could have fooled me," he said dryly.

She flicked him a glare that should have peeled the hide off him, except that she was still sucking her finger, which spoiled the effect. She turned back to the wagon and moved along the side, peering in. "There's got to be a way to get the boxes out."

"Get some shovels, Russ."

Within minutes Brit had two men using the shovels to slide the heavy wooden boxes out of the wagon. The first one they flipped to the ground broke open, spilling books across the sand like leaves of green and blue and burgundy.

The girl knelt among them as if they were old friends and began flipping pages in book after book. "They look all right. Not even singed. Wait, here's one." She riffled the pages. "No, even this one isn't bad." Standing up, she moved toward the second box.

Brit stepped into her path. "Before you open that box, you may want to think about how you're going to transport them. The men's saddlebags will take just so many. You'll have to leave the rest."

Dismay washed across her features. "Leave them? Now? When they didn't burn?" She glanced around frantically, then pointed at the overturned carriage. "The barouche!" She flashed him a triumphant smile.

"The seats lift up. There's storage underneath."

"For all of them?"

"We'll see how many—"

"Callista, are we ready to go yet? Why is everyone just standing around?" A white-haired patrician-looking woman emerged from the rocks. "Let's depart before those savages return."

Callista, eh? He'd remember that. Even if she hadn't been wearing white gloves, Brit could see the physical resemblance immediately, but the older woman had much more meat on her bones and walked with a stiff, slow gait, as if from rheumatism or illness.

"Look, Mamere." Callista gestured at the books tumbled into the sand. "My books didn't burn. They're all right."

"Books? We're standing around here because of books?" the older woman said in a trembling voice. "When those savages could return at any moment?"

"The books aren't holding us up, ma'am," Brit said. "We'll be righting your carriage and leaving presently. In the meantime, some of the men are chasing the Apaches away right now."

She picked up her lorgnette from where it rested on her ample bosom and peered at him. "And who are you?"

"This is Mr. Chance, Mamere." The girl mouthed *thank you* at him as she walked over to take her mother's arm. "He's the man who broke up the Apache attack. Why don't we wait for our carriage over in the shade of that tree?"

"Russ, check on the men who followed the Apaches and see if they're headed back to us," Brit said, easily slipping back into the habit of giving orders. Russ hurried away, while Brit turned his attention to the overturned carriage.

As the women walked away, Brit heard the mother say, "I wonder how long we'll be out in this wild country."

"Probably not long. You know Papa wants us here when he captures Geronimo. The newspapers will hail him as the hero who saved Arizona, and we'll be the family who believed in him and braved this wild land to be with him. Then we'll go home."

The women moved out of earshot. Did General Crook know that Warwick thought he'd capture Geronimo? Brit wondered. No, he would have told Brit when they'd talked. And it sounded as if Warwick thought it would be as simple as snapping his fingers.

As she walked away with her mother, Callista glanced over her shoulder at Britton Chance. To her eyes he'd seemed a giant charging down that slope, scattering Apaches like tenpins. She'd never in her whole life been so relieved to see anyone. It was mind-boggling to think that a single man had routed the Apaches. And frightening to realize how little the situation had changed if they attacked again.

"Callista." Her mother stopped abruptly. "If your books didn't burn, maybe our clothes are all right, also. Did you check our trunks?"

"I forgot about them, but I will." She'd packed her pretty dresses and worn the most drab, conservative ones she could find on the journey, in hopes of fading into the background, so the soldiers would forget she was around and she could listen to their conversations.

"What am I going to do with you?" her mother

said, shaking her head even as she smiled. "How can you forget about our clothes?"

"I was mentally composing a dispatch about the Apache attack. You know I would have remembered them eventually." She led her mother into the fernlike shade of a mesquite tree. "Let's get you settled until we're ready."

Callista knew her father wanted to join the long line of military heroes who'd become president of the United States. And he intended to make the capture of Geronimo his stepping-stone to becoming president.

In the meantime, Callista would be sending dispatches back to the Chicago and Washington newspapers about life in Arizona. Only she and her Washington editor knew about the other story she was after: to expose the traitors who were selling guns to the Apaches.

Her mother brushed a persistent fly away from her face. "Oh, dear me, my special mattress, it's gone. And . . ."

Callista's attention wandered from her mother, and she studied Mr. Chance while he directed the men who were righting the carriage.

He was whipcord-lean, as though the fiery desert sun had burned away any softness in him, leaving nothing but muscles and sinew. She'd felt positively tiny talking to him, and she wasn't used to that. Usually she looked men almost straight in the eye, but she'd had to look up at him.

With rattles and a thud, the barouche settled back on its wheels. Mr. Chance circled the open carriage, inspecting the spokes and hubs on each wheel. Harnesses jingled as troopers led over a team of horses and hitched them up.

Finally, he looked up, directly at her, and she realized he'd been aware of her scrutiny all along. He gestured at the carriage.

Callista glanced at her mother, who had closed her eyes and rested her head against the tree trunk. She started toward Mr. Chance, then hesitated. She didn't want to ask him to help load her books, she realized. Actually, she didn't want to ask him for anything.

She'd felt a flash of dislike from him when she told him her name. It had been as clear as a slap in the face, then it was gone—or hidden, she cautioned herself. But she couldn't forget it. Especially since she was positive they'd never met before.

She would have known, because he wasn't the kind of man a woman would forget.

Lieutenant Caruso came back around the landslide, and she rushed toward him, passing Mr. Chance as if he were invisible. "Lieutenant, could you assist me in retrieving my volumes?" The hair on the back of her neck warned her that Mr. Chance had turned to watch her.

"I'll be happy to help, Miss Warwick."

As they walked toward her books, the men who'd chased the Apaches returned in a cloud of dust and noise. They drew rein amidst jingling bits and stamping hooves.

"Lieutenant, Mr. Chance, come see what we found," one called, brandishing a rifle.

"I'll see to them; you take care of Miss Warwick," Mr. Chance said to Lieutenant Caruso as he passed.

Callista gave Russ Caruso her most brilliant smile. "After what we've just gone through, why don't you call me Callista?"

"If you'll call me Russ."

"It's a deal." She held out her hand, and he shook

it. "Thank you, Russ, for helping. My mother reminded me that we also have a trunk of clothes in that wagon. Would you see what condition it's in?"

"Sure. I'll check it after we're done." Arms loaded with books, he followed her to the carriage.

Callista climbed in and lifted the bench seats, removing her archery bow from the storage area in one. As Russ handed the books up to her, she stacked them inside the benches. Within minutes they'd loaded all her books, and she'd closed the seats and laid her bow across the backward-facing one.

Then Callista went to get her mother. Mr. Chance was still talking to the men, which was fine with her. The less she had to deal with him, the better.

By the time she returned, Russ was lashing their slightly scorched trunk to the back of the carriage. Callista settled her mother in the carriage, then sat beside her.

Mr. Chance passed the carriage on his big red charger. The horse was impatient to go, prancing and rearing, but he moved with the animal as though he was part of it, like a centaur.

The carriage tilted as the driver climbed up onto his high seat. In front of them, the troopers paired up and began moving forward, up the canyon, toward the wall of snow-topped mountain peaks.

"Where's my parasol?" Callista's mother felt around on the leather seat. "Callista, do you have yours?"

"No, Mamere." She peered at the spot where the barouche had overturned. "But I see them." They had been thrown out of the carriage and had rolled into the shadow of a boulder. "Driver, stop," she called over her shoulder.

Opening the low door after the driver reined in the

horses, she stepped down. She had only taken a couple of steps when the red horse came galloping back.

"What the hell's going on," Mr. Chance snarled, reining in his horse beside her. "What are you doing?"

She had to tilt her head far back to look up at him. "I'm getting our parasols."

"Your what?" His voice dropped in disbelief.

"Our parasols. They fell out of the carriage when it overturned."

Resting his elbow on his saddle horn, he leaned down until his face was so close to hers that his hat brim shaded her. "We're traveling through Apache country and you are searching for parasols?" He bit off each word.

"I'm not searching," she snapped. "I know exactly where they are." How dare he assume she didn't know what she was doing! She marched over, picked them up, then marched back to the carriage.

She climbed the two steps into the carriage and slammed the door, then, still standing, used her height to look down at him. "Why are we proceeding deeper into this canyon? Aren't the walls going to get higher and closer together, giving those savages more places to ambush us?" *And now that he was riding with them, there would be no one to surprise the Apaches and drive them away.*

"This canyon leads to a pass through the mountains. It's much shorter to reach the fort if we go this way."

"If we survive. Why not go back out to the plains and circle the mountains? We could see the Apaches from much farther off that way." She handed a parasol to her mother.

"If we can see them from farther off, they can see

us, too, can't they? So what good would that do?"

"I concur with your logic in reaching that conclusion." Callista sat down beside her mother and opened her parasol with a decisive snap. "You may proceed, Mr. Chance."

He gave her a long look, then touched spurs to his horse and galloped away. Callista watched him until he disappeared around a curve in the canyon.

"That man is dangerous, Callista. Stay away from him," her mother said quietly.

"What?" Astonished, Callista turned to her. "Mamere, what are you talking about?"

"That man is like a granite boulder, hard clear through. Lieutenant Caruso shows hints of what he was like as a boy; that man doesn't. I seriously doubt if he ever was a boy."

"He's older than Lieutenant Caruso by six or seven years. Maybe that's why."

"I don't think so." She tapped her fingers against the handle of her parasol. "It's something that comes from deep within him. He's as hard as those mountains blocking our way."

Callista leaned back against the brown leather. So Mamere had sensed something, too. That was interesting, because Mamere's hunches about people were usually right, and Callista had long ago learned to listen to them.

But in this case she'd already decided to keep an eye on Mr. Britton Chance. After all, he was the first bona fide hero she'd met in the Wild West, and he was going to be the subject of her first dispatch from Fort Bowie.

Yet she also felt an uneasiness—for she had a feeling that he was as fierce as the Apaches he'd driven away.

And as dangerous.

Chapter 2

Dispatch to the *Times/Tribune* Newspapers

Today a most distressing incident interrupted our journey to Fort Bowie, Arizona Territory.

My mother and I, and our escort of soldiers, were traversing a narrow, winding canyon when we were set upon by renegades of the Apache tribe and pinned down behind a barricade of boulders. The troopers held them off for long hours, but could not gain the ascendancy. Just when I thought we would be overrun and that I would be meeting my Maker, a hero appeared and drove them away.

Yes, dear readers, a true-life hero. He appeared on the ridge above the Apaches and sent his flame red stallion charging down the slope among them, firing guns from each hand. I thought he was leading a cavalry charge and the Apaches must have also, for they fled to their horses and galloped away.

Only later did I learn that he rode alone. His amazing act of bravery saved the day. Because of him, I will be able to continue to write about my adventures out West.

This is Callista Warwick, reporting from Arizona.

She was going to be trouble, Brit thought as he guided his horse past the troopers. Trouble with a capital T.

It wasn't bad enough that she was Warwick's daughter. He was sick and tired of prim-and-proper Eastern ladies who came out to experience the so-called Wild West simply because it was the thing to do. But they were so frightened by real wilderness, real Apaches, real snakes, that at the first sign of danger they turned tail and scurried back to the safe, tamed East.

She was by far the worst he'd seen, though. She'd come to Arizona only as window dressing for her father.

"Bah—women!" he muttered as he joined Russ in the lead. Callista and her mother obviously expected Warwick to capture Geronimo. Did they know about the family's dismal finances and real situation?

General Crook had called him to a meeting in Tucson because of Warwick. For almost twenty years Warwick had stayed in the power centers of New York, Washington, and Chicago, and had avoided duty on the frontier. Suddenly he had requested duty at Fort Bowie, claiming he wanted to fight the Apaches.

Warwick's sudden desire didn't ring true to General Crook, so he had quietly investigated. He'd found that Warwick was teetering on the edge of bankruptcy and was borrowing huge sums to keep up appearances. Yet within two months of arriving at Fort Bowie, he'd stopped borrowing and started to pay off his debts. At the same time, someone had started selling rifles to the Apaches.

General Crook had asked Brit to return to duty to track down Warwick or whoever was selling the guns and stop them.

Turning in his saddle, Brit glanced back at the carriage—and Warwick's daughter.

But General Crook didn't know that Brit knew Warwick from the War Between the States. Warwick had been hailed as a hero for the cavalry charge he'd led during the battle for Atlanta. But Brit had been there, and knew what Warwick had *really* done that day.

Several hours later, as they followed the rutted track up the last bit of slope out of the canyon, Brit turned to Russ. "This is where I'll be leaving you. I need to get back to my ranch."

"Thanks again." Russ held out his hand. "We would still be pinned down if you hadn't surprised the Apaches."

Brit shook it. "Glad to help. I'll—" He broke off as he sighted a dust cloud behind them. "Hell and damnation!" he muttered.

Russ looked back, too. "Think we might have company?"

"Could be. I'll ride with you for a while longer, and see what happens."

By midafternoon Brit had led them into the open oak forest that covered the lower slopes of the mountains. He called a halt to rest and water the horses at a stream that was close to a promontory where he could get a good look at their backtrail.

As the men cared for the horses, Miss Starch set up folding canvas chairs for herself and her mother in the shade, then she took out a notebook and began to scribble in it.

Brit pulled his binoculars out of his saddlebags and entered the forest, following a faint trail toward the promontory. He hadn't gone far when he heard someone crashing along behind him. A glance told him it was Callista Warwick.

Well, he'd just speed up and she'd turn back.

But she didn't.

Finally, he stopped and turned. "Miss Warwick, stop following me and go back to your carriage," he growled.

"Why?"

He hadn't expected her to question him, just turn tail and run. He hooked his thumbs over his gun belt, rocked back and forth on the balls of his feet, and gave her his most hard-eyed stare. "Because you're making so damn much noise you're scaring away all the game."

"You're hunting?" She kept coming until she was almost nose to nose with him, and she didn't look the least bit intimidated.

"Certainly, I'm hunting." Couldn't she tell when she wasn't wanted?

"Ah, I see. You're going to club the animals to death with your binoculars." She arched a golden brown eyebrow at him. "Right?"

She had him, dammit—and he'd walked straight into her little trap. He swallowed a smile. "Lady, I'm busy." He tried his hard-eyed glare again.

"Don't let me stop you."

If the Apaches were still following them, he didn't want her seeing them and getting hysterical. He removed his Stetson, raked his hand through his hair, and resettled it. He finally said, "I'm going a fair distance, and you'll get tired and whiny."

"Whiny!" She clamped her hands to her waist and leaned forward slightly, like a teacher getting ready to lecture him. "I have never in my whole life been whiny! And I'm used to perambulating."

Lord, she was persistent. "Not over rough trails, you're not. And I won't stop and walk you back to camp if you get tired."

"I can live with those conditions." Her eyes narrowed. "Especially the part about not having to walk back to camp with *you*. That's definitely a plus."

"Ah, hell! Come on then, but be quiet and don't bother me." He turned and strode off.

"You are the soul of graciousness."

He snorted. Loudly.

She fell back bit by bit, but not as quickly as he'd expected.

Emerging from the forest onto the bare rocks that jutted out from the mountain like a ship's prow, Brit walked to the edge. Immediately he raised the field glasses to his eyes and began to quarter the ridges and canyons that lay below, looking for any sign of Apaches. He wanted to find them before Miss Starch joined him.

In a few minutes, she came huffing and puffing up beside him. He caught a whiff of starch, which was only to be expected. He'd lay odds she dabbed it behind her ears instead of cologne.

"We're looking east, aren't we? Good heavens, I've never seen anything like this. You must be able to see for a hundred miles from here." The awe in her voice made him lower the glasses and look at her.

"You can." The wind blew her dress back against her, revealing nicely rounded hips and high, surprisingly curvy breasts. Not bad for a woman with such a damn prissy knot in her hair.

She pointed to a thin white scar winding across the green ridges below them. "Is that the track we were on?"

"Uh-huh." She was more observant than many people he'd met; he'd give her that.

Callista tried to catch her breath as she gazed at the blue ridges and purple canyons that marched rank upon rank to the horizon. She'd originally followed him merely out of curiosity, but when he'd so obviously not wanted her along, she'd become determined to see where he was going.

She had to trot to keep up with him and he *had* gone much farther than she'd expected. But there was no way she'd ask him to slow down—not after his *whiny* comment.

Callista didn't look at him. She didn't need to, for she was too aware of him as it was—of how the scent of horses and gunpowder clung to his broad shoulders, of how he stood, with his feet planted arrogantly wide.

She tried to ignore the fact that he was looking at her, but finally she couldn't stand it. "What is it, Mr. Chance?" she asked, turning to him.

He studied her with an unnerving intensity that made her mouth go desert dry. "You're bleeding."

He took a step towards her and cupped her cheeks between the palms of his big hands. Instinctively, she grabbed his wrists and felt the strength in the taut tendons.

"B-badly?" His palms were rough with calluses, yet he held her gently. As he bent over her, the sun limned his coffee black hair, bringing out red highlights.

"No." He brushed his thumb over her cheek, then held it up for her to see the red streak.

His soft touch sent a shiver through her. "A branch must have scratched me," she said with a nervous laugh, trying to cover her reaction.

"Maybe." He swiped his thumb over her cheek again and checked it. "It's stopped."

Her fingers slipped a bit on his wrists, and she felt the steady beating of his pulse. He slowly loosed his hands, as though reluctantly, and stepped back. Then he raised the binoculars to his eyes.

"I'm impressed," Callista said, trying to sound cool and calm. "You didn't try the old let-me-kiss-the-hurt-away routine."

"It wasn't that bad a cut," he said dryly.

She gazed at the landscape spread before her and tried to concentrate on it, but his presence kept intruding.

"Well? What should I be looking for?"

"Nothing in particular. Anything that doesn't look right." His tone was distant, as if he was preoccupied.

She watched him out of the corner of her eye. He was slowly scanning each ridge and canyon with a thoroughness that told her he knew what he was looking for. And he didn't want to miss it. Her knees went weak as she realized why he was scrutinizing their backtrail.

"Oh, my God," she whispered. "You're searching for Apaches, aren't you?"

He remained silent, still scanning the land.

"You think they'll come after us and attack again?" An icy blade of fear knifed through her.

He finally met her eyes. "No, not at all. I don't see any sign of them on our trail."

His gaze was clear, yet she felt that he was holding back, hiding something. She decided to trust her instincts.

"You're quite good. I can't tell if you're lying or not." She watched for the blink of surprise that would tell her if he was.

A very male smile flickered across his stern features. "You don't beat around the bush, do you?"

"No. So are you lying?"

"Nope. I don't see any sign of Apaches."

Callista crossed her arms and tapped the fingers of one hand on her other arm. "Why do I still feel there's something you're not telling me?"

He shrugged. "Beats me."

This time she was sure: he was hiding something.

"Come on," he added, "let's get back. We've got a long ways to go before nightfall."

"I hope *you* don't get whiny on the walk back." She gave him her very sweetest smile.

"All right, I concede that you didn't get whiny on the way out here." He headed back into the forest with his long, ground-eating strides. "Let's see how you do going back."

Once again, she hurried along in his wake. By the time they returned to the others, Callista was breathing hard and had a stitch in her side. But she'd kept up with him.

Mamere was already seated in the carriage. Some of the troopers were policing the area, while others tightened the horses' girths in preparation for continuing into the mountains.

"Here you go," Mr. Chance said, opening the carriage door and holding out his hand to steady her on the narrow iron steps.

When she grasped his hand, a tingle sizzled from his fingers up her arm. Feeling shocked and disoriented, she sat down on the leather seat. What was happening to her? Was she ill?

Pursing her lips in thought, she watched Britton Chance walk over to his horse, grasp the saddle horn, and swing up without stepping in the stirrup.

"I brought a canteen of water in case you were thirsty when you returned, Callista," her mother said. "Where did you go?"

"I followed Mr. Chance to a lookout where he examined our backtrail for Apaches. He didn't find any." She snagged the canteen and uncorked it, then drank. When she finished, she held it out to her mother. "Thirsty?"

"Not right now, dear." Her mother closed her eyes and leaned back in the seat.

Callista wedged herself into the other corner and gazed unseeingly at the rocks and trees they were passing. Had she really felt that strangely pleasant tingle when Mr. Chance held her hand?

No! Why would she have? It didn't make sense. She'd never been attracted to rough, uncivilized men. She liked men who'd read the classics and were sophisticated enough to enjoy an evening at the ballet or opera. Why, even the way he stood, with his feet planted far apart, was an arrogant challenge.

It had to be her imagination. She'd just spent hours fearing for her life; naturally she was oversensitive and on edge. That was all it was. Nothing more.

Relieved, Callista laid her head back against the leather cushion and gazed up at the blue sky. Now she could relax and get on to more important matters, like the feeling that Mr. Chance wasn't telling her everything when he said he hadn't seen any Apaches.

She'd learned to trust her instincts from interviewing people for the newspaper. Sometimes she'd finish an interview, feeling triumphant that she'd asked such tough questions and gotten the answers. Then she'd wake up in the middle of the night and her instincts would be chattering that the person she'd interviewed had told her lies, all lies. And nine times out of ten, her instincts were right.

If Mr. Chance left camp again she would follow him. Only this time, she wouldn't be so obvious.

As they climbed the mountain slopes the oak forest gave way to Ponderosa pines and Douglas firs. Brit chose a grassy, sun-drenched clearing for their camp. A stream flowed through the trees nearby. He directed the men to put the women's tent at the opposite end of the clearing from where the men would be sleeping. The campfire would be between them.

While the men were seeing to the horses and setting up the tent, Brit grabbed his soap, towel, and toothbrush and toothpowder, and walked downstream.

Where the creek fell over a large boulder, forming a churning pool, he stripped off his dust-coated clothes and waded in. He gasped and shivered as he began to wash, for the water was pure snowmelt, cold as a banker's heart.

As he washed, his thoughts turned to Miss Starch.

"Whoa up, right there," he muttered to himself. He couldn't allow himself to think of her as Miss Starch. She was Warwick's daughter. That was how he should be thinking of her.

She'd surprised him when she kept up with him all the way out to the promontory. And when she'd realized he was looking for Apaches, she hadn't gotten hysterical; she had wanted to know the truth. She hadn't shied away from it, like some people would have.

He soaped his chest. When he tried to reassure her about the Apaches, she'd been wary, as if she sensed that he wasn't telling her everything. Which he wasn't. For it was when you didn't see the Apaches that they were the most dangerous.

"Enough," he muttered as he returned to the bank and toweled off, taking care to thoroughly dry the medallion that hung around his neck. He stepped into clean pants, buckled his gun belt, and tied the holster strings around his thigh. Then he sat down to pull on clean woolen socks and his boots. Kneeling beside the water, he shaved and brushed his teeth. Then, draping the towel over his shoulders, he bundled his dirty clothes and headed back toward camp.

Mexican jays fluttered along his path, cawing an alarm and scolding him. Suddenly they fell silent, as though listening. He heard it, too. Someone was coming through the pines toward him. And they were accompanied by a strange sound, like a swarm of angry bees.

From the amount of twigs snapping underfoot, he had a good idea who it was. Still, this wasn't the place to take chances. He drew his revolver and backed behind a tree.

Soon Miss Starch—correction, Miss Warwick—passed him, humming. That was the swarm of bees. He couldn't help smiling: she clearly couldn't carry a tune.

"What are you doing so far away from camp?" he asked, stepping out from behind the tree.

She gasped and whirled, clutching a toothbrush, towel and bar of soap to her breasts. "You startled me."

Her gaze went to his medallion, then skimmed across his chest with a look that made him wonder what her fingers would feel like following the same track.

"And a good thing it was me, not someone or something else." He holstered his gun.

She stiffened and blanched noticeably. "You had your gun drawn?"

"I didn't know who was coming. It could have been an Apache or a wild animal." Neither of which would have made half the noise she had. Not even a drunken Apache.

"I see." She shifted her soap from one hand to the other. That was when he noticed the soft curves of her bosom and realized she was corsetless. That meant she intended to bathe in the stream. She'd change her mind once she found out how cold it was.

"You really shouldn't hum when you're alone. It gives away your position."

"That's why I was doing it. I just had to go for a walk. Doesn't the forest smell wonderful? Just like Christmas. And I didn't want to surprise any bears with cubs, so I thought if I hummed, they'd hear me coming and move out of my way. That's what a friend told me to do."

"Bears aren't your worry right now. Apaches are."

She glanced around fearfully. "Do you think they—"

"Probably not. But it's better to be safe."

"I suppose so." Her gaze fastened on his medallion again. "Do you carry pictures of your wife and children?"

"I don't have a wife. Or children. At least, none that I know of."

Her cheeks reddened becomingly. "I wasn't fishing for information."

"Yes, you were." But for some reason, it didn't bother him at all. In fact, he liked her flustered expression. It was the first time he'd seen her composure slip, and he found it intriguing. "It's pictures of my mother and father," he added, surprising himself.

She waited, as if expecting him to show them to her.

He had no intention of doing that, because he knew she'd then start asking questions and want names and the places where they were from, and he wasn't about to get into any of that. "If you want to wash up, I'll stand guard."

She blinked but didn't move.

"The stream is over there." He pointed.

"Do you think I should carry a gun in this wilderness?" she asked, her brow knit in thought.

Her question surprised him, and he thought about it before he replied. "A lot of women do. Especially if they're going to be riding or doing anything alone. After all there's snakes, bears, mountain lions, and—"

"But then," she went on thoughtfully, almost as if she were talking to herself, "I'd have to learn to shoot."

"Either that or throw the gun at whatever was attacking you."

She eyed him suspiciously. "Are you funning me?"

"Me?" He raised his eyebrows in an exaggerated look of innocence. "Never."

"Hmm, I'll have to think about it while I wash . . ." she murmured to herself.

"The stream is—"

"Yes, Mr. Chance, I remember where it is." As she edged between the bushes, she looked back over her shoulder. "And you really need to work on your innocent look," she added tartly. "If that's what it was."

He smiled as she disappeared. Maybe there was more to her than he'd originally thought.

"My name's Brit," he called.

"Callista," floated back to him.

"The fourth?"

"The one and only."

Smiling at her reply, he listened to her progress through the brush, then the silent pause as she pulled off her dress and knelt beside the stream, dipping her washcloth in. Her gasp told him the exact instant when she found out how cold the water was. He expected her to put her dress right back on and come back, but she didn't.

He leaned against a pine, his arms crossed over his chest. She was a brave woman to bathe in that icy water. And she was definitely beginning to intrigue him.

He listened to her splashing and pictured her running her soapy hands up her long, long legs. Then she'd soap them again and run them over that long swan neck, then down over those round breasts. Finally, she'd soap her hands and wash her thighs, moving higher until—

He straightened away from the pine abruptly. "Hurry up before you attract a bear," he growled.

"Sounds like I already have," she shot back.

Chapter 3

⌒⌒◦◎◦⌒⌒

Callista ate her dinner slowly, thinking about her encounter with Mr. Chance, who was turning out to be more interesting than she'd expected.

He'd looked much more civilized after he shaved. She might even go so far as to say he looked handsome—in a rugged way, of course.

His medallion intrigued her. It had the nicks and scratches that accumulate over years of wear, so it must have sentimental value to him. Yet he had struck her as a hard-riding, practical loner. To think he might be sentimental about his parents was unexpected.

Why hadn't he shown her their pictures, though? Most people would be proud to show off photographs of their family and talk about them.

"Callista, isn't that a beautiful sunset?" her mother said, leaning back in her canvas chair.

"Yes, it is. Did you have enough to eat, Mamere?"

"Plenty, although I shall be glad to get to Fort Bowie and eat something besides stew or beans."

"I'll get you some dried fruit. Do you want your shawl? It's beginning to get chilly." She stood up, and was amazed at how exhausted she felt. She

33

hadn't realized until that moment that she was bone-tired.

"Just sit still, Callista, and enjoy the sunset. If I want my shawl, I can get it. This chill in the air is quite invigorating, don't you think?"

Callista sank back into her chair. "Why, Mamere, you sound as if you're enjoying yourself."

"These last few days in the carriage have reminded me of the days when your father and I were first married, and I would follow him to his new posts. I was so young when Marsh was born, and then four years later, you arrived."

She stared off into the distance, but Callista had the feeling she was seeing a different time.

"Did you like following him around?" She'd never heard her mother talk about those days.

"Oh, yes. Seeing different parts of the country, meeting people we'd met at other posts. There was always something new to do." She glanced at Callista.

"It would have been nice to come out West before this, but your father wanted to be in Washington. I did, too, to be honest. We needed to make the contacts we've made over the last few years. He's wanted to be President Warwick for so many years that it's become my ambition, too."

"You've both worked hard laying the groundwork for his run ever since I can remember. And we're almost there. Next year at this time he'll be running for president."

"You've worked hard, too." Silence fell between them. The sunset deepened from pink and lavender to scarlet streaking across a purple sky.

"That was quite a scare we had this morning," her mother added in a pensive tone. "I thought it was the end for all of us, Callista. And I kept thinking that you'd had so much sorrow and so little joy. I wanted you to live so you could experience all that life has to give you."

"I've had happiness."

"Not enough. You deserve so much more. To fall in love and then to lose David the way you did—"

"Please, Mamere, I'm over him," she said. But there was a sudden lump in her throat. Why did Mamere have to bring him up now, when she was so exhausted from all that had happened that day? "It's been four years."

"While we were under attack this morning, I cried," her mother confessed in a low voice. "No, don't get up. Just sit down and let me finish, Callista. I wasn't crying for me or from fear, but for you, dear, for all that you haven't experienced yet. I've lived my life, but you haven't yet known the joy of a man who loves you or the joy of babies at your breast."

"Now you're going to make me cry, Mamere." Callista fought the salty sting of tears. Why did Mamere have bring up love and babies now? Her emotions were too close to the surface, too raw after her brush with death. "I have to wash these," she mumbled, gathering up their dishes and hurrying away.

Kneeling beside the stream, she gathered up handfuls of sand and scrubbed their plates. She scrubbed and she scrubbed, but she couldn't wash away the memories.

Finally she put the plates aside and sat back against a tree trunk. Drawing up her legs and wrapping her arms around them, she rested her head on her knees. And she let the memories of David come.

That year spring had been wonderful, full of soft breezes and lovers' dreams.

She'd been sitting at the Queen Anne desk in the study, writing out their wedding invitations, when Papa came home long before his usual time. She heard him and Mamere whispering, heard her mother gasp, then Papa came into the study. When she looked up, he was so white, she knew something terrible had happened.

"It's David," Papa had said.

And her heart had stopped.

He'd been taking a steamboat up the Missouri to his new duty post when the boilers blew up. As flames raged through the wooden boat, David had managed to save two women, but he died saving a little girl.

David. Her knight in shining armor, her hero. Her dead hero.

She'd stood up from the Queen Anne desk and stared at those invitations.

David was gone. Gone.

Then she had picked up the invitations one by one and torn them to shreds. But she hadn't cried; not then. Later she shed oceans of tears for David and the dreams that had died with him.

But that was four long years ago, and she was a different person now. Stronger. Harder in some ways. Less trusting.

This morning she'd faced death for the first time in her life, and fear had robbed her of strength, of thought, of breath. She'd been a boneless mass of fear, unable even to stand on her own two feet.

Now she knew what David had faced. Had he felt the same breath-stopping, strength-robbing, heart-screaming fear?

No, he couldn't have! After the boilers blew, he'd faced the flames and run back into them. She'd been paralyzed by fear, but he'd been thinking, running, saving two women.

He'd felt none of the fear she'd felt. Because he was a hero.

Tilting her head back against the rough bark, she let out a long sigh. She'd thought she'd worked through her grief long ago, but after facing death herself, she felt a need to say good-bye to David one last time, letting him go.

Callista didn't know how long she sat there beneath the pine. It could have been five minutes or five hours. When she finally stirred, sunset was long gone, and thousands of stars sparkled in the night.

And she was filled with an inner peace and tranquillity she hadn't known in years. It was as if a weight that had been clamped around her heart had fallen away. Her fatigue had melted away, and she felt extraordinarily clearheaded.

It wasn't a difference that anyone would have noticed; only she could feel it. But it was real, and she felt that she was looking at the world with sharper eyes, a sharper mind.

Retrieving the dishes, she started back toward the camp. She halted when she heard men's voices.

"Chance is a hard-nosed bastard," one was saying. "Be glad he's not still commanding our unit."

"A by-the-book fool?"

She backed behind a tree as the soldiers came toward her.

"Worse—he's a goddamn Indian lover. He made us share our water with Apache prisoners when we were crossing the desert in July. Hell, he treated them like they was human.

"Then last year Corporal Thompson was living with an Apache girl. When she got pregnant, he kicked her out. Chance found out and saw to it that the girl gets part of every paycheck Thompson gets."

"He can't do that! Can he?"

"All I know is that he did."

They walked past the tree where she hid.

"And Thompson's paying?"

"Nope. He quit. I hear he's working a silver mine down near Tombstone."

As their voices faded, Callista returned to the path.

How strange; they called the man who'd driven off the Apaches an Indian lover. They'd cheered him that morning when he saved their lives; now they called him a bastard.

Outside the tent she paused, and saw that Russ and Brit were still standing by the campfire, talking. Pushing aside the flap, she went in. Her mother had left the lantern lit but was already lying on her cot, bundled up against the cold.

Callista was full of energy and too restless to sleep. She pulled a paisley shawl out of her carpetbag and wrapped it around her shoulders against the evening chill.

"Where are you going?" her mother asked as Callista lifted the tent flap.

"Out to the fire. I'd like a hot drink."

She walked toward the men clustered around the fire. As she neared, she realized Brit was speaking. Every time she heard Brit's voice, she liked it better. Something in his low, gravelly rumble stirred something deep within her. She stopped outside the circle of light, letting his voice wash over her.

"Armed with these repeating rifles, the Apaches are a threat to everyone in Arizona," Brit said. The rifle he held glinted in the firelight as he turned it over and studied it. "Hell, these are better than the ones the army is issuing to enlisted men and—" He broke off and looked directly at her. "Are you going to join us or stand there all night?"

How did he know she was there? She was in darkness; there was no way for him to see her.

As she glided into the circle of light Russ Caruso leaped up from his camp stool. "Callista, how nice of you to join us."

Brit ignored him. "Where's your lantern?"

"I left it for Mamere, in case she awakens and is frightened. How did you know I was there?"

"I heard you coming, then you stopped." The flaring light accentuated his high cheekbones.

"Oh." So there'd been nothing unusual, no sensing of her before he saw her. "Don't let me stop you. You were talking about rifles, I believe."

"Someone is selling new rifles to the renegade Apaches," Russ explained.

"Isn't selling guns to them illegal? Who would do that?" A log broke in half and crashed into the fire in a fountain of sparks.

"That's what we're trying to figure out," Russ replied.

"Who would benefit from selling them rifles?"

Brit snapped a sharp look at her, as if her question had surprised him.

Russ's brow furrowed in thought. "That's a good question." He glanced from her to Brit, then yawned and rolled his shoulders. "Tomorrow is going to be a long day, so I'm going to turn in. I'll see you both in the morning." He waved and walked into the darkness.

Callista watched him go, wishing he'd stayed. He was a buffer between her and Brit, and she was more relaxed when he was there. Without him, her consciousness of Brit went up several notches.

"Would you like some coffee?" Brit asked.

"Yes, please. Normally I wouldn't drink it so late, but tonight I'd like the warmth." She unsnapped the small leather pouch on her belt, pulled out her collapsible metal cup, and handed it to him.

"Are you cold?" Brit crouched beside the fire and poured from the dented gallon pot, then rose and walked toward her with a lithe grace that was full of tension and power.

"It seems a lot cooler than at sunset."

"It is. You're high in the mountains. As soon as the sun goes down, the temperature drops like a rock." He halted close to her, but not so close that she felt the need to back up a step. "You should be wearing something warmer than that shawl."

"I'll know better tomorrow night." He was still in shirtsleeves. "Aren't you cold?"

"No, I'm warm enough." The fragrant steam from the coffee enveloped them as he held out her cup.

"You look tired," she said, taking it. His eyes were red-rimmed from dust and fatigue.

"I am."

A lock of dark hair fell across his forehead, and she reached up to brush it back.

He ducked away from her hand.

They froze. Tension sparked between them. A muscle pulsed in his jaw. Slowly, she lowered her hand.

"Sorry," he finally said, "You startled me."

"It doesn't matter anyway," she murmured. Good Lord, what was she thinking of? He was a stranger, for heavens sake! Turning away, she settled on the folding camp stool and, clasping her cup with both hands, leaned forward, staring into the fire as though fascinated by it.

She'd never brushed any man's hair back, except for David. Then to try to do it for a man she'd just met! Worse, it had seemed so natural to brush it back, she hadn't realized she was doing it until he recoiled. That was the scary part—that it had seemed so natural.

Brit sat on the ground, leaning against his saddle and contemplating the fire.

An owl hooted from one side of the camp. An answering hoot came from the other side. The pine trees behind them rustled, but there was no breeze.

"Are those really owls?" Callista asked, glancing around fearfully. Brit hadn't looked toward the noises, but they were surrounded by dark forest perfect for hiding attackers.

"Yes. The Apaches consider owls bad luck. They wouldn't use their hoots to signal to each other."

Callista relaxed a bit. "What does the Chief of Scouts do? I've never heard of that postion at any of the other army posts I've been at."

"I lead the Apache scouts who work for the army. That is, I used to."

She looked up, surprised. "The army employs Apaches? Why? Aren't they who we're fighting?"

"Only Apaches can track Apaches. They know this country better than we'll ever know it. And some would rather work for the army than fight it." The fire had died to glowing red embers. He stirred it with a stick, giving new life to the flames.

The comment Callista had heard earlier came back to her. "As I was coming back from the creek, I overheard a couple of soldiers talking." She'd found she sometimes got the most honest answers when she surprised people. She watched Brit as she continued. "Some of them don't like you."

He grimaced wryly. "Some of them hate me."

"They also called you an Indian lover. Why?"

"I respect the Apaches. I think we have to find a way to live with them, not exterminate them, which is what many people want. If that makes me an Indian lover, so be it."

He wasn't afraid to say what he thought, even if it was an unpopular belief. Standing up to people's scorn took a different kind of bravery than the physical courage he'd demonstrated that morning. To her mind, it took even more courage.

She'd often heard Papa say that a leader's job was to lead, not to be liked by his men. Still, she would have been bothered.

"Do you have any idea who's selling new rifles to the Apaches?" Maybe he heard rumors from the Apaches.

His shoulders squared, as if he'd tensed. He took a swallow of his coffee before he answered. "Nope."

All right, he didn't want to share who he suspected. She'd play along for the time being. After all, she didn't want to appear too eager. "Too bad."

The fire was fading, the circle of light shrinking around them.

"Russ was right, you know. Tomorrow will be a long day." He stirred the fire again, but it only flared weakly and died back to embers.

"It can't be any longer than today was." Had it been less than twelve hours since she'd met him? So much had happened.

"That's true. But it'll be just as tiring." Rising to his feet, Brit threw the dregs of his coffee onto the embers, where they sizzled and steamed. "Come on, I want to go to bed."

Callista jumped to her feet. "Now see here, Mr. Chance, I don't know what kind of woman—" Belatedly she noticed that his upper lip was twitching. "You're funning me again, aren't you." And if she weren't so sleepy, she would have realized it.

He gave her such a wolfish grin that her heart turned over. "What did you think I meant?"

"Never mind; it seems I *am* getting tired." Callista looked away, hoping he didn't see her smile. She didn't want to encourage him. *Oh yes, you do*, said a little voice inside her. "You go on to bed. Don't let me stop you."

"But you are—I want to walk you back to your tent before I turn in." He held out his hand.

She didn't take it. "That's not necessary."

"Yes, it is, Callista." His voice caressed her name, yet there was a serious tone that told her he wouldn't sleep until after he'd walked her back.

"Oh, all right!" she grumbled.

But she liked it when he wrapped his hand around her elbow. His long fingers lay against the sensitive inner skin of her arm, sending a shiver of sensation up it. And this time she knew it wasn't her imagination.

He walked so close, she could feel his heat. And a tiny change in his balance with each stride. "Are you limping?"

His fingers tightened on her arm for just an instant, then she felt him loosen his grip, as if he'd been startled by her question and hadn't meant to do that. His profile changed in the darkness, and she realized he was looking at her. "You're very observant. I only limp when I'm tired."

"What happened?"

"I was trampled by a horse when I was a child."

"How awful!"

"You should have seen the horse," he said, making a joke out of it. "He was limping worse than me."

All right, he didn't want to talk about that, either. She understood, because she didn't like talking about things that were personal to her.

"Ow!" She stumbled over a sharp stone and swayed toward him. Instinctively he reached out to catch her and she clutched his wrist to steady herself.

"Are you all right?" He steadied her with his other hand.

"Yes, but it felt like that stone came right through the shoe leather." She was holding on to his wrist like it was a lifeline, she realized, and dropped it like a hot potato.

"It could have. You need sturdier shoes or boots for walking around out here. We have rattlesnakes who can bite through thin leather."

"I shall definitely have to learn to shoot," she said, trying to sound nonchalant.

"I'll give you your first lesson tomorrow."

She stopped dead. And spend all that time with him alone? All her talk about learning to handle a gun was pure bravado, because she had no intention of ever touching one. "Oh, I couldn't. I wouldn't want to take you away from your duties."

"You won't."

She was silent as they approached her tent. The lantern was still lit inside, so it cast a yellow glow through the canvas walls.

"I can find my way from here," she murmured

dryly, stopping far enough away that they wouldn't disturb her mother.

"Are you sure?" A smile played across his surprisingly full lips, and she wondered how they would feel against hers.

Good Lord, where had that thought come from? There was no way on God's green earth she could be attracted to him!

"Good night. I want to thank you again," she said, retreating behind her wall of words. "It was remarkably gracious of you to interrupt your peregrination to come to our assistance and harass those Apaches until they decamped."

He just smiled. "Do you scare men away with your big words, Callista?" he drawled softly.

"If I do, then I know a lot about them, don't I?" she replied just as softly.

His voice feathered across her skin, as soft as a caress. "And I'm not running away."

Chapter 4

Brit headed for his bedroll, still smiling. What kind of men was she used to, if that silly tactic worked?

She was damned observant to have noticed his limp. It was almost imperceptible, and most people never did, which was fine with him. He didn't want anyone's pity.

Still, he wondered what she would have said if she'd known it was her father's horse that had trampled him during the battle for Atlanta.

Yawning, he shook out his bedroll, then stretched out on his side, resting his head on his crooked arm. He could see her shadow moving around in the tent until she turned the lantern down and the light faded to darkness.

It had been a day of surprises, and Callista Warwick was the biggest one.

All afternoon she'd carried her ridiculous parasol around to shield herself from the sun. Would she insist on carrying it tomorrow, too? He smiled at the image of her trying to hold her parasol and fire a rifle at the same time. He had a feeling she'd do more damage with the parasol.

Russ had told him that she was writing little vignettes about their journey to send to newspapers back East. He was curious about them—and her. She'd surprised him with her question about who would benefit if the Apaches had rifles. It was a smart way of looking at the problem.

So she was sharp as well as observant. He liked that.

In fact, he was beginning to like many things about her—which was a hell of a problem. She was Warwick's daughter, and he wanted to dislike her. He'd expected to dislike her, because she seemed such a prig with her starchy attitude and words.

But that wasn't what was happening. She'd shown a lot of courage and spunk today.

He was beginning to think she wore her starch as armor. But starch could wash away—and then what would be left? Backbone, he suspected from what he'd seen of her.

Callista. He liked the way her name felt on his lips when he said it.

Damn, he should be sleeping, not thinking about her! He rolled over on his back and folded his arms beneath his head. In the morning, when he was rested, everything was bound to look different.

The next morning Brit was standing by the fire, drinking his coffee, when Callista emerged from her tent. Her breath steamed in the frosty air. She locked her hands together and stretched her arms high overhead, as if beginning morning exercises.

But she must have felt his gaze, because suddenly she turned and looked directly at him. She smoothed her hands over her skirt as if that was what she'd intended all along, and walked toward him.

Despite the sleep, things didn't look at all different

from yesterday. In fact, *she* looked better.

She was wearing a lavender dress that was as plain as the brown dress she'd worn yesterday. But the sun's low rays picked up vivid jewel tones of emerald, ruby, and sapphire in the shawl she'd wrapped around her shoulders, making it glow against her delicate white skin. Yesterday he'd compared her to a brown wren, but now she reminded him of a hummingbird, whose iridescent colors flashed only in sunlight.

Brit stiffened. What the devil was he doing, noticing things like that? He gulped his coffee and choked, it was so damn hot.

"Good morning, Callista," Russ Caruso said.

"Morning, Russ." Her husky voice was still sleep-slurred, and it curled through Brit like warm honey. "How soon will we be leaving?"

"As soon as your tent is struck and the horses are harnessed to that damned carriage," Brit growled, feeling completely out of sorts. "We need every minute on the road with it slowing us down so much."

"Nevertheless, my mother requires a carriage," Callista snapped in that starchy tone that had made him want to laugh yesterday. Today he didn't feel like laughing, though. Instead he felt like pulling her into his arms and kissing the starch out of her.

Callista walked past him, trailing a faint flowery fragrance. At the fire she knelt on one knee to pour coffee, and her skirts pooled around her in lavender waves. Her grace reminded him of a flower bending in the wind, and his fingers tightened on his cup.

"I could have gotten that," he said, more harshly than he'd meant to.

"But you didn't need to." She stood up, but didn't move away. Instead she sipped her coffee, eyeing him over the rim. "My mother is afraid of horses. She feels much safer in the carriage," she said quietly.

"I see." All right, so they had a reason to use the damn carriage. "I'll give you your first lesson tonight, when we camp."

"About my lesson, I . . . I'll be ready."

He nodded, surprised by how pleased he was. What the hell was the matter with him? "I need to check the horses," he muttered and walked away.

Callista stared at Brit's back, her mouth open. Heavens, she'd done it now! How could she have said *I'll be ready?* when she'd intended to tell him she didn't need to know how to shoot. What was wrong with her?

After she'd slipped beneath the blankets last night, she'd lain there for the longest time, thinking about him. She could see how Brit could be appealing to some women—if you liked men who were rough and rugged. Which she didn't.

Yet she had to admit, there was something about him that she was beginning to like. There was a you-can-lean-on-me steadiness to him that she found very attractive. Not that she intended to lean on him. Still, it was nice to know.

And she was touched by his limp. That must have been an awful experience for a child. She didn't pity him, he wouldn't have wanted pity. But she felt for the child and the pain he must have endured.

Still, she needed to steer clear of the man, not seek out more time with him.

They made camp that evening on the other side of the mountains in a parklike oak forest. Some troopers began to set up the tent, while others cared for the horses.

Callista looked around, but didn't see Brit. After the men had set up the tent and gone off, she set up her folding table and stool in front of the tent and began making notes for future dispatches.

She was gazing at the ground, chewing the end of her fountain pen, when she noticed someone's dusty boots beside the table. She looked up slowly, past tan pants that were tight enough to cling to muscular thighs, past a four-button fly, to big, square hands with their thumbs hooked over the large belt buckle engraved with the words, WEST POINT.

"Are you almost done?" Brit asked.

She hadn't heard him walk up, but she was glad to see him. "Have you been there long?"

"A couple of minutes."

"And you didn't say anything? Goodness, I didn't realize I was concentrating so."

"Russ tells me you're writing notes to send to the newspapers back East." He moved to look over her shoulder and she caught a whiff of his pine-and-sagebrush scent. "What were you working on?"

"Nothing." She closed her notebook before he could see what she'd written.

"What's the big secret? I thought you wanted people to read what you write." He stood with his feet spread wide.

She straightened her notebook so it lined up neatly with the edge of the table before she answered. "I don't show my work to anyone. I've found it's easier that way."

"And you've sent your writing to newspapers before?"

Callista smiled. "Yes. I'm writing dispatches for Washington and Chicago newspapers about what I encounter in wild Arizona."

"And they buy these dispatches from you?"

"I'm afraid Russ misunderstood. I'm a reporter, Mr. Chance, employed by the *DC Tribune*. They sent me out here to write dispatches."

His silver eyes widened in surprise. "Damn! You must be good if you write for the *DC Tribune*. It's a helluva paper."

"You've heard of it? Way out here?" He must have it mixed up with another paper.

"A friend back East sent me some articles about fraud and bribery in military contracts, written by R.C. Wickwar."

Callista dropped her pen and it rolled across the table. He caught it as it fell off the edge. "You've read R.C.'s articles?" she asked faintly.

"Yes. They were fascinating." He handed the pen back to her. "They resulted in the conviction of a congressman, didn't they? And some officers. That was damn fine work."

"I thought so, too." She picked up her notebook and clasped it against her breasts like a shield.

"Wickwar sounds like he's been around the block a few times," Brit continued. "He must have gone undercover to get his information."

"He did." She quickly added, "Not that he ever confided in me, but that was the rumor around the office. I'm just a junior reporter, while he's been around for a long time."

"I can see that from his writing. The man speaks from years of accumulated knowledge and careful reporting."

"He does indeed. One day a congressman came in looking for him because he wanted to horsewhip that 'damn scoundrel.' "

"That shows you he's doing a good job."

"Next time I see R.C., I'll tell him that his name is known even out in Arizona."

"Known and respected. We need more reporters like him, who tell the truth. Is that what you aspire to, exposing fraud like he does?"

"Yes, I'd like to very much. Of course, I need years more of experience and contacts to do what he does."

"Good luck. From what I've seen, you certainly have the courage to do that kind of reporting."

"Why, thank you." She could feel her cheeks heating up, but she was so surprised by his encouragement. Other than her editor, no man had ever encouraged her. Not even David. "When you're a writer, every word of encouragement is important."

"The pen can be a damn fine weapon. It works best in places where there's rule of law. But in other places, like here, the rifle is a better weapon. It can stop an attacking mountain lion or bear before they reach you. A pen wouldn't be much use in those circumstances."

"Hmm, I never thought about it like that, but you're right. I need to put my notebook away, then I'll be ready for our lesson."

She pushed aside the flap and ducked into the tent, where she checked her image in the small mirror she'd hung from the tent post. "Well, R. C., you're known out here, too," she murmured as she tucked a loose tendril back into her knot.

Brit was waiting with his rifle when she emerged. "We'll go over that rise so we're far enough from camp to avoid accidents." He wrapped his hand around her elbow again.

Yessir, she was definitely getting used to having

his hand there. "It's a short enough walk that I don't think I'll get too whiny."

He groaned. "How long am I—"

"Mr. Chance, sir, can you come?" a young trooper called as he ran up to them. "One of the horses is down, and Lieutenant Caruso wondered if you'd take a look at it."

"I'll be back as soon as possible," Brit said.

"Take your time."

Bracing one foot, she leaned back against a tree. Only her editor and she knew that she was R.C. She hadn't told her parents because she knew Mamere would worry and Papa would rant and rave, but underneath, he would be worried, too.

A shot echoed through the camp, and she flinched.

The sun was setting by the time Brit returned. "Sorry it took so long," he said, rubbing the back of his neck wearily.

"I'm sorry you couldn't save the horse." She wanted to soothe away his weariness.

"How did you—? Oh, the shot." He rested his hand against the trunk beside her head.

He didn't say anything, but tension lines bracketed the hard line of his mouth. The white track of a scar zigzagged from his eyebrow up into his hair.

"How did you get this?" she asked softly, tracing it with a finger. Was it the track of an arrow? A bullet?

The hard line of his mouth slowly eased into a wry smile. "I was rousting one of my men out of bed and his lady friend didn't like being interrupted. She hit me with a vase."

Callista snickered, then clamped her hand over her mouth. "I'm sorry. That wasn't polite, but I expected you to say an Apache arrow or something equally unusual." And heroic and romantic.

"Instead it's so ordinary," he said, finishing her thought. He shrugged. "What can I say? It's the truth."

Callista knew she was falling under his spell. He was a hero who could make fun of himself and she found that endearing. But she had no intention of letting him know that.

"I think it's gotten too dark for a lesson tonight," she said, glancing around.

"I'll give you one at Fort Bowie," he promised.

"You're staying on?" He wouldn't be riding out of her life tomorrow! A bubble of happiness went through her. "I thought you had to get back to your ranch."

"I'll have to stay over a day to pick up supplies, so I'll give you your lesson as well before I go on."

Her bubble went flat.

He glanced over his shoulder at the campfire visible through the oaks. "I haven't eaten yet. Have you?"

"No, but I want—that is—I'm going to keep my mother company." Though she wanted to talk to him, she wouldn't leave Mamere to eat alone.

"I understand. See you in the morning, then." He tipped his Stetson.

She watched him walk away with regret. Darn! She really enjoyed talking to him. Usually she just listened—even with David, she'd listened. But Brit was honestly interested in her work.

Could it be that she was beginning to like him?

She was in the carriage the next afternoon, watching Brit's broad back as he rode ahead of them, when they came over a rise and saw Fort Bowie sprawled before them.

It lay in a grassy green bowl, overlooked on all sides by ridges and hills. Patches of golden poppies and white marguerites waved a welcome from the green slopes. Bowie was like other forts she'd seen, with buildings and corrals clustering around the parade ground. She immediately picked out the line of two-story houses along one side of the parade ground that was Officers' Row. But as she looked down on the fort, Callista's hand tightened on the carriage strap. There was no stockade to protect it. How did they keep the Apaches out?

Finally the carriage rattled along the rutted road in front of the two-story houses and halted at the last one, larger than the others.

Her father stood on the front porch. Muttonchop whiskers came forward on his cheeks to meet his beard, and Callista felt a dart of surprise at how grizzled he was. She hadn't noticed Papa was going gray.

"Verlene, my dear." Colonel Marsden Warwick came down the steps and helped his wife down out of the open carriage. Clasping her hands in his, he kissed her on each cheek in the French manner. "I'm glad to see you made it here without any problems."

"We were attacked by Apaches, Marsden. That's not what I call *without problems*. They burned your chair and my special mattress and—"

"There, there, dear." He rubbed her hands gently. "Don't fret. I'll take care of everything. You're safe: that's what's important."

Callista had followed her mother down the carriage steps, and now her father held out his arms. "And here's my favorite daughter," he exclaimed, giving her a hug.

"And here's my favorite father," she responded, hugging him back.

Brit sat on Red, surprised by Warwick's affection for his wife and daughter.

What had he expected? he asked himself. A horned Satan? But in a way, he knew that was what he *had* expected. Maybe he needed to step back and take a good look at Warwick, instead of disliking him for what he had done twenty years earlier.

After all, maybe the man had changed.

Warwick escorted his ladies up the steps to the veranda.

Callista paused. "Thank you for all your help, Mr. Chance," she said, resting her white-gloved hands on the white railing.

"It was my pleasure, Miss Warwick." Which was the truth.

Warwick looked at him. "Well, well, so you're Britton Chance." There wasn't a bit of warmth in his voice. He walked to the railing and, crossing his arms over his chest, studied Brit with eyes that were as cold as a Rocky Mountain blizzard. "I've heard a lot about you, Lieutenant. There's a telegram for you from General Crook in my office."

"Do you know what's in it, sir?" Of course he did, but Brit wanted to see how he answered.

"I do. As a matter of fact, I just sent a trooper to your ranch with a copy of it. General Crook is ordering you back to active duty, because of the Apache situation and Geronimo's depredations."

"Does it say where I'm stationed and what my duties are?" He couldn't appear to know what the telegram said, even though he and Crook had planned it. He noticed that Callista was listening.

"You'll be stationed here. He wants you to take up your duties as Chief of Scouts again."

"I'll need to return to my ranch and get some clothes and supplies." He'd have been at the ranch when the telegram came except for stumbling over Callista and her mother.

"Pick them up when you're on patrol in that area." Warwick glanced at his wife and daughter. "I want to welcome my family to the fort. I'll see you in my office in two hours." He saluted and turned away, then turned back. "And get yourself a room in the Bachelor Officers' Quarters."

"Yes, sir." Brit saluted. He watched Warwick usher the women into the house.

Callista looked back at him, quickly, and smiled.

Grinning, he touched his Stetson, then headed for the stable. The telegram had worked. He was at Fort Bowie, seemingly to lead the Apache scouts and capture Geronimo. No one suspected that he was really there to find out who was selling rifles—and to stop them.

Slinging his saddlebags over his shoulder, Brit left the stable and walked across the parade ground to the two-story house that was home to the bachelor officers. Banging through the front doorway, he headed for the stairs. He automatically checked the parlor to see who was there.

Charlie Ward looked up from the poker game he was playing with two other officers and raised a dark eyebrow quizzically. "Brit, you're back, old chap? Ranch not going well?"

"The ranch is doing fine, old chap." Charlie came from old money, and he and Brit had never been more than speaking acquaintances. "I'm back temporarily. Is my room still vacant?"

Charlie studied his cards. "Righto, old chap."

Brit nodded at the other two lieutenants holding cards.

One was new and wore a crisply pressed uniform which looked brand-spanking-new and tailor-made. His blond hair was long, and he affected a flowing handlebar mustache that made him resemble General Custer.

Not a good omen, Brit thought. He'd read the report of the investigation into Custer's defeat at the Little Bighorn River. He'd recognized the crucial mistakes Custer had made that fateful June day seven years ago when he led his men to their deaths. But the newspapers had made Custer into a hero, and many officers used his defeat as an excuse to continue the campaigns against the Indians.

"Care to join us?" Charlie asked.

"Not right now."

Up in his room, Brit dropped his saddlebags beside the bed. Going to the window, he absently peered across the backyards toward the commanding officer's home. What was she doing now? Unpacking her books, if he knew anything about her.

When he went downstairs later, the buzz of conversation in the parlor ceased as if cut off with a knife, and he knew they'd been talking about him.

Brit didn't even nod as he crossed to the front door. He paused on the porch to pull on his leather gauntlets, then headed toward the headquarters building.

It didn't bother him anymore that even though he'd graduated from West Point, he was still an outsider. He'd received a battlefield appointment to the Academy during the War Between the States. He'd only been fourteen then—though no one knew it—a drummer boy who saved a general's life.

That single moment of decision had changed his own life immeasurably, for it had given him entry to a new world. One he'd only dreamed of when growing up in the brothel.

In an odd way the brothel years had been the good times, when his mother was still alive and working at Madame Claudine's. He fingered the medallion she'd given him, then pushed the memories away.

Brit opened the headquarters door and removed his Stetson as he entered the main office. A wooden bench still sat outside the commandant's office. The few changes he spotted were sparkling-clean windows, no dust anywhere, and a new wooden railing separating the desk and telegraph key from the rest of the office. The only pictures were of U.S. Grant and Sherman.

"Sergeant Mac—I should have known you'd still be here," he said to the gray-haired man seated at the telegrapher's desk.

"Yes sir, Lieutenant sir, good to see you, sir." Sergeant MacDonald pushed himself to his feet and held out his hand.

"Same here." Brit clasped it and shook. "You're looking younger than when I left. Fewer wrinkles. You taking care of Sue Beth?"

"Yes sir, I am for sure." He gestured at a spindle on his desk piled high with yellow telegrams. "I've become a telegrapher, too, sir."

"And I understand you have a telegram for me."

"I do, sir." He looked through a pile of telegrams not yet spindled. "Here it is." He pulled out one of the flimsy yellow papers and handed it to him.

"Looks like you've got a lot of traffic on the military telegraph."

"Reports about Apache raids all over Arizona and New Mexico. I'll tell the colonel you're here." He limped around the end of the railing and knocked on the closed door.

Brit turned his attention to the telegram, as if he didn't know what it contained.

"The colonel will see you now, sir," the sergeant said, standing in the open doorway.

"Thanks, Mac." He patted the sergeant's shoulder, then went in and closed the door behind him.

Colonel Warwick continued writing at his desk. He didn't look up or invite Brit to sit.

If the colonel was trying to put him in his place by making him wait, the colonel had better think again. The ploy told him a lot about Warwick. In his experience, officers who were spit-and-polish and by-the-book often weren't good leaders. They used regulations to hide their own incompetence.

Brit gazed past him. Only one picture on the wall. George Armstrong Custer—in all his cocky vanity. *Also not a good sign*, he thought. *In fact, very bad.*

He studied Warwick out of the corner of his eye. If he was selling guns to the Apaches, he had to have accomplices who could leave the fort without being noticed. As commanding officer, Warwick couldn't disappear.

Warwick put his pen back in its holder, carefully standing it upright, before he looked at Brit.

"Sit down, Lieutenant." He folded his hands on his desk, and his West Point ring flashed in the sunlight, streaming through the window.

Brit took one of the wooden captain's chairs in front of the massive desk. The chair hadn't changed a bit—uncomfortable as ever, he thought, as he slouched in it and rested his ankle on his knee.

Warwick's lips thinned noticeably as he took in Brit's slouch and his nonuniform of tan pants and blue shirt. He didn't say anything, but as if setting an example, he sat up very straight.

"Colonel Warwick, the Apaches who attacked your wife and daughter had brand-new repeating rifles," Brit began, taking the offensive. "Rifles with a longer range than the ones the army has. We need to find out who's selling them to the Apaches and stop them. That'll save a lot of lives."

"That's not important right now." Warwick drummed his fingers on his desk, perused some papers, then looked up. "General Crook tells me you're the best Chief of Scouts he's had in a long time. That the Apaches respect you."

Brit shook his head. "He's only talking about the Apaches who are scouts, Colonel."

"Ah, yes. The tame Apaches." There was a sarcastic edge to his tone. "Are they loyal? Dare we trust them when we go after Geronimo?"

"Go after Geronimo, sir? Is that what you plan to do?"

"By God, yes! It's time someone caught that scallywag and taught him a lesson." Warwick banged his fist down on the desk. "Why hasn't anyone captured him yet?"

"Geronimo's a wily old fox. Whenever we get too close, he hightails it over the Mexican border." Did the man really think he'd capture him?

"We're going to take away that refuge, Lieutenant." Warwick tapped an official looking paper with a red seal. "We can now pursue him into Mexico."

"His strongholds down there are in even rougher country than in Arizona, and he's got more warriors there."

"Nevertheless, here's what we're going to do . . ."

A few minutes later, Brit shook his head. "That won't work, Colonel. There aren't any roads, so you can't get the cannon down there. And even if you could, they'd be useless in those narrow, twisting canyons."

"Lieutenant, you haven't captured Geronimo, have you?"

"No, but I know the terrain where you want to go. It's not country where you can use West Point tactics. Geronimo didn't go to West Point. He fights any way he can to win."

"Well, now I'm here, and we're going to do things my way, Lieutenant. And we will capture Geronimo." Warwick moved to a map of Arizona hanging on the wall. When Brit joined him, he drew a circle on it. "This will be your patrol area." The region included the main route for Apaches fleeing the reservations and heading for Mexico. "I expect you to stop escaped Apaches and send them back, while you're patrolling the border."

"Sir, I don't have enough scouts to cover both the border and stop the people fleeing the reservation."

"I don't want excuses, Lieutenant. I want results. Do I make myself clear?"

"Yes, sir. Perfectly clear." Warwick didn't have the least understanding of what it was like to pursue the Apaches across Arizona's mountains and deserts. Brit saluted and turned to leave.

When he opened the door he saw Callista, wearing a vivid raspberry-colored dress with white collar and cuffs, leaning against the railing and talking to Sergeant Mac. The mere sight of her lifted his spirits.

She glanced over her shoulder, her eyes lit up, and she gave him a smile. "Hello, Brit." He liked the

warmth in her voice. "I just filed my first dispatch.
Sergeant MacDonald here sent it on."

"Not wasting any time, are you?" She reminded
him of raspberry ice cream he'd had once—all lick-
able and luscious. He blinked, surprised by the
thought. And liking it. Raspberries were tart, with
just the right amount of sweetness. His mouth was
already watering.

The rest of his body was responding, also.

"Sergeant Mac is sending my next two right now."

"Good work." Damnation, he wanted to pull her
into his arms and kiss her, not say *good work*. He
put his Stetson on, winked at her, and walked out on
the porch.

The first thing he needed was a cold shower. Because Callista Warwick was becoming a hell of a
distraction.

Chapter 5

Dispatch to the *Times/Tribune* Newspapers

Among the heroes I have personally known, dear readers, was General Custer, who often dined at our home. And I can tell you that the man who saved us from the Apaches is cut from the same cloth as Custer. He's broad of shoulder, piercing of eye, a marksman without parallel. What the many men of my escort couldn't accomplish, he did through surprise and bravery.

Then he put aside his own business to accompany and protect my mother and me on the remainder of our journey. As we traversed the mountains, he was gracious enough to impart some of his vast knowledge of the territory. He even convinced me that it would be wise to learn how to use a gun in this wilderness. And yes, our hero is indeed instructing me in marksmanship.

This is Callista Warwick, somewhere in Arizona Territory.

It was already dark when Brit came out of the Bachelor Officers' Quarters. He walked along the wagon road, headed for the camp of the Apache scouts, downhill from the fort.

As he passed the commandant's house he noticed it was all lit up, as if they were having a party. In honor of Mrs. Warwick and Callista? What would she be wearing? Though any dress was simply a frame for her beauty.

"Brit!" boomed a gruff voice behind him.

He turned at that welcome voice. "John, I was going to come over and see you and Emmy later."

"I was headed for the BOQ to find you, then I saw you walking." John Piney slapped him on the back with a hand as big as a Smithfield ham. "How are you?"

"Fine. And you?" Brit studied the tall, beefy man who'd been his friend since he'd joined the army.

"There've been a lot of changes since you left. Let's go have a drink, and I'll tell you about them." Instead of turning back toward his house, he walked toward the cantina.

"You don't want to drink at home?" Over the years, John had often invited Brit over for dinner and drinks, but he'd never gone out drinking.

"Nah. Want to talk to you without Emmeline fussing and—Well, you know how she is."

"Yes, I do." He'd never seen Emmeline fuss over anything.

Ahead of them, yellow light spilled out the swinging doors of the cantina. The tinny sound of an out-of-tune piano mingled with the deep murmur of men's voices.

"Crowded in here tonight," Brit said, as they paused in the doorway, looking for an empty table. Smoke formed layers in the air, and the smell of beer was so strong, it roiled his stomach. Brit took a deep breath and told himself the smell didn't mean anything anymore. "There's a table in the back corner."

"I see it. I'll pick up a couple of drinks and join you," John said, heading for the mahogany bar.

Brit pulled out the wooden chair and sat down, tilting the chair back against the adobe wall as he studied the crowd. Enlisted men and noncoms, as he'd expect, but more of them than he'd ever seen on a weeknight before.

"What's going on, John?" he asked when the other man plopped two shot glasses of whiskey on the table.

"Everything is going to hell in a handbasket." He sat down opposite Brit with a weary sigh. "The colonel's more interested in spit and polish than the morale of the men. He even insists on drilling them every day."

Brit snorted with contempt. "These men are used to fighting Indians, not drilling on some damn parade ground. Doesn't Warwick know that?" It sounded as if Colonel Marsden Warwick IV hadn't learned a damn thing about being a good officer in the twenty years since Brit had last seen him.

"Nah. And he doesn't care to learn." John hunched over his whiskey, toying with the glass. "I'm retiring, Brit."

"You?" The front legs of Brit's chair hit the floor with a thud as he leaned forward and stared at his friend. "After thirty years in the army? Why? I've never heard you talk about retiring."

"I've been thinking about it since Warwick arrived." John didn't look up from his whisky. "We could move back East. Emmeline would like that."

Brit drained his whiskey in one swallow. "What does Emmeline think about—My God, she doesn't know, does she? That's why you wanted to come down here."

"I didn't want her fretting. Anyway, I wanted you to know there would be a captain's vacancy coming up so you could apply for it."

"Thanks, John, but I'm only back temporarily. I like being a rancher." He made wet rings on the table with his glass. "Besides, I can't support what the army is doing to the Apaches. It's wrong." His words fell into one of those silences that occur in crowds, and men at three tables turned and looked at him.

"But while you're back, you'll do your duty, I know," John said immediately.

"Of course." But it was already too late. The silence had been replaced by people talking, and no one heard him.

John shook his head. "I wish you hadn't said that, Brit. A lot of people heard you."

"I don't care. I'm not going to lie and say I support a policy that's trying to kill off the whole Apache tribe. Men, women, and children—all of them."

"You know that's an exaggeration."

"Not by much, John. And you know *that*."

Someone spilled a pitcher of beer at the next table and the toasted hops stench washed over Brit, but this time he couldn't keep his memories at bay. They boiled up like a pack of ravenous wolves howling for his blood. His heart pounded and his palms went clammy and—

He gripped the edge of the table as he fought them down, beating them back into the dark dungeons of his mind. Shuddering, he took a deep breath, and locked the doors of his memory on them.

"What just happened?" John asked in a low voice, concern furrowing his broad forehead.

"What?" Brit felt as if he were coming back from

far, far away. "The stink of the beer got to me. It was nothing."

"Look at yourself, man! You're wet with sweat, and you were gripping the table so hard your fingers went white. That's not nothing."

"Let's talk about your retirement," Brit said, desperate to change the subject. "Where do you want to go?"

John studied him with a grim expression. "You know, sometimes talking can help. I'm here, Brit."

"I know you are. And I appreciate it. It's just that I can't—" He gestured, as though he could wave everything away. "I haven't reacted like that in more years than I can remember. I didn't think I was tired, but maybe . . ."

"Maybe it was the strain of escorting the colonel's wife and daughter into the fort. I hear the daughter is a pain in the butt—just like her father." He leaned back in his chair.

Brit frowned at him. "Where did you hear that?"

"Gossip."

"Callista isn't like her father at all. But she can be a pain in the butt, all right." He smiled absently as he searched for words to describe her. "She's a skinny blond reporter for a Washington newspaper and she's always asking questions. Too many. She's no dumb bunny; not much gets by her."

"You're on a first-name basis? Sounds like you spent some time with her."

"Not by choice. I went out to a lookout to search for Apaches, and she insisted on going with me."

"Insisted? Couldn't you stop her?"

"Only if I hog-tied her," Brit said with a rueful grin. Last night he'd been standing by a campfire enjoying talking to her. Who was she with tonight?

John smiled. "And you're not interested in her, are you?"

"Good God! Miss Starch? No way in hell."

"No way in hell? You need to take a look at yourself, Brit. You were smiling the whole time you were telling me about her." John finished his drink and stood up. "Come on, I want to go talk to Emmeline."

Brit walked out on the porch with him. "I'll miss you, John," he admitted.

"What you'll miss is Emmeline's cooking."

"That, too," Brit said. "I'm going to have a cigar and do some thinking before I go back. Say hello to Emmy for me."

"Do it yourself. Come to dinner on Sunday."

"Will do."

"And bring Miss Starch."

Brit chuckled. "That'll be the day!"

He walked down to the corrals, where he'd be alone. Resting his hands on the top rail, he thought about his reaction to the beer. It had been a long time since he'd reacted like that. He'd hoped he'd finally forgotten those terrible years after his mother died. And the unrelenting loneliness and—

Think about the ranch. About how much work needs to be done before next winter. Pulling out his cigar, he bit off the end, then drew a match along the rail and lit up.

What was Callista doing this evening?

Damn! What was she doing in his thoughts? Wasn't it bad enough that she'd invaded his dreams?

Last night she'd visited him again. He had been sleeping soundly when she stole through his dream like a wraith, veiled in golden hair and wearing white gloves. He shook his head, thinking of how incon-

gruous those damned white gloves had been in the
midst of an Apache attack, and yet how like her they
were.

He'd enjoyed talking to her. Which wasn't supposed to happen, dammit!

Was she the prim-and-proper Easterner he'd first
seen? She'd given him several looks that had left his
heart thumping like a runaway train and wondering
if there was passion beneath the starch. What would
her lips feel like against his?

Bah! Too many questions, not enough answers.

Maybe he would try kissing her. Odds were she
would be prim and stiff as a board—but at least he
would have satisfied his curiosity.

Maybe then he could get her out of his mind.

Dinner that first night wasn't at all what Callista
expected. She came downstairs a few minutes late
and everyone was already seated at the table.

Papa sat at the head of the table, but instead of
having the senior officers over to meet Mamere and
her, only one guest joined them.

Callista's stomach clenched into a tight knot when
she saw him. Lieutenant Fowler Stanhope! The
basta— She'd always prided herself on never swearing, and now she couldn't say it, even in her mind.
But the word fit him perfectly. His actions made him
a walking, talking definition of the word.

"Surprise, Callista." Her father beamed at her. "I
know you haven't seen Fowler since we both left
Washington, so I invited him to join us."

Why in the world had Papa invited him? She'd
only gone out with him a few times, and then the last
time—Shuddering, she pushed that memory away.

"I was looking forward to seeing you tonight,

Papa. It's been so long since we were all together as a family." She knew she was skating perilously close to impoliteness, but she didn't care.

"But now you can see us both, my dear. Sit down so we can start. I'm starved."

She had to force herself to walk across the room and sit directly across from him. "Hello, Fowler," she said through tightly clenched teeth.

"Callista, my dear, as beautiful as ever." Fowler smirked at her, knowing full well that she hadn't told her father what had happened that night.

He watched her with bulging, froggy eyes. He'd let his blond hair grow until it brushed his shoulders, and he'd grown a long, flowing handlebar mustache, like General Custer had worn.

At first she hadn't told anyone because she was ashamed. She'd gone back over her actions time and again, wondering what she'd done that made him think he could do that. But she could find nothing that would have led him on.

Then she began to get angry. And her anger grew and grew. But still she didn't tell her father, because by that time she'd realized that Papa would confront Fowler.

"Ahh, put that roast right here, Josephina."

As the housekeeper carried in a huge rib roast, her father banged the table in front of him with the carving knife. The rich aroma of roast beef filled the dining room. "Smells good, doesn't it, Fowler?"

Callista glanced at her father as he began to slice the roast. What was going on?

"Remember those balls we went to in Washington, Miss Callista?" Fowler gave her another smirk.

"As clearly as if they were yesterday." She wanted

to lean across the table and slap that smirk right off his face.

"Good. Good. Here you go, Fowler." Her father passed a huge rib of beef to him.

"I'll just take a small slice, Papa," she said, passing her mother's plate and hers to him. She wasn't going to eat anything anyway. She'd lost her appetite.

"It's good to have you here, Verlene." Her father placed a thin slice of beef on the plate. "You too, Callista."

"Thank you, Papa. I'm glad we're finally here."

Fowler broke open a hot roll and slathered butter on it. The warm yeasty scent of hot bread floated up to her. Callista busied herself moving the peas around on her plate, rather than look at his damn hands and remember what he'd tried to do.

If she told him, Papa would take action against Fowler, and those actions would break up his friendship with Fowler's father, Senator Hiram Stanhope. And the senator was Papa's strongest supporter.

But the senator was a lying, conniving man who would support whoever could do the most for the senator once he was president. So if Papa and the senator weren't friends, then they would be enemies. And that would be the end of any chance Papa had of becoming president of the United States.

Everything Mamere and Papa had worked for the last twenty years would be gone. Everything. So she had remained silent.

Silverware tinkled against the Wedgwood serving bowls as the peas and mashed potatoes were passed around. Like an eight-year-old, Fowler poured so much gravy over his potatoes they floated in a pool of gravy and looked absolutely revolting.

"The trip was quite eventful, Marsden," her mother

said. "I could have done quite well without meeting those awful savages. And they burned my special feather mattress."

"I'll get you another." Papa cut a sizable chunk off his slab of beef and popped it into his mouth. "I hope you're ready for a full schedule of entertaining, ladies."

"Of course, Marsden. Aren't we, Callista?"

She looked at her mother absently. What was she asking about? "Certainly," she murmured.

"The governors of both Arizona and New Mexico will be visiting us soon," Papa announced.

"Is General Wallace still governor of New Mexico?" she asked, clutching at straws to get her mind off Fowler. "I couldn't put down that book he has written, *Ben Hur*."

"The general has gone to Turkey as ambassador, Callista."

"Too bad." Callista looked past Fowler's left shoulder and out the window at the darkness.

What was Brit doing this evening? At least he wouldn't be riding out of her life tomorrow. She smiled absently, knowing she'd see him every day, because the Bachelor Officers' Quarters were only four houses away along Officers' Row. Would he remember his offer to teach her to shoot? If only he were sitting across from her, what an interesting dinner she'd be having.

"Ladies," Papa announced, "I want you to know that Fowler has been to Mexico and found a gold mine for me to invest in. And it's already beginning to pay back my investment. This was a wonderful opportunity, and we have Fowler to thank for it."

"How brave of you to go down into Mexico, Fowler. Tell us about your adventures," Verlene said.

In between forkfuls of dripping mashed potatoes, Fowler talked about his trip and droned on and on and on.

Callista stared out the window, not listening. *Where is a good Apache attack when you need it?* she thought glumly, then almost laughed out loud. She preferred an Apache attack to listening to Fowler! That said a lot.

She ran her finger along the edge of the massive mahogany table. From the feel, she could tell it needed a good waxing. That was her job, but it had been months since she'd done it. Papa had taken most of the furniture with him—which had turned out to be a blessing, considering that the Apaches would have burned it, if it had accompanied them. She'd wax it—

Papa's fist banged down on the table. Callista jumped, startled.

"Yessir, by God, I'll catch that damn Geronimo," Papa thundered. "Lucky for me, these frontier officers are so damn incompetent they can't catch him. But I'll send him and all his kind to prison."

"Or hang 'em all," Fowler added enthusiastically. "Or put them in front of a firing—"

"Gentlemen, please." Mamere rapped her sterling-silver knife against her Waterford water goblet. "I won't have such talk at my dinner table." Callista wanted to clap. *Good for Mamere.*

"You're right, Verlene. It's been so long since I sat down with a lady—"

"Never mind, Marsden," Mamere said in her slightly imperious I'm-in-charge-of-the-house voice. "I've forgotten it already. Callista, is something wrong? You're not eating."

"I'm not hungry." Fowler had extended his foot

under the table, and was running it up and down her ankle.

"I hope you're not getting sick."

"I'm just tired." Tired of that smirk plastered on Fowler's face, she kicked him, hard.

"Which is quite understandable, after the journey we had." Mamere shook the bell that rested beside her plate until its light tinkle filled the room. "Where is that woman? It's time for her to clear the table."

Soon Josephina bustled in, wiping her hands on her white apron.

"Fowler wondered if you'd like to go horseback riding tomorrow," Papa said.

Why didn't he ask himself, then? But all she said was, "I need to get settled and rested first, Papa." She'd go to Hades before she'd go anywhere with Fowler.

"Tomorrow, Callista, I'd like you to go down to the sutler's store and see what fabrics he has," Mamere added, as Josephina cleared the table. "We're going to need new morning dresses."

"I'll do it first thing, when I take my daily constitutional." Her walk would give her a chance to become better acquainted with Fort Bowie.

Her mother's chair screeched on the wood floor as she pushed it back and stood up. "Come, Callista, let's repair to the parlor and leave the gentlemen to their cognac and cigars."

"Of course, Mamere." Dropping her crumpled napkin beside her plate, Callista followed her, glad to get away from Fowler.

In the parlor, Mamere settled down in the wing chair beside the fireplace and picked up the sweater she was knitting for Papa. Callista took a corner of the green-velvet sofa and pulled out the square of linen she'd been embroidering for the past month and stretched it over an embroidery hoop. Taking a crewel needle, she threaded it with wool yarn and began her embroidery.

As usual, the peacefulness of sitting quietly and embroidering began to seep into her soul and calm her. Slowly her stomach unclenched.

She pushed the needle through the cloth and brought it back to the right side of the embroidery directly into her finger.

"Oh, applesauce!" Even though the needle was blunt-tipped, it still stung, and she sucked her finger.

"Something wrong, dear?" Mamere glanced up.

"No." Callista examined her stitches. They were as ragged as a five-year-old's, and she threw the embroidery down, suddenly bored to tears with it.

She heard footsteps tromping loudly in the hall and looked up.

Her father flung the double doors open and walked in smiling. No, it was more than a smile. He was grinning.

"Ladies, I have wonderful news." He glanced at Fowler, who'd followed him into the parlor. "Callista, my dear, Fowler has asked for your hand in marriage, and I've said yes."

What was he talking about? She could have sworn he said—No, she had misunderstood him. He couldn't have. "My hand . . . in marriage?" she repeated faintly.

"Oh, that is wonderful," her mother exclaimed. Standing up, she hugged Fowler. "Welcome to our family, Fowler."

"Wait!" Callista gasped. He *had* said marriage! "You want me to . . . married?" No! How could he talk of marriage without discussing it with her? And to Fowler? Over her dead body!

"You'll be a June bride. We can have the nuptials here. I think this calls for a toast to—"

"No! You will not!" Callista cried, as she leaped to her feet. "I can't. I will not!"

"What?" Mamere asked softly.

"What are you saying?" her father asked, his brow furrowing in surprise.

Everyone looked at her as if she'd suddenly grown two heads.

"I mean—" Clasping her hand to her breast, trying to calm her wildly beating heart, Callista took two deep breaths. "I mean, everything is moving too fast," she said in a more normal voice. "Don't I get any say in the matter?" She had to talk to Papa alone, make him understand.

"Of course." Her father sipped from the glass he carried before he continued. "What do you want to say?"

"That I want—I want—" A thousand emotions welled up inside her, leaving her speechless. She tried to put order in her thoughts, tried to get the words out, tried to explain.

Both Papa and Fowler wore smug, closed expressions that said they were just indulging her whims. Even Mamere looked discomfited. Oh heavens, they didn't want to hear her protests!

"Oh, God," she whispered, hurting so badly inside. They were backing her into a corner, and panic set her heart to pounding. No!

She fled the parlor, hurried out the front door, and down the steps. The full moon lit the road, and she started walking blindly down it, trying to calm herself.

The mournful sound of a mouth organ drifted on the wind, as if someone were crying far away.

Oh Lord, what was she going to do? Hades would freeze before she'd marry Fowler. She had to explain to Papa. But she couldn't tell him the real reason!

Brit was twice the man Fowler was, with one hand tied behind his back. Heavens, where had that thought come from?

She saw a man and woman walking arm in arm ahead of her and turned toward the corrals. She didn't want to talk to anyone.

The horses were quiet as she walked between the enclosures. Finally, she slumped against a rail fence.

A horse ambled over and snuffled at her fingers, and she scratched its chin. "I don't know what to do," she murmured. "I want children and—and—"

And Brit, a little voice inside her whispered. Her eyes opened very wide. *And Brit?*

Another horse stuck its head over the rail, and she petted it as she sobbed quietly. "Maybe I want too much."

"Callista?" Brit's low voice came out of the darkness. A whiff of cigar smoke, then the aroma of soap and the faint rustle of broadcloth told her he was beside her. "Are you all right?"

Oh God, she didn't want to be caught crying. Not by him! Not now! Looking away, she brushed her fists over her eyes, wiping away the tears. "I'm—" She choked down a sob. "I've never been better. Excellent, in fact. Superb."

"Like hell you are," he growled.

"As subtle and courteous as ever," she managed, caught between a shocked laugh and a sob.

He stood behind her, not moving, not touching her. Thank heavens. If he'd touched her, he would have felt the tension in her, the sobs she was holding back. She didn't want him to wrap his big hands around her shoulders. She didn't want him to pull her into his arms. She didn't want— Why didn't he touch her, dammit? She *needed* his touch.

"Turn around." His voice was low.

She shook her head. "Go away." She squared her shoulders and pretended to study the horses.

Oh God, why didn't he go away? She didn't want to talk—Not now, not to him. Well, if he wouldn't go away, she would. She took a step away from him.

"Don't run away." He caught her wrist, stopping her. But she still wouldn't turn around, wouldn't look at him. He reached past her and laid his cigar on the rail.

Brit curved his hands over her shoulders and drew her back against him, then he wrapped his arms around her waist, holding her. His arms were warm bands across her midsection. That's all he did.

In spite of her determination to keep up appearances and not to let him know how she was hurting, she felt better with his arms around her, with his warmth enveloping her. She rested her hands on his. But she still stayed stiff and erect.

"What's the matter?" His warm lips brushed her ear, light as a butterfly.

"I can't—" she whispered, then gave up trying to speak and shook her head. Her tears were too close to the surface to talk.

Slowly, with tiny kisses, he worked his way down to the hollow of her shoulder. The stubble on his cheek tickled, and she shivered and arched her head back against his shoulder.

Callista wanted to turn toward him, to have him put his arms around her and his lips on hers.

But when he finally did turn her, she bowed her head a bit so he couldn't see the wetness on her cheeks. He crooked his finger under her chin and lifted her head until he could see her face in the moonlight.

Gently he brushed the tears off her cheeks with his thumbs. "Actually, you don't look half-bad for someone who's been crying. Your nose isn't even red."

She gave a choked gasp and hid her face against his shoulder.

"Was that a laugh or sob?"

"I don't know." And she didn't. "Oh, Brit, I—"

"Ssh." He gathered her into his arms and held her close. His big hands moved over her back in gentle, soothing strokes.

She smelled beer and whiskey and cigars on his shirt, but underneath, she smelled his clean pine-soap scent. "You went out to a bar tonight," she murmured.

"I went to the cantina with another officer."

So he hadn't been out with a woman. Slowly, tentatively, she let her head rest against his chest. He didn't seem to notice. She listened to the steady beat of his heart. Finally she sighed and leaned against him wholeheartedly, wrapping her arms around his waist. Again he didn't seem to notice.

She didn't know how long he held her, only that she began to feel heartened, as if she were absorbing strength from him. He made her feel less alone. Finally, she leaned back, against the corral rails.

"Thank you." She patted her upswept hair, looking for stragglers. "I must look a sight."

"You don't see me running away in horror, do you?"

She chuckled.

"Do you feel better?" His deep, dark voice wrapped around her like the warm quilt her grandmother had made for her when she was five.

"A thousand times better." She drew her hand down his jaw, then stood on tiptoe and brushed a quick kiss over his cheek.

Instantly he pulled her back into his arms. "Nice try," he murmured, "but it's a lot better on the mouth." With a devilish smile, he pointed to his lips. "Plant one here, lady."

Her breasts were pressed against the thick muscles padding his chest, and she could feel the steady thudding of his heart.

"I'm waiting," he murmured. His eyes glittered with silver fire in the moonlight.

She swallowed, trying to wet her desert-dry mouth. "So am I," she whispered.

With a single finger he traced the line of her throat down to the pulse point. That intimate touch made her heart leap like a startled deer.

"Your heart is racing," he murmured as he nuzzled the side of her throat, then strung tiny kisses along her jaw to her mouth, brushing it just once with his lips.

Raising his head, he gazed at her in the moonlight for an eternity, as though studying each of her features, and all the time, anticipation built for that moment when their lips would meet.

She couldn't look into his eyes; he was too close. Her eyes drifted shut, and she waited and she waited. And then when she thought he wasn't going to—

His lips crashed down on hers.

His kiss was hard and powerful, and she sank beneath the hot waves of desire washing over her. She gripped his shoulders tightly as the stars spun overhead.

His tongue swept inside her mouth, and after a moment of shock, she met his thrusts and parries with her own. His rumble of approval, deep in his throat, vibrated through her. She wrapped her arms around his neck as she sought to bring him closer.

He thrust deeper into her mouth, then his tongue retreated. She gave a tiny cry, far back in her throat. And he returned.

When he finally lifted his head they were both breathless and panting as if they'd run miles, and she was shaking with exhilaration and excitement.

Slowly she realized his arms were wrapped around her so tightly she could barely breathe. Though she knew her legs wouldn't support her, she stirred, pressing her hand against his chest.

"Don't ask me to let you go." He brushed kisses as light as snowflakes along her temple.

"You must," she whispered. "We can't stay here all night."

"We could try." He smiled against her lips.

"Please, let me go." She wanted him to, yet she didn't.

He shook his head. "I can't," he whispered in a moment of unexpected truth. "Damn it, I can't."

But he did, loosing his arms and taking a step back and leaving her feeling cold and bereft and melancholy.

"Brit, I—" Reality crashed through her passion-muddled brain. This was Brit. Uncivilized. Rugged. Dangerous.

A hero!

She wrenched away from him and took a hasty step back. "Oh God, Brit, I can't. I mustn't."

A sob filled her throat and she clamped her hand over her mouth. Lifting her skirts, she turned and fled.

But she slowed after a few steps. Stopped after a few more. Looked back. Brit stood where she'd left him.

She flitted back to him—like a moth going to the flame—quickly kissed him on the mouth, then flitted away again. Only this time she didn't stop.

As she rounded the last corral, she couldn't help glancing back. The red glow from his cigar gave his rugged features a satanic look.

All too appropriate, she thought. She might as well be attracted to the Devil as to him.

Chapter 6

Dispatch to the *Times/Tribune* Newspapers

We have arrived at our destination. Fort Bowie is a large garrison in high rolling desert, surrounded by mountains. Yes, dear readers, I am learning that Arizona is more than desert. It has the most rugged, forbidding mountains I've ever seen. They are green islands, rising out of the sea of desert.

When we arrived, the commander was most pleased to see our hero. It seems that General Crook, who is leading the fight against the Apaches, has been long acquainted with him. And in the present emergency, the general saw the need for men of such stature to stem the tide of Apache raiding and has called upon our hero to once again serve his country as Chief of Scouts. He will be based here at the fort, so I shall be able to keep you informed of his further exploits.

From Arizona Territory, this is Callista Warwick.

Early the next morning, Callista marched purposefully along the wagon road. She'd been up with the dawn after a long, sleepless night.

When she'd returned last night, she'd seen through

the window that her mother had already gone to bed, but Fowler and her father were still in the parlor, talking. Not wanting to talk to them, Callista had slipped in and tiptoed upstairs.

She'd sat on the stool in front of her dressing table and unpinned her hair, then brushed it one hundred strokes. With each stroke a name echoed in her mind—Brit.

Brit and the mind-stunning kiss they'd shared. She touched her lips with a sense of wonder. Yes, shared. She had given and taken, just as he had.

Before Brit she'd mainly *been* kissed. Oh, she'd kissed back a few times, thinking she was missing something since she hadn't felt the fireworks her friends bragged about. But she'd found that just kissing back didn't turn a so-so kiss into an entire body-tingling event.

But with Brit it was different. Never before had she felt breathless and dizzy and hot and cold all the way down to her toes.

When she'd finally gone to bed, her dreams had been invaded by Brit bending over her, blotting out the stars with his kisses. Brit holding out his hand to her. Brit inviting her to go where she'd never gone before.

He appealed to something in her, something that was wild and free and daring and all the things she wasn't. She was torn between wanting to experience his kiss again and fear of experiencing his kiss again.

It had been a turning point for her. No longer could she deny that she was attracted to him.

"Enough," she muttered, feeling dangerously close to tears from the emotions seething in her. "You have work to do. Put him out of your mind." As if she could!

Sighing wearily, she started down the hill toward

the Fort Bowie Mercantile. She hadn't even given a thought to Fowler yet. Not that she needed to; there was no way she'd ever marry him. The mere thought of him made her stomach knot up.

The store was a wide, sand-colored adobe building. A porch extended across the whole front, with two sets of widely separated steps. Over one set of steps, the word CANTINA was sloppily written in bold red paint. Over the other set, the word MERCANTILE was printed in sturdy black letters. On those steps, clay pots filled with bright yellow, white, and purple pansies nodded a cheery good morning to her.

Those flowers had to be a woman's idea—for even women who couldn't read would know which set of steps led to the store. Calista walked up the wide steps to the shady porch, where large windows flanked the open door. An inviting sit-a-while bench sat in front of one window, and axes, shovels, and hoes leaned against a large flour barrel in front of the other.

At the other end of the porch, two more large windows framed the swinging double doors of the cantina. She winced as someone pounded out discordant notes on a very out-of-tune piano. Good heavens, someone was in there at this early hour?

When she walked into the store, she had to pause to give her eyes a chance to adjust after the bright sunlight. The aroma of cinnamon and coffee beans welcomed her.

"Good morning," said the storekeeper from the back of the store. "You're new here," he added, coming around the counter and walking up the center aisle toward her with a smile and an outstretched hand. "I'm Justin Porter. My sister Hester and I run this store."

Blond and blue-eyed, he was in his late thirties. If it hadn't been for the white butcher's apron over his plaid shirt and jeans, she would have taken him for a cowboy.

"I'm Callista Warwick." She shook his hand.

"Ah, the colonel's daughter. We've been expecting you and your mother."

"We arrived yesterday and needed a few things, Mr. Porter."

A large woman approached them from the back. As she barreled past a table piled high with work shirts and denim jeans, she knocked some onto the floor.

"Let me be the first to welcome you to Fort Bowie, Miss Warwick," the woman gushed, elbowing Mr. Porter aside and extending her hand. "I'm Augusta Kreutz. My husband is Captain Kreutz. Did you have a pleasant journey? How is your mother? Not too tired by the trip, I hope."

"My mother is fine. Thank you for asking," Callista said pleasantly but formally.

"My, my, white gloves." The gray-haired woman grabbed Callista's hand in both of hers and pumped it up and down. "I haven't seen white gloves since we left the East. They won't do out here, you know. They get dirty almost as soon as you put them on, what with all the sand and dust."

Callista smiled frostily. "I would feel undressed without my gloves." Ladies always wore gloves.

"Oh." The older woman looked taken aback for a moment, then recovered. "Well, that's how I felt, too, when I first arrived. But I soon saw it was futile to wear them. You will, too," she finished with certainty.

"Ah, I see I have another customer." Mr. Porter

broke into the conversation smoothly, saving Callista from having to reply. "Ladies, feel free to look around. Take your time. I'll be here to answer any questions." He hurried off to wait on a young woman who leaned against the counter at the back and waved a pair of men's leather gauntlets.

"Humph!" Mrs. Kreutz sniffed as she eyed the woman with dislike. "That's our schoolteacher. She's not very good, if you ask me. But at least our boy, Harold, has had the same teacher all year. Last year we had three."

"Why?" Had the Apaches scared them off or—?

"They kept quitting to get married." Drawing herself up to her full height, as if she were getting up a head of steam, she glared at the young woman. "At least Miss Hendricks has had the decency to put educating our children ahead of her primitive urges."

Callista pressed her lips together to stop the words that wanted to roll off her tongue. *Primitive urges indeed!*

"Excuse me, I see some fabric I want to look at." She edged past the woman and went to the sidewall, where bolts of cloth were stacked.

To her dismay, Mrs. Kreutz dogged her steps. "They don't have a good selection here. You'll have to go into Tombstone for that. There's a dressmaker there, and she has ready-to-wear dresses, too."

Callista ignored Mrs. Kreutz's chatter as she pulled out the bolts. She had a choice of checkered gingham in blue or red, coarse black muslin, and a few others.

The cuckoo clock at the back of the store began to bong.

"Oh, dear me." Mrs. Kreutz patted her chubby cheek with a flustered air. "I didn't know it was already eight o'clock. I must go. Have work to do, you know."

Callista nodded and watched her bustle away, then turned back to the cloth. It was a small selection, but the ginghams would work, and maybe she could order fabric.

Mr. Porter was still talking to the young woman when Callista arrived at the counter, and he turned to her.

"Miss Warwick, this is our schoolteacher, Daisy Hendricks."

"Hello." Daisy flashed her a grin that did nothing to hide her slightly protruding front teeth or the freckles dancing across her nose and cheeks. "I see you finally got away from Mrs. Kreutz."

"It was the clock that sent her off, not me." Callista couldn't help smiling back.

"Humph!" Daisy sniffed in a perfect imitation of Mrs. Kreutz. "Have to go. Have to go. Work to do, you know."

Callista laughed. "You *do* know her." The sharp aroma coming from a wheel of cheddar cheese reminded her she hadn't eaten breakfast.

"Everyone knows her. She's on every committee known to man." Daisy had startlingly blue eyes. "Anyway, welcome, Miss Warwick." Her carrot red hair was piled atop her head in a haphazard upsweep that looked as if it would come down any second.

"It's Callista." She held out her hand.

"Daisy, here," she replied as they shook. "I understand Britton Chance escorted you and your mother into the fort after an Apache attack?"

"Yes. Then when we got here there was a telegram waiting for him, ordering him back to duty."

"It'll be nice having Brit around again," Daisy

said. She glanced at the clock. "I'd better be going off to school myself. I wouldn't put it past some of my young charges to get into trouble if I'm not there."

"Before you go—" Callista rested her hand on the other woman's arm. "I'm reporting on the West for newspapers back East. Would you have time to talk to me about your experiences?"

"I'd love to. Come by school any day after two."

"Why don't you come to tea at my father's house tomorrow after you finish?"

Daisy blinked. "Tea?" she said weakly. "I've never been to tea."

"No, no." Callista waved away her misgivings. "Not formal high tea. I just thought we could sit and have a cup of tea and talk without being interrupted."

"Since you put it that way, that sounds nice. I'll see you then. Bye." She waved as she grabbed her package and hurried toward the door.

Callista turned to Mr. Porter. "I need staples, Mr. Porter." She went down her list. "Canned milk. A wedge of that cheese that's making my stomach rumble. A brick of Arbuckle's Coffee. And do you have Twinings teas? Perhaps some Hires Root Beer and Durkee's Sauce?"

"Yep." Mr. Porter moved a ladder over to his tallest shelves. Climbing up two steps, he paused with his hand on the milk. "How many do you want? Find any cloth to your liking?"

"Three cans. Just the gingham, and that's only good for morning dresses. We'll need more than that. Some of our clothes burned when we ran into Apaches."

The cans clattered as Mr. Porter set them on the

counter. "Apaches, you say? You're lucky you could drive them off."

"Actually we didn't. Mr. Chance scared them off." Her heart skipped a beat at the thought of him.

"Brit, eh? That sounds like something he'd do." He added a tin of tea and sacks of beans and rice to her pile. "Shame he decided to get out of the army. It needs more mavericks like him."

"Mavericks?"

"People who think for themselves instead of believing everything they're told. The army needs more thinkers in these times. People who can find new solutions to the Indian problem instead of just trying to kill 'em all off."

"I hadn't thought about it, but you're probably right."

He pulled a pencil out from behind his ear and began totaling her purchases. "There's a dressmaker over in Tombstone. You might want to go see her if you need dresses made."

"Is she the closest?"

"Yep." He folded her material and tied it with string.

"I just might do that. I'll take these now," she said, dropping the tea and milk into her wicker basket and picking up the cloth. "I'll send someone for the rest."

As she was walking out, Callista spied the denim jeans and work shirts Mrs. Kreutz had knocked off the table earlier. She turned to tell Mr. Porter, but he'd disappeared into the back. Kneeling, she began picking them up and putting them back on the table.

She reached for the last pair of jeans just as a copper-skinned hand grasped them. Startled, she looked up. . . .

Straight into the obsidian eyes of an Apache war-.

rior in tan pants and a dirty white shirt. A blood-red headband kept his hair out of his eyes, and a huge nasty knife hung from his belt.

She gazed at him in shock. Her handbag and basket fell from her numb fingers. Without taking her eyes from him, she reached behind her, braced her hand on the table leg, and stood up.

He had to be one of the scouts Brit had told her about. But he looked just as savage as the Apaches who'd ambushed them.

He crouched, with his hand still on the pants, watching her. Rising to his feet, he picked up her handbag and basket and held them out to her as he spoke.

She couldn't understand his language, but she shook her head anyway. There was no way she'd get close to him.

"There you are," Brit's familiar voice made her whirl. "I've been looking for you." He stood in the doorway, silhouetted against the bright light.

"Oh, thank heavens. How did you know where to find me?" Relief flooded her. Brit would know what to say to his scout.

"Callista?" He walked to her side. "What are you doing here?"

"I-I thought you were talking to me. Just now."

"No, I was looking for Walks-with-Horses, my sergeant of scouts. I see you two have already met."

"Not exactly." He'd casually rested his hand in the small of her back, and it felt wonderfully reassuring.

"Then let me introduce you. Callista, this is Walks-with-Horses." He talked to the Apache in another language, but she recognized her name.

"You speak their language?"

"Some. After all, I am Chief of Scouts." He inhaled her woman scent mixed with a light lilac scent. And no starch, he thought with a smile.

"I tried to give her the things she dropped," Walks-with-Horses said in Apache.

"I'll take care of it," Brit replied in the same language. He took the handbag and basket and handed them to Callista. "He just wanted to give these to you," he explained.

"Thank him for me, please." The Apache was almost as tall as Brit, she realized. His bronze features betrayed no emotion as he gazed at her.

"No. *You* thank him. Try *grácias*. He understands Spanish better than English."

"*G-grácias.*" She smoothed a hand down her raspberry dress nervously, not sure what to do. "They speak Spanish, too?" she said in an aside to Brit.

"Uh-huh. They've been fighting the Spanish for two hundred years. We're newcomers in comparison."

"So he speaks three languages?"

"Yes."

The savage spoke three languages, while she, the civilized person, spoke one. She found that fact strangely disorienting, as if the world had been turned upside down.

The Apache eyed her for a searching moment, then he nodded abruptly. He said something to Brit, then stalked past them, taking care to give her a wide berth.

Callista caught a whiff of rancid bacon grease from his hair. She watched to be sure he was leaving, before she turned to Brit.

He was smiling. "Walks-with-Horses said your hair is the color of *hoddentin*. That's the yellow of corn pollen. It's sacred to the Apaches."

"Really?" Surprised, she glanced at the departing Apache. "How nice of him. And thank you, Brit, for coming in when you did. I didn't know what to do when I looked up and saw him. I guessed he was a scout, but that knife of his—" she shuddered.

"It can take a while to get used to dealing with the Apaches." He rested his hand on her back, but she was so stiff with tension he began massaging her in ever-broadening circles.

"I admit I was afraid. He looked just as fierce and dangerous as the Apaches who attacked us, and there was that little niggling doubt in my mind. *What if he wasn't a scout?* All right, now you can call me a fool for being afraid."

"I don't think you were a fool, nor do I think you were afraid. I think you were wary. Being wary is not stupidity, Callista. It's a lifesaving alertness. Did you need it with Walks-with-Horses? No. But you didn't know that."

"But I will next time." Callista could feel much of her tension melting away under the soothing massage of his fingers.

"Now come with me." With his hand in the small of her back, he guided her to the wall where stacks of straw and felt Stetson hats were arrayed on the shelves.

"Here." Grasping a creamy white felt by the creased crown, he turned and plunked it down on her head.

It was too big and rested on her ears. She didn't have to look in a mirror to know she looked silly in it. "What are you doing?"

"Finding you a hat. But this definitely isn't the one." He returned that hat to the shelf and stood, stroking his chin as he contemplated the others. "Do you have any preference for color?"

"Whatever you think will work." She reached past him and picked out a hat and plopped it on her head. "How does this look?"

"Like hell."

"Maybe I don't need a hat. I have my parasol."

"You don't have it with you now, do you? Anyway, it won't do the trick here. Especially if your're riding and the wind starts blowing. Here, let's see how this one fits." He plunked a natural straw squarely on her head.

"Well, it's not sitting on my ears, at least," she murmured dryly. She pushed the front brim up.

He smiled down at her. "Now you look like a farmer. Try it this way." He tilted it rakishly to the side.

His fingers trailed across her shoulder, awakening a fluttering butterfly in her stomach. "Does it look all right?"

"Looks fine." He tapped the crown a couple of times. "Always wear it with the chinstrap out, so if it blows off, it doesn't blow away. In some of the winds we get here, you could chase it all the way back to St. Louis."

He caught her hand and turned it over, smoothing his thumb over her palm. "Do you have riding gloves? Real leather riding gloves. Not white cotton."

"Yes, I do," she said briskly, touched and not wanting to admit it. With all the other things he had to do, he was worrying about her hands.

"Good. Learn to keep them with you, because between riding and the thorns on cactus and trees, you can rip your hands up if you don't have good protection."

She went up to the counter. By the time she finished paying and turned around, he was gone. Disappointment nudged her, but she shoved it away. What did she expect, for him to wait for her? Why? She marched resolutely outside.

And he was there, leaning against a pillar, his arms crossed over his broad chest.

"I'll walk you home," he said, not giving her a chance to say no.

"It really isn't necessary." But, oh, she wanted him to.

He led his horse, and they walked along the dusty road, side by side. Whenever the breeze stirred, Callista's skirt brushed his polished black boots. Sometimes her skirt wrapped completely around his leg, as though clinging to him. Her next step would pull it away.

"Careful," he murmured, taking her arm as she stepped over a particularly deep rut.

If she'd thought about it, she would have wondered what to say and do when she first met him today. After their kiss last night she wasn't sure how to act. In a roundabout way, the Apache had saved her from those dilemmas.

Only now she was thinking about it and feeling awkward and gawky and—For Pete's sake, she chided herself. She was twenty-six. Gawky was a word for teenagers, not women. But it was how she felt.

At the white picket fence that surrounded the commander's house, Brit turned to her.

"I promised you a shooting lesson. The men are using the firing range this morning, but we can use it this afternoon."

"Good. I'm anxious to start my lessons."

Though she needed to be careful around him. After last night, she was playing with fire. And she was liable to get burned.

He pushed the picket gate open for her. She gazed down at his strong hand, at the sprinkling of dark hair on the back, then drew a single finger along it as she went by and had the satisfaction of watching his fingers tighten on the gate.

"This afternoon, Callista."

His low voice was rich with promises, and a frisson of excitement went through her. But she didn't look back.

Brit watched Callista walk up the path. Last night's fireworks had floored him.

He'd suspected there was passion beneath Callista's starched exterior. But he'd found much more than he'd expected—and been knocked for a month of Sundays in the process.

He'd paced away a large part of the night thinking about the sparks ignited by their kiss. The kiss that was supposed to satisfy his curiosity and get her out of his system. Ha!

He shook his head in wonder. Hell, there'd been more fireworks than in a cow town on Saturday night.

But she wasn't the reason he was at Fort Bowie. He had a job to do. If he succeeded, he'd stop the Apache wars and the killing. If he failed, many people would die.

He couldn't let his attraction to her interfere with the job he had to do. He couldn't!

Chapter 7

Dispatch to the *Times/Tribune* Newspapers

The Fort Bowie Mercantile is well supplied with dried foods and canned goods. The wives on the post who must cook three meals a day depend on this selection, since the nearest town is fifty miles away. Many of the enlisted men's wives also tend gardens and sell the surplus, so fresh peas, lettuce, carrots, and potatoes are available now. In a few months, I understand we'll have corn, tomatoes and watermelon. I must confess finding fresh vegetables in the desert was a pleasant surprise.

Especially after seeing what passes for kitchen arrangements here. All the cooking is done in a tin-roofed shack set a distance behind the house.

I thought it extremely inconvenient, until an Arizonan pointed out that cooking outside in the summer didn't heat up the house. Ladies who've survived the summers here say these separate kitchens are a godsend. In July, I will let you know if I agree.

This is Callista Warwick in Arizona Territory.

As Callista walked up the steps, she noticed Mamere sitting on the porch drinking her morning coffee.

"Good morning, Mamere. Isn't it a lovely morning?"

"Quite refreshing. Would you like some coffee? Did you find any fabric we can use?"

"Yes and yes." Callista took the white-wicker chair across from her mother and broke the string tying the fabric. "I found these two ginghams for morning dresses," she said, opening them up on the table.

She sipped her coffee as Mamere looked them over.

"These will do temporarily, but we need more dresses. Is there a dressmaker on the post? Maybe she'd have a better selection."

"The storekeeper said the closest dressmaker is in Tombstone."

"Then I think you should go there and order dresses for us. You know what I like." She leaned back in her wicker chair, holding her cup with both hands. "Where did you get your new hat?"

"Do you like it?" Taking it off, Callista rested it in her lap. "Mr. Chance picked it out for me. He said I needed a real hat to protect me from the sun here."

"Did I see him walk you home, too?" Mamere buttered a slice of toast.

"You know you did." Sometimes Mamere was as subtle as a sledgehammer.

Mamere frowned thoughtfully. "He disturbs me, Callista. I feel the icy wind of danger from him."

"I *know* he's dangerous." But dangerous didn't begin to cover it. He was interesting and smart and so many other things. "You don't have to worry about me."

"That's just it, dear. I don't know if he's a danger to you or to our whole family." Putting her toast down, she wiped her mouth with her napkin. "I also think we need to talk about last night."

Callista gazed at her in horror. How did she know about their kiss? "Last night?" she said faintly.

"Fowler's marriage proposal," her mother prodded. "You do remember it, don't you?"

A shudder of revulsion went through her. She'd tried not to think about Fowler all morning. "I know that Fowler proposed to Papa," she said, choosing her words very precisely. "He didn't propose to me."

Her mother gave a long sigh. "Why are you splitting hairs, Callista? And what were you so upset about last night?"

Callista sipped her coffee slowly, trying to find a way to gently tell her mother that she wouldn't marry Fowler, but she couldn't. "I really don't want to talk about it."

"All right, Callista." She wagged her finger at her daughter. "But only for the time being. Whatever the problem is, I'm sure we can solve it if we work together."

Not this time, Mamere.

"Have you decided what you're going to tell Fowler?" her mother added.

"I will consider his proposal very carefully." She had to find a way to say no without angering Fowler or his father.

"Thank you, Callista, I hope you do." Her mother watched a squad of men marching back and forth at the other end of the parade ground. "Your father didn't mention it at dinner, but later he told me that the senator has agreed to run his presidential campaign next year. And you know that the senator has never lost a race."

"That means he thinks Papa will win." When she'd

been working on the articles about fraud in military contracts, she'd run into Senator Hiram Stanhope's name more than once.

"The senator thinks you'll be a wonderful hostess at senate functions, after you marry Fowler."

"That's nice. I'm going to the stables to see if there are any good horses available." Rising, Callista put on her hat. Mamere was too astute, her questions too probing. She couldn't answer any more without revealing her loathing of Fowler. "When I come back, I want to put away my books and see that the mahogany table gets a good waxing. Last night I noticed that it needed one."

The stable doors were wide-open and Callista walked into the alleyway that ran down the center. She ambled down it, smelling the horses and leather and just-cut-grass scent of hay. They were familiar scents amidst the strange, pungent odors of the desert.

Halfway down the row of box stalls, she spotted a dappled gray mare with an alert look in her eyes that Callista liked. Opening the stall door, she went in and petted the mare. Callista ran her hands over the horse, checking it out. She was bending down, running her hand down the mare's leg, when she heard voices and recognized Brit's deep rumble.

She had her hand on the stall door, ready to go out and greet him, when she heard the other man say, "Who do you suppose is smuggling guns to the Apaches?"

"Warwick is my prime suspect."

Shocked, she froze. Then she crouched down behind the stall door and listened.

"Warwick? Hell, I don't like the man, but I can't believe that. He's incompetent, but he's not a traitor."

"Why did Warwick request assignment to Fort Bowie when he's avoided frontier posts for twenty years? He's got to have a hidden reason."

"Good question," the other man said. "It's obvious he thinks the officers who serve out here are a bunch of stupid hicks. So why would he come out?"

"He's used to living high on the hog. What if he's suddenly broke and has to make money fast?"

The mare lipped Callista's ear and sniffed her hair. She pushed the horse's muzzle away, hoping Brit didn't come over to see what the mare found so fascinating on the floor of her stall.

"He was stationed in Washington, and there's always bribery going on there with military contracts. Why not get cash that way?" the other man said.

"That source of money has dried up. A newspaper reporter exposed the corruption last year, and a congressman and several officers went to prison. No one dares to offer or accept bribes now."

"So, if you need money fast and you can't rob a bank or solicit a bribe, what do you do?"

"Exactly." Brit's voice kept coming closer and closer. "I tried to tell him yesterday that the Apaches had a longer range with their guns than the army's rifles have, but he said that wasn't important." She heard the squeak of a door and realized he must be near the tack room. "And maybe it isn't, if you're the one selling the guns."

"What are you going to do?"

"I have to stop that source of rifles for the renegade Apaches. Otherwise, a lot more people will die."

"It'll be tough."

"I know. That's why I'm going to do some nosing around now. Maybe my scouts can learn something."

"I'll see you later, Brit."

She heard one set of footsteps recede. The other pair came close to the stall where she huddled, and she crouched even lower, trying to make herself smaller. A whiff of leather told her that Brit had walked by carrying a saddle.

Callista heard him open a stall door and the rumble of his voice as he talked to Red, followed by the slap of a saddle blanket going on a horse's back. There was silence, and she pictured him smoothing out the wrinkles, then came the jingle and creak as he swung the saddle up on the big horse.

Finally, she heard him open the stall door and the clip-clop of hooves as he led the horse outside. She waited until she heard his horse trot away before she emerged and hurried to the stable door.

How could he think Papa was selling guns to the enemy? Why, the idea was ludicrous! She'd set him straight.

But as she walked across the the parade ground, something else Brit had said nagged at her. He'd implied that Papa was broke. But that couldn't be; she would have realized it.

Her steps slowed. Or would she? Papa always handled the money. She and Mamere knew nothing about their finances. Papa always saw to it that Mamere had money for herself and to run the house. And she had insisted on living on her salary, since she started working.

If he was in financial trouble, he'd never admit it.

When she was investigating bribes in the War Department she'd learned what to look for. Had there been a change in spending habits during the last year or six months?

Papa had sold the foursome of flashy, high-stepping hackney horses that pulled the carriage and replaced them with two much cheaper horses a few months ago. He'd asked Mamere to cut down on their food bills, but not to stint on parties. And he'd changed cigar brands. He'd been smoking Cubans before, was he still? She'd have to look.

Maybe there was something to Brit's speculations about Papa's finances. But that had nothing to do with his ridiculous suspicion that Papa was selling guns to the Apaches. Brit might as well suspect her, too. She was as likely as Papa!

She walked up the steps to the front door, still thinking about their finances. She could contribute to the household expenses if Papa was short. Though how would she bring it up? She already knew exactly what Papa would say: that dealing with grubby money wasn't something ladies should have to do, and everything was fine.

That afternoon Brit led Red and a docile mare up to the Warwick's white picket fence. As he walked up the gravel path he saw a shadow behind one of the first-floor lace curtains.

When he lifted the knocker on the front door and rapped, the door opened almost instantly.

"Hi," Callista said in a soft voice that put a hitch in his breathing. She was wearing a starch-stiffened white apron over a purple riding skirt and white shirt, yet she looked soft and beautiful.

"Hello." There was a smudge of dirt on her right cheek, and she'd tied a red-and-white bandanna around her hair.

She held her finger up to her lips. "If you would keep your voice down, please," she whispered. "My mother is taking a nap, and I don't want to disturb her."

"Is she ill?"

"No, she tires easily, that's all. She was devastated when Marsh died, and she never fully recovered."

"Marsh?" Taking his Stetson off, he held it by the brim.

"Marsden Warwick the Fifth, my brother."

"I'm sorry."

"Thank you. It was many years ago. I was only eight when it happened." A wave of pain swept across her features. "Won't you come in?" She stepped back and gestured him in.

Her hips swayed an invitation as she led him across the entrance hall into the parlor. He dropped his Stetson on the hall table beside her white gloves as he went by.

"I'm looking forward to getting out of the house. After you left I spent the morning waxing the dining-room table and I just started putting my books away."

Stacks of books littered the floor, two tables, and the dark green sofa. Brit moved closer to the mahogany built-in bookcase that occupied one wall and scanned the volumes that were already shelved.

"Have you read all these?"

"My mother was ill for a few years, and I would sit by her bed and read to her. It entertained both of us." She smiled. "It's much safer exploring imaginary worlds than the real one."

"These are arranged alphabetically by author?"

"It makes it easy for me to find a book," she said crisply. "You know, a place for everything and everything in its place. That way there are no surprises."

"Sounds like you don't like surprises."

"I don't." Untying her apron, she slipped it off and dropped it on a stack of books.

"Why?" She'd surprised him several times and he'd liked each one. "Surprises can be fun, you know."

"Not the ones I've met up with." She crossed her arms over her bosom and raised her chin as though the subject was closed. He wondered how many surprise kisses it would take to change her mind.

"Surely you're not equating surprises with disasters. They're not the same thing at all. Surprises can be fun. Haven't you ever had a surprise birthday party?"

"No. Have you?"

"No." He'd never even had a birthday party.

"See."

He shook his head, even as he smiled. "I'll just have to show you."

He heard movement behind him and turned to see the Mexican housekeeper standing in the doorway, twisting her apron in her hands.

"Do you need me, Josephina?" Callista asked.

"*Sí. Sí.*"

"If you'll excuse me, Brit, I'll be back shortly."

"I think there's enough reading material here for me." Her soft scent lingered, like an airy caress.

He skipped Dickens—never could stomach him. But Tennyson was a different story. Brit pulled out *Idylls of the King*. He'd carried it when he'd been a drummer boy in Sherman's army.

At night he would lie by the campfire and read it to get away from the stench of unwashed bodies and blood and death. There had been passages that carried him over the sea to King Arthur's kingdom. In fact, the small volume had been what stopped the bullet and let him rescue the general.

He opened to one of his favorite passages. Brit

didn't know how long he'd been reading when he heard the tap of Callista's boots as she came down the hall. He closed the book and shoved it back on the Tennyson shelf. It was one thing to read a romantic like Tennyson; it was another thing to admit it.

"Are you ready to go?" he asked when she bustled in.

"I think so." She shrugged into her purple jacket and buttoned it as he retrieved his Stetson. The jacket was form-fitting and did an excellent job of emphasizing her elegant curves. She pulled on soft leather riding gloves. As they headed for the door, he picked up her new hat and plunked it on her head. "Your mount is the gentlest horse on the fort," he reassured her.

"I'm a good rider," she replied, grasping the sidesaddle horn. "A Prussian cavalry officer taught me."

"Why didn't you say so? I would have gotten you a more spirited horse." Brit clasped his hands together for her to step into, then boosted her up onto the saddle.

"It's all right. This old girl will do." She stroked the mare's neck.

Brit swung up on Red, and they followed the wagon road out of the fort and down the hill into a long, wooded valley.

"Which one is the road to Tombstone?" Callista asked when they came to a fork in the road.

"That one."

"Race you," she yelled as her mare took off at a dead run, with Callista leaning low over her neck.

"You're on!" He sent Red bounding after the mare. He would have caught her in a couple of strides, but he kept a tight rein on Red, letting her stay ahead.

She looked back at him, laughing with such pure joy, he couldn't help smiling. They were neck and neck when they came sweeping around a curve and saw the rickety old wagon stopped in the road and a man in uniform on horseback, talking to the driver.

Brit put Red into a sliding halt as Callista reined in the mare, and dust ballooned up around them. By the time it cleared the rider had disappeared, as though he'd never been there.

In Brit's experience, anyone who disappeared that quickly was hiding something. "Follow the road back to the fort," he yelled at Callista as he touched spur to Red. The big horse leaped forward at a dead run. He came up beside the wagon, looked at the driver, trying to memorize his features, and was past him.

The brush was still moving where the rider had gone into the mesquite trees, and he sent Red onto the same path. He caught glimpses of the rider, but couldn't get close enough to recognize him. They dashed down a narrow, twisty side canyon, then burst out into the Silver Springs Valley.

There was no one in sight. He reined Red in.

"Good boy!" he said, rubbing the neck of the foam-flecked horse. "It's not your fault we didn't catch him."

Dismounting, he crouched to study the other horse's hoofprints. If there was something distinctive about them, it would help to identify them later. The horse was shod and a V-shaped wedge was notched into the print of the right-front horseshoe.

"Where is he?" Callista called as she galloped up on her thoroughly winded mare.

He rose to his feet, staring at her, shocked. "Where the hell did you come from?"

"I followed you."

"I told you to go back to the fort!" He grabbed her mare's reins under its chin, taking control of the horse. "What if you'd fallen? Or gotten lost? I didn't know you were out here. I would have gone back to the fort and left you out here."

He was surprised by the wave of fear that washed over him. But what she'd done was dangerous. A woman didn't go riding alone in Arizona.

She laughed and shook her head. "I'd have to be dumber than a stump to get lost coming down that canyon, Brit. And if I got lost in the mesquites, I just had to wander around until I hit the road, then I would have taken it back to the fort. Either way, I was fine. And in the meantime, maybe I could help you."

"Help me? How?" He was damn angry at the risks she'd blithely taken. "With what? And what if whoever I was chasing had doubled back and ambushed me—or you?"

Tilting her head, she considered that possibility. "Yes, that might have been a problem. But since it didn't happen, it isn't."

"Or what if you had run into Apaches while you were blithely riding across the countryside alone?" He was overreacting, but he also knew the hazards she could have faced.

"I didn't, so that's that," she snapped, plainly at the end of her patience. "Did you get a good look at him?"

"Who?"

Callista rolled her eyes. "Do you have a memory problem? Whoever you were chasing. *Why* did you chase him?"

"I couldn't get close enough. He was in' uniform, though. All I was saw was flashes of him and his horse through the brush and trees. And I took off after him because he was beside the wagon when we came around the curve, but by the time the dust cleared, he was gone."

"Which means he had something to hide. Was there anything distinctive about his horse's hoofprints?"

"There's a V-notch in the right front shoe. Where did you learn to look at a horse's hoofprints?"

She shrugged. "When I was following a fraud story in Washington. Let's go back and get a closer look at that wagon. The driver has to stick to the road and he can't get far, even though the horses pulling it were in good shape."

"You noticed that, too? It wasn't as rickety as it looked either." He swung up on Red and edged up beside her. "There's a shortcut to the Tombstone road. Stay close to me. I don't want you to get lost." They followed a sandy dry creek bed until Brit halted.

"Let me go ahead." He rode up on the Tombstone road and waited in the middle for the wagon. Callista didn't come up on the road with him, staying out of sight until they knew the situation with the wagon. His respect for her went up a notch.

Finally, the wagon came into view and he waited until the driver stopped the horses. He moved up close and tried to talk to the driver, but he was a Mexican who didn't speak English, and Brit's Spanish was poor. He saw Callista come out on the road behind the wagon and walk her horse up to it. As he and the driver talked and gestured, she lifted a corner of the tarpaulin covering the bed and peeked under.

He thanked the driver and wished him a good journey, then backed Red away from the wagon. As it rolled away, Callista joined him.

"What was under the tarp?"

"Hundred pound bags of cornmeal, beans, and rice."

"The driver didn't know anything." He urged Red into a trot as they headed back toward the firing range and fort.

"Do you think they were connected to the gunrunners?"

He considered the odds. "Maybe. Something about that wagon doesn't add up. Those horses were well fed and in good shape to pull heavy loads. And I've never met a Mexican who doesn't speak English this far north of the border. If he gets lost, how does he get directions?"

"So let's trail him," she said eagerly.

"No." That's just what he needed, having her along when he caught up with gun smugglers. "The man who got away is the one who'd have the information. He's the one I want to catch."

Her hat had blown off and hung down her back, and her hair looked as yellow as just-picked corn.

"Now, it's time for your shooting lesson." He urged Red into a trot as they followed the road back toward the fort.

Callista followed Brit as he turned off the road onto a trail that led through horse-high bushes.

He'd looked so ruggedly handsome when she'd finally caught up with him after the chase that a sizzle of awareness had gone through her. His hair was windblown, and he was standing beside his horse like a hero who'd stepped from the pages of a dime novel.

So far there hadn't been a chance to tell him that he was wrong about Papa. But telling him wouldn't convince him, anyway. He would have to discover for himself that he was wrong. And the only way to do that was to find the real gun smugglers.

They emerged in an open area surrounded by low hills and carpeted with tall grass that was knee-high. When Brit halted, Callista lifted her leg free of the sidesaddle rest and slid down the horse's side. Brit took both sets of reins and tethered the horses in the shade of a tree.

He returned, carrying the rifle he'd had stowed in his saddle scabbard. "Callista, you're going to be aiming at those targets." He pointed at paper bull's-eyes attached to stacked bales of straw at the far end of the field.

"But they're so far away."

"That's what you want: to stop something before it gets close enough to hurt you. Now watch closely."

He cradled the rifle against his shoulder, supporting the barrel with his left hand. "See how it's pressed against my shoulder? That's to absorb the kick." He went on giving her instructions. "Then you just squeeze the trigger gently and—"

Even though she was expecting it, the rifle's boom startled her.

"All right. Your turn." He handed the rifle to her, got her holding it correctly, showed her how to squeeze the trigger, then stepped back. "Keep the stock firmly against your shoulder. Aim for the middle bull's-eye. Fire whenever you're ready."

The rifle was heavier than she'd expected and awkward to hold, and she was trying to follow his instructions and squeezing the trigger, but the rifle didn't go off, and didn't go off, and the end of the barrel was beginning to waver and she was getting tired and—

Boom!

A giant fist slammed into her shoulder, knocking her off her feet. Callista landed flat on her back, staring up at Brit.

"Callista! Are you all right?" Kneeling beside her, he helped her sit up.

She leaned against him. The rifle's kick had knocked the wind out of her, leaving her shaken. He'd warned her, but she hadn't taken him seriously enough. And her shoulder hurt like the devil.

"That must have hurt." He began kneading her shoulder to ease the ache. "Better?"

She could hear his heart beneath her ear, and it was beating as rapidly as hers. She wanted to stay there, nestled against him, but she couldn't. "I'm fine. Really." Pushing away from him, she sat up straight. "Let's get on with my lesson."

"We can continue another day." He didn't move. One leg was crooked, and he rested his arm on his knee.

She shook her head. "I want to go on, not quit."

"Good girl." He helped her to her feet. "Okay, we're going to do this a little differently this time," he said, picking up the rifle and handing it to her. "Bring it up against your shoulder, just like last time. Good. Now just hold it."

He moved behind her, then enfolded her in his arms, his left hand supporting hers under the barrel, his right hand covering hers on the stock, his chest against her back. "Now, we're going to try this again," he said against her ear. "All right?"

His voice was low and soothing, and she could feel its vibrations through her whole body. She nodded.

"You are in charge. You are doing everything. I'm

just here to hold you. Now start squeezing the trigger."

Callista squeezed the trigger, and tensed, waiting for the rifle to slam into her already-sore shoulder.

"No, don't tense." His lips brushed her ear. "It'll be all right. It won't hurt like last time."

The gun went off, surprising her as usual. But this time, with Brit's support, the rifle's kick wasn't nearly as bad. "That didn't hurt much," she said. "Let's do it again."

"First I want to see how you did on the target, then we'll repeat." His long strides took him to the target and back quickly.

"You hit the target to the right of the one you were aiming at."

She grinned. "That's why I want to practice."

Once again Brit wrapped around her, steadying her hands and aim. His warmth enveloped her. Callista could feel his whole body against hers. And she liked it.

Cheek to cheek, Brit sighted down the rifle with her. This time she didn't hesitate, just squeezed, and the rifle boomed.

"Good, you hit the target that time."

"Of course," Callista said, already feeling more confident about handling the rifle. "Let's do it again."

When Brit finally called a halt they were both dust-covered, but Callista was hitting the target.

Pleased with her improvement and knowing it was due to the confidence she'd absorbed from Brit, she turned to him. "That was—"

A gun boomed and gravel spurted up beside Brit's boot.

"Get down," he yelled as he knocked her to the ground.

It happened so fast she didn't understand.

He sprawled over her in the grass, one leg between hers, pinning her to the ground with his weight. He pressed his cheek against hers, even as he wrapped his hand around the exposed side of her head. "Don't move, Cally. Someone's shooting at us."

"I-I won't." She shivered with fear. His hard body blanketed her protectively. She could feel every move he made, every muscle tensing, even his ribs moving in and out with his breathing. His racing heart thudded against her ribs as well as his.

The gun boomed again and again, and she heard gravel spattering up all around them. He flinched and his arms tightened around her, as if trying to protect her even more than he already was.

"Thank God this grass is so tall," he said against her ear. "He can't see us." He felt around beside her for the rifle. "I'm going to slide off you. I'm going to draw his fire, then disappear and try to circle behind him. Whatever you do, don't move; you'll stir the grass. Stay here so that you're out of the line of fire."

Then he slid off her. The grass rustled as he snaked through it, then it grew silent. Callista didn't dare move; all she could do was listen.

A gun boomed.

She heard running feet.

Another gun boomed.

Then came the thudding hooves of a distant horse.

"It's okay, he's gone," Brit called. She sat up as he reached her. "Are you all right?" He offered her his hand and pulled her to her feet.

"I'm fine," she said, and walked into his waiting arms. Now that it was over, she trembled violently in reaction. Someone had shot at them. It brought home to her how dangerous life could be in Arizona.

"It's all right," he murmured as he held her close. He smoothed his hands over her back. "Ssh, you're okay." He murmured soft words, soothing her with his voice and hands. She didn't know how long he held her before she finally straightened away from him.

How could he be so calm, knowing someone had just shot at them? "Who was it? An Apache?"

"Not from the sound of the rifle. It was an army-issue weapon. He was up on the hill, and ran before I could get close enough to see him."

Reluctantly she pushed away from him completely. "Do you think it was the man you chased?"

"Maybe." He kept his hand on her elbow as they hurried toward the horses. "But there would be no reason for him to circle back after I'd lost his trail."

Once in the shelter of the trees, Brit slowed. Lord, he'd been scared when that bullet kicked up gravel right beside them. When he'd pushed Callista to the ground and covered her, she'd had the sense to remain calm instead of fighting him. Still, it had been a dicey few minutes, with the bastard's bullets striking all around them.

He flicked her a glance. Dried grass and leaves clung to her dress. Part of her hair had come loose and tumbled over her shoulders in wisps and tendrils.

He wanted to get her back to the fort before anything else happened. Then he was going to see if he could pick up the trail of whoever had shot at them.

He helped her mount, then swung up on Red.

"Brit, I can help you find the gun smugglers," she said as they headed for the fort. "When I'm interviewing people, I can be looking for clues."

He wanted to yell at her that that was a stupid,

risky idea, but at the same time, he didn't want her going off on her own to see if she could ferret out the gunrunners. So he chose his words very carefully.

"These are very dangerous people we're dealing with, Callista. Only people who aren't afraid to kill at the drop of a hat trade with the Apaches. And gun smugglers are the very worst of the lot."

"I wouldn't do anything other than look, Brit. You've admitted I'm observant. Let me put my training to use helping you."

Maybe it would be better to agree with her. After all, she couldn't get into any trouble at the fort. "All right, we'll try it for a couple of weeks and see what happens."

Maybe by that time she would have forgotten about the smugglers—although he doubted it. She had too much courage and determination.

He'd learned something today. The fear that had flooded him when she was in danger meant that he couldn't deny it any longer: he was attracted to her.

Attracted—what a weak word to describe all the emotions he felt when he thought of her or saw her or talked to her.

Or held her. Then he felt a connection with her at a primitive level that was extraordinary.

Chapter 8

As they trotted along the road, Callista was glad Brit had taught her how to fire a rifle. Not that she ever expected to use one; still, her instincts said it was good to be prepared.

Now that she'd admitted she was attracted to him, she could see that it was on many levels. She enjoyed being with him, and talking to him, and matching wits with him, but she also was attracted to him on a much deeper level—one she had never been aware of until she met him.

When he'd knocked her to the ground and covered her with his own body, she hadn't panicked, as she would have if it had been Fowler. Instinctively she'd trusted him—not consciously, but at a bone-deep level.

In the heat of the moment, he'd called her something. What was it . . . ? Cally. Hmm, she liked the sound of it. Cally. She'd never had a nickname; her parents were too formal for such things.

When Callista drew rein in front of the white picket fence, both her mother and father were on the front porch. They hurried to the railing and watched Brit and her intently.

Brit dismounted and came around to help her down. "Looks like you have a welcoming committee," he murmured as he reached up and grasped her waist.

"And they look grim." Callista braced her hands on his broad shoulders as he lifted her from the sidesaddle. "I wonder what's wrong."

She marched up the gravel walk and hadn't taken five steps when Papa said in his normal voice, which could carry across a parade ground, "Callista, are you all right? Your mother was worried to death about you."

"I'm fine," she called gaily, knowing Brit was still within hearing. "Why?"

"You disappeared. No one knew where you were."

"Oh, my Lord," her mother gasped, as Callista walked up the stairs. "Look at your clothes. And your hair." She gave Callista a stricken look. "He forced you, didn't he? It's all right, you can tell us."

"Forced me to do what? What are you talking about?"

"Did Lieutenant Chance force you to go with him and then—then—" Her father looked past her as Brit rode away. "Did he force himself on you?"

"No!" How could they think such a thing? "I felt like going riding after working indoors all morning. Why did you think he'd forced me?"

"Well, the way Fowler talked—"

"Fowler? How did Fowler get into this?"

"Ladies, let's finish this discussion in my office," Papa said firmly. He held the front door for Mamere and Callista, then followed them into the room off the entrance hall that served as his office.

"How did Fowler get involved?" Callista asked.

"He saw you riding with Mr. Chance while he was

exercising Papa's horse." Mamere clasped Callista's hands with hers. "Are you really all right, dear?"

"Did he see who shot at us? That's why I'm all dusty. Brit pushed me to the ground to protect me."

Mamere went white. "Shot at you?" She sat down abruptly on the black leather chair.

"These damn Apaches!" her father muttered. "Bold and deadly."

"Papa, it wasn't Apaches. It was someone with an army rifle, Lieutenant Chance said."

"Hogwash! Of course it was Apaches. Fowler didn't see anyone other than you and Lieutanant Chance. And he was quite displeased that you went riding with him." Papa walked over to the sideboard and poured himself a shot of whiskey. "Especially after you claimed you were too tired at dinner yesterday."

"I *was* too tired yesterday. But after a good night's sleep, I wasn't." She glanced from her mother to her father. What was going on here? "Now, what is wrong with that?" She perched on the small leather sofa.

"You're practically engaged to Fowler." Her father leaned against his desk. "How do you think it looks for a young lady to go riding with someone other than her fiancé?"

"I'm not engaged, and we only rode out to the rifle range. Mr. Chance is teaching me how to shoot."

"He's teaching you to fire a gun?" Mamere said faintly. "I don't think it is wise to be seen in Mr. Chance's company." She glanced at her husband. "He's quite unsuitable, you know."

"Unsuitable? Why? What's he done? Rob a bank?" Though she was being sarcastic, her parents exchanged a strange look that put her on alert.

"I can't tell you, dear. But it's something in his record that Papa knows." Mamere folded her hands in her lap and gazed at them. "Every wife on Officers' Row saw you go by with him today. And I don't want you to be the subject of rumor and conjecture."

"Don't beat around the bush, Verlene," Papa said. "He's unsuitable, Callista. I know that for a fact."

"All we did was go to the rifle range for a lesson. That's all."

"On a post this size gossip spreads as fast as cheap perfume," her father said. "And with your being engaged—"

She held up her hand, palm out. "Stop right there. We need to talk about Fowler and me, Papa."

Still holding his whiskey, her father crossed his arms over his chest. "Go ahead, Callista."

She took a deep breath, trying to decide where to start. "Papa, I don't understand why you talked to Fowler about marriage without talking to me first. I only went to a few balls with him in Washington, and those were because you wanted me to. I know you're good friends with the senator, but that doesn't mean I like his son."

"Don't act coy, Callista. Fowler told me that you two were very close to getting engaged before he left Washington. If I'd known, I wouldn't have taken him with me, but I wanted him here as my aide."

Callista jumped up and began to pace the room, rubbing her hands over her arms. Fowler had *lied*, downright lied to Papa.

"What is it, Callista?" Her mother's voice was shrill with fear. "What's wrong?"

She stopped and squared her shoulders. "I'm afraid Fowler has misled you, Papa. We were not ever close to being engaged. I haven't spoken to him in months."

"Are you saying he lied to me?"

"Ssh, Marsden, keep your voice down. Maybe he misunderstood Callista's intentions."

"My intentions were never to see him again," Callista said quietly. "And I made that very, very clear to him. There was no way he could misunderstand." She had kneed him, and while he'd been doubled over, she had fled.

"He lied to me! He led me to believe—Well, this is a hell of a kettle of fish." He stared down at the dark red carpet, deep in thought. Finally, he looked up. "He's in love with you. He wants to marry you. He considers you two engaged. His father is already looking forward to your being his hostess at senate functions."

"Do you like him a little bit, dear?" Mamere asked hopefully. "Is there a spark of affection that could grow—"

"No." She looked at her mother and father, but didn't have the heart to tell them that she'd never marry Fowler.

"Are you going to tell him that you can't marry him?" her father asked quietly. He moved to the sideboard and poured himself another drink.

She couldn't do what they wanted. They'd always been good parents, and it saddened her to know she couldn't do it. She gazed out the window at the distant mountains with their jagged peaks. That was how she felt inside, all jagged and jumbled up.

"You know I've always tried to do what you wanted—"

"I couldn't ask for a more wonderful daughter," Mamere broke in. "When I think of all the days you spent at my bedside, and you were so young—"

"What were you going to say, Callista?" her father prompted.

"This time I can't do it. But I know what would happen if I broke the engagement, Papa," she said, acknowledging that she knew it would be the end of his hopes for the presidency. Her father let out the breath he'd been holding. "However, I will want a very long engagement."

"Go on." He sipped his whiskey.

"I need time, and you'll have to back me up, Papa. We've got to find a way to end this engagement without making an enemy of Fowler's father." There, she'd gotten it out in the open.

"We'll work together," Mamere said. "Like we've done with everything else since the Lord took your brother. If you can just hang on until your father is president—"

"Verlene, that's a year and a half!"

"I know, Marsden. What else can we do?"

"There's one other thing." Callista intended to ask them to never leave her alone with Fowler.

She looked from Mamere to Papa, at their wrinkled, careworn faces, at their gray hair, and it was as if she was seeing them for the first time. *Why, they're old*, she thought, feeling a sense of shock. *When did they get old?*

"Never mind." She would take care that she wasn't alone with him.

"We're a family, Callista," her mother said in her firmest voice. "We will do what we have to do."

"Yes, we'll work together, like we always have. And now, I think we all need a drink. Sherry, anyone?"

"I'll take some, Marsden," her mother replied.

Absently Callista watched him pour the sherry from its brown bottle. Slowly she realized something was wrong with the array of bottles on the sideboard. Her gaze sharpened and she studied them. Something was missing.

The ruby decanter! Two hundred years old, made of ruby-colored glass with a real ruby in the stopper, it had belonged to the first Marsden Warwick and had been passed down from father to son. But now it was gone.

She glanced around the room. Papa's gold desk set was gone, too. He wouldn't have parted with either unless their financial situation was precarious. But the Wedgwood china was untouched. Why? Then she realized that Papa would never touch anything that would alert Mamere to their situation. He wouldn't want to worry her.

Her father poured himself a third drink, something she'd never seen him do. "There's one other thing, Callista. Stay away from Mr. Chance. I suspect he may be involved in illegal activities."

"Really?" Her eyebrows raised. "What kind?"

"I know he saved you and your mother, but don't let gratitude blind you. He may be very dangerous. No one knows where he got the money to buy his ranch—but someone started selling rifles to the Apaches a few months after he left the army.

"And I happen to know he's sympathetic to the Indians. Plus he's leading Apaches, not real troops. I know they and he are supposed to be working for the army, but until I see proof, I have my doubts."

"I think you've misjudged him, Papa. I've talked to him these last few days, and he's one of the most honest men I've ever met." And one of the most honorable, she thought. "He thinks we should learn to live with the Apaches, instead of trying to kill them all."

He took a hefty swallow of his drink. "You tend to look for the good in people, Callista, rather than seeing them as they are. He's dangerous."

"I'll remember," Callista said noncommitally. But she couldn't resist adding, "But I think you're wrong."

"It's time for dinner." Her mother rose and glided to the door.

Callista didn't follow her. "I'll be along in a minute, Mamere. I want to talk to Papa."

After the door closed, her father flicked her a wary glance. "What is it, Callista? Do you have another problem?"

"No, I don't, but I wonder if the family has one." Better to say the family than to ask him if he needed money. "I've saved up quite a bit of money, Papa."

"And?" His West Point ring glinted as he put his glass down beside the lamp.

He wouldn't take the money if she offered it to him straight out, so she needed to have a reason to give it to him. "Could you invest it for me? You've always been so good at investing and—"

He gave her a bittersweet smile. "I used to be, but that was in the days when there were a lot of investment opportunities in Washington. Then that damn Wickwar person insisted on writing about how we did business."

"Pardon me?" What did R.C. have to do with his investments?

"People in Washington have an old-fashioned way of doing business, Callista, but when Wickwar came along last year investigating military contracts, several people went to prison, and now everyone's afraid to do business the old way. I'm surprised you don't recognize the name. He works at your newspaper."

"I didn't realize he'd affected anything you did." Good lord, had Papa been involved? She hadn't seen his name on anything, but—No! Not Papa!

"Never mind. It's not something you need concern yourself with. I'll look around for an investment for you."

"Thank you, Papa." She gave him a quick kiss on the cheek and walked out.

There was a cold feeling in the pit of her stomach that she didn't like one bit. Papa hadn't told her or Mamere much about his last job in the War Department. Was he one of the shadowy, nameless people that she'd never been able to identify in the scandal? Was that why they were in financial straits this year?

Callista laid the napkins and silverware on the silver tray beside the Wedgwood china. There, it was ready for Daisy's visit. She wore her emerald green day dress with its white collar and cuffs, and was waiting out on the veranda when Daisy walked through the gate.

"Daisy, I'm so glad you could come." Callista went down the front steps to welcome her. After they were through with the pleasantries, she gestured to the white-wicker furniture on the veranda. "Why don't we sit out here?"

"I'd love to. You have a a great view of the whole parade ground."

Callista turned as Josephina carried the tea tray out. "Ah, here's our tea." The fragrance of Earl Grey tea filled the air.

"That tea smells wonderful."

Callista nodded as she draped her napkin across

her lap. "I think so, too. It's my favorite."

Daisy watched intently as Callista poured from the Wedgwood teapot into the cups, then handed her one.

"I've never had tea before," she said as she lifted the cup to her lips and sipped cautiously. "It tastes as wonderful as it smells."

"It'll be a new experience to tell your students about." Callista passed the strawberry biscuits and scones, then took one. When she broke it open, the rich fragrance of strawberries was like a taste of spring.

"Where did you get strawberries at this time of year?" Daisy watched what Callista did and did the same thing.

"Mamere canned some last year. Now, Daisy, where are you from?" Callista took out her pen and notebook. "And why did you come out here?"

"I grew up on a farm in Ohio, but I felt like everything always stayed the same there. Nothing ever changed, including the people. Some might say that's stability, but I found it boring. I like change.

"I came out to Arizona to visit a friend, and I liked it, so I stayed." She gestured at the mountains, blue in the afternoon sun. "After all, where else can you sit on your front porch and see mountains a hundred miles away?"

Three cups of tea later, Callista laid down her pen and closed her notebook. "That was fun, Daisy. I hope we can talk again."

"I hope so, too." Daisy drew aimless patterns on the table with her finger as though debating whether or not to say something.

"What?" Callista prompted.

"At the mercantile, you said that Brit saved you from the Apaches."

"Yes, he saved all of us. We were pinned down by the Apaches. Then he came charging down the slope where the Apaches were and changed everything. He was quite spectacular." A thrill went through her as she remembered.

"Like something out of a dime novel, huh?"

"Yes, but don't ever tell him I said so."

Daisy grinned. "I won't." She broke off a piece of scone and dabbed strawberry jam on it. "That's exactly the sort of thing Brit would do, you know. The army lost a fine officer when he left, but he was always a maverick."

"Do you know why he resigned?"

"He had the opportunity to buy a ranch from the people who settled it. They were giving up and going back East."

"Do you think it had anything to do with the fact that he thinks the army policy toward Apaches is wrong?"

Daisy shrugged. "I don't know. But I've heard gossip that he's good friends with a woman doctor."

Callista put down her tea cup. "He's friends with a woman doctor?"

"Yes. I've never met her, but I understand she's beautiful." She snapped her fingers. "I'd forgotten, but I think she lived here at Fort Bowie while her father was commander. Then she up and married an Apache chief. An Apache—do you believe that?"

"Do you think she's why he isn't married?" Callista brushed crumbs off her skirt.

"I don't think so." She shook her head. "Jack told me Brit was sparking a girl a few years ago, but she went back East and nothing came of it."

"Jack?"

"He's my fiancé. Brit bought the ranch adjoining

his, so we'll be neighbors soon." She folded her napkin and laid it beside her plate.

"Buying a ranch must be a very expensive proposition," Callista said carefully, recalling what Papa had said.

"It is. It's a wonder Brit was able to do it, being without family and all. Jack borrowed from his family to get the money, and he's still paying them back."

"What about filing for a homestead? I thought there was free land for people who want to settle out West."

"There is, but it's only enough for a farmer, and you can't farm this land. It's too dry. You have to buy thousands of acres more if you want to run cattle. That's why you wind up buying from people who are giving up and from the railroads."

"The railroads?"

"Yeah. Washington gave them millions of acres to get them to lay tracks out here."

"Hmm." Callista absently drummed her fingers on the table. "Thanks, Daisy, I didn't know any of that. Now, when are you getting married?"

"As soon as school is over. And I'll be moving to the ranch—I can hardly wait." She stood up. "Thank you, it's been so nice to talk to someone my age."

"I'm glad you came." Callista also rose. "Because I feel the same way."

Daisy gave her a quick hug. Then she took a step back. "I hope you don't mind. I've wanted to do that the whole time we've sat here. You looked like you needed a hug."

Callista smiled weakly. "You know, I guess I did. And I didn't even know it."

She accompanied Daisy to the gate and watched

her walk down the road. Then she sat on the porch steps and leaned against the post, deep in thought.

She had never realized how much money it would take to buy a ranch. What Daisy had told her jibed with what Papa had said.

And who was this lady friend of Brit's?

Chapter 9

Ten days later, Callista and Russ Caruso rode down Allen Street, the main street in Tombstone. Callista was surprised by the activity. Heavy freight wagons, buckboards, and men on horseback crowded the street, and women and men hurried along the boardwalks. The buildings were a mix of adobe and unpainted wood that had weathered to a soft gray. Tinny music issued from the saloons they passed, and Callista pretended not to see the half-dressed women sitting in the second-story windows above the saloons.

"This is a respectable establishment," Russ said, dismounting in front of a two-story hotel that was tarted up with garish bright red paint with white trim.

"Could have fooled me," Callista said, eyeing the paint.

He untied her carpetbag from behind her saddle. "No one will bother you here."

Callista led the way up the steps and across the veranda. She pushed open one of the double doors of heavily carved wood and entered. Two ladderback chairs and a wooden bench were drawn up before the fireplace on her right. To her left was the entrance to a restaurant, and the registration desk—a massive dark walnut monster—took up all of the back wall except for the stairs.

"Any boxes you have can come on the freight wagon that brings supplies to Fort Bowie every week. Just arrange their transport with the hotel clerk," Russ said as he placed her carpetbag beside the registration desk. "The next patrol returning to the fort will stop for you in five days."

"That will be you, won't it?" It hadn't occurred to her until that moment that it might not be nice, safe Russ.

"Probably, but it could be another officer."

"All right. I'll be here and ready." And ready to find an excuse not to go, if it was Fowler.

Callista watched Russ remount and ride away to join his patrol, then turned to the registration desk. Within minutes she was upstairs in her room. She dropped her carpetbag beside the bed, then went to the window which looked down on the street. It would be a good vantage point to watch the goings-on in Tombstone, but just then she wanted to wire her editor in Washington.

And while she was in Tombstone, she'd do a little snooping around herself and see if she could find out anything that would help her expose the gun smugglers. The dressmaker might be a very good place to start, because like bartenders, she overheard conversations while she was working.

Entering the telegraph office four days later, Callista closed the door behind her. Weak light struggled through the dust-caked front window, illuminating the high counter that separated the telegrapher's work area from the customers. The reek of stale cigars and coffee and other odors she didn't want to identify revolted Callista every time she walked in.

Usually the telegrapher was alone, but today a tall, black-haired man in desert tan clothes stood with his back to her at the high counter, writing on a yellow message pad.

"This is important," he rumbled, tearing it off and handing it to the telegrapher. "See that it goes to—"

Happiness darted through her at that familiar voice. "Brit, what are you doing here?"

He stiffened, then he turned and smiled at her. "Good afternoon, Callista, I didn't know you were in Tombstone."

"I didn't expect to see you, either. What are you doing here?"

"I stopped in Tombstone to take care of some business before we headed back to Fort Bowie."

"Oh, good. I'll go back to the fort with you, then."

"Sure, if you don't mind riding with the Apache scouts."

"I don't mind at all." The scouts were far better than riding back with Fowler.

"Sir." The telegrapher, a scrawny young man wearing green suspenders and a green eyeshade, tapped Brit on the shoulder. "Who is this addressed to?"

Brit half turned and took the message out of his hand. "Forget it, son. I've changed my mind." He crumpled the paper and stuffed it in the front pocket of his pants. "Are you free for dinner?" he asked Callista.

"Yes. Just let me send this message off." As she was writing, all her senses were focused on Brit. He'd probably run out the door if he knew how glad she was to see him. But she'd missed talking to him—more than she'd realized until she heard his voice. She handed her message to the telegrapher and paid him.

"I have a telegram for you, Miss Warwick," the young man said, pulling it off a spindle on his desk. "It came in about ten minutes ago, but I haven't had a chance to send it over to the hotel yet."

"Thanks, and see that that other one goes out quickly, please." Callista scanned the telegram, then slipped it into her purse.

Then she turned to Brit. He was leaning against the door, his arms crossed over his broad chest, the corners of his mouth turned up into a ghost of a smile.

"Telegrams coming and going? It sounds like you've been very busy, Callista." He opened the door for her.

"I've sent some dispatches from here, that's all." Her editor had wired her that her dispatches about *our hero* were drawing new readers every day.

As they walked down Allen Street the boardwalk echoed hollowly beneath the thud of Brit's boots. Their hands brushed several times, but she didn't widen the space between them, and Brit didn't either. They passed the bakery, rich with the scent of cinnamon and apple pie.

"I need to stop at the dressmakers on the way back to the hotel."

"And I'll bet you could use an extra pair of hands to carry boxes."

Callista laughed. "I certainly could."

Ladies in various stages of undress sat in the windows above the saloons. "Hey, Brit," one called, waving a scarlet boa furiously at him. "Are you coming up to see me?" She leaned so far out she was in danger of tumbling out.

"No, Soldier Blue, come see me." Another young lady called from a second-floor window on the other side of the street. "I'll give you a better time."

"It seems you have several admirers here," Callista said dryly. She should have been insulted that they were calling to her escort, but it was too amusing.

"I've hauled my men out of a lot of beds here."

"Well, you certainly made an impression on the ladies of the night."

"What can I say?" Brit flashed her a lopsided grin that made her heart strings flutter. "You're one of the very few respectable ladies I've met who's even acknowledged their existence."

"I'm a reporter, and I'll talk to anyone who has an interesting story to tell. Anyone."

They passed the gunshop she'd gone into the day before, but she didn't say anything. The tiny derringer she'd bought was her secret. It fit in her purse or even a skirt pocket. She'd bought it on a whim, then was glad she had, although she couldn't say why.

Once they picked up all her boxes, Brit accompanied her to the hotel and carried them up to the room for her, then arranged to pick her up for dinner.

As usual, she was ready early. It had always been a failing of hers. She didn't like rushing at the last minute, whether writing her dispatches or getting dressed to go out. When she rushed, she made mistakes. So she was always ready early and pacing. All her girlfriends said she was silly, that beaux expected to be kept waiting, that they wanted to wait.

She stood in front of the mirror, fiddling with her dress. It was simple, with none of the gewgaws and bustles so popular back East, allowing the color, a daffodil yellow, to shine and contrast with her lilac eyes. She was happy to get away from the somber colors of winter. She wanted happier colors to match the new lightness in her heart.

The bodice was scooped daringly low, but a white lace underblouse took the daring out of it before it ended in a high choker collar.

She'd brushed her hair until it shone, then wound it up into a complicated new figure-eight chignon she'd seen a woman wearing in Tombstone. She even wore some lip rouge.

She paced in her room until it was time, then went as far as the landing and peeked down into the lobby to make sure Brit was there. He was standing with his back to the stairs, deep in conversation with three other men. He was wearing a black suit and stood almost a head taller, and she would have known him anywhere.

But as soon as she started down, one of the men looked up and stopped speaking. Then another and another.

Finally Brit turned. She cared only what he thought, she realized. At first he looked stunned, then his eyes lit up with pleasure. That was when she decided that every second of primping had been worth it.

He walked to the bottom of the staircase and waited for her. As she reached the last step he held out his hand, palm up, and when she laid her hand in it, he raised it to his lips.

"You are very beautiful," he murmured. "Of course, I already knew that, but tonight I am dazzled."

To have him tell her she was beautiful gladdened her heart in a way that no other man's words ever had. They were standing in a hotel lobby surrounded by people, but Callista felt as if they were alone in some magical place.

"Thank you, Brit. I've never dazzled anyone before," she said with a smile. She handed him her soft wool challis shawl.

He moved behind her, to wrap it around her shoulders with fingers that lingered in a slow caress. He bent his head until his lips were close to her ear as he whispered, "Then they were blind."

Then he swept her through the lobby and outside.

"Where are we going?" She felt as if she were floating a few inches above the ground, rather than walking. She was the one who was dazzled!

"To a restaurant run by a man who knows how to cook steaks." His eyes flickered with warmth. "And who also knows how to give a couple privacy."

They strolled two blocks arm in arm. It was after dark, but men and women still crowded the boardwalk. They passed a mercantile store still open and a saloon that buzzed with men's voices. And Callista floated past all of them.

The restaurant was lit by candles rather than with bright oil lamps, and linen tablecloths covered the tables. The men wore suits, and the ladies wore evening and afternoon dresses. The murmur of conversation was hushed with good manners.

"I'm impressed," Callista said. "A French restaurant in Tombstone?"

"People have come here from all over the world because of the silver strike. And they all like good food."

The owner led them to a private alcove screened by potted palms. Soon they were seated on adjoining sides of the tiny table, the owner had taken their orders, and they were alone.

"You're very handsome in that suit." He was striking, with his height and austere features. "Several women watched you walk through the restaurant."

"I didn't see them," he said in a lazy drawl. "I was watching all the men watch you."

"Did you kiss the Blarney Stone while you were out on patrol?"

He laughed. "Nope. Only the stone of truth."

She didn't know what to say to that, so she said nothing.

The owner returned with a bottle of wine and uncorked it for Brit's approval. After pouring a glass for each, he left.

Callista sipped her wine. "While you were on patrol, did you come across anything that would help identify the men selling guns to the Apaches?"

"Nope. Not even my scouts were able to uncover any new information, except that the younger man has light hair." That was what he'd been about to telegraph to General Crook when she walked into the telegraph office. But lieutenants didn't telegraph officers who weren't their immediate superiors. They certainly didn't telegraph generals.

"Can't they be more specific? Blond or gray or light brown?"

"The Apaches don't have words for any of those. They have black and white and the man's hair is closer to white than black." He picked up his wine. "But I may have a lead on the horse with the strange shoe."

Good Lord, what was he doing telling her that? Next thing he'd admit that it was her father's favorite mount—although he still hadn't been able to identify who the rider had been.

"It was my father's horse, Brit. And Fowler was riding him." She leaned back in her chair, watching him with a triumphant smile.

"Fowler? That's interesting."

"So you knew it was my father's horse." It was a statement, not a question.

He lifted his wine in salute. "Lady, you are fast."

"I've learned to listen to what people say and what they don't say. Do you think Fowler could be involved?"

"It's possible," he said carefully.

"Personally, I don't think he's stupid enough to come back and shoot at us," Callista said. "But I could be wrong. I'm willing to share what I learn about the smugglers with you, if you'll do the same with me."

"Why are you so interested in them?"

She leaned forward earnestly. "I want the story. It'll make the front page of my paper and lots of others."

He saw her determination. "So you'll go looking whether or not you're working with me? Is that correct?"

She lifted her wine in salute. "You're fast, Brit."

He smiled. "I'm damned if I do and damned if I don't."

"Uh-uh. You're getting a partner who's very good at gathering information."

"All right, it's a deal. What else have you got?"

"I didn't know if you'd done any nosing around Tombstone, so I did. But I couldn't come up with anything useful. I couldn't even uncover any rumors, and there's often enough truth in rumors to check them out."

He drank his wine, then put the goblet down. "I'm regretting this arrangement already. I don't think you understand how dangerous these people are."

"Please, give me some credit for knowing how to ask questions without being obvious. Do you think I can get straight answers from politicians by asking straight questions? Of course not." She chuckled. "Once my question was so convoluted the senator couldn't figure it out, and he accidentally gave me a straight answer."

"These smugglers aren't politicians." His low voice was graveled with anger. "They deal in guns and bullets, not words. And there's a damn big difference in their lethalness."

"All right, all right." She raised her hand palm out in surrender. "I've been circumspect, but I'll be even more careful from now on."

"Please, let me handle it." He clasped her hand between his. "I guarantee that you'll have your story as soon as I know who it is."

"You don't understand. I'm not only after the story; I want to see these smugglers exposed and in prison. Their rifles are killing people. Someday it might be my father or . . . you—" Her voice broke. Embarrassed by her show of emotion, she picked up her wine and sipped it, hoping he hadn't noticed.

When had he become so important to her? Minute by minute, hour by hour he was in her thoughts. But she knew that she could be hurt—and badly—if he crept into her soul. Why wasn't her heart listening?

"Will you do it for me, Cally?" He raised her hand to his lips and kissed the back gently.

A butterfly fluttered in her. "Cally. I like that

name," she said. Was she becoming special to him? "I have been careful all along, Brit. I'm not foolhardy and I don't take chances. I'm a devout coward."

He smiled. "Not from what I've seen. And I like Cally, too."

He slowly drew a single finger along her arm. "Have I told you how beautiful you look tonight?"

The breath thickened in her throat. "I-I can't think when you do things like that."

"Don't think, Cally," he whispered. "Feel."

That's what she was afraid of: feeling. After David, she'd spent years walling herself off from feeling. But she couldn't avoid it when she was around Brit.

She looked up with relief as the waitress brought them a basket of warm French bread. The aroma filled their little alcove.

"This bread reminds me of how the house smells when Mamere makes bread. We bake it every Thursday morning. The aroma of bread in the oven makes me feel—" She buttered the crusty end piece. "I can't explain it. It's as if I'm a little girl again and my world is a warm safe place and nothing bad will ever happen and—Well, we all grow up, don't we?"

She knew she was babbling, but she felt off-balance, as if she'd revealed too much of herself. "How about you, Brit? Did your mother have the same sort of routine, always baking bread the same day?"

"Nope." Brit tore off a piece of the crusty bread. "We bought our bread at a bakery down the block. Although I do remember, about seven every morning, the aroma of baking bread would wake me up."

"You were still sleeping at seven? You must have had a pampered childhood."

He laughed. "Boy, have you got that wrong." Living at Madame Claudine's meant he had kept brothel hours. The girls would sleep in and it would be noon before everyone gathered for breakfast.

"Do I?" Callista said softly. "I'm sorry. Everyone deserves a wonderful childhood."

"Some of us grow up faster than others. Don't get me wrong; I had six mothers." He was tempted to tell her about Madame Claudine's, and what he really was. He didn't want lies between them; only the truth. That had never happened with a woman before.

Concern pleated her brow.

"Please don't, Cally," he said softly. He gently smoothed out those wrinkles. Her concern bothered him, it was too close to pity. And he didn't want that. Not from anyone, least of all her. "Don't trouble yourself about me. I can take care of myself."

"I don't worry about you, but when I think of a young boy who didn't get to enjoy being a child, I—" She turned her head and brushed a kiss across his palm.

He stilled, absorbing the feel of her lips on his flesh. This was his chance.

"Callista, there's something I'd like to tell you." He studied the linen tablecloth for a long moment. How did he tell someone? He'd never told anyone but John, and he'd been a child then.

"Yes, Brit?" She ran her fingers across the back of his hand.

"I'm a bastard." He wanted her to know the worst about him, and he wanted her to hear it from him. "I grew up in a brothel. That's why I had so many mothers."

Would she faint or scream or run from the restaurant? If she did, so be it. But he didn't want to lie about it; not to her.

She propped her elbows on the table and clasped her hands together in front of her mouth. But she didn't faint or scream, and he thought that was a good sign. He *hoped* it was a good sign.

"I've heard the men call you a bastard," she finally said, "but I didn't know it was true."

"Is that all you're going to say?" Needing to do something, he sipped his wine.

"Do you start every dinner with a revelation like this or is it a one-time thing?"

He choked and grabbed his napkin. "I can't believe how calmly you're taking this."

"I do feel stunned and a bit numb." She buttered a piece of bread, then her gaze came up to meet his and he saw wariness there. "Why did you tell me?"

"I want no lies between us, just truth. I want everything up front and out in the open. If I told you and it made a difference and you ran out of here, I wanted to know now."

She smiled. "The food is too good. I wouldn't run out until after dinner was over." She fiddled with her fork, then said, "I keep coming back to the fact that you're *you*, no matter what name anyone gives you. It's your deeds and how you live your life that make you who you are. Not a label. You're no different than you were a day ago or a week ago or a minute before you told me."

The waitress appeared with their onion soup, and for a few minutes they didn't talk.

But he was glad he'd told her.

"What's your ranch like?" Callista asked as she sipped the steaming soup.

He had to think about that, because there was so

much about the ranch he could never put into words. "It's a long, boring story," he said.

"I have all the time in the world."

Would she like the ranch or would the isolation frighten her as it frightened so many? "It's a horse that needs to be fed, a calf that needs to be weaned, a gate that needs to be fixed, a barn that needs to be finished, a house that needs to be built. And it's mine."

It was a dream that would take a lifetime of hard work. But that was all right, because he had a lifetime of hard work to give it.

She leaned back in her chair. "You love it, don't you."

He buttered a piece of bread as he thought about it. "Yeah. I do."

"Don't you have a house? Are you camping out?"

She'd been listening closely if she picked up on that. "I have a two-room adobe that was built by the original owners. But I want to build a bigger house up on the ridge." That was the home he'd build for his bride.

"If they settled it, why did they sell?"

The waitress replaced their soup bowls with sizzling steaks that gave off the aroma of mesquite smoke.

"A lot of people come West looking for the land of milk and honey," Brit said as he cut into his steak. "But Arizona is the land of rattlesnakes and Apaches. And loneliness. A lot of women, and men, too, can't take the isolation of living on a ranch that may be forty miles from your closest neighbor. That's what happened to the Burleys. They went back to Ohio."

"It sounds like your ranch is never-ending work. How many hands do you have?"

"I can't afford any right now. It'll be a couple of years before I can sell enough cattle to pay a cow-hand's wages." And that was if he had good years and the Apaches didn't run his cattle off.

"Aren't you lonely, out there all by yourself?"

"I don't have time to be lonely." He chewed a piece of his steak. "Callista, I'm curious about something. I've never met a woman reporter before. What made you decide to become one?"

She made wry face, as if she didn't like talking about herself. "I don't know."

"Yes, you do. A woman doesn't choose to go into a man's profession and face all the opposition she's going to face on a whim. So you'd thought about it." He'd seen some of the prejudice Aurora Spencer had faced as a woman doctor. And he'd often wondered if his mother would still be alive if she'd had a real profession to fall back on when his father abandoned her.

"You must know another woman who's done something similar. Most men aren't even aware of what a woman faces."

"Maybe, but I want to know what made you do it."

"It's a long, boring story," she teased.

"I'm eating a large steak. I have plenty of time. If I fall on the floor and start snoring, then you'll know it's time to stop."

She giggled. "I kind of fell into it. I was visiting a friend from Miss Porter's Academy for Young Ladies. Don't look at me like that; Miss Porter's really did give me a good education." She sipped her wine.

"Go on," Brit said. The candlelight from the wall sconce behind her curled through her upswept hair, turning it a fiery gold.

"One evening we took dinner down to her father, who worked in a newspaper office. He was short-handed and I helped a bit, and I was hooked."

"More wine?" Brit refilled her glass.

"That's enough. I don't want to get intoxicated."

She was intoxicating him with her perfume and her beauty and the endearing way she had of putting her hand in front of her mouth when she laughed. "I'll carry you back to the hotel."

"A truly gallant offer, Mr. Chance." She chuckled behind her napkin. "But I must refuse."

"The evening is young. I'll keep working on you."

"You do that," she challenged, but her eyes sparkled with laughter.

He caught her hand and raised it and kissed the satin-soft skin on the inside of her wrist. "I'm glad you wore your hair up tonight."

"Why?" The air throbbed with her question.

He leaned close to her. "Because I'm going to take it down later." He felt her shiver and when she turned to him, her eyes were large and dark.

Damn! He wanted to kiss her. Right there, in the middle of dinner, in the restaurant.

"Ready for your coffee?" the waitress asked as she placed a fresh basket of bread on the table.

"Yes." He didn't look away from Callista.

Callista broke the connection, picking up her glass and sipping her wine.

A rosy drop of wine glistened on her lower lip. He cupped the back of her head with his hand and leaned over and licked it away. Her lips were warm and moist, and he danced his way across her mouth to the corner, then back.

"I didn't expect to feel like this," she murmured leaning back against his hand. Then slowly, she threaded her fingers into his hair and drew him back to her lips.

He stopped thinking and just felt. Felt the rapid flutter of her pulse in her throat, felt her lean into him, felt her fingers sliding through his hair, felt her yearning and matched it with his own.

By the time he lifted his head they were both breathing hard, and she reclined languidly against his arm, her lips kiss-swollen and her eyes heavy-lidded.

She was made for loving. For his loving.

"Are you ready to go?" he asked huskily.

"Yes."

He paid the bill, and they left, his arm around her waist. The boardwalk was deserted and the stores dark, their wooden signs creaking in the slight breeze. Lanterns hung at regular intervals to light the street.

He thought of pulling her into one of the dark doorways for a quick kiss, but decided against it.

He couldn't keep his hands off her as it was. Her hair was already beginning to come down, and he didn't want her walking into the hotel looking as if she'd been mauled. Even if she had.

"Now listen to me," he murmured between tiny kisses to the shell of her ear. "We are going to walk down the street with great decorum."

"I can do that," she said with a laugh, "but I'll bet you can't."

"What would you like to bet?" He wrapped his hand around her elbow as they descended the two steps at the end of the boardwalk.

They crossed the darkened side street and were going up the two steps on the other side when he heard a dull thud—the kind that came when a fist hit flesh. He looked down the side street, but couldn't see anything in the darkness. But he heard another thud and grunt.

"Take that, you damn savage." Another thud.

"And that!" Another voice said.

He halted. "Stay here," he told Callista. "I think there's a fight going on, and it's at least two against one."

He slipped down the street, silent as the shadows around him. When his eyes adjusted he made out three men punching and kicking a gray-haired man who was bent with age. The old man was trying to fight back, and he would have been all right against one opponent, but not against three. As Brit neared, a punch knocked the man to his hands and knees, then one of the others kicked him in the ribs.

Brit launched himself into the fray. He was in the midst of the fight, pulling one assailant off the old man and punching him, before the three bullies even knew he was there.

They transferred their punches and kicks to him. "Won't work," he gritted. "I'm not an old man, and I'm going to beat the hell out of each of you."

One bully melted away into the darkness, then another. Only one was left. Brit grabbed him by his shirt and dragged him up to the lights of Allen Street, where he could see the man.

"Thompson," he snarled in disgust. "I should have known you'd be beating an old man in a dark alley."

"He was a damn Apache, Chance, you goddam bastard." He lashed out with both fists, catching Brit by surprise and landing a blow to Brit's temple that staggered him. He let go of Thompson's shirt. Thompson would have landed another blow with his other fist, but Brit blocked it with his arm.

Thompson turned and ran back into the side street.

Brit chased him for a block, then let him go. The old man was gone, too, he noticed as he walked back to Allen Street. Apparently he'd hightailed it out of there while Brit was fighting with his tormentors.

Callista stood on the boardwalk, trembling with fear for Brit. How like a hero to run to the aid of someone he didn't even know. She strained to see into the side street's darkness as footsteps approached. Brit emerged from the darkness and walked up to her.

"Are you all right?" She wanted to wrap her arms around him and make sure he was all right.

"I'm fine." He stopped at the bottom of the steps, so she was eye height with him. "Are you shaking?"

"I'm frightened. I told you I was a devout coward."

He tapped her nose gently. "Don't be silly. You're as little a coward as I am."

Ha! That showed how little he knew about her. She'd known she was a coward since the Apache attack, when she was paralyzed by fear.

She pulled her linen handkerchief out and dabbed at his cheek. "You're bleeding from a cut near your eye, and you've got a split lip and—"

"Don't worry. I've been in worse fights." He stepped up on the boardwalk. "Come on, I want to get you back to your hotel." His hand was a square of warmth in the small of her back.

"I'll take care of that cut when we get to my room."

"I'm not *that* injured. Besides, you have a reputation to protect. I'll say good night to you in the lobby."

Callista smiled to herself. He would be escorting her up to her room, whether or not he knew it just yet.

He would have walked straight into the hotel, but she stopped him. "Wait, Brit, I want to see who is in the lobby." She pulled him back away from the doors and cautiously peered through the window. If Fowler was there she wouldn't even go in; she'd just camp with Brit and his scouts. He wasn't, and she breathed a sigh of thanks. "All right, we can go in."

He pushed the double doors open and ushered her in. Callista walked in limping. "Ow! I think I turned my ankle. Would you mind helping me to my room, Mr. Chance?"

"Of course, Miss Warwick," he murmured dryly as he gave her an I'll-get-you-for-this look. He crooked his elbow for her and helped her up the stairs and down the second-floor hall to her room. Taking the key from her, he opened the door, then followed her in.

"What was that limp for?" He dropped the key on the small round table.

"My reputation is intact. You just helped an injured lady up to her room." She crossed to the windows and closed the curtains. "Sit down, and I'll take care of those cuts," she added as she lit the oil lamp on the table. She picked up the water pitcher and basin from the chest of drawers and brought them over to the table.

Brit sat in the straight chair and rested his arm on the table. "I can do this myself," he said. "You don't have to fuss over me."

"I know, but I want to," she admitted quietly. She wet a towel and dabbed at the diagonal cut along his cheekbone. "This came very close to your eye."

As she dabbed his cuts and bruises, her breasts brushed against his arm. His hand twitched, but he didn't move. Still, she felt awkward and tried to be more careful as she dabbed at a cut along his jaw. She bent lower to see it, and in the silence she heard his tiny, indrawn breath as she brushed against his arm again.

This time he moved, quick as a cat. He encircled her waist and tipped her into his lap. "Enough, Cally," he growled, leaning over her.

She froze. She could feel his hardness beneath her, and one of his hands splayed over her breast and her heart was racing.

He gazed down at her and his expression softened. "I didn't mean to frighten you."

"You didn't." She traced the line of his upper lip slowly.

A muscle tightened in his jaw. He surged to his feet still holding her, then carefully set her on her feet. "I'm leaving, Cally. Now. Before I do something one of us will regret."

"You don't have to." She felt so aware of him that her skin cried for his touch.

"Yes, Cally, I do," he whispered. He touched her cheek with such tenderness that he took her breath away. "And we both know why."

In the middle of the night, Callista bolted upright in bed. *She* was the reason Brit hadn't sent his telegram!

"Callista, pinch yourself, you're dreaming," she muttered. She did. And she wasn't.

He'd said that it was important to the telegrapher. But after she'd greeted him, when the telegrapher asked him who it was addressed to; he'd changed his mind.

She was definitely the reason. But why? What

hadn't he wanted her to see? The contents? She wouldn't have anyway.

So that meant he hadn't wanted her to know who it was going to.

She lay back down, but she didn't sleep for the rest of the night. Who could it have been going to?

Chapter 10

The Welcoming Ball was held two weeks later in the enlisted men's mess hall, the largest building at the fort.

It had been a very long two weeks for Callista. After they returned to Fort Bowie she had avoided Brit, afraid of the feelings he aroused in her.

She knew better than to give her heart to a hero.

So whenever she saw him, she went in a different direction. When she accidentally met him, she'd nod crisply and keep going. He would tip his hat and keep going.

Yet the more she avoided him, the more she was aware of him. She would be standing talking to someone and the hair on the back of her neck would warn her that someone was watching her. She would turn and he would be there, maybe across the room, maybe across the parade ground.

Their eyes would meet, and she would long to run into his arms, to have him hold her and kiss her, to feel his heart beating against hers. But she would steel herself and turn away.

Coming back from Tombstone with Brit had turned out to very smart, even though it threw her together with him. Fowler had stopped at the hotel the next morning and been furious to find her already gone.

Fowler was a very big problem. He was as persistent as a fly in the kitchen, only much more bothersome. He'd wanted to take her to the ball, but she'd managed to put him off, telling him that she wanted to go with her father since it was in his honor. Papa had done his part, keeping Fowler occupied by sending him on patrol.

Already Callista could see that her hopes of holding Fowler off through a long engagement wouldn't work. She had to find a way out soon.

The evening of the ball she walked up the gravel path beside her father, resting a white-gloved hand on his arm, as did her mother on his other side. The band was tuning up inside, but Callista knew they wouldn't start playing until her mother and father—the guests of honor—arrived.

They paused just inside the doorway. The officers' ladies were a garden of turquoise, ruby, sapphire, and emerald ball gowns. The officers were clustered around the punch bowl in a knot of army blue.

She wore her new amethyst silk gown with its plunging, scalloped neckline—and she was the only one in that color. She thought of it as her secret indulgence, because its color brought out the color of her eyes. The skirt had three tiers of silk ruffles, the top one being lavender, shading into a violet, shading into a deep purple.

And she wore twenty-button white kidskin gloves that sheathed her arms high above the elbows. Pearl teardrop earrings matched the pearl-bejeweled combs securing her upswept hair.

The officer's wives had gone all out decorating.

They'd pushed the long trestle tables and benches back against the walls, then strung bunting in shades of pink, yellow, green, and aqua across the beams until the room looked like a spring bower. Callista liked the soft, gentle colors that were such a change from the harsh, sun-bleached sand outdoors.

They'd even strewn fresh sawdust across the graying wood planks, and its woodsy scent filled the room.

As Callista looked around she felt Brit's gaze on her for long seconds before she casually turned, seemingly occupied with straightening her white-silk shawl. Slowly she stopped combing her fingers through the fringe. Slowly, compelled by an irresistible force, she looked up.

Into Brit's steely gaze. He was in his dress blue uniform with a bright yellow cummerbund, matching the yellow stripes on the outside of his pant legs that proclaimed him a cavalry man.

He stood tall, near the officers crowding around the punch bowl, but clearly not a part of their group. Clearly an outsider.

When her eyes met his, he didn't pretend to be doing anything other than looking at her. His gaze was so intense that her pulse quickened.

Standing with him, but with their backs to her, were a tall man in a black suit who wore his black hair in a thick braid that hung down his back and a petite woman with flaming red hair. She wore a strikingly simple royal blue gown that was the height of fashion, and Callista knew she had to have bought it in New York.

The tall man must have said something because Brit looked at him, breaking the connection that flickered between him and Callista like living fire.

She studied Brit as he talked. He was so different from the men she had known in the East. Too rugged and stern-looking to be called handsome, his features were angular, as though hewn with an ax.

The desert seemed to have burned every bit of softness out of him. His bronze flesh was drawn taut over high cheekbones and a square, very determined chin. There was no looseness that might develop into jowls or a double chin, only tautness. And strength and power.

He held a cup of ruby red punch that contrasted with his blue uniform. Looking directly at her, he lifted his cup in a casual salute.

Callista turned away, looking for someone to talk to. Russ Caruso was nearby, and she waved gaily and smiled her most carefree, happy smile.

Out of the corner of her eye, she glimpsed Fowler heading toward her.

Hastily she stepped toward Russ. "Dance with me, Russ."

"With pleasure," he said, pulling her into his arms and whirling her away. "I don't know who you're avoiding, but I'll be happy to help you all evening."

She laughed. "Avoiding someone? Never."

As they circled she saw Fowler speaking to her father and knew her father had called him over. If only he could keep him occupied until she'd filled her dance card.

"You look utterly enchanting tonight," Russ said, as the first dance ended. His gaze flowed over her, warm and slow as molasses in January. "Utterly enchanting."

His words didn't have half the impact of Brit's. But she didn't care, she told herself. Brit was too dangerous to her heart.

"You look quite handsome yourself," she replied, as she filled in his name for the second dance on the tiny card ribboned to her left wrist.

Then the other officers swarmed around her like bees around a rose, and her dance card was soon almost full. She didn't look at Brit again, although she knew he was watching her. She tapped Russ's arm with her folded fan and smiled up at him as if he were the only beau in the world.

The second dance was a fast polka, and he whirled her around the room in a foot-stomping rhythm that left her laughing. When the music slowed into a waltz, another officer claimed her. And so it went, officer after officer, dance after dance. Once Brit whirled by with Daisy in his arms, laughing up at him. Twice with the beautiful, red-haired woman in the blue dress.

But he never approached her. For which she was grateful, she reminded herself. Very grateful.

She was back in Russ's nonthreatening arms, enjoying the beautiful "Blue Danube Waltz" as they glided around the room once more, when Brit's rugged features loomed behind Russ as he tapped the younger man's shoulder.

"I believe this is my dance," he said, eyes only for her.

"I don't think so," she said, feeling seared by his look. "You're not on my dance card." She flicked the tiny card open and studied it. "No. I don't see your name at all."

"Maybe you forgot to write it down."

Heavens, her heart was beating faster, just talking to him. What would it be like to dance with him? Would they mesh or clash? "You must be mistaken."

"Mistakes happen," he said blandly. He slid his big hand around her waist.

She straightened to her full height and stopped dead, challenging him in the middle of the dance floor. "This really isn't your dance, Brit," she said sweetly.

Other couples swirled around them, but they could have been the only people on earth.

The corners of his eyes crinkled with his smile. "I'm making it my dance. Shall we?" He held up his other hand, fingers spread, palm toward her.

Reluctantly, relentlessly drawn to him, she threaded her fingers through his. When his fingers curled over the back of her hand, she knew he wouldn't let her go until he was ready. And she didn't want him to.

They were glove to palm. She looked up at his hard features. The silver fire in his eyes set her pulse to pounding.

Brit lowered his head and sniffed at the place behind her ear, where she'd applied her perfume. He did it so subtly, only she and he knew he'd done it. "You make lilacs smell like an entirely new scent," he murmured.

His fingers trailed down her back in an unmistakable caress that shimmered down her spine. His scent mixed with the pine soap he'd used. She stared at the cavalry's crossed swords decorating the brass buttons on his jacket.

He rubbed his jaw over her ear as he murmured, "Am I going to look at the top of your head for the whole dance?"

"You may peruse whatever you wish," she said in her best princess-talking-to-commoners voice.

He snorted and tightened his hand at the small of

her back, urging her closer. Wanting to keep him at arm's length, she pulled back, inadvertently jerking her head up and hitting his chin with an audible clink. It hurt, and she wanted to rub her head, but wouldn't give in.

"Did you hurt your head?" His low voice vibrated through her.

In spite of her intentions, she looked up at him. "Of course not," she snapped.

"Too hard, eh?" he deadpanned.

She looked away, afraid she'd laugh. It was no use. She snickered.

"Ah, the lady can laugh, after all." Then he whirled her with abandon, so fast her feet left the floor, and she couldn't help looking up at him and laughing. And she finally admitted to herself that being in his arms was heaven.

When the music slowed into another waltz, he nestled her closer. As they passed the front door, he whirled her out onto the porch.

"What are you doing?" Callista gasped.

Brit gave her a long, slow smile that would have put the devil to shame. "What would you like me to do?" He waltzed her the length of the porch, past the windows, to the shadows at the end.

"I want you to myself," he murmured. He didn't want anyone cutting in on them the way he'd cut in on Russ.

In the two weeks since they'd returned from Tombstone, he'd missed that flirty little sideways glance she had, her laughter, talking to her, and holding her in his arms. Hell, he'd just plain missed her.

He felt such a chaotic mix of emotions when he was with her. Pleasure, that edginess that came from having to be alert and on his toes when they talked, tenderness, and, deep down, passion. She could infuriate him and charm him—sometimes at the same time.

Life was never quiet or dull when he was with her. She could change before his eyes, and yet no matter what she did, he sensed a core of sweet innocence. She hid it with spunk and determination, but he was certain it was there.

He slid his hand down her back and drew her close, feeling the softness of her breasts against his chest, feeling the fluttering of her heart.

She felt so right in his arms.

Callista closed her eyes and absorbed the feel of him as they danced breast to chest, hip to hip, thigh to thigh, swaying in the darkness, barely moving.

"You look beautiful tonight." He nuzzled his way down to the hollow of her shoulder and kissed her. A frisson of awareness shivered through her.

His arms tightened and he waltzed her around the corner. There were no windows on that side of the building, and it was pitch-black.

Then he crooked his finger beneath her chin and tilted her head up and his lips met hers. It was a kiss as gentle as spring rain. Enticing, inviting her to come explore with him. Callista leaned into him and speared her fingers through his hair and answered with her tongue and lips and whole desire.

He groaned far back in his throat and his tongue sought hers, and their hunger met and exploded in flame. His hand settled at her breast and she turned toward it, wanting his hand there. And his lips.

He slipped his hand inside her gown and cupped her breast. The combination of his rough, callused palm against her sensitive flesh and the gentleness of his touch left her breathless.

Callista's bones began to soften, and she wanted to curl around him and hold him forever. Even as the thought surfaced in her mind, she stiffened.

There was no forever with men like him. There was only today.

"Let me go." She pushed against his chest, hard. "Let me go!" She couldn't let herself be seduced by the magic of his kiss, the touch of his hand.

"Cally, what's wrong?" When she remained board-stiff, he loosened his arms around her until she could step back away from him. "Mind telling me what just happened?"

Not trusting her voice, she shook her head. Turning away, she leaned against the porch railing and stared at the quarter moon coming up over the Chiricahua Mountains.

When she thought she could speak without a quaver in her voice, she said, "I'd like to go back, please."

She didn't want to go back; she wanted to stay with him, but she didn't trust herself.

She tensed when Fowler passed the window inside, circling the dancers as if looking for someone. Her?

"Is he looking for you?" Brit asked, following her gaze.

"I don't know. Probably. Yes."

"Tell me what's going on."

"Nothing." She looked back at him over her shoulder and met his unwavering hard gaze. "Really, nothing."

"Brit, is that you?" A woman's voice came from shadows beneath a sycamore tree in front of the building.

Brit leaned over the railing. "Aurora? Is Ethan with you?"

"Yes." The woman's and man's voices mingled.

"Stay there. I'd like Callista to meet you both." Brit turned to her. "I'd like you to meet Aurora. She's like you, a brave lady who's working in a man's profession."

"Then I want to meet her." Was this Brit's lady friend?

He kept her on his right since he wore his sword on his left. As usual, he wrapped his hand around her arm and as usual, she liked it there.

Once they walked beneath the leafy limbs of the Arizona sycamore, Callista found that enough light spilled from the mess-hall windows to make it easy to see the other couple.

As she'd expected, it was the tall man with the braided hair and the redheaded woman.

"Callista, I'd like you to meet Ethan and Aurora Winthrop, from Boston," Brit said, gesturing at the couple

"How do you do?" Her white-gloved hand was engulfed in Mr. Winthrop's large bronze one.

"Miss Warwick." He gave her a formal bow and a kiss on the back of her hand, which told her he'd been well educated at private schools.

"The Winthrops have a ranch north of here in the mountains, near the Apache reservation," Brit explained.

"Really? Do you have any trouble, living in such close proximity?"

"I'm a doctor," Mrs. Winthrop replied, "and I work on the reservation almost every day."

"I'm impressed." Brit was right; she was a brave woman to work on the reservation. "I'm a reporter for the *DC Tribune*, Mrs. Winthrop, and I'd like to interview you about what it's like being a woman doctor in Arizona." There was something else Daisy had told her . . . what was it? The doctor had married a . . . a . . . it was coming back. She'd married an Apache chief!

Callista tensed. The man standing next to her, who'd known how to kiss a lady's hand was an Apache chief? Impossible. She had it wrong.

"I'd be happy to talk to you. And please, call me Aurora."

"I'm Callista." She was dying to turn and look at Mr. Winthrop, but she didn't dare.

"Ethan and Aurora came in for the christening of their newest son," Brit explained. His hand settled in the middle of her back, a patch of warmth.

"And Brit agreed to be the godfather," Aurora added.

"Congratulations! What did you name him?" She stared steadfastly at Aurora, afraid to look at Mr. Winthrop. What if she offended him, or God forbid, she stared? He didn't seem like a savage, but . . .

"Britton Nathan Winthrop." Aurora slipped her arm through her husband's, and her eyes met his with such warmth that Callista felt a sudden lump in her throat, wondering if she'd ever have such a loving marriage. "By the way, Brit, I received a letter from Pincus. He's coming out in a few months."

"Good. I'll look forward to seeing him."

"He's a photographer," Aurora explained to Callista.

"A photographer? I know a Pincus Jones who's a photographer."

"That's him," Aurora replied. "How do you know him?"

"We worked together on several stories for the newspaper. How do you all know him?"

"It's a very long story," Aurora said with a laugh. "I helped him when he did a book of photographs about the Apache lifeway. So did Brit and Wolf." She gave her husband a conspiratorial smile. "Actually, Wolf arranged for Pincus and me to live among the Apaches for a time."

"Wolf?" Callista asked.

"Ethan," Brit replied without explaining further.

"Now I *really* want to interview you, Aurora."

"Spoken like a dedicated reporter." Brit slid his arm around Callista's waist. "Callista writes for the same newspaper as that R.C. Wickwar fellow," he said proudly. "I showed you his articles about fraud in military contracts last year."

"He ought to come out here and write about fraud in the contracts and supplies on reservations," Aurora said. "It's a national disgrace!"

"That's a good idea, Aurora," Mr. Winthrop said. "Do you think you could convince him to come out, Miss Warwick?"

"I-I can try. And, please, call me Callista." What would they do if they knew they were talking to R.C. Wickwar?

"If you'll call me Ethan." A half smile lit his copper-colored features.

The announcement gong rang before she could reply. Callista could see through the mess-hall windows that everyone had stopped dancing. "If you'll excuse me," she said. "I'd like to hear the speeches welcoming my father."

"Of course." Aurora slipped her arm through her husband's. "Besides, it's time for us to go back and feed the baby."

"See you two tomorrow," Brit said to the Winthrops. He kept his hand in the small of Callista's back as they went up the steps.

"Is Mr. Winthrop really an Apache?" she murmured.

"Yes. And he kidnapped his wife." Brit chuckled at her wide-eyed look. "He's also a Boston Winthrop."

"I've *got* to hear this story!" She'd seen the love that glowed between Aurora and Ethan.

"Ask Aurora. She's the one who lived it."

Callista turned her attention back to the raised dias on the other side of the room. Her parents stood at one end, while Mrs. Kreutz fluttered at the other with a sheaf of papers in her hands.

"Ladies and gentlemen," she started, but no one quieted. "Esteemed officers," she tried, with no effect. "Listen up all you Indian fighters!" she finally shouted as she banged a wooden gavel down on the table. "I know you have already met Colonel Warwick since he's been here for several months, but I want to introduce his lovely wife."

Callista and Brit watched as the officers and their wives were introduced to her mother.

After that, Fowler stepped to her father's side and announced, "And I have an announcement to make." He searched the crowd and spotted Callista. "There you are, my dear. Come on up here." He walked across the room to her and, ignoring Brit as if he were invisible, took her arm, and led her through the crowd.

Her heart thumping in horror, Callista tired to subtly jerk her arm loose, but his hand tightened painfully on her flesh. She glanced at him and saw in his eyes that he knew he was hurting her.

But by that time, they were stepping up on the

raised platform, and Fowler was turning around to face everyone. "Callista Warwick has graciously consented to marry me," Fowler announced, giving her a triumphant grin that didn't quite hide the darkness in his eyes. A darkness she wanted no part of.

Callista stood there immobile, trying desperately to smile coolly at the people who crowded up to the platform to wish them well.

"And when is the happy day?" Mrs. Kreutz asked.

"It's—" Fowler began.

"We haven't set a date yet," Callista spoke over his voice. He squeezed her hand. In warning? She already knew it wasn't in affection.

"And I have an announcement, too," Daisy Hendricks said loudly as she threaded her way through the crowd, holding the hand of a handsome cowboy. "Jack, here," She grinned at him, but it was a genuine grin, not like Fowler's, "and I are getting married."

Callista was shocked by the groans that came from all parts of the room. She looked around in dismay. What was wrong with everyone?

But Daisy seemed unfazed. "I've taught almost the whole school year, longer than any other teacher, but now I need to go with my soon-to-be-husband as he builds his cattle herd on his—our—ranch."

More groans sounded. Callista glanced around at the crowd. Was no one going to wish her well?

"Congratulations, Jack," she said, stepping away from Fowler. "You've got a wonderful lady. And—" She looked around at the crowd. Here was a built-in excuse to extend her engagement. "I'll be happy to take over for Daisy."

"But we're getting married," Fowler snapped.

Callista blinked innocently at him. "But, Fowler dear, you know I need time to plan my wedding. And school will be over in June." That would give her time to find something else to delay her marriage.

"But—" Fowler began.

"That's a marvelous idea, Callista. I'm sure the children will love having a new teacher." Mamere's clear voice cut through the buzz around her. Her face was serene, giving away none of her thoughts.

"That's wonderful!" Daisy Hendricks exclaimed. "I was so worried about the children." Smiling, she took Callista's hand in hers. "I know you'll be a good teacher. Would you like to come Monday after school, so I can show you around?"

"Yes. That would be fine."

"Now see here, Callista," Fowler began angrily, "I won't—"

Mamere doubled over in a sudden coughing attack.

"Here, Mamere," Callista knelt at her side, rubbing the older woman's back. "What happened?"

"Don't . . . know," her mother gasped. "Out . . . side."

"Of course." She helped her mother up and guided her toward the door. As she did, she glanced over her shoulder. Papa and Fowler were engaged in conversation. As her gaze slid over the other officers, she was startled by Brit's cold glare.

Outside, her mother sat down on a bench near the door. "I'm fine, dear," she said, smoothing the skirt of her satin gown. "You go do what you need to do."

"Not until I know you're all right."

Mamere patted her hand. "I am, dear. I am." She drew a deep breath. "See?"

Callista gasped. "You were faking."

"Yes. I wanted to get you out of there before Fowler said too much."

Callista grasped her mother's hands and leaned

down and kissed her on the cheek. "Thank you, Mamere."

Through the window she could see couples whirling by. She had to get away before Fowler came looking for her. Callista rubbed her forehead. "I believe I'm getting a headache. I'm going to go home. Will you make my apologies for me?"

"Of course, dear. You go. Just one thing."

"What, Mamere?"

"Remember what I told you about Mr. Chance. I still feel that he's dangerous."

Callista smiled down at her. "You're right, Mamere, he is. But don't worry, I won't take any chances. And that's not a pun."

At the edge of the porch, Callista hesitated and looked back at her mother. "Had Fowler talked that announcement over with Papa?"

"Absolutely not! Didn't you see your father's face? He was as surprised as you were. Now, go along with you, and I'll tell anyone who asks that all the excitement gave you a headache."

"That's the truth." But she wasn't talking about the same excitement her mother was. She blew her mother a kiss. "Night, Mamere."

Callista hurried past the homes on Officer's Row. A row of sycamores shaded the road from the weak light of the quarter moon. Out beyond the stables, a wolf howled. It was answered by one in the mountains behind the fort.

She drew her silk wrap closer around her shoulders and hastened on. Ahead of her, the lanterns hanging from the porch posts threw feeble light that didn't extend into the shadows beneath the sycamores.

She was two houses away from home when a man stepped out of the shadow of a sycamore. Callista gasped and stopped short. "Who are you?" she demanded, her heart bucking like a wild bronco.

"Brit," he said, apparently recognizing the terror in her voice. "I want to talk to you," he growled.

There was anger in his voice. Real anger. Callista straightened, taken aback. "What are you so angry about?"

"You." Good Lord, how could she act so innocent when she'd led him on as she had? And he'd been only too happy to follow. What happened to his thinking ability when he was with her? Hell, he was letting his balls do his thinking!

"Me? What ever for? What did I do to you, Mr. Chance?"

He clapped softly. "Another outstanding performance, Miss Warwick. You sound so puzzled, as if you really were innocent. You lie better than any trooper I've ever known."

She stared at him, her brow furrowed and her mouth slightly open, as if inviting the touch of his lips. Oh for God's sake, how could he think of that now!

"I have never lied to you." Her lower lip quivered. Just once.

"What do you call forgetting to tell me about your engagement?"

"Fowler made that announcement without discussing it with me," she bit off each word as if it were a bullet. "I am not engaged. Do you hear me?"

"I hear you, I just don't happen to believe you. How the hell could you kiss me like you did an hour ago? What kind of woman are you?" When Fowler announced their engagement, he'd felt a stabbing pain deep inside him. He marked it down to shock and buried it under anger. Hot, bone-deep, fury.

"Now listen to me, Britton Chance." Her voice shook with a righteous indignation that almost convinced him. "I do not lie. Nor am I engaged. Fowler did that on his own." She turned and started to walk away.

He hooked his arm through hers and turned her back. "Running away?" He didn't know if he was angrier at her or himself, for believing her lies. She blinked furiously, and he realized her eyes were brimming with tears. "Yet another performance? Spare me the tears—they don't bother me anyway." Talk about lying through his teeth!

"I'm not crying! I just have something in my eye." She rubbed the backs of her hands over her eyes quickly, furtively, like a seven-year-old.

"Here, use my handkerchief to get it out." He pulled it out of his chest pocket and threw it at her.

She caught it and threw it back. "I don't need your help, thank you."

He plucked it out of the air and slowly crumpled it in his fist. "Are you engaged or are you not engaged?"

"No! Yes!" She rubbed her temples with her fingers. "It's so very complicated."

"How the hell can you call it complicated? Being engaged is like being with child. Either you are or you aren't."

"You don't understand."

"I understand only too well." She was a damned liar. And he was damned fool.

"No. Please, Brit, trust me." She rested her small hand on his arm. "My father is—" The faint moonlight showed him the sheen of tears in her eyes. "It's a family problem."

"I'm listening." He clasped his hands behind his

back to keep from reaching for her, damned fool that he was. "What's your family problem?"

"My heart is not involved." She placed her hand over her heart. "I promise you that."

"That's a damn cold-hearted admission to make, Callista. I sure as hell wouldn't admit something like that, if I was engaged."

"No! It's not like that at all."

"Then what's it like? Explain it to me."

"Oh, Brit, I want to. Don't you know me well enough by now to recognize that?" She leaned against the sycamore trunk and held out her hands to him, as if asking him to take them—and trust her. "I can't. It's—my father—Please, trust me."

"How can you ask for trust when you're not willing to give it?" He rested a big hand on the trunk beside her head, and pictured pulling the hairpins out of her hair and letting it cascade over his hand.

Suddenly it hit him—The officer she'd avoided by coming back from Tombstone with him was Fowler. And she'd shuddered when she saw the man through the window not an hour earlier. "Good God! Fowler's who you've been avoiding!" She was silent. "What the hell's going on here, Callista? You're avoiding him, and he's announcing your engagement?"

"Brit, I want to explain, but I can't. You see, my family needs—" She broke off and tried again. "There are obligations and—" She dragged her fingers through her hair, pulling half of it down, but she didn't seem to notice. "I—Trust me, please."

Then she ducked under his arm and ran toward her father's house. The picket gate banged behind her.

Callista ran through the house, up the stairs, and slammed the door of her bedroom. It flew open and she slammed it again. She kicked off her shoes and began pacing, too angry to sit. Damn him! How could he accuse her of lying to him? Couldn't he see that she loved him?

Callista went very still. She stopped pacing and stared unseeingly into the soft darkness. She sat down on the bed, feeling dazed and as if she were in a dream. She loved him? No! It couldn't be. She couldn't!

She must be hysterical—that's all it was. She'd even sworn at him mentally, and she never swore. She had to calm herself. Once she was calm she'd be more rational and she'd be able to see that it wasn't true.

She padded around her room in the dark, taking off her gown and hanging it up. Then she curled up, in her chemise and drawers, in the window seat and gazed out at the moonlit mountains. In love with him?

She'd hoped two weeks without contact between her and Brit had dimmed the attraction she felt for him. Instead it seemed to shine even brighter. But it *wasn't* love.

Her dreams had been filled with Brit saving her from the Apaches. Brit bending over to kiss her, blotting out the stars. Even a misty vision of Brit making love to her. But she wasn't in love with him.

Never had she dreamt of a man as she dreamt of him.

It was so unlike her, this awareness of him. She was a rational, educated woman. She thought things through, acted on logic, not emotion. Yet when she was with him, she became a creature of the senses: the sky was bluer and the grass greener, roses more fragrant, the "Blue Danube Waltz" more beautiful, food more flavorful. When she was with him she absorbed him through her senses, and every breath she took filled her with a fierce longing for his touch.

But she wasn't in love with him. She couldn't possibly be.

Chapter 11

Dispatch to the *Times/Tribune* Newspapers

Dr. Aurora Spencer Winthrop ministers to all the people of Arizona. And she hastens to emphasize ALL, whatever their skin color—white, bronze, black, or copper. These are her remarks from an interview at Fort Bowie.

"I am appalled at the terrible medical conditions I see all over Arizona. We have known for many years how to stop childbed fever, but I still see women die of it.

"We've known for thirty years that simple attention to sanitation and cleanliness will stop many diseases before they start. Yet I see people, even doctors, ignore these rules. So I say to everyone reading this: Always, always, always wash your hands before touching wounds, dealing with illness, preparing food, or eating.

"We've made so many advances in medicine that I feel my job is part medicine, part education. Wash your hands!"

This is Callista Warwick, washing my hands in Arizona.

"I didn't realize you had so many students, Daisy." Callista stood at the front of the schoolroom, looking down four endless rows of desks that went all the way to the double doors at the back, which seemed at least a half mile away. Maybe she'd bitten off more than she could chew. *It doesn't matter, you've got to stay busy and hold off Fowler until you find a way to break the engagement.*

"There aren't as many as it seems. No one sits in the front two rows except goody-goodies, and I don't have any this year. But I—" She broke off when she glanced at Callista. "Uh-oh. You sat in the front row, didn't you?"

"Always," she replied with a guilty chuckle.

"And see? You turned out all right, in spite of it."

"I don't know about *that*."

"You did." Daisy clasped Callista's hand in both of hers. "Otherwise, you wouldn't have volunteered to take over for me."

"Thank you. Where are the chalk and erasers?" she asked, uncomfortable with Daisy's praise when she'd had a hidden reason for volunteering.

"They're around here somewhere." She looked around, then scooped a small basket off the windowsill next to the blackboard at the front of the room. "Here."

Daisy perched one hip on the desk and crossed her arms over the bosom of her soft yellow dress. "Let me fill you in on the students before Jack gets here. Most of them are wonderful kids, but you need to keep an eye on a couple."

"Why?"

"Well, take Harold Kreutz: he's big for a twelve-year-old and a bully. Takes after his mother," she added dryly, "if you know what I mean."

"I do." Callista flipped open the spiral notebook she'd brought with her and wrote in it.

Daisy filled her in on several other students. "I

can't tell you how relieved I am that you're taking over. I've heard about your book collection, and I know the children will be in good hands."

"My books? How did you hear about them?"

"When you arrived at the fort, the troopers were talking about the books you'd salvaged."

They both turned at the jingle of harness and clip-clop of hooves. The doors at the back were wide-open, and Callista had a good view of Daisy's fiancé as he drove up in a buckboard. Stopping his bay horse at the hitching rail in front, he jumped down, then bounded up the steps into the schoolroom.

"Ah, there you are, Daisy darlin'," he said in a deep, Southern drawl. "Ready to go see the preacher?"

The warmth in his eyes when he looked at Daisy was almost palpable. How lucky they were to have found each other, Callista mused.

"I'm just about through here, Jack." Daisy returned his look with one of her own. "Do you have any questions before I go?" she added, turning back to Callista.

"You're getting married today?"

Daisy grinned unabashedly. "Right now. I wouldn't go out to the ranch without being hitched. Don't know when I'd be able to get back here. There's a lot to do at a ranch in the springtime, what with calving and roundup."

"But . . ." She glanced at Daisy's yellow traveling dress. "What about your wedding dress?"

"We didn't have time for such frills." Jack moved to stand behind Daisy, resting his hands on her shoulders.

"It takes weeks for a dress to arrive after it's ordered. And that's from a catalog, and who knows what it's going to look like anyway," Daisy added.

And they didn't have the money, Callista thought. "I have a white Sunday church dress that I got in Tombstone. It's nothing fancy, you understand, but it's new, and I believe it would fit you, Daisy. Why don't you make it your wedding dress?"

"We couldn't—" Daisy began.

"That'd be wonderful, ma'am." Jack brushed Daisy with his warm gaze. "I know Daisy's been hankering for one."

Raising her chin, Daisy glanced over her shoulder at him. "I don't take charity, Jack. And neither do you."

"Nonsense! This isn't charity, it's my wedding present to you. I can give you a wedding present, can't I?"

"I don't know," Daisy murmured thoughtfully. "Still sounds a lot like charity to me."

"No, it's an investment. I want to see you married, because then you'll leave, and I'll have a job." Callista smiled. "You'll look lovely in it."

"Do it, darlin'," Jack added.

"Come on, Jack," Callista said, wanting Daisy's day to be perfect for her, "drive us to my house and we'll get it."

Jack smiled down at Daisy. "It'll be my pleasure. I'm looking forward to seeing your wedding dress, darlin'."

"So am I," Daisy said with a new sparkle in her eyes.

Within minutes Callista ushered Daisy and Jack into her father's house. Leaving Jack sitting stiffly on the green-velvet sofa in the parlor, Callista hustled Daisy upstairs to her room, where she swept Daisy's curls up in a stylish hairdo.

When they came downstairs a half hour later, Callista paused, letting Daisy go ahead. She watched Jack's face as he saw his bride come down the stairs in her wedding dress. The love lighting his face brought a sudden tightness to her chest. Daisy was a very lucky woman.

"Darlin'?" Jack stood and gave her a slow as molasses up-and-down look. "We were wrong. You deserve a wedding dress that's almost as beautiful as you." Grinning, he started to wrap his arms around her.

"Wait," Daisy yelped, laughing as she slapped his hands away. "Don't muss me. I'll never get my hair to look like Callista did."

"That's the truth." Jack nodded. Unable to take his gaze off Daisy, he said to Callista. "Thank you, ma'am. You were right about the wedding dress. I've never seen my Daisy look so beautiful."

"Come on, you two," Callista said, shooing them toward the front door. "You don't want to be late for your own wedding, do you?"

"Shucks, they can't start without us," Jack replied.

"You're coming with us." Daisy grasped her hand and tugged her along.

"Me? I can't." She tried to dig in her feet, but the waxed wood gave her no toehold.

"Yes, you can. Besides, we need another witness." She glanced at Jack. "And we want that witness to be you."

"She's right, ma'am—so you might as well give in and come along. 'Cause we're not leaving without you."

"Oh, all right." Carried along on their happiness, Callista grabbed her white gloves from the hall table as she went by and pulled them on.

That euphoric feeling lasted the whole time they were driving around the parade ground. In the sunlight, the whitewashed post chapel gleamed like a wedding cake. The double doors were open in welcome.

Then Britton Chance emerged from the chapel. Her treacherous heart leaped at the sight of him. What was he doing here? Heavens, he was the other witness!

He held a bouquet of lavender and white flowers that looked lilliputian in his large hands. "About time," he growled as he came down the steps to the buckboard. "Where the hell have you been, Jack?"

"We were getting a wedding dress for my bride." He reached up to help Callista out of the buckboard. "And we've got our other witness."

Brit had been standing in the vestibule, looking out through the open doorway, when he saw Jack drive up with Daisy and with—Callista?

Callista, who was engaged, but told him her *heart wasn't involved*. Callista, whom he craved like a man lost in the desert craved water. Not just her kisses, but everything about her. Damn her! Damn him!

Why did she have to wear her hair all piled atop her head in loose golden yellow curls that invited his fingers?

"Daisy, you're beautiful," he said, not even looking at Callista, although all his senses were focused on her. "Here, these are for you." He held out the flowers.

"Brit, they're lovely." Daisy sniffed the sprays of lilacs and white roses. "I don't know how you even found flowers."

"I have my ways. But you're lucky the lilacs were early this year. That's a beautiful wedding dress."

"It's courtesy of Callista," Daisy said, smiling.

Just what he needed—to witness a wedding with *her*. Consciousness of her already throbbed in his blood.

"Ready, sweetheart?" Jack asked, as he crooked his arm.

"Ready." Daisy rested her hand on his arm. For a trembling second, they just looked at each other, then together they started up the sunlit steps to the chapel.

Brit turned to follow them. They deserved a fine wedding day, and he wouldn't spoil it for them. He'd be polite to Miss Warwick if it killed him. *And it just might,* he thought ruefully.

Callista couldn't help envying Daisy and Jack their happiness. Would she ever know such a love as theirs?

Brit started up the brick steps behind them, then paused and looked back at her. "Are you coming, Miss Warwick?"

"Of course, Lieutenant Chance." She didn't want to spoil Daisy and Jack's wedding, so she'd be polite to him, even if it killed her.

He waited, half-turned with one foot still on the lower step. Chin up, she swept up the three steps to him, nodded sharply, and kept going.

The steps were uneven, and her foot wobbled when it landed on a loose brick. Instantly Brit's hand was at her elbow, steadying her. She jerked away, not even deigning to look at him.

Side by side they marched up the steps and crossed the broad terrace to the open double doors. Brit stopped her there with a hand on her arm. It was a different touch than she was used to, cold and impersonal.

"What?" she snapped. He smelled of pine soap and

leather and horses, ordinary scents. How could they smell so sexy on him?

"You're going to Daisy's wedding, not a firing squad," he murmured.

"Oh, shut up!" But he was right. She couldn't let her anger at him spill over into Daisy's wedding. And it made her even angrier to know that he was right.

When she walked into the chapel, she found it cool and quiet. And tranquil, oh, so tranquil. Callista absorbed the peace, needing it to soothe the chaotic emotions filling her. If only her treacherous heart hadn't leaped with joy at the sight of Brit.

The interior was whitewashed, like the outside. It was very simple, with dark pews facing the altar. Behind the altar, a window let in light and a view of the Chiricahua Mountains, blanketed in the glorious greens of spring.

A house wren flashed its red breast as it flew past, and she tracked its swooping flight up to a nest on one of the high wooden beams beneath the roof.

"The eaves are open for air circulation in summer," Brit explained quietly. "Birds can get in and out."

Standing in front of the altar, the black-suited minister watched Daisy and Jack progress down the aisle.

"Come on," Brit murmured. "We don't want to hold up the ceremony."

They quietly walked down the aisle in step, which surprised Callista until she realized Brit had shortened his stride to accommodate hers.

She and Brit stood beside the happy couple. The fragrance of lilacs and roses enveloped her. Callista clasped her hands in front of her waist and listened to the quiet words of the marriage ceremony.

What would her marriage be like? Would she fall in love and marry the man she loved, as Daisy was doing? She listened to the steady breathing of the man who stood beside her.

Could she picture herself walking down the aisle to meet him? It would be a tranquil chapel like this one. She'd be wearing white, of course. A floor-length dress and a veil of white. She would walk down the aisle slowly as an organist played.

In her mind's eye, she saw Brit waiting for her. Her eyes would meet his silver gaze. Would he make a good husband? Would he be there for the children they would have, to teach the boys how to throw a baseball, and how to fish and shoot, to give the girls the secure love of a father? Then as they grew up, to teach the boys about the love and respect they should feel for their wives, and to teach the girls about the love and respect they should expect from their husbands?

Would he stand beside her through the years? They were in the spring of their lives—would he be beside her during the richness of their summer, through the autumn harvest of grandchildren, would he hold her and warm her and have a rocking chair beside hers during the winter of their lives?

To all her questions, she had the same answer. Yes. A thousand times yes.

Her heart swelled with a joy she could barely contain. For she knew he would not only stand beside her; he would hold her hand, and make her laugh, and be her friend.

She tilted her head a bit so she could study him.

Until then, whenever she thought of walking down the aisle as a bride, she hadn't been able to complete the picture. The face of the man she walked to meet, the one she would marry and spend her life with, had always been blurred. Never before had she been able to see him clearly. Until Brit.

She'd always wanted children, but never before had she been able to picture a father for them. Until Brit.

Never had she been able to complete the mental picture of lying in a bed with a man and making love with him. Until Brit.

She felt stunned, picturing herself making love with him. That simple act of overwhelming trust and vulnerabilty and intimacy had always been her winnowing tool. If she cringed away from the thought of sharing a bed with a man, she knew she couldn't marry him. And always before, she had cringed away from every man she'd met.

Oh Lord, *was* she falling love with Brit? Callista looked at him, really looked at him with her mind as well as her eyes. And she faced the truth. She was already in love with him.

Brit eyed the minister, and tried to listen intently. Instead he pictured Callista walking down the aisle to place her hand in his. To pledge her troth, her faithfulness to him.

It was a shocking thought, like being struck by lightning. Never before had he pictured any woman walking down the aisle to him. Never before had he even pictured a wedding ceremony, with its commitment of love and trust for a lifetime.

Yet he could almost feel her hand in his, its softness and its strength. Like her—softness and strength.

But she came from a wealthy family; she'd grown up with privilege and servants. He could offer her nothing—nothing but hard work. And a loving husband?

He shied away from the thought, unable to answer that question. It was too astounding.

Besides, it was an impossibility. She was the kind of woman who didn't give her love or trust lightly. But once she did, it would be his—forever. But if he ever violated her love or her trust, he knew it would be gone—forever.

He looked at her. Really looked at her, with his eyes and with his mind. Was he falling in love with her?

Callista took a deep breath and pushed thoughts about marriage to the back of her head. She was there to wish Daisy well. Not to speculate about a man named Britton Chance.

Beside her, Brit stirred restlessly. He was holding her elbow so close to his side, she could feel his heat.

She glanced at him and found him looking at her. Hastily, she looked away, afraid he'd see too much.

The minister closed his book and clasped it in both hands as he bent his gray head and said a final benediction. Then he nodded to Jack. "You may kiss your bride."

"With pleasure," Jack drawled as he grasped Daisy's shoulders and hauled her up in his arms.

Daisy squeaked with mock fear and threw her arms around his neck and hung on.

Their kiss went on for so long, Callista looked away. She didn't dare look at Brit, for his thumb was stroking the inner skin on her arm. So she stared at the mountains visible beyond the minister.

Finally, Daisy and Jack parted, laughing and gasping.

"I just have to share my joy," Daisy said as she hugged Callista. Then she turned to Brit and hugged him, too.

Stepping back, she shooed them toward the back of the chapel. "Okay, go sign that you were a witness, Callista. You too, Brit. I want this all legal."

"Come on," Brit said with a smile, wrapping his hand around Callista's elbow. "Let's go sign so the two lovebirds can be on their way."

Callista didn't say anything as she and Brit walked back up the aisle to the high, dark Spanish sideboard near the entrance. She was still feeling stunned by her discovery.

Brit opened the large leather-bound register. Dipping the quill into ink, he signed below where the minister had already entered Jack's and Daisy's names. Turning, he held the pen out to Callista.

When she took it, his fingers brushed across the back of her hand in a caress that sent a wave of tingles flowing up her arm. Grasping the pen, she signed her even, controlled signature beneath his big, bold scrawl.

Then Daisy hugged her again enthusiastically. "Thank you, Callista, for making my wedding day more perfect than I ever dreamt it would be."

Callista shook her head. "Your wedding day is perfect because you and Jack are meant to be together. It has nothing to do with me."

"Then I wish you a wedding day as perfect as mine has been." Daisy gave her another hug, then turned to Brit. "And to you, Brit, I wish as perfect a wedding day as mine has been. May you find a woman worthy of you." She hugged him.

Callista looked at their signatures again. Her neat, carefully formed letters and his bold strokes. Two different ways of doing the same thing. They had two very different ways of looking at life. Could they ever reconcile them enough to live together?

To marry and live together forever? She wanted a man who was there all the time, being a husband to her and a father to their children. Not riding off being a hero—and getting killed.

"Well, Callista?"

She came back with a jerk and found everyone looking at her. "I'm sorry—what?"

"I've invited Jack and Daisy to the cantina for a celebratory drink."

"What a good idea," she said.

"So you'll come, too," Daisy said as she drifted toward the door. "I'm glad. Somehow it seems fitting for our two witnesses to have a drink with us."

"Drink with you?" Callista hesitated, almost stumbling. Beelzebub, she didn't need a drink with Britton Chance. Not with all she had to think about.

"That's what you said you wanted to do," Brit said. The deep rumble of his voice was impersonal, without a hint of warmth.

"Oh, it is. I want to toast the happy couple. But you don't have to hold my arm and help me down the steps like I was an invalid." And she pulled away.

"Fine." He walked toward his horse without looking back.

Brit followed Jack's buckboard on horseback. A few minutes later they were walking up the steps of the cantina. Callista was surprised to find that it was very clean, with no drunks lying on the floor sleeping off a binge.

Brit held her chair for her and took the chair next to her. Instead of the buxom saloon girl Callista expected, Hester Porter took their order. She returned with sherry for Daisy and Callista, and whiskey for the men.

"To Daisy and Jack, here's to a long and prosperous life together." Brit lifted his glass and clinked with Jack and Daisy's glasses, then hers.

Callista proposed the next toast. "May you find much happiness in each other," she said, clinking her glass against the others. She didn't dare look at Brit, afraid her eyes would telegraph her stunning discovery.

"There you are, Brit," said a gray-haired, beefy officer who had just come through the swinging doors.

"John, come join us for a drink."

"Don't mind if I do." The officer grabbed a chair from the next table and swung it around between Brit and Callista, and sat down.

"You know Daisy and Jack. We're here celebrating their wedding," Brit said. "But I don't know if you've met Callista Warwick yet. Callista, this is Captain John Piney."

"Congratulations, Daisy, Jack. Hope you'll be as happy as me and the Missus have been." He hooked his hat on the spindleback of his chair. "Miss Warwick."

"Don't stand on formality, Captain Piney; please call me Callista," she said, recognizing his voice. He was the John Brit had been talking to in the stables and he knew about Brit's suspicions about Papa and the gunrunners. She moved over to give him more room.

"Before he received a battlefield commission during the War Between the States John was a recruiting sergeant in Chicago," Brit explained. "He recruited me as a twelve-year-old drummer boy."

"I recruited you as a sixteen-year-old drummer boy," John corrected. "We didn't take twelve-year-olds."

"But I lied about my age."

"And I pretended to believe you." He looked around and signaled to Hester for a drink.

"Which saved my life."

Callista frowned at Brit. "How?"

Brit drained his whiskey in one swallow. "Kids living on the streets of Chicago didn't last long," he said in a carefully neutral tone that told her not to pursue the subject.

She took a sip of sherry and sat back, listening to the two men banter and hearing the affection flowing between them.

"How's Emmy?"

"Trying to decide what we'll pack and where we'll go. Amazing what you accumulate in thirty years in the army. But I'm retiring." His gaze met Brit's. "I've got the paperwork started. Have you uncovered anything more about the smugglers since they shot at you?"

"No," Brit said, "but there are more and more Apaches slipping away from the reservation and joining the renegades in Mexico. The smugglers have to be stopped, or we'll have a full-scale war on our hands."

"That's bad news, Brit," Jack said. "I'll tell my men to be alert all the time." He turned to his new wife. "And, darlin', we need to get on the road. We've got miles to cover before dark."

"I'm ready." She stood up. "Before we go, Callista, I've been thinking about your dispatches. Why don't you come out to the ranch and interview me when school finishes and see what it's like?"

"That's a good idea, Daisy. I think I will." She slanted a mischievous look at Jack. "That's if Jack wants company so soon."

"You're always welcome. It can get kind of lonely for a woman out on the ranch, with no one but me and the hands to talk to."

"I'll see you in a couple of months, Daisy." Callista walked around the table and hugged the other girl. "I think the second interview idea is marvelous, and I'll—"

"Miss Warwick!" Fowler Stanhope's voice thundered across the cantina, stopping all conversations as everyone turned to look at him.

He strutted toward Callista in his newest uniform like a flashy bantam rooster, spoiling for a fight. "Hello, Fowler." What was the matter with him?

"What are you doing in this . . . this . . ." The whiskey on his breath was strong enough to start a fire.

Wrinkling her nose at the smell, Callista recoiled. "Cantina?" she supplied coolly. Behind her she heard Brit snort.

"Does your father, our commanding officer, know you're here?" He swayed, and she realized he was already drunk.

"I know he's the commanding officer, Fowler."

"Come." He crooked his elbow out at an odd angle. "I'll escort you home."

"No." She had to count to ten before she could add, "Thank you."

"No?" He opened and closed his mouth several times, like a fish gulping for air. "But—"

"I'm here with my friends, Fowler," Callista said in a very quiet voice. "I shall leave with them."

"Now, see here, Callista, this is no place for a lady."

"There is nothing wrong with this cantina." She was beginning to get up a head of steam. How dare he shout at her? "And no one would even have known I was here, Fowler, if you hadn't shouted my name."

"I won't have you—"

"Enough is enough," Brit growled, standing up and kicking his chair back.

Callista glowered at him. That was all she needed, Brit having words—or worse trading punches—with Fowler. In a cantina, yet. Couldn't he see that Fowler was drunk?

"I've had enough too, Brit," John Piney said, standing up beside him. "Miss Warwick, I believe you asked me to escort you home. Are you ready to go?"

"How kind of you to remember, Captain. Yes, I am."

Ignoring Fowler, they all walked out together, wishing Daisy and Jack well. After the newlyweds drove off, Brit mounted his horse, nodded to Callista, and rode away.

That was when Fowler joined Callista on the porch. "He's a bastard, Callista," Fowler said, watching Brit. "A real bastard—illegitimate. Doesn't even know who his father is."

"I know, Fowler," Callista said quietly. What a mean, miserable excuse for a man he was.

"You know?" He held a fresh drink.

"Yes, he told me." And she wanted to clap for Brit, that he had told her.

"Did he tell you that he grew up in a brothel?" He swayed precariously.

"Yes, that too." She almost laughed at the disappointed look he gave her. "Shall we go, Captain Piney?"

"With pleasure, Miss Warwick," John Piney said,

as he clasped Callista's arm and started down the steps.

"I am impressed, Miss Warwick, by your performance just now." He chuckled. "You didn't give Lieutenant Stanhope a bit of satisfaction over his news."

"Brit *had* told me." She lifted her skirt to step over a deep rut. "And it's a good thing he did."

"Brit told you?" He stopped in the road. "He's never told anyone but me. You must be special."

She could only hope she was. "Thank you, Captain Piney, for averting a fight. I also suspect that it was no accident that you sat down between Brit and me."

"Brit's right—you *can* add two and two, Miss Warwick. I was at the ball Saturday night, and I seem to remember an engagement announcement," he added gently.

"Brit and I were witnesses at the wedding. That's why we were in the cantina, Captain Piney. Each of us wanted to wish the newlyweds happiness." There, she'd made it quite plain that she and Brit weren't together.

They stopped at her father's house. "I hope you'll enjoy your retirement, Captain."

"I'll be around for another few months, Miss Warwick, so I'm sure we'll meet again."

Callista watched Captain Piney walk up Officers' Row. She'd never seen Brit speak to anyone with such open affection before. And everything she'd learned intrigued her more.

So Brit had been living on the streets of Chicago. No wonder he was so hard. And no wonder Mamere had sensed that he had no traces of child in him. Maybe he'd never had the freedom to be a child.

She still had a slightly dazed feeling, as if she'd

been struck by lightning. How had love crept up on her without her realizing it?

And what was she going to do about it?

For the time being, she would keep her shining discovery locked in her heart.

Chapter 12

~~~∽◡◠◡∽~~~

Dispatch to the *Times/Tribune* Newspapers

Miss Daisy Hendricks, teacher at the Fort Bowie school, shared the following information in an interview.

The men of Arizona are gallant gentlemen who treasure their women. They have to. Otherwise, they'll be replaced by a man who does. Women who dare the dangerous journey to Arizona have a most enviable task of choosing from among a multitude of suitors.

Miss Hendricks's students arrive each morning eager to learn. Although in need of books and supplies of all sorts, she teaches first grade through ninth. With a few picture books and a world map, she has taught her students about the people, animals, and countries of the world. Even more important, her students leave her classroom knowing how to read and write: such a hard skill to teach, yet so necessary in our increasingly technical world.

Miss Hendricks is leaving to get married. I will teach her students until a new teacher arrives.

This is Callista Warwick, reporting from Fort Bowie.

A week after she took over for Daisy, Callista picked up the bucket of erasers and went out to the secluded area behind the school. A sycamore shaded a picnic table for the students, and bushes screened the area.

The past week had been a blur, teaching her students in the morning, doing her interviews in the afternoon, making sure Fowler's path didn't cross hers, looking for clues to the gun smugglers, and most of all thinking about Brit, speculating about Brit, missing Brit.

Busy as she was, it didn't fill the hole in her heart left by Brit's absence. She didn't know which was worse: when he was gone on patrol and she worried about his safety, or when he was at the fort and she'd see him, but not speak to him.

She didn't want a repeat of Fowler's actions in the cantina. If she was going to say she was engaged, she had to act like it. But it was so much harder than she'd expected. Fowler expected to spend some evenings with her. She'd pleaded that she was too tired at night for socializing and Papa had concurred—to Fowler's frustration and her delight.

But she still had the problem of breaking her engagement.

She picked up two of the erasers and spread her arms wide, then brought them together. Splat! A puff of chalk dust erupted from the erasers. If only Fowler was out of her life. Splat! Take that, Fowler! Splat! And that! Splat! Splat!

She dropped them in the bucket and picked up two more.

"You," a low guttural voice said.

Startled, she dropped the erasers and whirled.

An Apache stood there watching her, his dark copper arms crossed over his chest. He wore a white shirt and a white breechcloth hung over tan pants tucked into knee-high moccasins. A blood-red bandanna was tied around his head.

She thought it was the Apache scout she'd met in the store, but she wasn't sure. What had Brit called him?

"Walks-with-Horses?"

"Umm." He nodded sharply, just once. "You teach?"

"Yes, I'm the teacher now." She ran her palms down her blue-denim skirt, wiping away sudden perspiration. What did he want? Why hadn't he come during school hours?

"Teach son."

"Teach your son?" Callista digested his request. Teach an Apache child with the other children? Her first thought was that there'd be fights; her second was that maybe they could get to know each other as individuals instead of as the *enemy*. It might work. It was worth a try.

She could imagine what the parents would say to having an Apache in the classroom. Mrs. Kreutz would be the loudest. Still, if she didn't try, she'd always wonder if it would have worked.

"Yes, Walks-with-Horses, I will—"

"Callista, you're here already," Brit said, as he rode his horse around the corner of the schoolhouse.

"Of course. I'm getting ready for school." She clasped her hands behind her back to keep from running to him and throwing her arms around him.

"I told Walks-with-Horses that I would see if you would teach his son." He dismounted and walked up to her, holding the reins. "He's only eight and—"

He hadn't even asked her how she was. "Yes, Walks-with-Horses and I have already discussed it. His son can come at eight o'clock tomorrow so he can meet the other children before class starts."

"Good, I'm glad you agreed." His silver eyes held hers for a heartbeat, then he spoke to Walks-with-Horses in Apache. The Apache shook his head and replied in Apache.

"His son doesn't speak English."

"He won't be able to participate in the class, then." She was disappointed, she realized. She would have liked the challenge of teaching him. "What if I taught him after the regular school day is over? Just him and me. Wait! If he doesn't speak English, I don't have any way of communicating with him."

"You could learn Apache."

"That's a possibility, but I can't learn it fast enough." His blue shirt was open at the throat, revealing his silver medallion and dark curls.

Brit began explaining to Walks-With-Horses, but paused and frowned at her thoughtfully. "Could you come two hours early, before school? I could act as interpreter on days when I'm not gone on patrol."

"That would work." It would be a chance to spend time with him, but did she want that? Well, she couldn't deny the boy a chance to learn just to avoid Brit. "You'd only have to come in the beginning, until he begins to understand English."

"And you begin to understand Apache." His horse rubbed its head against Brit's back, shoving him against her. He grasped her arms to keep her from falling. "I didn't train him to do that." He gave her a lopsided grin that launched a fluttering butterfly in her stomach. He held her a heartbeat longer, then he released her. "It's not an easy language. There's lots of z's."

"W-what?" She tried to remember what they'd been talking about. "Oh, yes, of course, I'll learn

Apache." Actually, learning a little Apache would make for interesting dispatches to send back. What better way to broaden her horizons than to learn the language of the savages? She would write about teaching the boy. "Tell Walks-with-Horses that he should bring his son tomorrow. If you can come?"

"I can. We're not scheduled to leave on patrol for a few days. Maybe in that time I can help you two begin to communicate."

He swung up on Red. Callista watched him until the horse cantered past the school and disappeared. Could she see him every day, talk to him every day, when she was in love with him?

Or was she daring fate?

The next morning Brit saddled Red early and rode out to the abandoned homestead where the lilac bushes grew, and cut a large armful of the fragrant blossoms.

Brit had spent the days since Daisy's wedding on patrol, riding hard, working hard, looking for signs of the smugglers, and dealing with his shocking thoughts during Daisy's wedding.

He couldn't believe that he had actually pictured Callista walking down an aisle to meet him as his bride. He hadn't been drinking; he hadn't eaten locoweed. Why would he have had such a clear picture of her as his bride? Unless . . . No, he didn't want to go down that trail. Not yet.

He reined in at the schoolhouse and dismounted. This was the first of many mornings when he'd be seeing Callista. His hummingbird, with her golden hair and jewel-colored eyes. And her sharp little tongue that could make him laugh and long for her at the same time. He bounded up the front steps two at a time, eager to see her.

The door was open and she was erasing the blackboard. She was wearing a deep, sapphire blue dress with white stripes, which looked cool and crisp. Like her. Holding the lilacs loosely, he leaned a shoulder against the doorjamb and watched her.

Instead of the tight, prim knot she'd worn yesterday, she'd swept her hair up into a loose gathering of curls on top of her head, which allowed some tendrils to trail over the back of her neck. He itched to pull it all down and fill his hands with it again.

He knew the passion that simmered beneath her oh-so-in-control facade. Her fire tantalized him. Along with her mind and—

But she was engaged—to a man she avoided. What was going on? Had everything she'd said when they were together been lies? Had the response he'd felt from her when she was in his arms been a lie? His head said no, she wasn't an actress. She was an honest lady.

So why was she engaged to Fowler Stanhope? He shook his head. Fowler would never have graduated from West Point if his father wasn't such a powerful senator. Brit had heard rumors about the threats the senator had made to the commandant at the Point.

Hell, Fowler was so incompetent, he was a menace to every patrol he led. He'd gotten lost on his last one. Brit had had to send an Apache scout to find him and his men, and lead them back. As it was, Fowler would have shot the scout if one of his men hadn't stopped him.

Callista began to write a new lesson on the blackboard.

Don't waste the morning leaning against the door.

He paced forward and saw the tiny hesitation in her hand when she heard his steps. So, she was aware of him. Good.

He didn't say anything until her curiosity got the better of her, and she turned in a swirl of skirts that revealed shapely ankles.

"These are for you." He held out the flowers.

Her face lit up when she saw them. "Lilacs! My favorites." She swept up the sprays and plunged her face into them, inhaling deeply. "Brit, thank you." She looked up at him, her features aglow. "They're lovely."

His mouth went dry. "You're lovely," he growled. Next year he'd pick enough lilacs to cover his whole bed and then he'd make love to her on a bed of fragrant lilacs and—

"Shit," he muttered, shifting restlessly as his pants grew taut. What did he expect, with an image like that in his mind? He breathed deeply, and the fragrance of the lilacs seemed to mock him.

Or were they a promise? Next year. Next year in lilac season.

"Where did you get them?" Her soft voice wrapped around him like a siren's call.

"At an abandoned homestead. Settlers who gave up and went back East. The wife planted two lilac bushes."

"And they couldn't make it? That's so sad." She brushed a finger over the delicate velvety petals.

"They probably brought lilac cuttings west, coddling them all the way. Better put them in water, Cally." He walked around the room, noticing the changes she'd made.

She pulled a glass out of her desk, filled it with water from the bucket, and put the lilacs in. She sniffed the fragrant flowers again before placing the glass on the front corner of her desk.

"This is the first thing I've smelled in ages that smells like home."

"Where's home?" He rested one hip on her desk.

"We've lived in Washington and Chicago a lot, but Galena, Illinois, is really home. There are lilac bushes all over town and in the spring it's wonderful." She moved away from her desk to lean against the cabinets beneath the windows and crossed her arms.

It looked so casual that most people wouldn't have noticed it. He did. Was she backing away from him?

"Galena is where President Grant is from, you know," she said in a rush, "and I grew up hearing all about him. Especially with Papa being in the army. Everyone was always comparing him to Grant. And everyone always said Papa would make a better president."

"Did they?" Picking up a couple of sprigs of lilacs, he paced over to her and saw her eyes widen as he drew near. He held the sprigs up beside her eyes. "When I saw these, I thought they were the same shade as your eyes."

Her eyes darkened. "Are they?" Her voice was soft, throaty.

"I was right." He threaded one sprig into her hair over her right ear, then let his finger trail down her silken throat to the tiny hollow where her pulse throbbed against her ivory skin.

He heard the clip-clop of approaching horses and stepped away.

Leather creaked as the riders dismounted in front of the schoolhouse. Callista hurried to meet them. Walks-with-Horses walked up the steps, but his son stomped. She understood *that* in any language. So, George didn't want to be there.

Walks-with-Horses stopped in front of Callista. His son was dressed like his father in a white shirt and tan pants under a white breechcloth. Like his father, he had tied a red bandanna around his head to control his long hair. He stopped beside his father and stared at her skirt hem.

"Will my son learn valuable things from this White-eyes woman?" Walks-with-Horses asked in Apache.

"Yes," Brit replied. "She will teach your son much."

"Will you see to it, my friend?"

Brit nodded. "I will see to it, my friend."

Callista watched the Apache stalk away. "What was that all about?"

"He wants to be sure I supervise you well. And he wants his son to learn much."

"Well, of all the—" Clamping her hands to her hips, she glared balefully at the Apache's retreating back.

"It isn't personal. Warriors teach the Apache boys his age. You are obviously not a warrior."

"And you just as obviously are." Oh, Lord, how could she have fallen in love with him? It just wasn't possible.

He hunkered down in front of the boy and held out his hand. "*Buenos dias*, George." *Good day.*

George took his hand and shook it, but didn't look up. "*Buenos dias, Nantan*," he said softly.

"*Nantan*." Brit looked up at Callista. "There's your first word of Apache. It means chief or leader."

"*Nantan*, huh?" Callista tried it out. "All right."

"No, *enju*. That means good."

"*Enju*." She nodded. "*Enju*."

"Hello, George." She held out her hand.

George didn't move until Brit murmured something to him. Then he limply touched her hand with his, but instead of looking at her, he continued to gaze at the hem of her skirt.

He was shy. She could work around that. "I've been thinking about how to start since we don't have a common language. How about if we start with numbers? One, two, three?"

"Why don't you start off with concrete things? Let's bring my horse around back and we'll name the saddle, bridle, etc."

And they wouldn't be so visible in back, she thought. "All right. Let's see if that works."

Callista gathered chalk and a slate and joined them. Brit rested his hand on the saddle as he talked to George and it was clear that he'd already started his lessons.

Callista stayed in the background, making suggestions when Brit wanted them, but letting him get George started. She was amazed at Brit's patience. He would be a wonderful father.

After what seemed to be only a few minutes, Brit pulled his pocket watch out and checked the time. "I think that's enough for one day. Don't you, Callista?"

"Yes. You did *enju*, George." George dug his toe into the soil again, but still didn't look directly at her.

"What is wrong?" Callista said, exasperated. "Why won't he meet my eyes when I'm talking to him? Is he shy?"

"He's showing you respect, Callista. Apache children are taught not to return the gaze of their elders."

He spoke to George, then, grabbing the back of George's shirt and pants, he swung him up on his pony. Slapping the pony's rump, he sent him galloping away.

He sauntered back to where she sat on one of the benches beside the picnic table.

"I think it will be worthwhile for you to teach George," he said, propping his boot on the bench and resting his arm on his raised knee. "He's a smart kid."

"Me? You taught him."

"Tomorrow you'll do it. He doesn't want to be here right now, but give him time, and he'll come around."

"You did a great job. I was watching you, and you are going to be a wonderful father." An image of him holding their child flashed before her eyes.

"I like kids." He pulled a yellow bandanna out of his pocket and brushed dust off his boot. "Of course, lots of things have to happen before I'm a father. Like finding the right woman and getting engaged. You know, Callista, most people think an engagement is the last step before marriage. But apparently that isn't the case with you. Why are you engaged to a man you don't even like?"

Her smile faded, and she turned away. "I can't explain."

"Yes, you can." He kneaded her shoulder gently. "Are you going to marry a man you don't like? I don't think so," he said, thinking aloud. "So why would you be engaged to a man you don't like?"

"Because I can't figure out a way to break the engagement without bitter feelings," she snapped.

He continued kneading, loosening the tight muscles in her shoulder. "Why are you worried about hurt feelings?"

"Papa and Fowler's father are partners in a business. I don't want to ruin their friendship. That's all I'm going to say."

"So you want a way out of the engagement without Fowler—or his father—becoming angry. Right?" She nodded. "It's simple."

She turned to him, clasping his hand with both of hers. "You've got a way? How?"

"Fowler is a blatant snob. Do something that isn't suitable for his future wife to do, and he'll break the engagement."

She slapped her forehead. "Why didn't I think of that? It's so simple it's brilliant!"

"You were too focused on breaking the engagement to think of another way. I wasn't."

Rising, she hugged him in delight. But as she would have pulled away, he held her. Just for a heartbeat. Then he let her go.

Callista backed up, wanting to be in his arms, but knowing her students would be arriving. "I-I'll see you tomorrow?"

He nodded once. "Damn right."

He swung up on Red and rode away.

That night, as Callista unpinned her hair, a wilted sprig of lilacs fell to the floor. Smiling, she picked it up and brushed her finger over the limp but still silky petals.

Opening *Idylls of the King*, the book on her nightstand, she laid the sprig in it, flattened the tiny petals gently with her finger, then closed the book.

She was in love with him. There was no getting around it. He was all wrong for her, but that hadn't stopped her heart.

Several mornings later, Brit rode his big red horse directly into the school clearing. Callista looked up from where she sat at the picnic table.

"I'm taking the Apache scouts on patrol." He dismounted and came to her. "But I think you and George can communicate well enough to get along without me now."

Callista jumped up, her hand pressed to her bosom. "I'm sure we'll be all right," she said, trying to sound confident. "Are you going after—"

"Geronimo? Yes." He swept his hat off and flung it on the table. "He was seen over near Douglas. The scouts are the only hope of being able to capture him."

"Why?" How dangerous was it for him? That was the important thing.

"Because they're the only ones who can travel as fast as he through the rough canyons where he likes to hide." The morning breeze ruffled his hair.

"What about you? Do you get left behind then?" Please, say yes. She wanted to smooth back his mussed hair and to say, *don't go*.

He smiled and shook his head. "Nope. I'm either in the pursuit or up ahead, trying to set up an ambush."

"Sounds dangerous as all get out."

"Not really. It's not a matter of galloping along shooting at each other, but a dogged pursuit with ambushs and feints and more ambushs. It's a mental game of strategy."

Callista looked up at him, wanting to yell at him to be careful. "No, Brit, it's not a game. It's deadly serious business."

He eyed her thoughtfully. Then his eyes crinkled and a slow smile spread a slash of white across his sun-bronzed face. "Why, thank you, Cally. I do appreciate your worrying about me."

Damn him, how could he stand there and look

pleased because she was worried? "Oh, puleeze. Me worry about you? Don't flatter yourself." She walked away a few steps before she trusted herself to turn and face him. Nothing in her expression would give her away, she thought.

"Callista, Callista, Callista," he murmured as he closed on her, step by step. She stood her ground until he was just a stride away. Then she backed up a step. He advanced. She backed up. He kept coming.

And with the next step she was backed against the tree.

Brit's smile howled of wolves and promises as he rested a big hand on the trunk beside her head. "I was hoping you'd worry about me, Cally."

His soft drawl purred with heat and passion, and sent a shimmer of awareness skittering through her. She swallowed against the sudden dryness in her throat.

"You shouldn't have done that," he murmured, his gaze on her throat. He trailed a single finger down her skin, then his lips followed the same trail.

Callista's head fell back as he scattered kisses across her throat like flower petals. She gave a soft moan and ran her hands over his powerful shoulders, drinking in his strength. His mouth found hers, and she sank beneath the heat and fierce need in his lips and tongue.

She clung to him, her fingers tight on his shoulders, giving and demanding in turn. Touching and tasting him in a delicious haze of feeling.

The hoofbeats of an approaching horse gradually intruded into her consciousness and she wrenched away from Brit, even as she savored the last lingering touch of his lips.

"Someone's coming," she gasped, dragging air deep into her lungs.

Brit nodded. "Probably our student."

She patted her hair, checking to see that all the strands were still neatly wound into a knot on top of her head. "Good thing he's late this morning."

"That's a great send-off you gave me," Brit murmured.

"Send-off? I did no such thing!" She glared at him before she noticed the teasing glint in his eyes. "Please, Brit," she said softly, "do be careful."

"I will." Grasping her arms, he brushed a last kiss over her lips. Then he turned away and mounted.

He was at the corner of the schoolhouse before she found her voice.

"Brit?" He looked back. "Take care."

He waved nonchalantly and rode away. Callista listened until the sound of his horse's hoofbeats faded.

Lord, when had her life gotten so complicated?

She was engaged to a man she hated, and in love with a man she couldn't have.

Chapter 13

~~~ ❦ ~~~

Dispatch to the *Times/Tribune* Newspapers

The Chief of Scouts has prevailed upon me to educate an Apache child. He is a boy of eight, straight and sturdy with lively black eyes. His father is an Apache scout in the employ of the U.S. Army.

Since the boy doesn't speak English and I don't speak Apache, the Chief of Scouts is acting as translator, and we meet every school morning. I am most impressed with the boy's intelligence.

The Apaches don't have a written language: they learn their history from tellers of tales. An alphabet and writing and reading are foreign concepts, yet George is a very quick learner, even though we are working in a language foreign to him. Seeing his ebony eyes shine when he understands something is wonderfully rewarding.

I am learning Apache from George. I can't speak a sentence yet in his language, but I'm trying.

This is Callista Warwick, reporting from Fort Bowie.

Callista took her writing materials out to the front veranda. Papa had gone to Tucson to confer with General Crook, and Mamere was upstairs reading, so

she knew no one would disturb her. She drew one of
the white-wicker chairs up to the round table and
settled down to write her next dispatch.

The parade ground was deserted. The only movement was the bright green leaves of the sycamores,
whispering softly in the afternoon breeze.

Fowler had taken leave to go back to Connecticut
to see his sick aunt. She didn't know how long he'd
be gone, but it was a welcome reprieve. When he
came back, though, she knew he would insist on setting a wedding date. That was when she had to break
off the engagement.

Fowler could be gone until hell froze over, but she
longed for Brit to return.

It would have been a perfect day if he were back.
He'd been gone on patrol for over a week, and the
days dragged on leaden feet. She taught school in the
morning and in the afternoon tried to pick up information that would help find the gun smugglers.

But without Brit, something was missing from her
days. She felt only half-awake. He could be exasper-
ating and overprotective, as when he had told her to
forget helping him with the smugglers, but he also
made her laugh. Now the days bled into one another,
with nothing to make them stand apart. She sent off
dispatches and the next day wondered what she'd
sent off.

When she was with him, she felt so alive. Colors
were brighter, fragrances stronger, food tasted better,
and sunsets were more splendidly, passionately red.

So this was what love felt like: this dreamy, float-
ing-two-feet-above-the-ground, can't-wait-for-him-to-
return feeling. She'd never felt like this before. Not
even when she'd been engaged to David.

It frightened her in a way. She couldn't picture him

as her husband. As a logical person, she'd made lists of the traits she wanted in a husband. Brit didn't have the right traits at all. In fact, he had the one trait that she most certainly *didn't* want in a husband: he was a hero.

She fished in her pocket for her linen handkerchief and dabbed at the moisture beginning to dew her upper lip. She'd dawdled long enough, Callista thought, opening her notebook. After working for a few minutes, she gazed absently across the parade ground. In the eight years since she'd graduated from Miss Porter's, she'd come a long way.

When she became a reporter, Callista had found she liked the challenge of writing stories and articles that people read. She'd started out writing the obituaries, but soon graduated to stories about living people. She enjoyed interviewing people and checking facts and everything about the job—including the money.

And here she was, eight years after writing her first article, writing dispatches that were being printed by newspapers in Chicago and Washington, D.C.

And she had one to write now, Callista chided herself, picking up her pencil. She was just putting the finishing touches on it when a door slammed somewhere.

Startled, she looked up in time to see Brit run down the steps of the headquarters building. He was back, her heart cried. He was back!

Swinging up on his red horse, he cantered to her house, dismounted before the horse stopped, and banged the picket gate open. He came up the walk with a very purposeful stride, took the steps two at a time, marched across the porch, and pounded on the front door.

"Are you looking for me?" She smiled in welcome and stood up to greet him. Just back from patrol and he couldn't wait to see her—so he *did* feel something for her!

"Damn right, I'm looking for you. I want to talk to you, *Miss Warwick!*" Letters stuck out of his chest pocket and his pants pockets, two were stuffed into his hatband, and he held a handful as well.

Was he frowning? No, he couldn't be; he was just squinting against the bright sun.

"When did you get back from patrol?" He was unshaven and coated with trail dust. And she caught a whiff of horses and leather.

"About an hour ago."

And he'd come straight to see her. She gestured at the wicker chair on the other side of the table. "Why don't you sit down?" She sat, too. Obviously this wasn't the time to run into his arms.

He swept his hat off. His hair was all rumpled and sticking up in spiky tufts, as if he'd been running his fingers through it before he'd put his hat on.

Then he sat down, leaned forward, and glared at her from beneath his dark brows. "I want to know what the hell you've been writing about me, *Miss Warwick.*"

"What are you talking about?" Callista straightened in her chair. "Writing about you? I haven't."

"You must have written something," he said in a hard tone.

"I haven't." She lifted her hands, palms up. "Really. Well, I wrote about you saving us, but I didn't mention your name."

"Then what is this?" He dug in his chest pocket and pulled out a handful of letters. Whatever he was looking for wasn't there, so he emptied his pants pockets of more letters. And more letters. He even yanked the ones out of his hatband and threw them on the table.

"My, you get a lot of letters."

He gave her a disgruntled look. "Don't push me, lady." He shuffled through them looking for something. Finally he pulled a newspaper clipping out and waved it at her. "Did you or did you not write this pack of lies?"

"Stop waving it around if you want me to read it." Heavens, why was he so upset? Just because she'd written a few dispatches about him?

"Here." He slammed it down on the table.

She only had to read the first couple of words to know it was her second hero dispatch, the one where she'd been especially effusive. "Yes, I wrote that. What about it? I didn't name you."

"You didn't have to. You wrote this." He pushed another newspaper clipping across the table—the one where she mentioned General Crook recalling him to active duty as Chief of Scouts.

"I still didn't name you."

"But you told your 'dear readers' that I was at the same post as you. I returned from a ten-day patrol and found my mailbox jammed with letters. Do you know what these are?" He gestured at the letters strewn over the table.

"No, of course I don't."

"These"—he leaned forward and pinned her to her chair with a steely glare—"are marriage proposals addressed to the Chief of Scouts at Fort Bowie."

Callista sank back in her chair, staring at him. "All of them?" she asked weakly.

"All of them." He shuffled through the letters.

"Here—read this one. And this one." He threw a couple of letters in her lap.

Callista read them, then carefully refolded them. She didn't dare look at him. If she did, she was going to laugh. She cleared her throat, folded her hands in her lap, and gazed at them. "Well." She vowed not to smile. "These ladies appear to be very sincere."

"They are all sincere. Some even included photos. And one, nude photos."

She choked and clamped her hand across her mouth to keep from giggling. It was obvious he didn't see anything funny about the situation.

"I am so sorry. I never meant for this to happen." His sleeves were rolled up, exposing his tanned arms dusted with dark hairs. She rested her hand on his arm and jerked back, shocked. His muscles were tense and hard, like touching iron. "What can I do to make amends?"

"I think you've done quite enough already."

She snapped her fingers. "I know. I'll put in my next dispatch that your wife and three children have arrived from your ranch."

He grimaced. "Hell, no! With my luck some woman will show up with a bunch of kids and claim to be my wife. But you could retract that bunch of lies you wrote about me."

She shook her head. "I didn't write any lies. I may have exaggerated a bit, but I didn't lie."

He glowered at her from beneath his dark brows. "Lady, they weren't exaggerations. They weren't even within shouting distance of the truth. They were poppycock. Hogwash. Rubbish. Retract them."

"I'm afraid I can't do that," she said, congratulating herself on her calm, rational manner. "I would lose my credibility with my readers."

"What credibility? You're feeding them a pack of lies."

She slammed her palm down on her papers. "No. You're forgetting that I'm reporting what I see. It's my opinion, that's all."

He cocked one dark eyebrow at her. "Now, let me get this straight, Callista." His voice went all silky smooth. "What you wrote is *your* opinion of me?"

"I was writing about a hero. My readers like to read about heroes." Good Lord, she hadn't seen that one coming. He must be addling her brains again.

"So you consider me a hero?"

"Yes. But don't get such a satisfied look on your face. My readers are impressed by heroes. I'm not."

He gave her a slow up-and-down look that would have melted the stays in her corset if she'd been wearing one. "Really? Would you care to elaborate?"

"You see, I happen to know that heroes don't live long. They're so busy being heroes, they get themselves killed."

"Want to give me some examples?"

"Let's start with Custer."

"He wasn't a hero, he was a hotheaded fool."

"Your opinion, Mr. Chance. There's also my fiancé, and my brother, and John Paul Jones and the men who died at the Alamo and—"

"Enough." He held up his hand. "I see the trend."

"Heroes are like dessert," she said, warming to her subject. "They're dramatic and wonderful to taste, but they're gone and forgotten the next day." Which she had managed to push to the back of her mind when she fell in love with him. "They're not the meat and potatoes of life that sustains you and sticks to your ribs. They're not the men who are there, day after day."

He tapped a folded letter on the table as he eyed her thoughtfully. "So you don't have a very high opinion of heroes. Is that correct?"

"Yes."

"And you're not attracted to them?"

"Far from it." She raised her chin. "Getting involved with heroes brings nothing but heartache. I want nothing to do with them."

He nodded. "Good. I'm glad to hear that, because I'm not a hero. I'm just an ordinary man. And I don't want you telling lies about me."

He wasn't ordinary, he was extraordinary. Not that she'd ever tell him that.

The front door opened, and Josephina came out with a large silver tray.

"Ahh, it's Josephina with afternoon tea." Callista gathered her writing papers into a single pile and stacked Brit's letters into two piles, giving the stout housekeeper room to slide the tray onto the table.

"You will take tea with me, won't you?"

"Tea?" He gave her a dazed look, like a man who'd just been bucked off a wild horse.

"Yes, afternoon tea. One of the most civilized habits known to man."

"Maybe to woman, but not to man," he growled.

"You'll enjoy it. Especially the scones and biscuits." She poured the fragrant Earl Grey tea, then picked up the sugar tongs. "One cube or two?"

"Are you serious?"

"Of course." She tapped the cream pitcher. "Yes? No?"

"This is the desert, woman. I'll die of thirst and you'll still be talking."

"Now who's exaggerating?" But she handed the cup and saucer to him.

"And you don't like it, do you?" He took a scone from the plate and broke it open and the scent of strawberries wafted by. Lord, he was hungry. For her, not food.

But why had she written those stories about him? Did she really see him like that? It had been a strange sensation to read about himself. Especially since he didn't recognize the man she described.

He drained his cup and held it out to her. "Don't go through all the damn rigamarole. Just refill it."

"Brit, I have an idea," she said as she passed him the full cup. "In my next dispatch, I'll tell my readers that because you are in hot pursuit of Geronimo's renegades, you can't reply to all the letters you've received, but you want to thank everyone. I'll also mention that you are engaged to a lady in . . . in Arizona." She'd started to say Fort Bowie, then decided that was too close to what she wished for. "Don't worry, I'll take care of it."

"That's what I'm afraid of," he said ruefully. He caught a whiff of her lilac scent, so refreshing after days of smelling sweaty horses and men.

Brit watched her sip her tea. Good Lord, it was wonderful to see her. The last ten days had been ten years long. Ten long days when she was in his thoughts all the time. Ten long days when her ghost rode double with him and lay in his bedroll with him. She had beckoned to him from his dreams for ten long nights.

And now he was here and he wanted her more than when he'd left. His hand tightened on the teacup. This was not the time or the place, he told himself sternly.

He glanced around. "By the way, is your fiancé going to show up like he did at the cantina?"

"No, he's taken leave and gone to visit his sick aunt in Connecticut."

He stiffened. "Did he say where he was going?" Connecticut was where Winchester had its weapons factories. And Fowler Stanhope had arrived at the same time as Warwick. Were they partners in gun smuggling?

"New Haven, I think. But I can't be certain. Have you found out anything more about the gunrunners?"

"No, they've been quiet, as if they know we're on their trail."

"I haven't come across anything in my interviews, either."

Brit sighed wearily. "Callista, please, don't try to find out who the smugglers are; you're playing with fire. Identifying them is a job for a man like R.C. Wickwar. He's used to working undercover and taking risks. You aren't."

"Brit, there's something I need to tell you." She stroked her cup handle absently with her forefinger and he wondered what it would be like to have her stroking him the same way, with only one tantalizing finger. He leaned forward, thinking about sweeping her into his arms. "I'm R.C. Wickwar," she said softly.

He must be more tired than he realized. He'd swear she just said she was Wickwar. But that was impossible!

"What did you say?"

"I'm R.C."

"You're—Oh, don't be ridiculous, Callista. Why are you—My God, you are!" Brit leaned back in his chair, studying her. "I thought I knew you. But I was wrong. You are a brave lady."

She drew her finger through a bead of water on

the table. "I've wanted to tell you, but I didn't know how."

"Why are you using a fake name, instead of getting credit for the investigative work you're doing?"

"So my parents and other people wouldn't know. There were death threats made against R.C. Only my editor and I, and now you, know who R.C. is."

"I suppose I should feel flattered that you told me. But don't expect me to back off and give you a free hand going after the gun smugglers and not worry about you. Whether you're snooping around as yourself or as R.C., it's still damn dangerous." He glanced out at the parade ground. "We won't talk about R.C. here, if you don't want your parents to know."

"No one will hear us. Papa's gone to Tucson to meet with General Crook, and Mamere's upstairs reading."

Brit went still with the teacup halfway to his lips. He carefully put it down and pinched the bridge of his nose wearily. General Crook was in New Mexico at the moment, not Tucson. So where had her father gone, and why did he want people to think he was in Tucson? There was only one answer that he could see.

Mexico. And why would he go to Mexico? There was only one reason: to smuggle guns.

It was the first real break he'd had—so why didn't he feel wonderful about it? Because he knew it would affect Callista.

And it would affect the exhilarating, wondrous attachment that was growing between them. Yet he had to bring her father in and stop the smuggling. That was the only way to stop the killing—on both sides.

"I need to get cleaned up." He stood up, needing to get away before she sensed something was wrong.

"I'll see you and George tomorrow. And stop writing lies about me."

The next day was the last day of school, and Josephina had baked cupcakes for her to take along. Callista came a few minutes early and set a cupcake on each desk, then made some notes at her desk for the teacher who would come in the fall. She heard George ride up and take his horse in back.

She was just finishing her notes when she heard an odd scuffling noise coming from behind the school. Going out the back door, she paused at the top of the steps, looking down at the three boys rolling around in the grass with George. What were they—?

"No!" she shouted when she realized they were beating the Apache child. Rushing down the stairs, she waded into the mass of arms and legs. Grabbing one boy by the back of his shirt, she pulled him off George and dropped him.

Callista waded back in, grabbing the stocky one, whom she'd recognized as Harold Kreutz. She grasped a handful of his shirt and yanked as hard as she could, but he swung around with a fist. She danced back, out of range. Off-balance from his swing, Harold staggered, and she grabbed the back of his collar and shook him.

"Stop, Harold, or I will tell your mother!"

He looked at her for a second and she could see the wheels going around in his head. "So what?"

But she was ready for him. She stepped forward until she was nose to nose with him. She was taller and looked down at him. "Go home, Harold," she said in a deathly quiet voice. "Tell your mother you're suspended for fighting."

He opened and closed his mouth twice, like a fish

gulping for air. Then he backed a step, and she knew she'd won. He picked his hat up and put it on.

"I'll tell her all right, and she'll back me up. My pop will, too. You'll see—you'll be sorry." He backed another few steps, then whirled and stomped away.

She looked for the third boy who'd been pummeling George, but he'd disappeared. Well, she'd figure out who he was when she took the roll.

Callista ran past the remaining boy and knelt in the grass beside the pitifully small, still body that lay belly down.

"George?" She rolled him over carefully. One eye was swollen, and he had a cut over the other. A trickle of blood seeped out of the corner of his mouth. "George, come on, let me see how bad it is."

She slipped her arm around his back and helped him sit up, then fished out her handkerchief and dabbed at the blood on his face.

He pushed her away and scrambled to his feet, yelling something. Although she didn't understand his language, she knew he was cursing all of them. He ran to his pony, swung up, and galloped away.

Callista swung around. "You may go home also, James, and tell your mother that you have been suspended."

"Aw, Miss Warwick. Ma will be madder than a wet hen!"

"You should have thought of that before you hit George."

Going inside, she slumped down at her desk. Resting her elbows on the desk, she cradled her head in her hands. What a way to end the school year.

She was glad she was going out to Daisy and

Jack's ranch soon. She needed a change from Fort
Bowie.

She needed Brit, is what she needed.

As if she'd conjured him up by magic, she heard
the hoofbeats of a horse, followed by jingle of Brit's
spurs as he dismounted and came up the steps into
the schoolroom.

"Callista? Are you all right?" His gravelly voice
was sharp with concern when he saw her slumped at
her desk.

She nodded, torn between anger at the bullies and
happiness at seeing Brit, and ran down the aisle into
his waiting arms.

Chapter 14

⎯⎯◯⌒◯⎯⎯

Callista and Russ Caruso sat their horses on a
ridge above a barren, sandy white valley.

"Is that it, Russ?" Callista asked, keeping her voice
even to hide her dismay and shock. She'd expected
Jack's ranch to be grassy green pastures full of fat
cattle.

She almost didn't see the house. Sand-colored, it
melted into the landscape near a rock-strewn stream-
bed marked by scrawny, low bushes. Near it were a
couple of corrals, and a second small building she
assumed was a bunkhouse. Mesquite trees made pitifully small circles of green beside the house and corrals. A fenced vegetable garden had a scarecrow in
each corner. But there were no cattle or horses in
sight.

"It doesn't look too good now, but when the summer rains come, it greens up right nice."

"Can you raise cattle on this kind of land?" Callista
asked, thinking of the fields in the Midwest where
cattle grazed knee deep in green grass.

"It's hard, but yes, you can." He shifted his weight
in the saddle, making it creak.

"But can you raise a family and make a living on it?"

Russ shot her a questioning look. "Do you have a reason for asking?"

Callista shook her head as she gazed at Jack's ranch. "Not really. Except that Daisy grew up on a farm in Ohio. I wonder what she thinks of land like this."

"Why don't we ride down and ask her?"

Callista flashed him a grin. "That would be a good idea, wouldn't it?"

Brit's ranch was next to Jack's. Was his land as barren? A wave of sadness washed over her as she pictured him struggling to build a ranch and make a life on land this poor.

As they rode toward the house, Callista noticed clumps of green prickly pear cactus mixed with dried, brown bunch grass. Was that the grass Russ had mentioned? How could anything live on that? When they crossed the stream, Callista found there was a trickle of water, maybe a foot wide, in the deepest part of the bed.

"Look at that: year-round running water." Russ pointed.

"Are you saying that's good?"

"Damn tootin'. You've got to have a supply of water year-round for the cattle."

As they neared the house, Callista realized it was made of adobe, but hadn't been whitewashed. It was an awful, dingy mud color that she would have painted the first day she was there.

They rode up to the porch, and Callista dismounted without waiting for Russ to help her. Her boots sounded unnaturally loud as she walked across the porch and knocked on the door. "Daisy? Are you here?"

She heard footsteps scurrying across the wooden floor and a shadow flitted past the lace curtains at the window, then silence.

"Daisy?" She knocked again.

This time she heard footsteps coming toward the door. When Daisy opened it Callista's first impression was that she'd lost weight, and her hair had a scraggly unkept look—which was unusual for Daisy.

"Callista, how wonderful of you to come." She flung her arms around Callista and hugged her tightly.

Almost too tightly, Callista thought. And her breath reeked of cologne.

"Russ, you came, too?" Still hugging her, Daisy called over Callista's shoulder, "Get down and come in. Come in."

"Let me look at you." Callista caught Daisy's hands as she stepped back and studied her. "Daisy, I must say you look like ranch life agrees with you," she said gaily.

"Aw, go on with you," Daisy said, but her voice wasn't as strong as it should have been. And there were grease spots on the bodice of her pink-striped dress, Callista noticed, surprised because Daisy was a fanatic about cleanliness.

Russ walked past her and held out his arms. "You do look wonderful, Daisy. Now do I get a hug, too?"

Daisy gave him a great big hug and he whirled her around until her feet left the floor and she squealed with delight. When he set her down, Daisy patted her hair in the old way that Callista remembered, but now her carrot red hair was dull, rather than shiny with life.

"Sit down. I'll make us some coffee."

Callista and Russ sat at the kitchen table. A narrow divan in the corner was the only sitting place other than the chairs around the kitchen table. At least the walls were whitewashed, so it was brighter than she expected from the small windows.

"I see you have another room."

"Our bedroom. You'll be sleeping on the divan. Oh, I'm *so* glad you came." Daisy dipped water out of a bucket into a coffeepot and put it on the cast-iron stove that took up a good portion of one wall. "Look at this stove, would you? Jack already had it when I came. He wanted to surprise me."

"It's beautiful." Callista patted the table. "Now come sit down and tell us what you've been doing."

"Oh, it's been so busy." The chair scraped across the floor as she pulled it out. "I've put in a vegetable garden, and we should be getting corn in a couple of weeks. We already have tomatoes, green beans, and strawberries."

"And I brought you some flower cuttings. They're in my saddlebags."

"I think that's my cue to go get your saddlebags and carpetbag," Russ said, rising and going out to the horses.

The women watched him through the open door as he picked up the bags and returned, kicking the door closed behind him.

"Did you two ride out here alone all the way from the fort? I kept watching for you after school was out, Callista, but you didn't come and didn't come. I had about given up hope that you were coming."

"I had to wait for a patrol coming this way. We split off from it this morning, and Russ accompanied me the rest of the way." She leaned forward and patted Daisy's hand. "If I could have gotten here any sooner I would have. I'm looking forward to a nice, long visit."

"Oh, so am I, so am I." Daisy started to smile, but her smile wavered and melted into a quivering upper lip. She jumped up and bustled over to the stove. Taking a pot holder from the upper shelf on the stove, she shook the pot. "Come on, coffee."

Callista looked at Russ. Had he seen that Daisy was close to tears? His soft brown gaze met hers and he shrugged. Callista unbuckled her saddlebag and took out the plants she'd wrapped in moist cotton. "Have you got a pan we can put these in? There's an assortment of marigolds, zinnias, and all sorts of summer flowers."

"Thank you. That's just what I need to brighten up the yard." She pulled a small pan off the shelf and put the cuttings in it. "I'll get these started tomorrow morning."

"Where's that handsome husband of yours?" Callista asked, trying to sound happy and relaxed.

"He and the men are up in the higher canyons with the cattle. They can't bring the cattle down here until the rains come and the range greens up."

"I thought for sure we'd have rain last night, with all the lightning and thunder," Russ said. "Especially because we were camping out in the open. But we stayed dry."

"We had a few sprinkles," Daisy replied, getting three cups down from the shelf. "But it wasn't worth spit."

"Here, let me help you." Callista rose and took two of the cups and brought them back to the table. Daisy followed with her cup and a silver sugar bowl that she plunked down on the table, along with three spoons.

"Help yourselves."

"Daisy, sit down. We came to talk, not drink coffee. When will Jack be back?"

"Normally he'd be home by now." Daisy didn't look up as she stirred her coffee.

"Do the men come back with him?"

"Sometimes."

Callista studied Daisy, who was usually so talkative. "Can I help you start supper?"

Daisy gave her a puzzled look. "Start supper?"

"Do you need to cook up some rice or beans?"

"I guess we could cook some rice," she said in a vague tone. "Let me see if we have any." She moved to a row of large metal canisters and opened one. "Yes, there's some."

Callista and Russ looked at each other. What was wrong with her?

"I think I'll go take care of the horses," Russ said.

Callista watched him lead their horses away, then turned to Daisy. "All right, what's wrong?"

"Wrong?" Daisy patted an errant strand of hair back into her loose upswept style. "What could be wrong?"

"Daisy, your breath smells of cologne. You ran into the bedroom and swished some in your mouth when I knocked. Now, the only reason for you to do that is that you had been drinking whiskey."

"Me?" She tapped her chest for emphasis. "Me?"

"Yes, you. And since you're not the kind of person who drinks whiskey, I know something is wrong."

Daisy focused on her coffee, stirring and stirring. Finally Callista put her hand over Daisy's, stopping her. "Sometimes it really helps to talk. Has Jack . . ."

Oh, lord she hoped he hadn't—She took a deep breath and plunged in. "Has he struck you?"

"Jack?" Daisy gave her a surprised look. "Oh no. Jack's wonderful. It's just that—" She drew her finger through a coffee puddle on the table, spreading the puddle in circles.

"What?"

She looked at Callista, started to say something, looked away, then tried again. "I—I—" She pressed her fist against her lips, trying to hold back a sob, then her whole face crumpled. She buried her face in her arms, sobbing so deeply her sobs were almost soundless. "Oh God, it's so *lonely* out here. Jack's gone from sunrise to sunset every day. There's no one to talk to. Ever."

"Oh, Daisy, I'm so sorry." Callista rubbed her back gently, trying to comfort her.

Finally, Daisy twisted away from her and bent down to wipe her eyes with the corner of her apron. She stared out the window rather than look at Callista and took deep, hiccuping breaths.

"And the only thing that kept me going was knowing you were coming. But you didn't come and didn't come."

"Well, I'm here now, and we'll talk until we have sore throats." Through the open door she saw Russ approaching and waved him off.

"But you can't stay," Daisy wailed. "And then I'll be alone with just the godawful wind."

"Hey, I'm staying now. And maybe you can come to the fort and stay with me. I should warn you, though. My father gets up when the bugler sounds reveille, and he stumbles around the house bumping into things in the dark." She deepened her voice in imitation of her father. "Verlene, who left that damn door open?" Daisy smiled through her tears. "Verlene, where is my underwear? Verlene, did I waken you? Go back to sleep."

Daisy was giggling by the time she finished. "Oh, Callista," she said, grasping her hands, "you don't know how much I needed to hear a woman's voice."

Two mornings later, Callista and Daisy were sitting on the porch having a cup of coffee and talking after Jack and the men left. It had rained during the night and the desert smelled fresh and clean. The pungent odor of creosote drifted by. Two adult quail and eight balls of fluff on matchstick legs pecked at the damp earth.

Callista noticed the lone rider first, when he was still far down the valley. "Rider." Heat waves rose from the desert floor, making his image waver like a mirage. Shading her eyes with her hand, she studied him, as did Daisy.

"He's coming this way," Daisy said. She went inside and returned with a rifle. "You never know," she explained as she sat in her rocker, resting the rifle across her knees.

"I have this, too." Callista pulled her derringer out of her skirt pocket. "But you don't have to worry, it's Brit."

Daisy frowned at her. "How can you tell? I can barely see him and you've already identified him?"

"He's riding a red horse."

"Lots of people ride red horses."

Callista squinted into the distance. Was it the breadth of his shoulders? The way he sat a horse? Or was it because she so desperately wanted it to be him? "I just know it's him." Daisy eyed her for so long that Callista glanced at her. "What's the matter?"

"You're in lust with him, aren't you? Like I was with Jack, before I fell in love with him."

"Me? For him? No! Don't be silly! We're too different. That's impossible. I—" She took a sip of coffee. "Yes."

Daisy started to laugh. "You should have heard yourself."

"That obvious, huh?"

"Uh-huh. What about him? Is he interested?"

Callista thought back to their kisses, their unforgettable kisses, to the fire in his touch when he touched her, the tenuous gossamer-like connections between them. To so many things she couldn't name.

"Never mind, I can see from your smile that he is."

"Am I really that transparent?" Callista asked, dismayed. She'd always prided herself on her quiet, dignified comportment, on her Mona Lisa smile that revealed nothing. "I do enjoy talking to him. And I respect him for his feelings about the Apaches and his willingness to stand up for his convictions and—"

"In other words, you like him because he's him." Daisy rolled her eyes. "Listen to my grammar! But there's something different about you when you're talking about him. You kind of glow, like—My God, you're in love with him!"

Callista stared at Daisy, dismayed that she'd guessed her secret. It couldn't show! "You're letting your imagination run wild. You're seeing mirages in the desert."

"Oh, Callista, take care. Being in love is so much more serious than being in lust."

Callista gave up pretending and shrugged. "Sometimes life doesn't go as smoothly as we'd like."

"Boy, you can say that again."

She rocked alongside Daisy and listened to the rhythmic creak of the rockers. And waited for her love to come to her.

He rode up to the porch and dismounted, casually tossing the reins around the hitching rail. "Are you two my welcoming committee?" he asked as he came up the two steps to the porch. Even though he included Daisy, he had eyes only for Callista.

"Hi," she said softly, putting a world of meaning into that single word.

"Hi," he replied, just as softly. He pushed up the brim of his hat with his thumb, revealing a tan line.

"We saw you coming for the last hour," she said in the same tone, feeling dreamlike.

"Did you?" The deep rumble of his voice caressed her.

Daisy clapped her hands sharply. Startled, they both looked at her. She smiled like a cat full of cream. "Sorry, but I figured it was the only way to get your attention. Brit, would you like some coffee? Maybe some leftover griddle cakes from breakfast?"

"Sure." He ushered Callista ahead of him as they followed Daisy inside. His warm fingers trailed down her back in a caress that sent a cascade of ripples through her.

She glanced at him over her shoulder. He was so close and the light in his eyes so intense, she wanted to turn into his arms right there.

Daisy put a plate full of flapjacks down at the head of the table. "So, Brit, what brings you over this way? As if I didn't know."

"I passed Russ's patrol and he said Callista was over visiting you, so I thought I'd see you both."

Daisy slid onto the bench opposite Callista. "And Daisy, you look a lot better than you did last week."

"Thanks to Callista. I've really enjoyed having her." She snapped her fingers. "Say, have you seen Brit's ranch, Callista? Why don't you take her over, Brit?"

"Do you want to see it?" he asked as he forked up a large bite of pancakes. His knee came to rest against hers under the table.

"Only if you want to. I mean, I don't want Daisy talking you into doing something you don't want to do." Daisy the matchmaker was as transparent as glass.

"I intended to ask you over, but—" He gave Daisy a mock glare. "Daisy beat me to it."

"Oops. Sorry." Daisy clamped her hand over her mouth.

"Now, are you sure, Cally? I wouldn't want you coming if you didn't want to."

Callista had to look at him twice to see the teasing glint in his eye. Two could play that game, she thought. "I don't have anything better to do this afternoon," she said offhandedly, as if going with him sounded boring. "Might as well."

"I might put you to work, you know. I have to clean some snags out of the creeks."

"What do you want me to do?"

Slowly his sensual lips tipped up at the corners. "I wouldn't want to shock Daisy." The promise in his dark voice wrapped around her, warm as a June evening.

"Hold that thought, Brit. I'll change while you saddle my horse."

"Make it fast." He forked up the last bite of pancakes, then pushed the plate away. "How about you,

Daisy?" He drank the last of his cooled coffee in large gulps. "Want to come? It'll be cooler at my place."

"Thanks, Brit, but not this time. I need to bake six loaves of bread. Might as well get it all done."

"The bread can wait. Do come, Daisy," Callista added her voice to Brit's. "It'll do you good to get away."

"I'm coming to visit you soon, remember? That's enough. I really do need to bake bread. Believe me, it's not my favorite chore, and if I could put it off, I would."

"All right, then I'll change." She retreated to the bedroom to put on her riding habit. By the time she came out, Brit was carrying in a load of wood for Daisy.

He stacked it beside the stove. "I left more wood on the porch, Daisy. It'll stay dry if we get a storm today." He dusted off his hands.

"You think we'll finally get a real gully washer?" Daisy didn't look up as she sifted flour into a metal bowl.

"Could be. I already see clouds building to the south. I'll have Callista back by dark."

"All right. Have a good time, Callista."

"Ready?" Brit plunked her hat on her head, then held out his hand to her.

"Ready." She placed her hand in his, wishing it could be for a lifetime. She pictured him holding his daughter's hand, a bright-eyed toddler with black-brown hair.

Outside, his gaze flowed over her like honey, slowly and thoroughly. "You know, I like that riding habit, but I think you're going to be too hot in the jacket."

"Maybe you just like what's in it." Callista walked out to the mare he'd saddled for her and gathered up the reins.

"That too." He gave her a leg up, lifting her onto the horse as if she were weightless.

"Thanks." She settled onto the sidesaddle, wiggling around a bit to get comfortable.

He led the way up the valley beside the stream that flowed past Daisy's home for a couple of hours. Then they left the valley and turned into the side canyon the stream flowed out of. The stream flowed along one side and the floor was strewn with rocks and house-sized boulders.

It reminded Callista of the canyon where the Apaches had ambushed them, except that now the trees that grew along the stream had leafed out, giving them some shade from the hot sun. The horses drank their fill, then carefully picked their way over the rocks and around the boulders. An hour later, Brit turned away from the stream and led her to a steep deer trail that zigzagged up the canyon wall.

By the time they topped out, the horses were hot and winded. They were on a grassy plateau that stretched to the horizon. Junipers and oaks dotted the open plain.

"We'll rest the horses here," Brit said, dismounting in the midst of a cluster of alligator junipers.

"Good. After almost four hours in the saddle I need to walk around."

He came around and settled his big hands at her waist and lifted her off, then slowly let her slide down.

She could feel every muscle in his hard body, and he smelled of sun-warmed leather and his own male scent—a very sensual combination.

She slid her arms around his neck and pulled his head down and kissed him, quickly, tantalizingly, then she danced away from him. He growled far back in his throat and reached for her.

"Don't you need to take care of the horses?"

"Not this instant." But he tapped her nose gently. "I'll be back as soon as I've seen to the horses. Don't go away." He loosed their saddle girths and tethered them in the shade of a juniper.

"Is this where your ranch is?" It looked like it had more grass for cattle to eat, which she was glad to see.

"Part of it's up here, part in a canyon where the house is sheltered from the winds." He uncorked his canteen and offered it to her. "Have a drink."

"Thanks." She took a few swallows of the flat-tasting water and handed it back to him.

He took a few swallows and recorked it. "Callista, I don't think you should ride sidesaddle in this kind of rough country. It's too easy to get thrown or pinned under your horse if he goes down.

"You said a Prussian cavalry officer taught you to ride, so you must know how to ride astride. Do that here. Don't worry about how it looks." He slid his hand along her waist and pulled her against him. "Do it for me."

"You're right, I can ride astride, and I've worried about riding sidesaddle on some of these trails. I guess I just needed a kick in the pants to change."

"Good." He brushed a kiss over her temple.

"I'm anxious to see your home," she said quickly, before she turned in his arms and kissed him, long and slow.

How did he live? She pictured him roughing it,

practically camping out even when he had a roof over his head.

"It's like Jack's place. Nothing to bring a bride home to." Why the hell had he said that? He'd never thought of what it would look like to a woman before. Why did he now?

Hell, man, don't lie to yourself. You know damn well why you thought of it now.

"Not even any of the ladies who wrote to you?" Callista teased.

"None of them ever held a candle to you." He trailed his fingers down the side of her face. "None of them."

Thunder rumbled in the distance, and he looked over his shoulder. "Damn, I don't like the look of those clouds over the mountains."

She looked too. They were iron blue and were boiling higher and higher into the sky above the mountains.

"Come on," Brit called, hurrying to the horses and tightening their girths.

He helped her mount, then set a fast pace as they crossed part of the plateau, then dropped down into a wide green canyon that was the prettiest she'd seen so far.

"Now this is more like it," she muttered.

They came to a pasture with thick grass that was belly high on the two horses in it.

"I just fenced this pasture in," Brit explained as they cantered by. "It's where I want to keep the mares who are in foal to Red. But with my being gone so much on army business, I turned the mares into Jack's herd. They'll be safer there, where he can keep an eye on them."

They continued along the road through oak trees.

"Slow down," Brit called. "We cross the stream on a wooden bridge, and it can startle your horse."

They walked the horses across the wooden planks, and Callista's mare shied at the hollow echo of her hooves. Finally, they rode out of the scattered oaks into a large clearing with a small adobe building, two empty corrals, and a half-built barn.

"This is home," Brit said, as they continued past the buildings.

"Aren't we stopping?"

"No time. I need to get up to the head of the canyon and make sure the creek is clear." He snapped his fingers. "What am I saying? You could stay here. You don't have to come with me."

"No, I'll come with you." She wanted to be with him. That was when her heart was full of joy and sunlight.

"I'm glad." He sent Red into a canter that covered ground fast.

The deep-throated rumble of thunder made her look back. Thunderclouds boiled high into the sky, but she couldn't see how close they were through the trees.

The road narrowed to a deer path past the buildings, and they climbed a gentle slope. Patches of sunlight broke up the forest into pools of shadow and light, while bushes and undergrowth kept it from looking like a park. Boulders, from chair-sized to house-sized, littered the forest, as though a giant had been bowling among the trees.

Brit kept looking back to make sure she was still with him, which gave her a warm feeling.

Mexican jays scolded and called and followed them as though warning the other creatures in the forest where they were.

The gentle slope leveled off, and Brit turned off the path and pushed through the underbrush toward the stream. Halting beside a placid pool, he dismounted.

She joined him beside it. "What are you looking for? I don't understand what you want to do."

"I'm looking for snags—dead trees or stumps that have fallen into the stream and gotten stuck. They can make small dams where the water builds up behind them until it floods over the top or cuts a new path for the creek. And I don't want either happening on this slope." He pointed at some tree limbs sticking up out of the water like gnarled fingers. "That could be a snag or it could be just a couple of broken branches."

He waded out to them and fished around in the murky water, then came back to her. "No problem. I'm going to follow the stream. You take the horses and keep me in sight from the path."

The stream was mercifully clear of debris, although it chattered and foamed over rocks and boulders.

"Bring Red up," Brit called as he spied a tree stump sitting almost upside down in the water, its twisted brown roots sticking out like snakes frozen in place.

Taking his lariat, he waded out to the stump, and leaned against it, rocking it a bit, then tied the rope around several of the thickest roots. He was wading back to her, when he suddenly went down on one knee. He stood almost immediately, then tested his footing with each step as he returned to her, completely soaked.

"What happened?" His wet jeans clung to him like a second skin, outlining every muscle and tendon and the bulge between his legs. She knew a polite person would look away. She didn't.

"The rocks in the stream can be slippery as hell. I didn't watch where I was stepping." He mounted Red, looped the lariat around his saddle horn, drew it taut, then backed the horse up slowly. He had to send the horse forward and back several times to rock the stump loose, then he pulled it out of the stream and up to the top of the bank so it couldn't fall back in.

Callista was sweating along with Brit when he dismounted and loosened his rope from the roots. "Whoo! That's hard work," she said.

"That was an easy one. Sometimes they get a root really dug into the mud and then it's hell getting them out." He coiled his lariat and gathered Red's reins, glancing skyward as menacing purple-black clouds scudded across the sky. Thunder rumbled over them. "You should have stayed at the house, Callista. This is going to be a bad gully washer."

"I'm better off here. I would have been worried about you."

"I can take care of myself; I've been doing it for years." He glanced over his shoulder at her. "Are you afraid of thunder and lightning?"

"No, but this storm seems more threatening than the ones I'm used to." If she were alone she'd have been frightened, but she knew she was safe with him. He would know what to do no matter what happened.

It began to rain—big, fat drops that felt wonderfully cooling in the heat of a June afternoon. "This is wonderful," she said, turning her face to the sky to enjoy the refreshing moisture. "Why are you complaining about a rain like this?"

"It won't stay like this; this is only the edge of the storm. Wait 'til it gets here."

Callista cringed as lightning flashed, followed almost immediately by the harsh crack of thunder.

"What's that?" She whirled when she heard the rushing roar of a train. Then the icy rain hit her, coming down not in drops, but in sheets. Lightning flashed and thunder roared.

"Brit!" she gasped, soaked in seconds.

He left the snag he'd just roped and pulled her into his arms, running his hands up and down her back, trying to warm her through her wet clothes.

She laughed and wrapped her arms around his neck. "I'm all right; I was just surprised. Lord, I must look like a drowned rat."

"We both do." He brushed a quick kiss over her temple. "Much as I'd prefer to stay here with you, this snag is calling my name. And I have to move fast. The stream is going to be flowing fast and deep soon."

She stepped back, which left him feeling damned cold all of a sudden. "What can I do to help?"

"Just stay out of the way." He mounted Red and urged the horse backward. The snag was all jagged wood at one end, as though it had been struck by lightning and part blown away. The roots were at the sunken end, and he was worried that they were embedded deep in the mud.

Red hunkered down on his hind legs and pulled, but it didn't budge. Brit slid down the bank and waded back in, leaning against it with his shoulder to rock it and break it loose from the mud.

"Callista, walk Red forward, then back as I rock this snag."

He felt it move. Just a bit, but it moved. "Good. Do it again."

She did and he put his shoulder to it and felt it move more. But he wasn't rocking it enough to break it free of the mud. "We're almost there. Just a little more rocking." He leaned against the trunk once again.

Out of the corner of his eye he saw movement. He snapped around and saw that Callista had slid down the bank and was beside him, pushing at the log with both hands.

"Get out of the water—this is no place for you." It was too dangerous. He didn't want her risking her safety to help him. She was too precious to him.

"Shut up and shove," she grunted, leaning into the log.

"Get out," he roared.

"Shove, dammit!"

She might be right. Just one more shove would do it. Besides, it would be the quickest way to get her out of the water.

"All right, but watch your footing. On the count of three: one." He turned away from her and he shoved his shoulder up against the log. "Two. Three!"

He felt the log move at the same time he heard her shriek.

Chapter 15

S he fell backward, arms windmilling wildly as
she tried to regain her balance.

Brit lunged toward her, trying to catch her hand as
she sat down in a splash of icy cold water.

"Oh, applesauce!" she sputtered. "How clumsy."

"Are you all right?" He splashed over to her.

"Just humiliated; my foot slipped right out from
under me. And this water is like ice." She held out
her hand. "Help me up, please."

"Gladly." He grasped her hand and pulled. But she
just came up a couple of inches, then sank back
down. She looked at her leg with a strange frown.

"I think my foot's caught."

"Don't worry. I've caught my foot lots of times,"
he said, surprising himself with the smooth way the
lie rolled off his lips. "I'll have you out in no time."

The rain was still coming down in sheets, and they
couldn't be any wetter than they already were. But
the rushing creek water felt damn cold as he knelt in
it and felt down her leg to her foot. Damn! It was
caught under a root—a very thick root. He tried
scooping mud away from under her foot, but as fast
as he scooped, the mud settled back around her.

"Brit, I think the stream is rising."

"Nah. It's your—" He snapped a quick look. She was sitting up, leaning back on her hands. The water had been at her waist before. Now it was almost an inch higher. He looked at her then, silver gaze to amethyst. "Don't worry, I'll get you out. I promise."

"I know you will."

She said it so simply that he felt as if she'd punched him in the heart. Her life depended on him, and she didn't have the least doubt in him.

Brit looked around for something he could use as a lever. A thick tree limb lay on the bank and he grabbed it.

"When I lever the log up, pull your foot free. All right?"

"I'm ready."

She was so calm. More calm than he was; his heart was racing. He jammed the branch into the mud underneath the log. He pressed down on it with both hands, using all the muscle power in his arms and shoulders and legs. The branch bent slightly with an awful screech.

"Get ready," he yelled. He pushed down as hard as he could. The branch bent more . . . more . . . and splintered into useless pieces! He fell into the water on his hands and knees.

"Hell!" He came up sputtering and swearing. "Damn! I have to go back to the ranch to get something to lever the log off you, sweetheart," he said, floundering to his feet. "I'll be right back." The water was higher, almost up to her breasts.

"I k-know you will." But her voice quavered.

He wanted to hug her, to tell her he wouldn't let anything happen to her. But he already had let something happen to her. And now she was in mortal danger.

He scrambled up the bank, swung up on Red, and sent him galloping down the narrow path. *Please, God, keep her safe until I get back.* He repeated the words over and over.

The rain was still coming down as if the heavens had opened up. How much time did he have?

He lashed Red with the reins, surprised by how slowly the horse was moving. "Damn it, Red, get your butt moving." Tree branches lashed his face, but he didn't even notice.

Red burst into the clearing and Brit turned him toward the half-built barn. *Please let the lever be where I think it is,* he prayed as he leaped off Red and ran into the barn, pawing through the tools stacked in the corner. A long-handled shovel. A pickax. A large saw and a keyhole saw. The lever.

He gathered them all up, mounted one-handed, then sent Red racing back along the path. "Come on, boy!" he urged Red, for the first time in his life afraid his horse couldn't run fast enough. "Please, God," he whispered. "Please, I need her."

The water was almost up to her throat when he dropped the tools on the bank. "I'm back, Cally. I'm here, sweetheart." He wanted to go to her and hold her. But he couldn't.

"Don't waste time talking," she gasped. Shaking violently from the icy water and icy fear, she watched him grab the narrow keyhole saw as another thunderclap rolled over them.

"Hang on, Cally." He jumped into the water, and felt around in the mud and tangled roots. The higher water level confused things. He had to reach deeper into the water, and though he had his hand on her foot, he had to cut through two other roots before he could get down to the right one.

"Ready?" He glanced at her and his heart fell into his boots. The water was up to her chin.

"Ready." Her voice was noticeably weaker.

"Hang on!" He sawed furiously at what he thought was the right root and felt it break away. But when he tried to pull her foot free, the root was still pinning her.

"Brit." Her voice was a bare shred of sound.

He glanced at her. The water was halfway up her chin. She choked as some splashed in her mouth.

"I will not let you die! Do you hear me?" he vowed through clenched teeth. "I won't let you die!"

"I . . . lo . . ."

"Hang on. I've got the right root this time, I know it." He sawed frantically and finally felt the root give. Dropping the saw, he groped in the mud with both hands, grabbed her foot and leg and pulled it back, away from the tangling roots. She was free!

He swung around and saw her blue lips and white face. Her eyes were closed.

"No!" He lunged on his knees to scoop her up out of the water. Her body was limp. One arm hung down, the fingers trailing in the water.

"No!" he whispered as he struggled to his feet and splashed through the water to the bank.

When he laid her down her arms and legs seemed to go in all directions in a limp, broken kind of way. Her head lolled to the side.

"Oh God, Cally, don't die. Please, don't die." Tears filled his eyes and made them burn, and he brushed at them absently. "I need you so much."

How much water had she swallowed? He placed his hands on her abdomen and pushed up, and a tiny stream of water trickled from her mouth. He did it again, afraid to do it, afraid not to. More water trickled from her mouth.

She coughed, and he felt his heart swell with joy.

He pressed upward on her abdomen once more. This time she coughed and spit up more water. He tried it again, and she moaned. Softly, but it was definitely a moan.

She was breathing!

"Thank you, God," he whispered. He held her in his arms, rocking back and forth on his knees on the rocky bank, not sure who was shaking harder, Callista or him.

But she wasn't out of the woods yet. He still had to get her inside and dry.

She weakly raised her hand to touch his cheek. Looking down, he saw that her eyes were open a slit, just enough to show the life in them.

"Brit." She sighed, and her eyes closed again.

He carried her to Red. "Callista?"

"I'm all right, Brit, just cold." Her voice was weak and thready, and she stopped to draw a breath between each word, but she sounded better.

"Can you sit on the horse for the few seconds it'll take me to mount, or don't you have the strength?"

She nodded.

She slumped like a rag doll when he lifted her astride the horse, and he took his hands away slowly, ready to catch her if she started to fall to the side. But she didn't.

He grabbed the horn with his left hand and swung up behind the saddle, then turned her into his lap as he slid forward onto the seat itself. He nestled her against his chest and wrapped his arms around her, trying to warm her with his heat through their soaked clothes.

"Come on, Red," he called, nudging the stallion with his spurs—which he never did. Red galloped down the path, as if he knew what a precious burden he carried. Brit rubbed his chin against her icy forehead.

The rain was still coming down. It was still lightning and thundering, and he realized that during the entire time he'd been trying to rescue Callista, he hadn't been aware of either.

He rode Red straight up to the adobe house. Lifting his leg over the saddle horn, he slid down with Callista in his arms and strode onto the porch.

She tugged at his shirt to get his attention. "I can walk."

He ignored her as he fumbled with the latch, kicked the door open, and carried her across the general room to his bedroom. There he gently sat her on the bed.

"You've got to get out of these clothes and boots." He started to unbutton her white shirt. It was plastered to her, and even without her shivers, he could see how cold she was from the peaks of her nipples, straining against the material.

She pushed his hands away. "I can do it."

"All right, I'll get your boots off while you work on that."

He knelt and got her black riding boots off; then he rolled down her soaked stockings. He toweled her legs and feet dry. Her small icy foot curled in his hand.

Finally, he stood up. She was still fumbling with the buttons on her shirt, and he realized her fingers were too stiff and numb.

"Cally, let me get that skirt off you." He tried to speak softly because tension and fear were making his voice harsh.

"I can do it." She yawned.

"The hell you can! It's way too heavy with water. Stand up so I can get it off you."

He pulled her to her feet. "Lean against me." He worked with his arms around her in case she became dizzy, ripping the two buttons at the waist off and letting the waterlogged fabric sink into a pool at her feet. He lifted her out of the trap of fabric and kicked it away, then set her back on her feet beside the bed.

"All right, now let me get that shirt off you." He had to get her dry and into something warm.

"I can do it." Her eyes closed, and she yawned again as she fumbled with the buttons.

He brushed her hands away. "Your fingers are too cold and numb, and we need to get you warm." He spoke slowly, calmly, although he wasn't a bit calm inside. "I have a shirt all ready for you."

He unbuttoned her shirt and pulled it off. Through her lacy camisole top, he could see the bluish tinge to her nipples.

She tried to cover herself with her hands, but she was clumsy and still shivering wildly.

"Just hold on, Callista. I have to get the rest of these wet clothes off you." He reached for her drawers' drawstring at her waist.

"Wait. Wait." Her hands fluttered against his. "Please close your eyes."

He didn't have the heart to tell her the wet cotton was so fine it was almost transparent. He just shut his eyes and worked by feel—which probably got him into a lot more trouble than if his eyes had been open. He untied the drawstring for her drawers and let them slide down to the floor.

Then he pulled the camisole off over her head and slipped his shirt over her shoulders. He opened his eyes then. It was huge on her, hanging down almost to her knees, but it was dry and warm.

"I can button this."

"But I can do it faster." He was all too aware of the way his hands brushed against her high breasts as he buttoned the first few buttons. Then it was smooth sailing until the last couple, way below her waist, and he buttoned them, too.

He whipped a blanket off the bed and swathed her in it, then carried her out to the other room and put her down on a chair near the fireplace. "You'll be warmer here as soon as I get the fire going."

It was twilight and with the storm, the gray light was fading fast. He lit the oil lamp, then went out to the porch and brought in an armful of wood. Stacking some in the corner fireplace with kindling, he took a match from the mantel and lit it.

He kept glancing at her, checking on her, but she didn't move, just slumped in the chair, her eyes closed.

He opened a cupboard and brought out a bottle of brandy and splashed some into a glass. "Here—drink this. It'll make you feel better." He shoved it into her hand.

"Or I'll feel nothing at all," she said, looking at the amount.

"Stay here by the fire, Cally. I'm going to get the horses and take care of them."

"But your clothes are wet," she said drowsily. "You need to get into some dry ones."

"I'll change as soon as I get back."

Once again, Brit had saved her life. Callista took a tiny sip of the brandy and stared into the flames. Today his words had implied much more between them—as if she were special to him. Or more than special.

From the very first day, attraction had sparked between them like fire, flaming higher and higher.

For her that attraction had bloomed into love. She'd known it ever since Daisy's wedding.

Had it deepened for Brit, also?

During those moments of hopelessness, when she thought she was going to die, he'd looked deep into her eyes and said he wouldn't let her die. He had said it with such fierce conviction that she'd believed him.

It was a promise. A pledge. And it came from his heart.

Callista took another sip of brandy. She'd never forget the way he'd held her, there on the bank. His arms had been so full of protection and . . . she'd felt a special warmth that came from inside him and embraced her, and made her feel more safe than she'd ever felt in her life. Was it his love that embraced her and warmed her?

Had she told him she loved him? She remembered thinking that if she was going to die, she wanted him to know. But had she said the words?

She took a swallow of brandy and contemplated the flames. They were warming the room quite nicely, she thought as she stretched out her legs toward the fire.

She'd discovered something else while feeling the water creep higher and higher. She didn't want to go to her grave wondering what might have been.

Fowler had almost taken her innocence from her once. He'd come as close to raping her as it was possible. Only another partygoer walking into the room had saved her that night. When Fowler had turned to snarl at the interloper, she'd kicked him as hard as she could and fled. And she wouldn't let that awful experience spoil what could be.

She desperately wanted to taste life, and she wanted to taste it with Brit. She wanted to experience all there was to experience with him.

Should she tell him that? No, somehow that seemed too cold and calculated. She wanted it to be magical and impromptu, just two people following where their hearts led.

Maybe she'd seduce him? She contemplated the shimmering topaz liquid left in her glass, then took another large swallow. The problem was, she didn't have the least idea of how to go about it.

"Callista, you don't even know how to enjoy life," she chided herself. "Unless . . . Maybe if you . . ." She sipped the brandy and smiled a very feminine smile.

"Brit, you'll never know what hit you."

Chapter 16

Brit blew in on a gust of cold rain a few minutes later. Rain dripped off his hat brim and his wet clothes clung to him. He sailed his hat onto a hook by the door.

Callista smiled at him. "Did you get everything done?"

"Yup." He backed one bootheel into the bootjack beside the door and pulled the boot off, then did the same with the other. Hopping on one foot, he pulled off his sodden socks, then left wet footprints on the planks as he crossed the room to her. "How are you feeling?"

"Much better." She sat in the ladderback chair, all bundled up in his blanket. "Do you have to go out again for anything?"

"Nope. I'm in for good."

"Good." She tossed back the blanket and stood up. "We need to get those wet clothes off you." She reached for his belt buckle.

Brit shied back, out of reach. "Whoa up, there, Cally." He grabbed her hands and held them as he frowned down at her. "What's going on here?"

"I'm helping you get out of those cold, wet clothes,

before you catch your death of cold." She batted her eyes like she'd seen her roommate do at Miss Porter's. "After all, turnabout is fair play."

"Have you got something in your eye?"

"No." She batted her eyes some more. "Let me help you out of your clothes."

His eyes narrowed speculatively, and he said, "Breathe on me."

"Breathe on you?" Her brow furrowed with confusion. How could she seduce him when he wanted her to do strange things? Was this part of some ritual he did?

"Yeah. Exhale. Right here." He pointed to himself. "Breathe."

"All right. But I don't understand." She blew a large breath at the middle of his shirt.

He crooked his finger under her chin and tilted her head up. "Try it again up here. Exhale."

"All right." She drew in the deepest breath she could, then blew it in his face.

"Aha! Just as I thought. How much of that brandy did you have?" He looked at the bottle he'd left on the table.

"Here's what's left, if you want it." She picked up the glass from the hearth and handed it to him.

He glanced at it. "You refilled it, right?"

"No. I only had a few sips." She shook her head, flinging her long hair back off her shoulders. She didn't want it getting in the way.

"Then what is this attempt to undress me?" Crossing his arms over his chest, he spread his feet arrogantly wide.

The way he looked at her sent butterflies tumbling in her stomach. "I don't want you to get sick, that's all. And if we keep talking, you will."

"Who's talking, you or the brandy?"

"It's me . . . mostly." She squinted and focused with great care on his belt buckle as she unbuckled it and pulled his belt loose. Then she undid the top button on his fly.

"How do I know that?" He braced his hands on his hips as he gazed down at her.

"You'll have to take my word for it." She swayed and grabbed his shoulder to steady herself. "See? Look at how you're swaying with fa—fatigue. Good thing I was here to hold you up."

"Yeah. Right." His upper lip twitched.

She unbuttoned his shirt until she could pull the tails out of his pants. Her breasts, covered only by his thin cotton shirt, brushed against his chest as she pushed his shirt back to his shoulders, and she liked the way it felt.

"Mmmmm." She rubbed against him again, like a cat. She felt him tense and looked up. His eyes were half-closed, glittering with a hot silvery light that washed over her like fire in moonlight.

She had to get very close to push his shirt off his shoulders. He grasped her shoulders in his big hands. "Do you know what you're doing to me?" he rasped.

The passion in his voice made her breath catch and her heart drum against her ribs.

"I'm getting you out of your wet clothes. Why are you having such a hard time understanding that?" She moved behind him and pulled his shirt off.

"Hard time is right," he growled.

"Come again?"

"That too, probably."

"What are you mumbling about? Why don't we finish this conversation after I've gotten you out of your pants?" She knelt in front of him and began unbuttoning the remaining five buttons on his fly.

"Good God, Cally, are you out to drive me crazy?" He grasped her shoulders and lifted her up off her knees and kissed her, hard and quick. Then he took a step away from her and hooked his thumbs over his pants and shoved them down in one swift move and kicked them aside. "Satisfied?"

Dark hair whorled and swirled all the way down his legs to his feet. Did it continue up under the cloth that hid his—she swallowed—private parts? Not that the white cotton hid much; it was stretched very taut in front at the moment.

"At last we're making progress," she said in her briskest voice. "I'm sure you got your pants down a lot faster than I could have."

"Yeah, I'm sure too," he growled, but there was a smile in his voice.

As she openly ogled him, she lost her nerve. "I'll let you take care of your underwear. I'm not up to that."

"And I most definitely am," he said wryly. He moved behind her and wrapped his arms around her, just below her breasts. "Are you by any chance seducing me, woman?"

"I hope so." She tilted her head as she looked at him over her shoulder. "I decided that I wanted to learn more about life, and I wanted it to be with you." He traced the hollow of her shoulder with a slow, gentle finger, and she shuddered in his arms. "S-so the next step was seducing you, but I'm afraid I don't know how." He nibbled her earlobe, and she arched her head back. "T-that wasn't something they taught at Miss Porter's Academy for Young Ladies."

"I'd say you're doing just fine." He filled his hands

with her hair, letting it cascade across his fingers in a shower of gold. He buried his face in it, inhaling sunshine and lilacs. "Just fine."

"R-really?" She turned in his arms and locked hers around his neck. Lordy, she felt all shivery and warm inside.

"You must be naturally talented." He closed his eyes and just absorbed the feel of her warmth and softness against him. Just holding her was enough. Holding her and knowing she was safe.

Her pulse fluttered wildly in the hollow at the base of her throat. He bent his head and lovingly tongued that hollow and she softened in his arms.

"Brit," she gasped, "I can't think when you do that."

"You're not supposed to," he murmured. He was only feeling, absorbing her into his senses like sunshine.

"W-will you let me know if I start to get things wrong?" she said in a breathy little voice that made his breath catch.

"Umm."

"Do you like this?" She walked her fingers through the curls on his chest in touches that made him shudder.

"I like anything you do." She was unbelievable. And he was unbelievably lucky to be wanted by her.

"I love your voice," she said softly. "It caresses me and vibrates through me and sings a siren song to me."

He traced the long sensuous curve of her back through the shirt, and she shivered. "My shirt looks a lot better on you than on me," he murmured as he dropped a kiss on her shoulder.

She bowed her head, but he could see the corner

of her mouth lifted in a smile. "Are you by chance seducing me?"

He shook his head. "It's not by chance at all. It's by choice." He kissed her other shoulder and felt her sigh.

"I'm glad."

"Cally, look at me." He cupped her face in his hands. "If you have any objection to making love, say so now, because I still have some self-control. But once I lay you down on the bed—" He shook his head. "I don't know about then." *I want you too badly.*

"I won't object." Tilting her head, she gave him a sideways smile that tempted him. "So what are you going to do to me?"

For answer he swung her up in his arms. Callista gasped and locked her arms around his neck. She could feel the muscles in his neck flexing as he walked across the room, and a primitive thrill went through her.

The room was dark except for the firelight spilling through the doorway, but he walked unerringly to the bed and laid her down as carefully as if she were the most fragile Wedgwood china.

He stripped off his underwear, then stood there for a heartbeat looking down at her, like a conqueror looking at his woman, and again she felt that primitive throb of excitement. The firelight gilded him in gold, highlighting his high cheekbones, every corded sinew in his body. And his arousal.

She felt a moment of fear at the unknown, then she pushed it aside. She wanted Brit to be the first. She didn't know how long she would have him to love; this might be their only time. She wanted to be able to look back on this shimmering moment and know that she had shared it with the man she loved.

She held out her arms to him. "Come. Make love to me." *For I love you so.*

He paused for a second, then he stretched out on the bed beside her. He braced his weight on his elbows as he leaned over her and filled his hands with her hair, toying with it and letting it flow through his fingers.

"Now I know how King Midas felt when he was counting his gold." He rubbed his cheek against her hair. "I love the smell of your hair." Then he leaned down and kissed her. His tongue slid into her moist warmth and danced with hers. He retreated, inviting her to come after him, and she did.

He slid a hand along her cheek and held her as he deepened his kiss, dipping into the soft warmth of her mouth. She moaned, far back in her throat, and tightened her arms around him. *I want to hold you always.*

She kneaded the thick muscles covering his shoulders, knowing she'd never get enough of touching him, feeling the different textures of him. His clean, silky hair brushed her cheek as he bent to tongue the pulse point at her throat.

Then his hand closed gently on her breast and he brushed his thumb over her nipple. She sighed as a ripple of exhilaration swept her. "More."

She could barely see him as he leaned over her in the darkness. "Not backward about asking for what you want, are you?"

"Should I be?" She smoothed her hand over his bushy eyebrow and down his beard-stubbled cheek.

"No—never. I want to know what you like, so I can give you the greatest pleasure."

He caught her hand and kissed her palm, then

slowly drew his teeth across it in a different kind of caress. Callista closed her eyes and just felt what he was doing to her.

He unbuttoned her shirt slowly, and followed every button with a hot kiss that made her sigh and shiver. "I feel like I'm unwrapping the best Christmas present I've ever gotten." When the buttons were all open, his hand moved tantalizingly slowly over her breasts.

She stirred restlessly, wanting him closer, wanting more, and arched up against his hand. "What are you doing?"

"It's too dark to see you with my eyes, so I'm seeing you with my hand. You are so beautiful, my darling. So very beautiful. You are worthy of your name."

"You know what it means?"

"From the first day," he said, lifting her up so he could pull the shirt away.

He seemed to be painting intricate patterns all over her with soft, feathery paintbrushes. She stretched sensuously and trembled as the nerve endings in her skin awakened with astonishing sensitivity.

"What is that?" she murmured, catching his hand and feeling his paintbrush. "My hair?"

"Surprised?" He drew the silky strands back and forth over her breasts. "From now on, wherever we are, even in a crowd, when I touch your hair, you'll think of what we can do with it."

She sighed at the image he painted and felt a throbbing begin deep inside her. This was what she wanted: this loving, this touch, this man.

Then his hands caressed her breasts—his large, powerful, callused hands, which were exquisitely gentle as he learned the contours and curves of her breasts, shaping and lifting and filling his hands with them, and sending sweet chills tumbling through her. "Oh, yes," she murmured when he brushed his thumbs over her nipples and they tightened into buds.

His hair brushed her skin as he took a nipple in his mouth. She moaned and went all soft inside as shimmers of pure pleasure swept her. She threaded her fingers through his hair and held him close. As he varied the pressure, and changed from one nipple to the other, she dissolved into a boneless creature of the senses.

"Oh-h-h," she whispered. "I didn't know it could be like this."

"We're just starting." He circled her budding nipple with his tongue, then blew gently across her moist, sensitive skin, making her tremble.

"Please," she moaned.

"That's what I want to do: please you." He kissed her breasts, then worked his way down her body with more teasing kisses that left her shimmering.

"Wait." She ran her fingers up and down his back in a caress that sent tremors rippling through his whole body. "I want to pleasure you, too."

"And I want you to, but it's not a good idea this time. Next time I will welcome your hands, your touch." He kissed each of her fingers.

"Why not this time? I-I want to know more about you." She drew her fingers through the curls on his chest with a natural sensuality that sent sunshine tumbling through him.

"A man is different from a woman," he said tightly, searching for a way to explain.

"I've noticed."

"A man is quicker to arouse. And when he wants a certain woman and then he waits a long time until she wants him, too . . . well, sometimes he's strung as tight as a hair trigger and—"

"Have you wanted me for long?" She drew him down and kissed him deeply. She ached for him, deep inside.

"Almost from the first time I saw you." He ran his hand down her abdomen, then lower. "Open your legs for me, love," he whispered between kisses.

She hesitated for several heartbeats, and he stilled, waiting. She felt completely vulnerable when she spread her legs. Never before had she trusted a man the way she trusted him. "Only because it's you," she whispered, trying to tell him what was in her heart.

He felt so exhilarated by her trust that he could have been floating a foot above the bed. Anticipation unlike any he'd ever before felt mixed with his exhilaration. She was giving him a gift more precious than all the jewels in the world. She was giving him herself.

"Cally," he whispered, "you are the greatest gift of all." *You fill my heart with joy.*

When he stroked her down there, the tension inside Callista spiraled higher and higher. The throbbing inside her grew. She stirred restlessly as he stroked her, and arched against his hand. Wanting more. Wanting him.

"Slowly, Cally, slowly."

"Now, Brit. I want you *now.*" Everything she was feeling was blending into a rising crescendo of tension.

"Patience." She felt him moving his finger over her, stroking her in a way that was making the throbbing inside beat ever faster, ever more insistently, ever more achingly.

"Spread your legs more, my love."

She did. She felt his knees between hers as he knelt over her. She trailed her fingers down his belly and found his hardness, and he shuddered and sighed.

He stretched out over her, supporting his weight with his hands, then sank down until he barely touched her. There.

She stilled, absorbing the warmth and feel of him. Absorbing his tantalizing nearness.

She lifted her head and kissed the side of his throat. "Tell me what you're going to do to me," she whispered.

"I'm not good with words, Cally. Let me tell you with my hands and my body and my heart." And he slowly rubbed against her. *I need you so much, Cally.*

She ran her hands over his shoulders, wanting more of him, wanting to be one with him. "Now," she whispered urgently. "Do it now."

She felt him push into her slowly, stretching and filling her. Then he retreated and came to her again, slowly, carefully, but she surged up against him.

"Callista," he cried through clenched teeth as he tried to hold on to his self-control.

"Now, Brit! Please!"

He drove into her with all his pent-up longing, drinking her gasps from her lips. *You are life to me, Cally.*

Deep inside her, she felt a ribbon of tension tighten. As he drove into her again and again, the ribbon spiraled tighter and tighter. She wrapped her legs around his waist and tried to move with him.

Panting, she clung to his sweat-slick shoulders, welcoming him and losing him, welcoming and losing, feeling the tension inside her spiral higher and higher.

She wrapped around him, wanting him deeper. Oh

God, it was like climbing a mountain. Just one step higher. One step higher. Higher. Tighter. Tighter.

"Brit!" She arched against him, rigid with tension as he surged into her again and again, filling her.

"Br-i-t!" And she soared off the top of the mountain and shattered into a thousand rainbows. Waves of pleasure tightened her around him, again and again and again. "I . . . love . . . you."

"Cal—lista!" He cried as he sank into her one last time, holding her tightly as he sailed on winds of glory.

They lay clasped in each other's arms, immersed in the special glory of joining, of two become one.

It was long minutes before either had breath to speak. Brit stirred first, moving to take his weight off Callista, but she locked her arms around his shoulders and held him close.

"No, don't go," she whispered. She ran her foot up his leg.

"But my weight—"

"Feels wonderful. It feels right." She relished feeling him in her.

"Did I hurt you?" They were becoming two again, and he felt the sadness of separating from her.

"Just for a second, then it was gone and you were filling me . . ." Her voice trailed away.

"My darling," he groaned deep in his throat.

"Is it always this . . . wonderful?" she whispered, running her fingers through his sweat-damp hair.

"No. Rarely." He rolled onto his back, taking her with him.

He was still floating. She'd said she loved him. Him! The bastard child of the brothel! He couldn't quite believe it. But his heart, his soul, his whole being was filled with love. He felt as if a piece of sunshine had settled in his heart, and her name was Cally.

She rested her head on his shoulder and her hair tumbled over both of them. He stroked the curve of her hip, just enjoying the satin feel of her.

Callista felt him relax into sleep and savored just holding him in her arms. Making love with him had been all she hoped for and much more. So much more, because it was Brit. Brit, whom she loved with every particle of her being, with every breath she took.

She didn't know she could feel such joy. Her heart sang with love for him.

She rubbed her cheek against his hair. It was her destiny to fall in love with him. And she would love him always—she knew that now with a certainty.

She would glory in loving him for all the days they had, no matter how few they might be.

But she was afraid. How long would she have him? How long would her heart sing?

It was still dark when Brit awoke. He came alert instantly, knowing something had awakened him. There was no sound. Then he felt a tiny shaking of the bed.

Callista had rolled away from him and was sleeping on her side with her back to him. He put out his hand to touch her, and felt the same tiny shaking.

"Callista, what is it?" Rolling on his side, he reached for her to pull her back into his arms.

"Nothing. Go back to sleep." She curled up in a ball, trying to stifle her sobs.

"It's not nothing. Oh God," he groaned, "did I hurt you, sweetheart? Tell me." He ran his hands over her, stroking whatever he touched.

"No! That's . . . not . . . it." She reached behind her and grasped his hand.

"Then what is?" He held her hand tightly.

"I was so-o-o-o afraid this afternoon." Words began to tumble out among the sobs. "Marsh . . . drowned. I . . . was afraid . . . I would, too."

"Marsh was your brother?"

"He was four years older than me. I was e-eight." Her voice quavered. "We were ice-skating on the pond behind our house, and I broke through the ice. He . . . he came after me and got me out of the water onto the bank. But . . . he was too cold . . . by the time Papa came and pulled him out . . . it was too late."

"Oh, Callista, I'm so sorry." He wrapped his arms around her as they lay spoon fashion.

"And . . . and today . . . I kept picturing you having to tell my parents their other child drowned, too," she sobbed, resting her head on his arm.

"Shhh, you're safe. It's all right." Brit felt her hot tears dripping onto his arm. He held her close, stroking and kissing and murmuring gently until she fell asleep.

But he didn't sleep.

Callista felt so right in his arms, in his bed. In his heart. So very, very right.

He had almost lost her that day. He thought back to those agonizing moments when Callista was trapped. Those moments when he'd been willing to bargain with God for her life. To beg, if that was what he had to do. Anything.

He'd never before desired anyone as he desired her. She was water in the desert, land for a shipwrecked sailor, the dawn after a dark night. He had been the desert, the shipwrecked sailor, the dark night. Until her.

But now, with every breath he took, with every beat of his heart—she was there. She was the fever in his blood. She was the cool hands that soothed him afterward.

She had opened herself to him. And then given him her whole being—because she wanted to.

For so long, he'd pretended to himself that he felt a passing attraction. But he couldn't keep up that lie any longer. His feelings went much deeper.

Though he lived in a land of sunshine, until she had come into his life, he hadn't seen the sunshine, hadn't basked in its light and warmth. She was the one who had brought laughter and sunshine to the darkest heart of him.

The place no one had ever touched before. The place he had never gone, because it was too lonely to endure.

He thought of the medallion he'd put on the night-stand before he made love to her. It had always been his badge of aloneness. And he'd worn his aloneness like armor, but his armor had had a price, separating him from people.

She'd pierced his armor, and it had fallen away in pieces. It was gone.

But her tears had confirmed what he'd feared with all his heart: she would stand by her father, no matter what the evidence against him was, for she loved him. When she loved, she gave her all.

Blood was thicker than passion. She would be loyal to her father out of love, not duty. Just as she would have been loyal to *him* in the years to come, if they had ever had a chance for a future together.

In the meantime, in the seconds and minutes and

hours and days they had together, he would love her. He would protect her, and keep her safe, and love her.

For that was all he would have of her.

Chapter 17

❧

Callista awakened slowly. Something was tickling her nose. She tried brushing it away, and her fingers tangled in surprisingly soft curls. Her eyes flew open as she remembered.

Brit lay on his back, while she sprawled over him, her leg thrust between his and her head pillowed on his shoulder. She listened to the steady beat of his heart with a warm satisfaction.

She'd heard her married friends talk about making love, but hadn't listened very well. It had made her uncomfortable to talk about such private things. So the sensations, the delicious tension, the joy of being one with another person, had all been unexpected. And it had been wondrous beyond her wildest imagination.

She toyed with the dark curls furring Brit's chest. "Brit?" she said on a bare breath of sound.

"Hmm?" He curled one arm around her and caressed the sleek curve of her bottom.

"Good morning." Her hair tumbled down over them, veiling them from the world.

It was light enough for her to see red marks on his cheeks and forehead. Frowning, she looked at them closer. "Brit, how did you get those slashes on your face?"

"Hmm?" He felt his cheeks. "I don't know. Maybe when I was riding down to the barn."

He must have been racing the wind, and he'd gotten lashed like that because of her. She blinked back tears. She leaned down and with a fierce tenderness kissed each slash mark.

Brit wrapped his arms around her and nuzzled her, and she ran her foot up and down his leg. He'd pulled the sheet halfway up during the night, but it did nothing to hide his arousal.

"Thank you for last night." She leaned over him and kissed his dark nipple, hidden among the curls.

"No, sweetheart, don't thank me." He slowly filled his hand with strands of gold. "I want to thank you for giving yourself to me."

"But you pleasured me so." She punctuated each word with a kiss on his chest. She kept moving, never kissing him twice in the same place and all the time brushing her silky strands across him.

"Oh, Cally." Raising his head, he kissed her. "Don't you know, it gave me pleasure to do it. You'll see. When we make love, the better it is for one, the better it is for the other." His hand glided along the curve of her back in long smooth strokes that shimmered on her skin.

She bent over him, using her hair to paint swirling tantalizing designs on him. Brit shifted his legs and caught her hand, bringing it to his mouth, where he kissed each finger.

She pushed the sheet away and worked her way lower, kissing each rib, then his flat stomach. She discovered that adoring him brought joy to her, too.

She explored the dark line of hair that arrowed

down from his navel, brushing tantalizing close to his hardness.

Brit stirred restlessly. "Do you know what you're doing?" he asked in a tight voice.

"No, what am I doing?

"You're driving me crazy." He pulled her down for a kiss that took her breath and left her toes tingling.

"Does this mean you're enjoying it?" she teased, slowly moving lower and lower again.

Brit groaned far back in his throat and gripped the sheet tightly. She looked up in alarm. "Did I hurt you?"

"Only with sweet torture," he rasped.

Her fingers brushed his shaft lightly, then circled around him, exploring.

"I won't break." He closed her hand around him and she moved it up and down. "Yes. Y-e-s. Like that."

She felt it enlarge even more in her hand, and felt the delicious throbbing growing deep inside her, too.

"Enough," he gasped. Grasping her waist, he lifted her up and over him.

He cupped and stroked her breasts and gently rolled her budding nipples between his finger and thumb.

"Brit!"

He eased her higher and took a nipple in his mouth.

"Y-yes-s." Callista arched against his mouth, her head thrown back. Closing her eyes, she absorbed the wondrous sensations. The throbbing in her grew more urgent.

Brit lowered her to his chest, then rolled over with her.

"Open for me," he murmured between hot kisses.

And she did.

"Come to me!" she demanded and pleaded at the same time.

He knelt over her, watching her as he surged into her, filling her with heat and passion.

Clasping his shoulders, she clung to him, wanting to feel him on her as he was in her. He began to move. Faster and faster. "Yes!" Higher and higher.

She panted as the exhilarating tension in her spiraled tighter and tighter.

Higher. Faster. She rocked forward and back with him, clinging to him. Higher. Faster. She was close to the peak, so close—

"Cal-lis-ta!" He locked his arms around her as he flew over the edge. He thrust fiercely into her as she drew her fingernails along his back.

"B-r-i-t!" And she soared high with him, locked in his arms.

As lightly and slowly as feathers, they floated down to earth again. Boneless, unable to move, locked in each other's arms. Sharing passion's afterglow.

When Brit awoke, he was still holding Callista, and her arms were locked around him. He lingered, savoring the closeness, feeling a beating heart and not knowing if it was hers or his. How many more times would he have the joy of holding her?

He feathered a kiss on the swell of her breast, then tried to ease his arm out from beneath her head without waking her.

She opened her eyes and tightened her arms around him. "Don't go."

"I don't want to." He wanted to stay and hold her and love her for the rest of their days. "But I must." He put her away from him reluctantly, wrenchingly.

Finally he made himself get up and move away from the bed. Because if he didn't . . .

"I'm going down to the stream to bathe before I get dressed, Cally." He glanced at her over his shoulder, which was a mistake. She was sprawled across the bed, all soft curves and hot passion. He almost went back to her, but knew if he did, he'd never leave.

"Do you want to come with me?" He congratulated himself on how normal his voice sounded.

She stretched, long and slow, sinuous and curvy as a cat.

He grabbed a towel and soap and marched himself out of there damn fast, not stopping until he was out the front door and standing in the sunlight. Circling the house, he walked down to the stream and waded in, gasping at the cold but welcoming it.

He was almost done when she came down the slope wearing his blue shirt and nothing else. Her high breasts peaked against the material. That familiar longing began to throb, deep inside him.

She unbuttoned his shirt and slipped it off before stretching out her leg to stick a single toe in. "That won't do it, sweetheart," he murmured and swept her off the bank into his arms.

She locked her arms around his neck. "This won't do it either, sweetheart," she echoed, smiling. "I came to bathe."

He sighed, knowing she was right. He let her legs slide down him into the water and she gasped.

"I'll soap you," he offered.

"If you do that, you know we'll be here all day." She held out her hand for the soap, but he could see sadness in her eyes.

The same sadness he felt as he gave her the soap.

He turned away, knowing that if he didn't, he would reach for her. That didn't help at all. She was splashing around, then silent.

He turned and she was standing there like a water sprite, drawing soap-slick hands over her breasts. "You are so beautiful, Callista."

"So are you." She had watched from the window as he walked down to the stream, naked. She'd seen statues of naked men before, but none had been as powerful and muscular, yet beautiful, as he.

Shivering, Callista ran out of the stream and snatched up her towel.

"Here, let me help you." Brit followed and dropped a towel over her shoulders and pulled her against his chest. "I'll keep you warm while I dry you." He used a corner of the towel to dry her breast, slowly, thoroughly. Then he did the other one. Slowly, sensuously, he slid the towel over every inch of her flesh.

"I don't need the sun to warm me when I have you," she murmured in a broken voice. Her nipples were tight buds of desire, and she wanted to hold him in her arms again. "Enough," she finally gasped, pulling on his shirt. "Your turn," she added, snatching up the other towel.

Brit sat down on a river-rounded boulder so she could dry his hair and then, slowly, sensuously, his shoulders and back. Then she knelt between his knees, toweling his chest and stomach and arousal.

He looked down at her with a heat that could melt glaciers. She watched the muscles of his face tighten with sweet tension.

"Enough!" he growled, grasping her shoulders and lifting her up to meet his hungry mouth.

She rose up on her knees to meet him, just as hungry.

All too soon, he lifted his head. "If we don't stop now . . .

"I know . . ."

Later, in the house, he made coffee while she dressed. Callista glanced around his bedroom, curious about how he lived.

A large rack of deer antlers hung on the wall and shirts and pants were hooked over the points. The bed had a large carved headboard. There was a two-door cupboard in the corner and a nightstand beside the bed. And that was it. There were no pictures on the wall, nothing on the nightstand except his medallion. And two logs stuck out from under the bed.

"Brit," she called, "why do you have two logs under the bed?"

"It's a ladder," he said from the doorway, sipping coffee and watching her. He came to the foot of the bed and pulled it out.

"What for?" she asked as she finished buttoning her own shirt.

"The escape hole." He pointed to a trapdoor in the ceiling. "The rancher who built this house put that in in case they were ever surrounded by Apaches. The hatch opens under the big tree, so even if you're standing on the roof, you're camouflaged from the Apaches."

"And?" She clasped her hand around his and sipped from his coffee mug. "You look like you've got more to say."

"That"—he pointed to the trapdoor—"isn't the real escape hole. It's a decoy. The real escape hole is through that cupboard in the corner. One half of the floor covers the entrance to a tunnel that comes out on the bank of the stream."

"I find it scary that someone had to think like that."

"Then you may be reassured to know that I've never used either one."

She picked up her hairpins from the nightstand and his medallion. "Here, I think this is yours." She slipped it over his head.

"Come on, let's have some coffee and breakfast. Then I have to get you back to Daisy's."

"Now, Daisy, you're going to come visit me soon, aren't you?" Callista hugged her friend. They stood in front of the ranch house, while Russ Caruso, Fowler Stanhope, and a mounted patrol waited for Callista.

"Of course. Just as soon as I can get away."

Daisy smiled, but Callista could see that she was close to tears and she hugged her again. "You'll be okay. It's only a couple of weeks until you visit me."

"Are you two done yet?" Fowler held the reins of the horse Callista was going to ride. "We don't have all day."

"Coming, Fowler." Callista rolled her eyes at Daisy, then walked to her horse, and gathered up the reins. She'd seen to it that it was a regular saddle rather than a sidesaddle.

"Are you going to give me a leg up, Fowler?" she asked.

"Since you are riding astride like a man, I thought you'd just swing up like a man."

"Actually, Fowler, that's a good idea." She stretched to get her foot in the stirrup, then bounced a couple of times on her other foot to get the leverage to swing her leg over the horse's back. She looked over at Fowler, who was obviously surprised to see her mounted. "I guess I didn't need you after all," she said in her sweetest voice.

"Humph!" He gave her a disgusted look. "I guess being a lady is only skin deep."

"I guess so." Had she actually stumbled on to behavior that would make him break the engagement?

She'd been shocked when he knocked on Daisy's door that morning. He was supposed to be in Connecticut! Her first thought was to refuse to go back with him; then, over his shoulder she had glimpsed Russ Caruso and knew she wouldn't be alone with him.

Callista suspected riding back to the fort with him wouldn't be a pleasant experience.

"Come on, men," Fowler yelled, riding to the head of the column of twenty men.

Callista waited for all the men to trot by before she urged her horse to follow them.

Russ had followed Fowler, but now he came back to where she rode. "What are you doing at the tail end, eating everyone's dust?"

"I don't mind. I want to watch them and see what they're doing and let them forget that there's a woman along on this patrol." She'd hoped that by riding at the back no one would join her, and she could treasure and savor her memories of her magical day with Brit.

Russ tilted his hat back and gave her a searching look. "You're going to write about the patrol?"

"I'm thinking about it. But the men won't act natural until they forget I'm along."

Russ was good company, and she was glad for his presence. She knew Fowler would never drop back to ride with her while Russ was.

He flashed her a grin. "Personally, I don't think they'll forget the colonel's daughter is riding with them. However, I'll be glad to keep you company."

She took off her purple jacket and tied it behind her saddle. "Why are you and Fowler on the same patrol? Wouldn't you cover more territory if you split up?"

"Well, I have the experience, so Fowler's supposed to be learning from me."

"But he has the seniority, so he can't be bothered to listen to a junior officer." Callista unbuttoned her cuffs and rolled up her sleeves.

"Correct. Of course, if anything goes wrong, then it'll be all my fault."

The sun moved higher in the sky and the breeze became dragon's breath, sucking the moisture out of their bodies.

They stopped at noon in a grove of sycamores alongside a wash, where everyone, even the horses, could rest in the shade. Callista slipped off her horse and sat down at the base of a tree, then leaned back against the trunk and closed her eyes. Traveling in the hot desert was damn tiring.

"We'll rest here for a few hours, Callista," Fowler said in a commander-in-chief voice that sounded utterly false to her ears. He sat down beside her, but she kept her eyes closed and pretended to be asleep.

On a ridge high above the patrol, Brit lowered his field glasses. "They're still resting." He shook his head in disbelief. "Didn't any of them notice the tracks when they crossed the trail of that Apache war party a couple of miles back?"

"Soldiers not say anything. Stanhope not notice. Only Caruso alert," Walks-with-Horses said.

"But not even he acts as if he's seen them." He was glad Caruso was on the patrol, so it wasn't left to Fowler Stanhope's incompetent leadership.

"What you do, *Nantan*?"

"We'll join them in camp tonight. Maybe that'll wake them up."

As he rode into their camp later, Brit scanned the men. It wasn't quite dark, but they had a large fire going and they were lolling around on their bedrolls. He halted outside the camp, counting, and saw a man for every horse on the picket line, which meant no sentries had been posted. And sentries should have been the first thing taken care of.

He urged his horse forward at a trot, watching to see what the men did. As soon as the men heard his hoofbeats, they scattered into the bushes and shadows.

He saw Russ hustle Callista away from the fire into the darkness. But Fowler just lowered his coffee cup and looked in his direction, not alert enough even to take the precaution of moving into the shadows.

"Ahoy the camp," he shouted. "This is Lieutenant Chance. I'm coming in with a couple of my scouts."

The men had returned to their bedrolls by the time he drew rein near the fire and dismounted. He saw neither relief nor welcome on their faces.

He tossed his reins to Walks-with-Horses. "Take the animals and camp at the far edge," he ordered in Apache.

"Evening, gentlemen, Callista," he added, turning to the fire, as Callista and Russ returned. The golden glow of the fire highlighted her delicate bone structure. Then her eyes met his, and the memories in them took his breath away.

"Where did you come from?" Fowler snarled.

"Out there." Brit gestured at the darkness. Smoke eddied around the fire, which was far too large. An Apache could spot such a fire from miles away. "Why haven't you sent men following that Apache war party whose trail you crossed earlier?"

"Lieutenant Caruso, why didn't you inform me we had crossed the trail of a party of the renegades? We could have gone after them."

"How far back were they, Brit?" Russ said easily, all but ignoring Fowler. "You're sure we crossed them and they didn't cross our trail?"

"Before you stopped at noon. And yes, my scouts have been trailing that band for days."

"Then why haven't you caught them, Chance?" Fowler managed to make his name sound like a curse.

"Trailing and catching are two different things."

"It appears they certainly are with you."

Brit counted to ten. He hadn't come into camp to protect Fowler's ass, but to guard Callista. He was sure the Apaches knew there was a woman traveling with this patrol, so he'd left most of his scouts posted as sentries in a large circle around the camp, in case the Apaches tried anything.

"Have you posted sentries for the night?"

Fowler smiled smugly. "Don't need them. Apaches don't attack at night."

Brit shook his head. "Apaches don't *like* to fight at night, but they will if it brings them the advantage of surprise."

Fowler turned to Russ. "Lieutenant Caruso, why haven't you posted guards around the camp?"

"Would you like some coffee, Lieutenant Chance?" Callista asked. She was standing off to the side, in the shadows between firelight and darkness.

"Thank you." He followed her the few steps to the coffeepot. She'd rolled up the sleeves on her white shirt, like a man would, but it only emphasized her femininity.

"I'm glad to see you," she murmured as she wrapped the edge of her skirt around the handle of the pot, and poured coffee into her folding cup. "I missed you."

Her fingers slid along his as she handed him the cup of fragrant coffee. "Same here," he said gruffly. Saying he had missed her sounded too namby-pamby.

Putting the coffeepot back on the coals, she laced her fingers together and stared at them rather than meet his gaze. "And I'll sleep a lot better tonight knowing you are on guard."

The V of her white collar led his eye to the throbbing pulse at the base of her throat. *Was* she safer? He could protect her from the Apaches, but could he protect her from himself?

"Are you staying the night, Brit?" Russ asked, joining them.

"Yup." Out of the corner of his eye, he saw Callista smile, then quickly look down as if to hide it.

"Good," Russ said quickly, not giving Fowler a chance to say anything. "It'll give us a chance to catch up and find out what you've seen on your patrol." He glanced around. "You rode in with only two scouts? Where are the rest?"

"They preferred to camp in a different spot." He didn't add that it was because he had set up a perimeter a good way back from the camp itself. Besides, he knew they wouldn't want to sleep around a fire that could have served as a signal beacon.

"So hunker down and talk." Russ Caruso sat down on the ground, tailor-fashion.

Callista sat down on a log at the edge of the light, Brit noticed, close enough to hear without appearing to be listening to army business.

Brit squatted down as he'd learned from the Apaches. It was a position from which he could react immediately if something happened. Sitting on the ground as Russ was doing would leave him seconds behind in dealing with an emergency.

He rested his coffee on his knee and contemplated it. "Geronimo isn't the only one who's escaped from the reservation. Nana, Ulzanna, Mangus, Loco, and other chiefs have broken out, too."

"Damn!" Russ dragged his hand back through his hair. "That's bad news. What's got them so riled this year?"

"They're not getting their rations of beef and flour, and people are starving on the reservation."

"Oh, come now, surely you don't believe that." Fowler leaned against a tree, his arms crossed over his chest. "The agents supply them with the allotment of beef. They're just saying that as an excuse to leave the reservation."

Brit tossed the last of his coffee into the fire and listened to it sizzle, then rose to his feet, before he answered. "They don't need an excuse to leave the reservation. You know what they call it? 'White-eyes cage.'"

Fowler stood away from the trunk. "You sound as if you agree with them, Chance. Maybe you can't catch Geronimo because you don't want to, eh?"

"And you sound like you're accusing me of treason, Stanhope," Brit drawled, hanging on to his temper with difficulty.

"If the shoe fits—"

"How far is it to Fort Bowie?" Callista said abruptly, moving into the circle of light.

Out of politeness, Brit turned to her. "You'll be there tomorrow afternoon."

She adjusted the light shawl that covered her shoulders. When one edge slipped down over her shoulder suggestively, he stiffened. Was that an invitation to—? He glanced at Fowler, and noted that he, too, was watching Callista. Just as quickly, Brit realized what she was doing. Damn, she was good. She'd set out to distract Stanhope and him—and she'd done it.

So he'd take advantage of her distraction to leave—for while they'd been talking, it had been deathly quiet beyond the camp. Other than the occasional stamp of a horse's hoof, he had heard none of the normal night sounds, the hoot of an owl, the distant yodel of a coyote, the rustling of mice in the grass—that told him it was a night like all others. He had heard only silence.

"Good night, gentlemen, Callista." Turning on his heel, he stalked to where Walks-with-Horses had dropped Brit's saddle and his bedroll. Instead of spreading his bedroll, he walked on into the darkness until he judged that he was well clear of the camp.

He made a cautious circuit, taking a step and listening, taking a step and listening. And the more he listened, the less he heard.

He was on full alert, using all his senses. Heavy clouds scudded across the sky, blotting out the feeble starlight, leaving nothing but his instincts to guide him. Heat lightning in the distance occasionally sent a flash of light through the darkness, so he moved cautiously.

And froze when he sensed rather than saw the out-line of a man sitting on a boulder silhouetted against the sky. He waited until a flash of the distant light-ning confirmed what his instincts had said. A brave sat upon a boulder, one knee drawn up, his rifle lean-ing against his leg.

Brit breathed an Apache word of greeting. The sil-houette of the brave's face changed, and he knew the man had turned toward him. A grunt answered him.

He eased up to where Walks-with-Horses sat. "What have you seen?" he breathed.

"Apaches not travel this night." In Apache fashion, he pointed his nose at the distant lightning. "Rain come soon. Lose tracks again. You shadow girl to-morrow?"

"Yes," Brit murmured, and returned to camp.

Picking up his bedroll, he used the light of the dying fire to scan the sleeping men. Callista was on the other side of the fire, kneeling on a blanket, brushing the wrinkles out of it.

As if she felt his gaze, she stopped, then slowly looked up—directly at him. An arrow of desire shot through him. He inhaled deeply, and would have sworn he caught a whiff of her scent. Deliberately turning his back on her, he spread his bedroll where he stood, rather than get any closer to her.

Lying down, he folded his arms beneath his head and stared up at the clouds. He and his scouts had been chasing a band of Apaches who had come north from Mexico when they crossed the tracks of the pa-trol.

Even though Fowler's group had crossed over the Apaches' tracks, he was certain they'd circled back and knew exactly where the patrol was. His instincts said they were close.

And the patrol presented a tempting target to the Apaches, with their guns and ammunition and horses and a girl with hair the color of *hoddentin*.

So he would protect Callista—at all costs.

Chapter 18

At breakfast the next day, Callista learned to her dismay that the whole patrol wasn't returning to Fort Bowie. She and Fowler would break away from the others and go to the fort, while the patrol continued on under Russ.

She was afraid of being alone with Fowler, and felt in her pocket for her single-shot derringer. It would give her courage if she needed it.

Two hours later, as they rode side by side, Callista said, "I've been wanting to tell you, Fowler, that you look quite resplendent in that uniform." It had the biggest brass buttons she'd ever seen. If Fowler fell into the water, the air pockets in his brass buttons would keep him afloat like water wings.

The furrow between his eyes deepened as he frowned at her. "Resplendent?" She saw understanding of the word dawn in his brown cow eyes. "Oh, yes. Of course."

"And there's something else I'd like to discuss with you." She took a deep breath. "About our engagement."

"After we're married, I won't allow you to ride astride, you know." Fowler gave her an up-and-down look that made Callista want to slap him. Hard.

She opened her mouth to give him a tongue-lashing he'd never forget, then glimpsed riders galloping down the hill behind them.

"Fowler! Are those Apaches?"

He glanced back. "Damn right!" he yelled as he whipped his horse into a gallop.

Callista whipped her horse too and leaned low over his neck. "Come on, boy! Come on!" She said a silent thanks to Brit for making her change to an astride saddle. Within a few hundred yards, Fowler began to pull away from her on his faster horse.

The Apaches were gaining on her. She spurred her horse, hoping it would put on a burst of speed.

Fowler looked back at her but didn't slow at all.

Shots boomed. The Apaches? Shooting at her?

As she looked back, she saw two riders on the ridge to her right, firing at the Apaches. They weren't close enough for her to recognize them, but she recognized the big red horse one rode.

"Brit!" Her love, her hero. Brit would save her.

A glance back told her the Apaches were only a couple of horse lengths behind. So close! She whipped her horse and leaned low over its neck, urging it to run faster.

Then the Apaches engulfed her. Surrounding her, they kept galloping with her in their midst. Their horses ran on both sides of her, in front and behind her.

The derringer's single shot wouldn't help her. She heard shots fired in the distance and gravel spurted up in front of them.

Oh God, what was she going to do? She flicked glances at the Apaches to the right and left of her, and saw nothing but hardened warriors.

No one touched her or her horse, but her horse turned when their horses did—as if they were all yoked together. Callista sawed on the reins, but no matter how hard she pulled, her horse stayed with the other horses.

The Apaches cut away from the trail and opened fire on the riders who'd been riding to aid her. They were much closer now.

She stared at Brit, willing their gazes to meet. And for a single searing instant, they did. Then his horse went down, somersaulting head over heels. Brit was thrown onto boulders, where he lay motionless. The scout with him leaped off his horse and ran to Brit.

She turned in her saddle, watching for as long as she could, while the Apaches led her away. But Brit never moved.

The Apache on her right reached over and jerked the reins out of her hand. They rode all afternoon without stopping. They'd trot, walk, then trot, but they kept moving. From the position of the sun, she knew they were headed south, toward the Mexican border.

No one spoke to her. She might have been invisible for all the attention they paid her. Finally, when the sun was close to the horizon, they stopped at a stream shaded by mesquites. In seconds they had all dismounted, swept their saddles off the horses and hobbled them, then turned them loose to graze.

A tall brave pulled her off her horse and shoved her toward the stream. Dizzy with fear, light-headed from lack of water, stiff from so many hours in the saddle, she sprawled on the ground.

He swooped down, grabbed her arm and lifted her up so roughly, she screamed at the pain. He back-handed her across the face, knocking her to the ground again.

This time he just nudged her in the side with his moccasin. Slowly, she got to her hands and knees, shaking her head to clear it of the fog that threatened to engulf her. She could taste blood. Her blood.

"Come," he ordered. In English, she realized dully. She looked at him as, holding on to a sapling, she pulled herself to her feet.

"Come." He grasped her arm and shoved her ahead of him, toward the stream.

She stumbled down to it, lay flat on the ground like the Apache beside her, and scooped water into her mouth with her hand. She was petrified, waiting for them to rape her—or to try. Now she was glad she'd saved the derringer's single shot, because she'd make them pay. But no one touched her.

The brave who'd captured her bound her hands behind her back. Then he went to sleep with his hand on her throat.

She lay there, knowing that Brit was dead. And knowing, too, that no one would be coming after her. She was so numb she couldn't even cry.

In the morning, the Apaches mounted and headed south again, still leading her horse. She'd been their captive for over a day and she was still unharmed and relatively unhurt. The longer they went without touching her, the more her terror mounted. She told herself to stay calm, but the pounding of her heart mingled with the pounding of her horse's hooves until they were one.

They rode until sunset. When they finally stopped beside a spring where water welled up, she dismounted, and fell in a numb heap.

The Apaches ignored her as they drank, then watered their horses. She managed to get feeling in her numb legs and stumbled down to the spring. She drank and rested, and drank more. Slowly, she revived—Although it seemed better to stay in a fog.

The brave shared a strip of jerky with her that evening, then tied her hands behind her. As though he knew how defeated she was, he didn't tie her feet. Then he joined the other Apaches, who were sitting around the fire passing around bottles of whiskey. She could smell the raw odor of the whiskey when they spilled it. What would they do when they were drunk?

She lay there in an agony of fear as they drank until they fell over. While they were intoxicated she had a chance to escape. She felt around for a sharp-edged stone and began to saw at the rope. She had to do something.

She didn't know how long she'd been sawing when a hand clamped across her mouth. She felt a warm breath beside her ear and knew this was it. *This was it!*

Then she made out the word being breathed into her ear. "Quiet." In English.

In Brit's voice. And she smelled his pine-soap scent.

She nodded against his hand. He removed it cautiously. Then she felt him cutting the rope binding her hands. It gave, freeing her.

She moved slowly, getting feeling back in her arms as he helped her up. Thank God the Apache hadn't tied her feet, too.

He led her downhill. "Oh God, Brit," she gasped as they ran. "I was so scared. I saw you go down and you didn't move and I thought the Apaches had killed you."

"I had to do that, so they wouldn't know I was in pursuit. I didn't want them traveling faster. Hell, they moved fast enough as it was."

He'd left the horses tethered downwind from the Apaches' horses so they wouldn't whinny at the scent of strange horses. There he wrapped his arms around her and his mouth came down on hers. Hard. Hot. Quick.

She kissed him back. Hard. Hot. Quick.

Then he threw her up on her horse.

As he turned to his horse, an Apache sprang upon him with a savage war cry that made her blood run cold. The other Apaches would soon be running to help.

And she could do nothing to help Brit. It was so dark Callista couldn't see the brief, fierce struggle. All she heard was the thud of fists striking flesh.

Then Brit was swinging up on his horse and reining him around. "That way," he yelled, pointing.

Rifles crackled behind them as they galloped away. A half-moon silvered the open grassland they raced across.

She was in the lead. Once, while the Apaches were still shooting at them, she thought she heard Brit grunt, and she looked back at him. "Are you all right?"

"Yes. Keep going." But his voice sounded strange.

So she galloped on, listening to the steady beat of his horse's hooves behind her. They rode through the hours of darkness, walking to rest the horses, then galloping on. Dawn slowly pearled the eastern sky.

It was light, although still a half hour to sunrise, when Callista drew rein at a stream. The horses needed water. Brit had been silent for a while and she glanced at him.

He was hunched over, almost lying on the horse.
"Brit!"

He raised his head weakly, as if it was a great
effort. Jumping off her horse, she ran to him.

"I stopped . . . a bullet." He took a long, shallow
breath.

"Where? Let me see." She rested her hand on his
shoulder, and felt something wet and sticky just as
she smelled the metallic scent of blood. She stared at
the dark red blood on her fingers. Oh God, no!

He shook his head. "Hide first. Walk horses upstream."

"Oh, my God," she whispered. Brit was wounded,
and she was alone with him somewhere in Mexico.
She pressed the back of her hand to his forehead. His
skin felt clammy and hot at the same time.

Keep calm, keep calm, she told herself. Her heart
was pounding like a runaway train. *Hide from the
Apaches in case they're on our trail. That's the first
thing. Then take care of Brit's wound.*

She waded into the icy stream and led the horses
upstream, walking in water to hide their tracks. The
oak forest was open and parklike, not a good place
to hide.

"Callista." Brit's voice was low, strained.

She splashed back to his side. "Can you hang on?"
He was hunched over, holding on to the saddle horn
with one hand. His wounded arm hung straight down,
useless.

"Have to." He paused for several breaths. "Look
for caves . . . in canyon walls."

"Don't worry; just hang on. I'll get us hidden before long." The canyon was narrowing, the walls
coming closer.

The creek twisted and turned with the canyon. She

scanned the walls, looking for the black hole of a cave. Brit was depending on her, and she couldn't let him down.

Not when he'd braved an Apache war party to free her. But they had to hide quickly. For if they were recaptured by the Apaches . . .

She shuddered as stories of Apache prisoners filled her mind. Resolutely, she pushed them away. First things first. Brit needed her.

A splash behind her made her turn.

Brit had fallen off his horse.

"Oh no!" She splashed back to him. The icy water had revived him a bit, and he was floundering weakly, trying to stand up.

"Oh, my darling, please try to hang on until I can get you to safety," she whispered as she knelt beside him.

He turned his head slowly. "Get shirt off." He paused and pawed weakly at his shirt with his left hand, his working hand. "Let water flush wound."

The shirt was stuck to him, and she was afraid to pull it away and start him bleeding more heavily. So she helped him lie in the icy water as it flowed over his shoulder. After a few minutes she was able to pull his shirt away from the wound.

"Rip it." He gasped. "Or cut it away."

She used her folding scissors to cut away as much as she could from his torn flesh. She peeled away his shirt and saw the surprisingly small hole in the back of his shoulder—at least for the amount of blood that he'd lost. Brit lay back in the stream, his teeth chattering, and let the water flow over his wound.

"H-help m-me u-up."

"Lean on me," she muttered, kneeling beside him

and sliding her arm behind him. He pushed himself up with his good arm, then slumped against her. He didn't have enough strength left to sit up by himself. Callista draped his good arm over her shoulders and wrapped her arm around his waist. "All right. On the count of three, let's get you up. One. Two. Three."

She got him three-quarters of the way up, but one foot went out from under him. He had to clasp her shoulder and lean on her heavily to keep from sliding back into the stream. She braced her knees and took his weight, but she could feel him trying to straighten away from her. "It's okay, lean on me."

"Too heavy."

"No, you're not. I'm strong—lean." But instead of taking a step with her help, he still struggled to stand alone and get his weight off her. "Damn it, Brit! You don't have the strength to walk by yourself."

He leaned forward, as if deciding how much strength it would take. "Won't lean."

"You *have* to." Finally, step by slow staggering step, they walked up the middle of the stream.

"Horses?" Brit got out through gritted teeth.

Callista stared at him and knew her eyes were getting big as saucers. Oh, Lord, she'd forgotten them completely.

"Around the next bend," she said, hoping it was true. Good Lord, she'd dropped the reins in her hurry to get back to Brit. Had she left Brit and herself afoot?

They took one slow step after the next, but Callista could see that they weren't going to get any farther than they were. Brit was too weak.

"Brit, let me leave you here and explore ahead myself." She angled toward the gently sloping bank. With the first bit of slope, Brit went down, taking her with him.

"Thanks." Brit reached over and squeezed her hand as she lay beside him.

"You're out of the water." She looked over her shoulder and found that his boots were still in the water. "At least most of you. Rest and I'll be back as soon as I can."

She splashed upstream. "Oh God, please let the horses be around the next bend. Please."

She waded around the bend. And they were there, grazing on the sparse grass that fringed the bank. But when she reached for the reins dragging along the ground, one shied, whirling away from her. She froze. If one bolted, the other would go with him.

"Easy, boy, easy," she murmured. He watched her alertly, ready to run at the least excuse. She held out her hand palm up and eased up to the other one, keeping up a continuous soothing murmur. When she caught that one, she exhaled a long, heartfelt sigh. Now she knew they wouldn't be afoot, no matter what.

Mounting, she grabbed the other horse's reins and tethered it to a tree, then explored a little farther up the creek, watching the canyon walls for any indication of a cave. All she found was a rock overhang that would have to do. At least it was well screened by bushes and large boulders.

Now all she had to do was get Brit. She grimaced as she turned her horse around. Getting him moved wasn't going to be easy for either of them.

When she returned, she found clawlike finger marks on the soft mud of the bank, where Brit had pulled himself along by his fingertips. He'd managed to climb the bank, then roll under berry bushes, so he wasn't lying in the open.

"Brit," she murmured, kneeling beside him and brushing a lock of black hair off his forehead.

His eyelids flickered. "Brush bank where we—" He lapsed back into unconsciousness.

Something she should have thought of. She led both horses up to where he was, then broke off a leafy branch and brushed away the marks they'd made on the sandy bank. Then, walking backward, she brushed out her tracks until she got back to Brit.

He touched her ankle with his good hand so she knew he was conscious. "Brit, I found an overhang where we'll be sheltered and I can take care you." Brushing his matted hair away from his forehead, she felt it. Too warm.

"Get horse." He sat up slowly, with great effort.

When she returned, he was holding on to a sapling and swaying, but he was standing. She held the horse motionless while Brit got his left boot into the stirrup, grabbed the horn with his left hand, and slowly pulled himself up. Tears burned her eyes as she watched the effort it cost him.

Though he hunched over, at least he was mounted. Callista mounted the other horse and led him back through the oaks, around the huge boulder that hid the entrance, and into the shade beneath the rock slab. With boulders hiding it on three sides and the canyon slope forming the back wall, they were effectively in a cave. One where she could hide the horses, too, if necessary.

"Stay on the horse," she said, as she pulled his bedroll off and spread it out near the back wall. Then she led his horse close and helped him down. He held on to the horse's mane, but even so, swayed. She wrapped her arms around his waist and steadied him.

Brit collapsed onto the blankets and lay back. He plucked at his shirt buttons. "Get it off."

Kneeling beside him, Calista unbuttoned what was left of his shirt and pulled it off him. The stream had cleaned away the blood on his chest and the front of his shoulder. Brit felt his shoulder. "Wound? In front? Look."

Callista's brow furrowed. What was he looking for? "There's no wound here."

"Only in back?" He grimaced as a wave of pain racked him.

"Yes." She gripped his left hand tightly, trying to give him strength. If only she could wrap him in her arms and hold him until the pain was gone.

"Bullet has to come out." He took a labored breath between each word. "You."

Callista's eyes widened. He couldn't mean that she'd have to get the bullet out of him. She had to have misunderstood. *I love you. I couldn't do something that would hurt you so.*

"Make fire."

He was right—she needed to get a fire started. "Hold on, Brit. I'll be right back." She kissed his cheek, then scrambled up. She brought the other horse into the shelter also, so they couldn't be spotted by anyone.

Next she collected dried wood and laid a fire near the edge of the overhang so the smoke would rise, instead of pocketing beneath the rock. Standing up, she stared down at the dry wood.

"Matches! Oh, my God, we need matches." Maybe Brit carried some. Kneeling beside him, she went through his pockets until she felt a small round canister. Pulling it out and unscrewing the top, she found matches.

She stilled for a moment, thinking how close they'd come to disaster—simply because she didn't carry matches with her. She gathered dried leaves and twigs for kindling, glancing at Brit the whole time she was getting the fire going.

He was so motionless, she feared he was unconscious.

Oh Lord, what was she going to do? No matter how many times she said I love you, it wouldn't help him now.

His life was in her hands, and she didn't know a thing about bullet wounds.

Chapter 19

～⁓⚬⁓～

"**C**ally." Brit's voice was a dry rasp.

"I'm here, darling." At least he was conscious. "Just lie still." She knelt beside him. Pulling her riding skirt out of the way, she began to rip the bottom ruffle from her petticoat. "I'll have you bandaged in no time."

"Get bullet out. Heat my knife."

She stared at him. *Oh, God, I can't!*

As though he read her mind, Brit opened his eyes and looked at her. "You have to." He moved his good hand to rest it on hers. "I can't. You must."

"I don't know if I can."

"If you don't"—he paused for breath—"I'll die."

"No!" she wailed. He'd voiced her greatest fear. "Oh God, what if I don't do it right?" she whispered. But she had to—they both knew it was his only chance.

She went through his pockets until she found his folding knife, then heated the blade at the edge of the fire. She helped him turn over on his stomach, and listened to his instructions.

Then, she took the heated knife and went back to

him. She closed her eyes, said a swift prayer, then went to work.

In seconds, Brit went from a knot of tension to relaxed muscles, and she knew he was unconscious. She probed and did what he'd told her to do. She had to get the bullet out: that was all she could think about. Finally, after what seemed an eternity, she found it and removed it.

She knelt back and watched the fresh blood well up. She'd done it. But she didn't feel a single bit of triumph, only overwhelming relief.

Standing up, she took the bloody knife and bullet and walked outside. She flung the damn bullet as far away as she could. Then, with deep, wrenching sobs, she stumbled down to the stream and washed her hands and the knife.

She'd never have believed she could do what she'd just done—yet there'd been no choice. She dried her hands on her bedraggled riding skirt and wiped her eyes with her petticoat. As she stood up, she felt something hard in her pocket and dug it out. And stared at the piece of white soap. It would come in handy, she thought, remembering Aurora Spencer's admonition to everyone—wash your hands.

She returned to Brit, who seemed to have fallen into an exhausted sleep. She covered him with a blanket, then turned to the horses and unsaddled them. And stared at the saddlebags on Brit's saddle. She'd forgotten them completely.

Feeling as if she might have found hidden treasure, she unbuckled Brit's saddlebags. Inside she found a clean shirt and socks and a nested mess kit. She pulled the tin pan out and thanked her lucky stars. At least she had something to boil water in.

Digging deeper into the saddlebag, she found several pieces of jerky.

While he slept, she took the ruffle of petticoat she'd torn off earlier down to the stream and washed it, so it would make a clean bandage. She filled their canteens and the pan from the mess kit with water.

Thunder rumbled across the sky, and she noticed dark clouds to the west of them. With a sense of unreality, she remembered they were still in the rainy season.

So much had happened, that it seemed as if it had been years since they'd made love. But when she counted, it was only five days. Five days and a lifetime.

She slipped around the boulder that shielded the entrance to their hideaway and went to check Brit. He was awake and had turned his head so he could see their hideway.

"How do you feel?" She sat beside him and brushed his hair back off his forehead.

"Like a herd of horses trampled me." His eyes drifted closed, then opened again, and she realized he was fighting sleep. "Did you get it?"

"Yes. And I've got a clean bandage here. Let me bandage your wound to keep it clean, then we can turn you over on your back."

"Deal."

She laid several layers of cloth over his wound, then wound the long strip over his opposite shoulder, then down and around his chest, sliding her hand under him to catch the ends, and finally knotting it. It looked awful, but at least it would protect his wound. He felt cool, rather than feverish, and she was thankful for that.

Getting her bedroll, she slipped it beneath his head

as a pillow when she helped him roll over. Then she sat beside him again, needing to touch him to reassure herself.

"Thanks," he said softly. He caught her hand in his and squeezed it.

Tears prickled her eyes. "I just did what I had to do."

Brit closed his eyes, afraid she'd see his weakness in them. The thing he'd always feared had finally come to pass. He was weak and helpless. Helpless!

Helpless like he'd been when he was ten years old and his mother was dying and he couldn't help her. *That* day when his mother had coughed up so much blood. She'd given him the medallion and reached out to him.

Automatically he felt for the medallion with his good hand. Then he remembered the Apache had ripped it off when they were fighting at the camp. There'd been no time to stop to grab it, not when he had to get Callista away from there.

When his mother died, he'd sat beside her, holding her hand until it was stiff and cold. He was ten years old and alone in the world except for Dog, a brown and white terrier. But somehow, knowing he was responsible for Dog as well as himself had helped him cope with the loneliness.

He had stolen food for Dog and himself, and on cold winter nights, he'd found places in doorways or under stairs where he and Dog were out of the wind and they'd sleep curled up together. Then Dog was run over by a goddamn freight wagon.

He had picked up Dog's poor broken body and gotten a last loving lick. Then he was truly alone.

In the months afterward, he learned the true meaning of loneliness. On too many nights, all he had to eat was the sweet hops smell from passing beer wagons.

He had vowed then that he would survive. He would stand on his own two feet and be self-contained. Needing someone else was a weakness he couldn't afford. Not when it hurt so damn much when they died.

But here he was, completely dependent on Callista—and he didn't like it one bit. Yet he trusted Callista more than he'd ever trusted anyone. She had a strength that he knew would get them though whatever happened. And he had come to need her in more ways than he could count.

Sleep claimed him. When he awoke again, he could hear thunder and rain and see the flash of lightning in the darkness outside.

"Cally," he said, surprised at how raspy his voice was. "How far away from the creek are we?"

She gave him a wide-eyed look, and he knew she'd never thought about flooding.

"I'll keep an eye out, but I think we're far enough away. Would you like some soup?"

"Yes." He wasn't a bit hungry, but he'd need it for strength.

She brought a steaming bowl of broth to him and helped him sit up. He was surprised to find that he still didn't have the strength to sit up by himself, and had to lean against her. Damn! It was humiliating.

After only a few spoonfuls, he was full and ready to lie down again. Not good, he thought. He was much weaker than he would have expected. Of course, he'd never been shot before, so he didn't have anything to compare with, but still, he didn't think he should be so weak.

He awoke sometime in the night. His first awareness was of Callista, curled against his side, her small hand resting on his chest. She had covered them both with a blanket. He turned his head just enough to smell her wonderful hair—a relief after the metallic smell of blood that had filled his nostrils for hours. He kissed her forehead gently.

She stirred and her fingers flexed on his chest, but she didn't waken.

The storm had moved on, although he could occasionally see a distant flash of lightning. They'd stayed dry, at least. But they were still somewhere in the middle of Apache country. And there was undoubtably a war party looking for him right now—which meant that she was in terrible danger. In the morning he would tell her to ride on, to get away while she could.

Callista raised up on one elbow and looked at Brit in the dim light of the dying fire. She'd thought he was awake. Strange, how she'd imagined his lips brushing her forehead. She spread her fingers across his chest, feeling for his steady heartbeat. Thank God he didn't feel feverish.

Tomorrow she would have to hunt. Brit needed more than jerky soup if he was to regain his strength. She'd never thought she'd need the ability to shoot, but now she needed it desperately.

She brushed her lips across his good shoulder and cuddled against him, and slipped back into sleep.

When she awakened in the morning, she saw that his eyes were half-open—although they had a dullness she didn't like.

"Brit, darling?" She stroked his cheek, wanting, needing to touch him.

He grimaced at her. Or maybe it was supposed to be a smile. "Thirsty."

"Of course you are." She slipped her arm under him, and, trying to stay away from his wound, lifted him. He slumped against her, but gulped several large swallows before he pushed the canteen away.

"Thanks . . . Cally." He rested his head on her shoulder. She thought he'd slipped into sleep, when he spoke again. "Apaches looking . . . for us. Take my . . . horse and . . . head north."

"What? Leave you? Absolutely not."

"Don't be . . . stupid. Go."

"Be quiet and save your strength for healing." Tears burned the backs of her eyes. He was so badly wounded, yet he wanted her to go, to save herself.

"The one time you need me, and you want me to leave you," she grumbled.

"Go. I will survive . . . or I won't." He rested his good hand on hers.

"You heroes are always so goddamned noble, aren't you?" She had to get mad at him; otherwise, she'd cry.

"I'm not a hero." He closed his eyes and rested for a moment, before continuing in a weak voice. "When are you going to understand that?"

"Right. Any coward would have dared to come into the Apache camp to rescue me."

"Yes." *Any coward who loved you*, he thought, as he fell asleep.

Callista watched him for a few minutes to make sure he was sleeping, then picked up his rifle and went hunting.

Two hours later, she headed back to their camp. She'd shot a rabbit, then cleaned it. Afterward, she'd walked behind some bushes and retched her insides out.

She walked into their shelter before she realized Brit wasn't alone. Her eyes widened with shock and she drew in a sharp breath. Then she looked each of the three Apaches in the eye.

"You should have gone, Cally," Brit said sadly. "Why didn't you leave me and go?"

At his words, an Apache aimed his rifle at Brit.

"No!" She screamed as she flung herself across Brit's broad chest. She heard his grunt of pain when her hand brushed his shoulder.

Behind them, the Apache spoke. She recognized one word: *hoddentin*. Beneath her, she felt Brit stiffen. Then he replied in halting Apache. Bracing her hand beside him, she moved off him, watching him. His expression didn't change, and yet she sensed something had.

"What is it?" She kept a hand on him—for her courage, not his.

"They know who you are."

"Of course they know. After all, my father is leading the campaign against Geronimo."

"No." He spoke slowly, with great effort. "The name they gave you is Woman-with-hoddentin-hair-who-saved-grandchild-of-Nana."

She looked over her shoulder at the Apaches, watching their impassive ebony eyes. "Who's Nana?"

"Important chief."

"You're saying that because I waded into that fight to help George? Th-that's why they didn't touch me?" She didn't want to think about what might have happened.

He nodded, then she saw his lips tighten with pain. The Apache leader broke the silence, speaking rapid fire words to the other Apaches. They approached Brit and she saw him clench his jaw, as if to prepare for what was coming.

She stood up in front of him, her arms out, trying to shield him. "No! Leave him alone. He's hurt."

The leader jerked her out of the way, and the other two got Brit to his feet with no care at all for his wound. When the Apaches dragged him to his horse, Brit's head lolled, and he didn't try to walk at all. That's when she realized he'd lost consciousness—which was just as well.

They threw him up on the horse and tied his hands in the animal's long mane. An Apache snagged her arm and pushed her toward her horse. She mounted quickly.

They rode south for the rest of the day, through a mountain pass, across a scorching desert valley. Finally the Apaches took Brit and her up a hairpin trail onto a plateau. She was exhausted and knew Brit was in much worse shape than she was, yet she looked around to get her bearings in case they had a chance to escape.

They crossed a grassy meadow, then entered a village of brush huts at the edge of an oak forest.

The Apaches came out to watch them, but were silent. Finally they came to a hut where a white-haired Apache, bent with age, stood. Their captors stopped to confer with him.

Callista reined her horse close to Brit's and reached over to feel his forehead. He was burning up with fever.

The Apaches finished talking to the old man and led Brit's and her horses behind his hut to another one. Their captors untied Brit and pulled him off his horse, then dragged him inside the hut and left him.

In seconds they'd dropped the saddlebags and bed-rolls in the dwelling, too. Callista dismounted and pushed aside the deerhide covering the opening.

Brit lay on his stomach on the dirt floor. Callista dropped to her knees beside him and rolled him over, and supporting him with her arm, got him to drink some water. But after only a few swallows, he twisted sharply in pain and again slipped over the cliff into unconsciousness.

She opened one of the bedrolls and spread it beside him, then carefully rolled him onto it. She left him lying on his stomach and grabbed one of the canteens.

Ducking outside, she looked around for a stream but didn't see one. A little boy about four or five years old stood in the shade of a tree, watching her. She put the canteen up to her mouth and pretended to drink. He watched her impassively. She held the canteen out to him and pantomimed drinking again.

To her surprise, he snatched the canteen and ran away.

Dismayed, she watched him disappear among the huts. "Damn, he didn't understand," she muttered, before going back into the hut.

She swished the other canteen around. Was there enough water to clean Brit's wound? Well, there had to be. She ripped away most of his bandage, which was now filthy with trail dust and perspiration.

A rustling behind her made her turn. The little boy stood in the hut holding out the canteen—and it was dripping.

"Thank you." She took the canteen. Remembering that many of the Apaches understood Spanish, she added, "*Grácias. Grácias.*"

He nodded and ran out.

Callista pulled the last layer of bandages away from Brit's wound. As she'd feared, it was an angry red, with red streaks radiating out from it. She cleaned it carefully and bandaged it with the clean strip of her petticoat that she'd stuffed into her saddlebag. Then she rolled him onto his back.

A small fire was already burning in the hut, so she added the remaining jerky to some water and put it to cook.

Then she lay down beside Brit, resting her hand on him so she could feel any movement. She'd just rest her eyes for a few minutes. Then she'd feed the broth to Brit.

"Mama, you've got to get well!" The desperation in the child's voice brought Callista bolt upright out of sleep. It was Brit's voice, but it was a child's, too.

"Ssh." She leaned over him, stroking his forehead in an effort to calm him. He was burning up. Oh God, he was burning up!

"Mama, you can't die. I need you." He was a little boy again, and she pictured him sitting beside his mother's bed, holding her hand. She'd sat beside her sick mother's bed, too, when she was a little girl. She knew the countless fears that went through a child's mind at a time like that.

He began to thrash about, flinging his arms out wildly. "I'll always wear your medallion. I promise. Just don't die. Please . . . don't die." The overwhelming sadness in his voice broke her heart.

"Brit, ssh. It's all right." She clasped his good hand with hers.

He quieted for a few minutes, then his eyes opened wide. But they were blank and she knew he was seeing another time. "Mama, don't leave me. Mama . . . ?" He gave an anguished cry.

His eyes closed and he seemed to fall back asleep, but even so he was restless. She wanted to hold him in her arms and soothe him. But first she needed to cool him down and break the fever.

Callista talked to him and used the light from the dying fire to find the canteen and pour water onto a cloth. Then she wiped his face and kept up a stream of nonsense, not even listening to what she was saying, just trying to soothe him. She poured more water on the cloth and sponged his chest.

Oh God, they were alone in an Apache village and he was depending on her and she didn't know what to do. She had to help him fight the infection. She pulled his pants off so she could wet more of him down. More water. Sponge faster.

Oh God, please, don't let him die!

"Dog!" Brit was back in that little boy's time. He whimpered and moved his hand as if he were petting a dog. "Oh, Dog, not you, too." She pictured a little boy kneeling over his dying dog. "Don't leave me, Dog. I'll be all alone. Don't leave me . . ." His hand stopped moving.

He sank back into sleep, and Callista continued to sponge him, silent tears flowing down her cheeks.

Getting the bullet out hadn't saved him.

She loved him, and she was losing him.

Chapter 20

Dispatch to the *Times/Tribune* Newspapers

Much has happened since my last dispatch. I was captured by Apaches, rescued by the Chief of Scouts, then he and I were recaptured by Apaches. We are still prisoners and I am writing this dispatch in hopes, that if we do not survive, my notebook will be found.

I am snatching time to write unbeknownst to our captors, so these dispatches will be brief and you, dear readers, will have to fill in my terror at these disastrous events. My first capture occured when I was returning to Fort Bowie from an outlying ranch. Lieutenant Stanhope and I were set upon by Apaches and he managed to out run them, while I did not.

As soon as the Apaches had me, they turned south and rode hard. There is no river, no fence, no ditch, not even a sign at the Mexican border, but somehow I knew I had crossed into a foreign country. My heart ached and I wondered if I would ever see my home again.

Someone comes! Until next time, this is Callista Warwick.

* * *

The deerhide rustled as someone threw it back and ducked inside. She turned to see a gray-haired, barrel-chested man stomp across the dirt.

Pushing her aside, he knelt beside Brit and examined his wound as carefully as if he were a doctor. Rising to his feet, he called out. A short, wide Apache woman with a basket joined him and they bent over Brit.

The gray-haired one drew a nasty, long knife from his belt and the woman laid it in the fire.

"What are you doing?" Callista demanded. The woman came over to her, turned Callista around, and shoved her outside. "Wait," she cried, turning back to the entrance.

But a warrior stepped in front of her and folded his arms across his chest and stared at her. She tried ducking around him to the right and left, but each time he was there, barring her way.

She paced back and forth outside the hut.

She heard Brit moan. Then silence.

"What are they *doing*?"

The warrior stared at her impassively.

Callista waited for an eternity, all her attention focused on the hut. Finally, the Apaches came out and walked away. They didn't say anything or look at her; they just walked away.

She ducked inside. Brit still lay on his stomach, but now his whole shoulder was coated with a slimy green substance. She went to wipe it off, but some instinct made her hesitate.

If they'd wanted to kill him, he'd be dead now. So the green had to be something they used for infection. If she waited until morning before wiping it away, she would see if it was helping.

Staying clear of the green slime, she sponged his

skin again and again, trying to cool him.

Finally, she spread her bedroll beside him, lay down on her side facing him, and rested her hand on Brit so she would awaken if he moved. When she closed her eyes, it seemed to her that his breathing was less labored, and he didn't feel as feverish. She prayed that it was true.

Dawn had lightened the eastern sky when she awakened. Her hand was still on Brit, and he felt cooler. She moved her hand and felt him again. He *was* cooler. His fever must have broken during the night, for he was definitely better. She covered him with her blanket and lay down beside him.

She awoke when someone kicked her. Callista's eyes flew open and she stared up into the flat black eyes of the gray-haired Apache who'd come last night. He gestured for her to move away from Brit.

Callista stood up with as much dignity as she could and backed away, keeping a wary eye on him. He didn't pay her any attention at all, just knelt and roughly pulled Brit closer and examined the bullet hole in his back.

He grunted. Whether it was a good or bad grunt she didn't know. He reached into a half gourd he carried and brought up a handful of the green stuff and slopped it onto Brit's shoulder again. He let Brit fall back, then left.

Callista returned to Brit's side. He'd turned his head and his eyes were open. "Brit?" she said softly.

"Hmm?" His deep voice was weak, but it was the first time she'd heard it in an eternity, and she wanted to dance around the hut with joy.

"You *are* awake!" She brushed his hair back from his temple and stroked his cheek.

"Umm."

"Do you want water?"

"Umm."

He took only a few sips before he stopped, letting his head loll against her shoulder.

"Is that enough?"

"Umm."

She helped him lie back down, and he was asleep in seconds. But this time she knew it was different. Brit would live!

The black cloud that had dogged her lifted. Her heart began to swell with the knowledge that he would live.

She clamped her hands across her mouth as she gave way to tears of relief. Sobbing so deeply she made no noise, she cried until she could cry no more.

Brit would live!

Brit lay there trying to remember why he felt like hell. Why was he so weak? And why was he lying on his stomach? He tried to roll over and pain knifed through him, paralyzing him. He waited for it to ease, then slowly let himself back down on his stomach.

He wouldn't be turning over for a while. His eyes closed as sleep claimed him.

When he woke the next time, he was lying on his back staring up at a brush ceiling. Where was he?

Someone was puttering around out of his sight. He caught a whiff of a familiar scent and smiled.

"Cally." His voice was a harsh rasp that he didn't recognize.

Then she was kneeling beside him. "Thank God, you're awake, darling." She smoothed his hair back from his face. "Are you thirsty? Hungry?"

"Yes." She looked good enough to eat.

"Good, I've kept broth warm for you, waiting for you to wake up. I'll get it." Rising, she moved out of his sight.

He had a hazy memory of her cradling him against her and feeding him broth before. "Did I have some before?"

"Every time you woke up for the last two days," she said, returning with a gourdful of broth.

He must have been one sick puppy if he had so little memory of two days.

She helped him sit up and held the gourd to his lips. Thirsty, he drank most of it before he pushed it away.

"Thank you. What was in it?" She helped him lie back down.

"Parched corn, venison, and roots that one of the women gave me."

"That one of the women gave you?" Her scent was like balm to him and Brit drew it deep into his lungs. "Where are we?"

"An Apache village."

"Good Lord! I've been sick for two days? I'm sorry I wasn't awake for you. You must have been terrified to be in an Apache village."

She gave him a shy smile. "Actually, I never thought about it. I was too busy taking care of you."

"I owe you a lot, Cally. A lot." He trailed his fingers over her hand.

"Do you remember being shot?"

"No." That would explain why he felt like hell.

"It happened when you rescued me from the Apaches. Only you didn't tell me for hours, and by that time you'd lost a lot of blood. So I found a place for us to hide, but I didn't hide our tracks well enough, and the Apaches found us and brought us here."

"Where's here?"

"Someplace in Mexico."

"Why would Apaches bring a wounded White-eyes to their village? Why not just kill him?"

"I don't know, Brit," she said quietly, "but I'm grateful they did."

"I am, too." He wanted to ask her more, but he was too tired.

Callista sat beside him, just watching him sleep. It was such a relief to know it *was* sleep, not unconsciousness. The old man had come every morning and night and applied more of the green medicine that had saved Brit.

She didn't want to look back on those bleak, black hours when she had been afraid he'd die. "Thank you, God," she whispered as she brushed a kiss over his cheek.

The next time he awoke, Brit felt better and managed to roll onto his good side. Callista was kneeling beside the fire, stirring a pot.

"Cally." This time he recognized his voice.

She hurried to him. "Feeling better? Ready for more broth?"

"Ready for more than soup."

"Have the broth first," she said as she helped him sit up.

That was when he realized he was naked. A blanket had covered him in the morning, but now it was hot enough that he'd thrown it off. When Callista brought him the broth she didn't avert her eyes or even seem to notice his nakedness—which told him he'd been naked for several days.

He knew he should just leave it alone, but he had

to ask. "Why did you take my pants off?"

"You were burning up with fever. I was sponging you, trying to cool you down."

"Cally, you are a hell of a lady."

She blushed and averted her eyes.

He was finishing the second gourd of broth when the gray-haired man entered the hut.

"This is the man who put the green medicine on your infected wound, Brit." Callista stood up and moved back, making room for the old man beside Brit. "I don't know what it is, but it saved you."

As the man entered the firelight and Brit got a good look at him, he gave a long, low whistle. "You're sure this is the man?" he said in a quick aside to Callista.

"Yes, why?"

"Judas priest, I don't believe this."

The Apache grunted something and Brit replied. "Cally, he says you got the bullet out of me. Is that right?"

"Yes, but the wound got infected, and that's when you almost died. This medicine man stopped the infection." She picked up the canteen.

"Geronimo says you were a good nurse," Brit said, as she took a drink from the canteen.

Callista choked and dropped the canteen. "Geronimo?" she said in a wispy voice. Her eyes were saucer-big. "Geronimo?"

Brit shot her a searching look. "Didn't you know?"

"No! Thank God, I didn't, I would have been scared to death. I just thought he was a shaman." This gray-haired man didn't look like Satan or the Scourge of the West, two of his many names.

The Apache grunted something, and Brit turned over on his stomach. "I can't believe I'm turning my back on Geronimo," he said. "By rights, I should be dead by now."

The Apache knelt beside him and examined his wound. He said something to Brit, then left.

Callista waited until she was sure he was gone, then turned to Brit. "What's going on? I can't believe that Geronimo saved you. Why?"

Brit turned onto his back and slowly sat up. "I don't know. And *that* worries me a lot."

After that, Brit regained his strength quickly. By the next day he was sitting up without Callista's help. By the third, he'd pulled on his pants and was sitting outside in the sun.

Callista sat with him, happy to do anything with him after the scare she'd had. Men and women walked by and riders galloped by all day. The people looked at them but didn't stop or speak, although she made eye contact with some of the women and smiled.

That night, when she lay beside Brit, he pulled her close, wrapping his good arm around her and resting his hand on her breast. He turned his head and nuzzled her hair.

Callista lay there thinking how possessive his hand felt on her breast. And how right. He ran his thumb over her cotton shirt until he found her budding nipple.

"Why don't you take that damn shirt off?" he murmured.

"Because you're not well enough yet." She turned on her side and caressed his rugged, gaunt face.

"I'm well enough to look at you," he growled.

"You wouldn't just look. And you need to conserve your strength."

"I will. You'll do the work."

"Sleep. You want to get better, don't you?"

"Do you think it can get better between us?" he asked, pretending to misunderstand her.

"I don't know. You're the one with experience." She rose on her elbow and rained kisses all over his face. "That's a little advance, though."

That night they slept tangled together. The next morning he walked around the village. Slowly, but at least he walked. She walked with him. Men and women passed them but didn't speak, yet Callista didn't sense hostility toward them. It was more a wary alertness.

Naked children ran around the huts, playing games.

"Maybe we should turn back, Brit. You don't want to push your strength too far these first few days."

"Yeah, you're probably right." He turned back reluctantly.

As they walked, Callista glimpsed a long wooden crate in the wood pile beside a hut. The red letters on the side drew her eye. WINCHESTER REPEATING ARMS COMPANY, NEW HAVEN, CONNECTICUT. "Look at that," she said, pointing.

Brit walked over. "It's a shipping box for rifles," he said, "and it's not weathered, which means it hasn't been here long." Feeling along the sides, he found a bit of blue cloth caught on a nail.

Callista knelt beside him and also examined the box, hoping she'd find something more that they could use to identify the smugglers. "Look." Some long strands of blond hair were caught in a split in the wood. She wound them around her hand. "I'll put these in your saddlebags. It's a long shot, but maybe we can match them with someone."

"It is a long shot, all right. But it's better than nothing."

He was ready to lie down by the time they returned to the hut, and slept for the rest of the day. The next day he walked farther. And he did it twice.

Each day he walked more until he was circling the village several times on each walk. He was alone on the day he stopped at the Winchester Arms crate again, and he went over it carefully. It was slightly askew, as if the sides were beginning to separate. He felt in the crevices looking for anything. He found nothing.

He was about to give up when he felt a metal band wedged deep into the bottom corner. It felt like a ring, and he wiggled it back and forth until it came loose.

He recognized it as soon as he saw it. A West Point ring. Elation burst through him. He had the evidence he needed to find the gun smugglers!

He read the date on the ring. Class of 1852.

Warwick's ring. He had him!

Elation warred with dejection. Here was the proof he needed to link Warwick to the gun smuggling and stop him. But when he did, he'd lose Callista. He'd known all along that when he confronted her father, he'd lose her. But that had been sometime in the future.

Suddenly the future was now.

He pocketed the ring and walked on, torn between happiness and sadness. By the time he returned to their wickiup, sadness had overwhelmed any momentary happiness he'd felt.

That night he held Callista close and wondered how many more times he'd be able to.

A hundred times in the following days he thought

of telling her about the ring. A hundred times he held his tongue. For the moment, no one knew he had the ring. That gave him time to think.

They were sitting outside in the sun a few days later, when an Apache galloped up and leaped off his horse. A red headband kept his long black hair out of his eyes, and he wore tan pants and a white shirt, like so many of the Apaches, but he seemed vaguely familiar.

"Callista, are you all right?" he asked as he strode toward them.

"Who are you?" she asked, jumping up. She was surprised he could speak English so well. Why did he look familiar?

"Stalking Wolf! Am I glad to see you." Brit slowly rose to his feet.

Callista looked at him, surprised. Was this Apache one of his scouts?

"Maybe you can explain what's going on," Brit added as they shook hands, clasping the other's arm in the way of old friends.

"Stalking Wolf?" Callista echoed.

The Apache smiled. "I forgot that you wouldn't recognize me. Does this jog your memory?" He bowed and kissed the back of her hand as he had done at the welcoming ball. And it came back to her. Aurora Spencer Winthrop and her husband, Ethan Winthrop.

"Ethan?" Callista couldn't believe the difference between their first meeting and now, when he seemed an uncivilized savage. "Is it really you? I don't know what to call you. Ethan or Stalking Wolf?

"I answer to both," he said. Then he turned to Brit. "I came because of you. A warrior brought me the news that you'd been badly wounded and were a captive. And he brought me this." He held out his fist and opened it, revealing Brit's medallion.

"My medallion." Brit's eyes lit up. He picked it up by the broken chain. It turned slowly, glittering in the sunlight. He glanced at Callista. "I lost it when I fought the Apache in the dark. I felt the chain break, but there was no time to stop and pick it up. I had to get you away."

He'd lost his most precious possession when he rescued her—and he'd never said a word. Her heart felt as if it would burst, she was so filled with love for him. She slipped her arm through his. "I discovered it was gone while you were delirious," she said softly, "but I hoped you didn't know."

"I knew," he said in that velvet-gravel voice she loved. Then he turned to Wolf, and his tone became brisk. "How did you wind up with it?"

"The warrior found it and opened it. He looked at the pictures and immediately brought it to Geronimo. And when Geronimo saw what was inside, he sent it on to me."

"Why? Is there some hidden treasure in it that I don't know about?" He ran his thumb over the medallion.

"Who are the people in the pictures, Brit?"

"My parents." He opened it and gazed at the fading photographs, yellowed with age. "My mother gave it to me when she was dying."

"Do you know your father's name?"

"No." Brit looked down at the picture for several long moments before he continued. "She was trying to tell me, when she died."

"Come, my friend, let us sit—for we have much to talk about." Wolf clasped Brit's good shoulder.

Brit gave him a wary look. "Why? What's going on?"

"You shall see."

Callista sat on a boulder while Brit chose the ground next to her, resting his good arm across her lap.

"Fire away," he said to Stalking Wolf.

Callista rested her hand on Brit's shoulder, hoping he understood that she was giving him her support and her love.

"Geronimo recognized your father, because long ago, he was married to Geronimo's younger sister—my mother."

Brit was silent for several moments. "Your mother? Good Lord, I am glad I'm sitting."

Stalking Wolf nodded. "His name is Tobias Winthrop, and he's one of the Boston Winthrops."

Brit frowned at him. "Say again? His name is Winthrop? How do you know?"

"He's my father, too," Wolf said gently.

"What?" Callista felt his hand tighten on her knee. "He was *your* father?" Brit shook his head, as if clearing away cobwebs. "We're half brothers? All these years I've known you and—We're really brothers?"

"We are blood brothers, my friend." Wolf was silent, letting Brit deal with the incredible news.

"Is that why Geronimo saved me? Us," he added, glancing at Callista.

"Yes, but it's more complicated than that. You see, Tobias's family had a gold mine in Mexico, and when he was visiting it, he was ambushed and left for dead in the wilderness. My mother found him and nursed him back to health—except that he'd lost his memory. He didn't know who he was. So he became an Apache.

"And your father," Brit clarified.

"Exactly."

"How do you know all this, if he lost his memory?" Brit asked. He felt stunned, as if a horse had thrown him. He'd looked for his bastard father ever since he could remember—twenty years. He'd intended to beat the hell out of him, for abandoning his mother. What the hell kind of man would do that?

Now, to learn not only his father's name, but who he was . . . to learn that he had a brother, when for his whole life he'd had no family except his mother . . .

"Our village was attacked by Bluecoats. The shock of seeing my mother killed restored our father's memory."

Rising, Brit began to pace. "Where is he now? I want to see him." Hate seethed through him like hot lava. Finally, he'd confront him; tell him what he'd done to the girl he abandoned.

Stalking Wolf stepped in front of him and clasped his upper arms. "Take it easy, my brother. You are wounded."

I am only wounded in the shoulder. Our father wounded my mother in the heart. It took her a long time to die, but it was because of him!

"Where is he?" Brit gritted. He stood, stiff and bristling.

"He lies in a grave in Boston." Wolf's voice deepened. "As soon as we returned to Boston, he began looking for a girl he'd loved there many years before, but she was gone."

Hope rose within Brit. "My mother?"

"She had gone to Chicago. Is that where you and

your mother were?" Brit nodded. "He must have loved her very much, because he went to Chicago twice a month, looking for her."

"If he really loved her, he would have found her. He didn't." His mother could have died happy if he'd found them. Maybe she wouldn't have died at all.

Callista cleared her throat and both men looked at her. "When did you go to Boston, Stalking Wolf?" she asked softly.

"The fall of sixty-four."

Brit's elation turned to sorrow. "It was too late. Mother died in sixty-two."

Silence enveloped them, each lost in their own thoughts.

Brit felt stunned. To know that his father had searched for his mother, that he hadn't abandoned her. A new wave of grief for his mother flooded him. She had gone to her grave not knowing that she was loved by the man she had loved for so many years.

Callista looked from one to the other. "You know, there is a resemblence. Really, there is. Look at yourselves in a mirror someday."

Her heart was filled with warmth, knowing that after all these years, Brit had found his family. Family was the arms around you, supporting you through life—no matter what you did. Brit had never had that. He didn't know what it was like.

She had seen him and Wolf clasp hands as friends. Now they would clasp hands as brothers.

Wolf finally broke the silence. "Our father loved two women, Brit, and he lost them both. His heart died with them. He became a shell of a man, withering away until he died."

Brit rubbed his hand over the back of his neck tensely. "You went back to Boston with him, didn't you? I'll bet his family welcomed you with open arms."

Wolf shook his head. "There was no room for him or me in that family. They had already decided who would inherit what. But he was the eldest son, so when he returned he inherited everything—the money, the ships, the hate, the envy."

"And you were his eldest son."

"We thought so at the time, but you must be older than me. Which means you are the eldest son—the inheritor of everything."

Brit shook his head. "My father didn't acknowledge me during his life. I want nothing from him or his family, least of all his name." He took a deep breath. "Do you know how I got the name Chance? My mother's father was a minister, and when he learned that his daughter was pregnant, he threw her out of the house. His parting words to her were, "You took a chance. Now live with it."

"Oh, Brit," Callista murmured, her heart aching for him. She wrapped her arms around his waist and leaned against him.

"Our Winthrop family is very wealthy. You could be a wealthy man."

"Did you want the money?" Brit asked curiously.

Wolf shook his head. "No. I am rich in the things that matter. I love a woman who loves me. We make babies together. And I am an Apache; I am surrounded by family all my days. Those are the things that are important." He paused, then continued. "Today I have added to my family a brother. What more could a man want?"

Brit nodded. "I started this day as I've started every day since my mother died: alone, with no blood relatives in the world. And now I have a brother. It has been a very good day," he finished with a lop-sided smile.

"I guess that explains why Geronimo nursed Brit," Callista said.

Wolf's brows rose in surprise. "Geronimo nursed you? You must have been very sick."

"He almost died." Her voice broke with emotion. She looked away, fighting the tears that burned her eyes as she remembered how close death had come to him.

Brit smoothed his hands down her back.

When she again had control of her voice, Callista said, "If you hadn't fought with that Apache that night, Brit, and if he hadn't grabbed your medallion, none of this would have come out."

"Sometimes the Great Spirit works in strange ways," Wolf said thoughtfully. "Especially when Brit rescued you, Callista. Because, you see, you didn't need rescuing."

Callista clamped her hands to her waist and gave him a disbelieving look. "Easy for you to say; you weren't there."

"You are right. I did not walk in your moccasins. However, you were under Nana's protection. His warriors would have done nothing to harm you."

"No one told me. I lived in terror from one minute to the next."

Wolf inhaled sharply. "For that I am sorry. There is no way I can take away the fear you felt. Capturing you was done on the spur of the moment. Nana had talked about thanking you for rescuing his grandson. When his warriors saw you riding alone except for the forked-tongue one, they decided to bring you to him."

"Isn't this an awfully long way for me to come for

him to say thanks?" Callista asked doubtfully.

"Nana is an old man. His world has changed around him. Sometimes he does things that don't fit with our modern times."

"So where is he?" She crossed her arms. "No one has spoken to either of us."

"I would like you to meet Nana." He looked from Brit to Callista. "Both of you."

Brit nodded. "All right. He started a hell of a chain of events."

After Wolf strode away, Callista and Brit went back inside the wickiup. There, away from prying eyes, Callista walked into Brit's arms. "Oh, Brit, I'm so happy for you. You've discovered a blood relative." She hugged him. "There's nothing so important as blood. It really is thicker than water, you know."

"Yes, I know."

Her words brought sadness that threatened to overwhelm his joy at finding a brother. They confirmed what he already knew and were a warning that his days of holding her and loving her were dwindling away.

He could feel her father's ring in his pocket and its weight seemed to grow with each passing day.

He hugged her to him with his good arm and buried his face in her hair. For as many days as he had, he would love her and cherish her and protect her.

For she was more important than breath. She was his heart.

Chapter 21

<hr />

Dispatch to the *Times/Tribune* Newspapers

We are still prisoners of the Apaches.

On the second night of my captivity, while the Apaches slept, I was rescued by the Chief of Scouts, who had been tracking them since my capture. We fled in a hail of bullets.

The Chief of Scouts was wounded. I didn't know this until hours later and by that time he had lost much blood. We hid and I removed a bullet from his shoulder.

The Apaches searched ceaselessly for us. Despite my care in hiding, they found us, and took us many miles deeper into Mexico. By that time, the Chief of Scouts' wound was badly infected and I feared greatly for his life.

It hung by a single frayed thread when we arrived here and I despaired of saving him. A shaman began applying Apache medicine to his wound twice a day.

We have been here three days now and I believe the Chief of Scouts will live. We are guarded, but not tied.

Callista Warwick, in an Apache village in Mexico.

Callista didn't know how long she'd been in Brit's arms, when she became aware of someone coughing outside the hut. Reluctantly she loosened her hug while Brit did the same.

When they came out, they found Wolf. She was struck anew by the resemblence between Brit and him.

"Are you all right?" Callista asked, concerned about Brit's new brother. "We heard you coughing."

He smiled. "That is the Apache version of knocking on the front door. Nana would like to meet you. I will translate."

The stooped, white-haired man Callista had seen on her first night in the village sat cross-legged on the ground before his wickiup. A red headband kept his white hair out of his eyes. Like Wolf, he wore tan pants and a white shirt.

"We will wait for Nana to speak." Stalking Wolf sat down next to Nana. "He is the eldest, so out of respect to him, it is the custom to let him choose to start and end our conversation."

Callista sat so close to Brit, their knees brushed. And that was just fine with her, because she loved touching him. And she loved having him touch her just as much.

Brit crossed his arms and sat very straight, giving no hint that he'd been wounded. The old man also crossed his arms and sat very straight, and looked at them for what seemed hours before he spoke.

"Nana says he is glad the woman with *hoddentin* hair and eyes like the flowers in the high mountain meadows is educating his grandson in the ways of the White-eyes, and he hopes that you will continue his education," Wolf translated.

" 'Eyes like the flowers in mountain meadows'? I like that, Cally." Brit's low voice stroked her, all sunshine and honey. "I'll remember that."

Callista felt her cheeks grow heated and knew she was blushing. "Teaching George was a pleasure. He's so bright. George is his White-eyes name," she added quickly.

Nana listened to Wolf, nodding all the while. Then he said something that surprised Wolf, for he glanced at the old man before he translated. "It seems Nana intended to ask you to teach the children here. But he has realized that White-eyes women are not adaptable like Apache women and that you would be more trouble than you're worth." Wolf's upper lip twitched. "Still, he wants to thank you for aiding his grandson when the bad ones fought with him."

Nana began to speak again, and Wolf questioned him before he translated. "Brit, Nana wants you to know that your woman fought for you when you were ill. He would have spoken to her before this, but she was busy nursing you. He wishes you well in your life together." Wolf grinned. "I'm just translating."

Callista eyed the ground, smiling.

As they walked back to the wickiup, Wolf said, "Can you be ready to leave by tomorrow morning? I'd like to lead you out of here myself."

Brit stopped and gripped Wolf's shoulder. "What's wrong, brother?"

"Many of the people have slipped away from the village over the past few days because the Mexicans are getting ready to raid this village. I want you out of here before they come."

"We will be ready."

Brit followed Callista into their wickiup. If they were leaving tomorrow, he had to tell her about her father's ring. He could no longer put it off. She deserved to have time to think, to decide what she'd do when they returned to Fort Bowie.

He caught her hand and swung her around into his waiting arms. "Callista," he said, wondering how many more times he would hold her, "we need to talk. Let's go for a walk."

She leaned back in his arms, giving him an assessing look. "This sounds important."

"It is." He wanted to tighten his arms around her and never let her go.

"All right, let's go." Would she finally find out why he'd been preoccupied for days? He held her and loved her with such tenderness and yearning that her heart sang. But even as her heart sang, she was afraid. There was a poignancy in his lovemaking that made her fear the future.

And there were times when she'd catch him unawares and there would be such a look of sadness on his beloved face that she'd want to cry out to him, ask him what was wrong.

But she was afraid she knew. Their days together were dwindling. She knew it with an instinct that was older than time itself.

The forest was rich with the wet, earthy scent of loam, but Callista also caught whiffs of Brit's sagebrush scent as as she followed him along the narrow, winding path. Sunlight splashed through the leaves, forming pools of light among the green shadows beneath the leaves.

They were far from the village when Brit finally stopped. "I think you should see this." He reached into his pants pocket and brought out a ring, which he dropped into her hand.

"I didn't know you had a West Point ring," she said, examining the ring. It was a bloodstone, like her father's, symbolizing blood shed for the United States.

"I don't. That's not mine. It's your father's."

She turned it over and read the tiny writing. Class of 1852. A cold knot formed in her stomach. She swallowed to wet her suddenly dry mouth. "Where did you get this?"

"I found it in that Winchester Arms rifle box."

"You did not! We searched that box together. This ring wasn't in there."

He rubbed the back of his neck tensely. "I went back later to look at the box again and noticed that it was beginning to come apart. So I felt in the crevices between the sides and the bottom, and it was wedged in there."

Callista wanted to yell at him that he was lying, but she knew he wasn't. He was too honorable to plant evidence and lie about something so important.

"How do you think it got there?" She crossed her arms over her stomach and rubbed her upper arms against the chill inside her.

"I don't know. Maybe the rifles were packed so tightly, he took it off and laid it on the edge of the box. Somehow it got knocked into the box and he didn't notice or forgot it was there."

This was the evidence Brit needed to unravel the identity of the gun smugglers. And it tied Papa to them. She shivered at the implications. Could he really be a smuggler, working against his own country?

Oh God, she wanted it not to be true. Just as she wished Brit had never found the ring. But he had.

She walked away from Brit to a pool of sunlight and stood in it, trying to melt the iceberg growing inside her. "What will you do with it?"

"You know what I'll do with it. Turn it over to

General Crook, since he's head of the Apache campaign."

And then would come General Crook's charges, and a court-martial. And that would be the end of Papa's career and his run for the presidency. All he and Mamere had worked for, for the last twenty years.

She knew the answer to her next question before she asked it, because Brit was an honorable man. That sense of honor was one of the things she loved about him. But she still had to ask it; otherwise, she would always wonder.

"Is there a chance that you could lose the ring?"

He was silent so long, she wondered if he *was* considering it. "I couldn't live with the kind of man I would be, if I did that, Callista." His voice was low, measured. "And I don't think you could, either."

"I'll take my chances," she said, beginning to get angry. *Why did he have to discover that damn ring?* she thought. "You've suspected my father from the beginning, haven't you?"

"What do you mean?" He didn't move, yet she knew he'd tensed. And he was watching her too intently. She was missing something—something that was out in plain sight.

"I heard you talking in the stable the day after we arrived at Fort Bowie. You said Papa was your prime suspect." She began to pace across the sunlit glade. What should she see that she wasn't?

"Callista, listen to me. I want to stop that flow of rifles to the Apache renegades. And yes, your father has been on my list of suspects. But Fowler Stanhope is also on my list."

"He's a much better candidate as a smuggler. I wouldn't be surprised if that blond hair is his."

"I wouldn't be either, but that's not relevant right now. We're talking about your father."

She turned and frowned at him. "How did you know he had financial trouble? Who told you he had money worries?"

"Callista, I—" He raked his fingers through his hair.

"My God, you've been spying on Papa ever since you came to Fort Bowie. Who are you working for? General Crook? Of course! That's why he ordered you back to duty at Fort Bowie, isn't it." She snapped her fingers as the pieces fell into place. "He's who you were going to telegraph when I walked into the Tombstone telegraph office that day! That's why you didn't telegraph him: you didn't want me to know who the telegram was going to." She paced away, furious. "Were you using me for your spying, too? Did you get anything useful?"

"Stop it!" He was right behind her as she turned. "You know what's between us has nothing to do with your father."

"The hell I do! You—"

He hauled her up in his arms and kissed her hard. Did she really think he'd use her to get to her father? At first her lips were ice, but he kissed her until he felt her begin to soften and respond. When he raised his head, her lips were rosy and waiting for him to return and her eyes were passion-darkened. "There were only two people in that kiss, Callista. You and me."

She snapped out of his arms as if he'd burned her and walked away without looking back. He waited for her, but she didn't return, and he realized she'd gone on to their wickiup.

Callista was a tumultuous, chaotic, seething mass

of emotions, from anger at Brit for finding the damn ring, to an overriding sadness for what she and Brit had had. She'd feared the future, but it had leaped up and bitten her before she even knew it was there.

She wanted Brit's arms around her, and felt like a traitor to her father for wanting them.

Brit was quiet that evening.

When they crawled beneath the blankets that night, Callista turned to Brit and he wrapped his arms around her and held her through the night.

Callista lay awake, absorbing the many textures of this man she loved: the steely hardness of his muscles beneath the tautness of his skin, the soft curls on his chest, the wiry hair on his legs.

In the middle of the night, she shook Brit awake. "Brit, do you remember what Wolf said about Nana's warriors?" She sprawled over him, her hair hanging down in a blond curtain around them.

"All right, I'll bite. What did Wolf say?" He filled his hands with her curves.

"Nana's warriors saw me riding with the 'forked-tongued' one." He nestled her down on his chest.

"Yeah, Fowler. So?"

"They had to have dealt with him! Why else would they have a name for him and know that he's a liar?"

"Which means that he's definitely smuggling rifles."

They were ready when Stalking Wolf came at dawn the next morning. He escorted them down the trail from the plateau, then north for several days.

"This is where I leave you," he said one afternoon, as they rested near a creek in the shade of a palo verde tree. "You're only about a day and a half south of the border. Just follow the trail and even if you lose it, keep heading north until you see the Chiricahua Mountains. You'll know where you are then."

"Where are you going, Wolf?" Callista asked.

"Back to the stronghold. I want to talk to Geronimo, and try to make him see that if he raids in both the United States and Mexico, both armies will be after him, and there will be no safe place for the Apaches who are with him. He must stop, or too many people will die."

Wolf hugged Brit. "Go with care, my brother." Then he hugged Callista. "You take care, too."

And he rode away, back to the south.

Brit led the way north. That afternoon they happened upon a tiny valley carpeted with wildflowers in white, gold, and purple, whose spicy scent perfumed the air. At one end, a waterfall leaped from a cliff and fell into a pool of turquoise water.

"We'll camp here," Brit said. He unsaddled the horses and hobbled them, then turned them loose to graze.

He took off his shirt as he walked into camp. He wanted to make love to Callista in this beautiful place. If this was their last time—No! He wouldn't think like that.

"Callista," he said softly. She turned toward him and he gathered her to his heart. "When we were at my ranch, I promised you that the next time we bathed together, we would do it right."

"Is that what you promised?" she said lightly. She rested her hand on his chest and twirled his soft curls over her fingers.

"It's next time now. And I keep my promises. Come on."

It was like walking through Eden, with the scent of the flowers rising from their footsteps. He held her hand in his and looked at her and knew she was his Eve.

When they reached the pool, Brit found that Callista had already been there—and laid out a towel and soap.

"I see you remember my promises, too." His heart swelled with need.

"Maybe." She gave him a come-hither smile that ignited a slow fire in his belly.

They sat to pull off their boots and socks, then Brit held out a hand to help her up. She took it, letting him pull her into his arms. "Let me do this," she murmured as she unbuckled his belt. "Save your strength for more important things."

She slipped her fingers inside the top of his fly. She could feel his skin moving against the backs of her fingers as she undid the buttons on his fly and opened it. She slid her hands inside, feeling the wiry, soft texture of his hair and the warmth of his skin, delighting in his swiftly indrawn breath.

"Woman," he growled, his eyes mere silver slits as he gazed down at her. He clamped his large hands over hers, stilling them, as he took her mouth with his and kissed her, hot and hard. Then he released her hands. "You are the most important thing."

She slid his pants down, ready with need for him.

"My turn," he said, reaching for her shirt. He unbuttoned it rapidly and helped her out of it, then her skirt.

"Cally, you don't know how much I've wanted to do this." He filled his hands with the fullness of her breasts and teased her sensitive nipples with his thumbs. Slowly he bent her back over his arm as he took a nipple in his mouth and suckled.

Callista sighed and floated on the beloved feel of

his mouth and hands on her. She felt her bones begin to soften.

One by one, he pulled the hairpins out of her hair, letting it fall in a golden cloak over her shoulders. "You don't know how much I want you."

"Oh, yes, I do." She pulled away from him and ran into the water. "Bet you can't catch me."

He picked up the soap and followed her. Callista turned around in the middle of the pool and waited for him. Sunbeams sparkled through her hair, falling over her shoulders.

She looked like a water nymph, bathed in sunlight. Her breasts were beautiful, and the nipped-in curve of her waist widened into luscious hips, framing the darker hair between her legs.

He wanted to explore every square inch of her. Several times a day. For the rest of his life. But he knew it wasn't to be.

So he would give her his love and take away memories to last a lifetime. For they were all he would have of her.

"Turn around," he said. "I'll do your back first." And he did, with long soapy strokes that made her shudder in his hands.

He paused, wanting her so much he ached. Yet in his heart, there was already the sadness of farewell.

He pulled her back against himself, savoring the feel of her against him, telling himself to live only for the moment.

Soon his soap-slicked hands slid over and around and under her breasts. "Oh, Brit, I can't wait much longer," Callista said breathlessly as she arched her head back against his shoulder.

He soaped his hands and slid them down between

her legs. Callista trembled as his fingers slid into her most secret places.

"Enough," she gasped, turning her soap-slick body in the circle of his arms. "My turn." She held out her hand for the soap.

Brit absorbed the sensations of having her pressed against him. Her nipples were pointy and hard against his chest. His own hardness was sliding over the smooth curve of her hip. She soaped his chest in circles that kept her hands moving over his skin in wide, erotic paths that didn't help his breathing at all.

Then she moved lower, soaping him with long, slow strokes that had him stopping her all too soon. "Stop! Or I won't be able to!"

She slid soapy hands over his abdomen and lower into the forest of hair, then knelt in the water to do his legs.

She only got partway up his second leg before he reached for her. She came up out of the water like a sea nymph, all wet and slick.

They stood under the tumbling waterfall to rinse off, splashing in the sun-warmed water, delaying what they knew was coming. Anticipating.

Passion had darkened Callista's eyes to a violet that was deep enough to swim in. Brit knew his eyes carried the same awareness. He lifted her high. "Wrap your legs around my waist and your arms around my shoulders," he said, as he positioned himself at her entrance.

After she did, he entered her in a long, smooth glide that made her shiver and exhale a long sigh.

"Yes," she whispered against the side of his throat, nipping him gently at the same time.

"Hang on, Cally," he murmured. "Hang on." He

felt her growing more and more tight around him as he moved in and out.

"Brit!" She clamped down on his shoulder with her teeth, but didn't bite. She went rigid, then she shattered into golden rain, falling all over him.

He yelled as he climaxed, holding her tightly as he felt her contracting around him.

He rested his forehead against her breasts, not wanting to let her go. She rested her head on his shoulder and held him.

Slowly he felt himself slip out of her, and felt a sense of loss and sadness. He needed her. He would always need her.

"Ready for one more dip?" he murmured against the satin skin of her breast.

"Yes." She sighed as he carried her underneath the waterfall again.

When they were clean, he swept her back into his arms. She threw her arms around his sturdy neck as he stepped out of the pool and kept walking. "Where are you taking me?"

"To make love in a field of flowers." He laid her down in the soft grass amid the white, gold, and purple flowers. Callista leaned back on her elbows and watched him pick large handfuls of the flowers, then he slowly showered her with them.

The petals were silky soft and clung to her still-wet flesh. Slowly, never taking his eyes from hers, Brit knelt between her legs.

He kissed the inside of her knee, then worked slowly up the sensitive flesh of her inner thigh, to the soft curls that guarded the entrance to her womb.

Callista closed her eyes and absorbed the myriad sensations of being adored and cherished, as only a man who loved her could do it.

She shivered and trembled. A delicious throbbing blossomed deep within her. As he brushed kisses up one thigh, then the other, his silky hair slid across her sensitive skin in haunting caresses. She wrapped her fingers in his hair, wanting him. Closer. Closer.

Then he kissed her. There.

"Brit," she gasped, bucking in surprise. "Don't . . . I . . . y-e-s." Her whole body arched away from the ground when his fingers entered her. Then she shattered into rainbows in his arms.

She was still flying when he slid into her and felt her immediate contractions around him. Brit gritted his teeth and fought for self-control and held her tightly. He suckled and tongued her aroused nipples.

"Oh, Brit," she said, gasping and laughing at the same time, "I can't believe I—"

He just held her and moved slowly in her, savoring the sensations welling up in him. Her eyes widened and went dark with passion.

"Not again." She sighed. "I can't."

"Yes, you can." He moved faster and she began to meet his rhythm with her own, arching up to meet him and take all of him. "You can." Faster. "You can." Faster.

"B-r-i-t-!" Her head fell back and she arched up and went rigid, then she came apart in his arms.

"Cal . . . ly!" he cried as he felt his explosion begin. She was locked in his embrace as he quaked with the force of his own shattering moment.

Brit didn't know how long it was before he was aware again. Callista's eyes were closed, and she was still panting.

"Darling, are you all right?" He brushed a golden curl away from her cheek.

"Yes. But I'm so boneless I can't move." She

locked her fingers around his neck and punctuated her words with kisses all over his sweat-slick body. He trembled with each kiss, savoring it, storing its memory away.

He didn't want to move while he was still in her. Only when he felt them becoming two again, did he roll to her side.

The spicy-sweet fragrance of the petals they'd crushed between their bodies enveloped them and mingled with the heady scent of their lovemaking.

He closed his eyes, knowing a special deep sadness. Was this their last time?

Was this their farewell?

Callista lay there, listening to Brit's steady breathing, touching him and wondering how many more times she'd touch him. Did they have any time left?

Or had they run out of time?

Chapter 22

Dispatch to the *Times/Tribune* Newspapers

I have learned that I was captured because of the Apache boy I was teaching. One day he was set upon by ruffians who ganged up on him. I stopped the fight and rescued him, which appeared to be the end of the incident. But it wasn't.

The child's grandfather is a great chief who wished to discuss the education of Apache children with me. That is why his warriors captured me and why I was unharmed throughout my stay in the Apache village.

After the Chief of Scouts and I conferred with him, we were released and headed north to Arizona with information about the traitors who have been smuggling guns to the renegade Apaches. The Chief of Scouts is in hot pursuit of these men as I write this dispatch.

The Chief of Scouts and I are not the only ones who have survived an Apache captivity. Dr. Aurora Spencer Winthrop, whom I introduced to my readers in a previous column, also survived one.

Callista Warwick, reporting from Arizona Territory.

* * *

It was after dark when they rode into Fort Bowie. Brit dropped Callista at her parents' house, then took the horses on to the stables.

"Mamere, Papa, I'm home," she called as she ran up the steps into their waiting arms. And even as she said it, she knew it was a lie. Her heart's home was with Brit.

After all the hugs and questions, Callista took her father aside. In his den/office, she told him about his ring and where Brit had found it. He said he'd lost his ring a month earlier and denied everything.

She tried to talk to him again at breakfast, and he angrily accused her of not believing him. When he left, she followed him down the steps and along the road to the headquarters building, trying to get him to listen. But he would have none of it.

Wearily she continued down to the stable, where she'd arranged to meet Brit. When she entered, she saw that he had a horse tethered in the alleyway and was grooming him.

As she neared, she recognized Red. "Red is all right? I'm so glad. I know he means a lot to you, and I thought the Apaches killed him when they snatched me."

Brit had a currycomb in each hand and was alternating long strokes over the red horse's sleek coat. "He was badly wounded, but Walks-with-Horses was able to save him."

He rested one elbow on the animal's broad back as he turned to look at her. "How did it go?"

"Not very well," Callista said in a small, defeated voice. That was how she felt, too. She yearned for Brit to hold her and soothe her, yet she knew she couldn't go into his arms until the matter of her father was settled.

She slumped down on a rickety old stool. "I talked until I was blue in the face, but Papa won't resign. He says he lost the ring over a month ago. He was insulted that I would even think he could be involved with smugglers. And he wants his ring back."

"That will be up to General Crook." Brit wanted to take her in his arms and comfort her, but knew he couldn't. Because once he had her in his arms, he didn't know if he would ever let go again.

So the court-martial of her father had to be finished before they could see if they had a future together.

He moved to the far side of Red, putting the horse between them as an added barrier. He was weak where she was concerned.

"Do you believe him?" he asked. Would she believe Fowler, if Fowler linked her father to the smuggling? Because his gut feeling said Warwick and Stanhope were in it together.

Callista's head snapped up. "Of course I believe him. He's my father."

"Ahh, such loyalty, Callista. Would you believe him if you weren't his daughter?" He groomed Red's back.

She stretched out her long legs, legs that held him so close when they made love. "Yes. Papa is not an actor. He was genuinely insulted when I questioned him about our money situation. He says he's been to the gold mine in Mexico, and knows the money he's been depositing to his account is coming from there."

"All right, let's see what we can shake out of Fowler." He was trying to help her, but if she'd said anything to him, he would have denied it.

Callista smiled up at him, her eyes sparkling more than he'd seen in the days since they'd left the Apache village.

"Thank you, Brit. Do you have a plan?"

"I have an outline." He led Red into a stall. "We'll fill in the blanks now. Let's go for a walk and work everything out."

Late that afternoon, Callista walked into the headquarters building with a dispatch. After Sergeant Mac sent it off, she stayed around, leaning against the railing that separated the desks from the common area and chatting with him.

Through the windows, she could see that the purple-black storm clouds that had been building over the Chiricahua Mountains all afternoon were rolling down the slopes and headed straight for the fort. The glass panes rattled with the low rumble of thunder.

"Looks like we're going to have a real gully washer," Sergeant Mac said.

"I'm afraid so," said John Piney as he walked in, according to plan. "I'm glad you're all right, Callista," he added with real warmth in his voice.

Would the storm affect Brit's plan?

Then Russ Caruso walked in, according to plan as well. "Hello, Callista, and welcome back." He hugged her. "Tell me about your adventures."

She was giving them a highly edited version when Fowler Stanhope entered.

"Callista, I heard that you'd escaped from the Apaches." He went to the table in the corner and poured himself a cup of coffee from the coffeepot that sat over a warming candle.

"Yes, I did." She wanted to add, *no thanks to you, Fowler,* but held her tongue. Would he apologize for leaving her when the Apaches chased them?

He leaned against the table and crossed his arms

over his chest as he contemplated her. "I hear you and Chance had quite an adventure."

"Yes, we did," Brit said from the doorway. "We found out who was smuggling guns to the renegades, Fowler."

"Who?" Fowler didn't stiffen or move except to drink some coffee.

"Officers in the United States Army. And trading with the enemy is treason. Those officers will be court-martialed and shot." His voice was steel-hard.

Fowler shrugged. "What the hell do I care?"

Callista saw her father's office door open a crack and realized he was listening.

"I'll show you."

Brit reached for something on the porch, then shoved an Apache, his hands tied in front of him, inside and followed him in.

Beyond him, wind-whipped dust devils whirled across the parade ground and thunder rumbled, close enough to make the whole building shake.

"Who's that, another renegade?" Fowler asked.

"Yes, as a matter of fact he is." Brit pulled his revolver, pointed it at the Apache, and cocked it.

Callista stiffened. Brit's acting was a lot more re-alistic than she'd expected. She felt the menace in him, even though she knew the Apache was a scout that Brit had recruited to play the renegade.

"And this one has been trading with the officers smuggling rifles to the Apaches. So he's going to identify them."

He spoke in Apache. The Apache scrutinized them all. He pointed to Fowler.

"That's ridiculous," Fowler snapped. "You can't believe some damn Apache over me." He looked around the room, at Russ Caruso and John Piney, at

Callista and Brit, but no one said anything. "You don't have anything connecting me to the guns," he sneered.

But he didn't deny it, Callista noticed.

"Yes, we do, Fowler," she said with great satisfaction. "In the Apache village we found a box from Winchester Repeating Arms Company, in New Haven. Isn't that where your sick aunt is?"

"You still don't have anything connecting me to any gun smuggling."

Callista opened her notebook and took out the blond hair strands. She'd glued one end of each strand to a piece of paper so they now formed a clump of blond hair. "We found these caught in that box. We all know how many blond Apaches there are."

"How do I know that? Besides, it could be your hair, not mine."

"My hair is a different shade of blond. Yours is much darker." She walked over to him and held the clump up.

"Looks like a perfect—"

He flung the coffee cup toward Brit and grabbed Callista with his left hand, jerking her in front of him. He wrapped his left arm around her throat, keeping her in front, shielding him. At the same time, he pulled his revolver and leveled it at Callista's head.

"Nobody move!" Fowler yelled.

In the silence, Callista heard the coffee cup rocking on the uneven floor and the spatter of the first raindrops hitting the roof.

The click as Fowler cocked his revolver was loud in her ear. She could smell whiskey on his breath.

Callista watched Brit, who watched Fowler with a deadly intensity. He would save her.

"Go ahead, Chance," Fowler goaded. "Shoot. Kill her."

"You bastard!"

Callista's father walked out of his office at that moment. "Drop that gun, Fowler," he ordered in his parade-ground voice.

"The hell I will." Fowler's eyes blazed with a strange fire. "I'm not going down for gun smuggling alone, Warwick. You were in it with me, and I'll tell everyone."

Everyone looked at Callista's father.

"Shut up, you two-bit liar," her father snarled.

"You knew our gold mine was repeating rifles. You're as crooked as me. Get over there with Russ. And everyone drop their weapons. You first, Chance. You too, Russ."

Brit's revolver clattered to the floor. Russ's followed.

Fowler's arm was pressing on her windpipe, cutting off her air, and Callista felt herself growing dizzy. She clawed at his arm and struggled for breath.

"You're choking her," Brit yelled.

Fowler eased up enough for her to draw a breath deep into her air-starved lungs. She tried to see what he was doing out of the corner of her eye, but he had the muzzle of his revolver pressed against her temple.

"Chance, you take your Apache and back out that door. Then turn around so I've got a good view of your back. Now!"

Fowler sidled along the wall, keeping his revolver pressed to Callista's temple. Callista would have kicked backward, trying to knock him off-balance, but his finger was on a cocked trigger. She didn't dare.

He pulled her out the door with him. As they

passed Brit, Fowler swung his revolver at the side of Brit's head. Brit went down in a limp heap. Callista was too shocked to react and in the next second, the muzzle was pressed against her temple again.

It was raining hard when Fowler pulled her off the porch.

"Mount," he yelled, grabbing her by the shoulder and her skirt and throwing her up on one of the two horses at the hitching rail. He mounted the other, grabbed her reins, and sent the horses galloping away.

Callista grabbed the horn and held on. She knew that when he regained consciousness, Brit would come after her. And when he caught Fowler—

Right now her father and Russ would be organizing a pursuit. But it didn't matter how many men they sent galloping after Fowler; she had no doubt in her mind that it would be Brit who found them.

Their horses galloped down the Tombstone road. Callista listened for the sound of hooves behind them, but the rain drowned out any other noise. She was soaked. Her hair hung down, and her shirt was plastered to her breasts. Steam rose from the horses. And the rain washed out their hoofprints as fast as the horses made them.

By the time the rain began to ease up, they were many miles from Fort Bowie. And their pursuers wouldn't know in which direction they'd gone.

They rode hard all night and most of the next day. The horses were staggering when Fowler halted at Brit's ranch house.

"Are you crazy?" she said, when he pulled her off her horse.

"On the contrary—I'm brilliant." His hand was hard on her arm as he shoved her toward the house.

"They'll never think to look for me here."

"Brit'll look for you here." She stumbled up the two steps to the porch. "Because he'll figure out where you think you'll be safe."

"Shut up or I'll gag you." He shoved her inside and pushed her down on a chair and tied her to it.

"I've got enough money stashed away in Mexico for a good life," Fowler bragged. Then he smiled a thoroughly evil smile as he looked at her. Callista tensed, ready to fight him as she'd never fought anyone.

He just laughed and went into the bedroom and went to sleep on Brit's bed. The bed where she and Brit had made love.

A cold fury such as she'd never known filled her, and she was waiting for him when he awakened hours later and came out, yawning. He drew his dirty fingers down her cheek in a parody of a caress. She jerked her head away.

"Make me something to eat, bitch," he said, untying her hands. "And get some coffee made quick."

Callista stood up slowly, rubbing her hands to get blood circulating in them. She was stiff and sore from being tied and from the hard riding.

She poured coffee beans in the grinder and turned it round and round. "You made a big mistake this time, Fowler," she said in a conversational tone. By the time she was through, Fowler would be spooked and running for his life. "Brit is related to an Apache. And his Apache relatives will be looking for you. Do you know what they'll do when they find you? Do you know how long it will take you to die?"

"Bitch!" He swung her around, and she saw his fist coming up—

When Callista came to, she was lying on the floor of the bedroom. And Fowler had forgotten to tie her. She listened for noise from the other room, but it was silent.

He was gone. But for how long?

She sat up cautiously, aware of a splitting headache. And bumped her foot against the ladder under Brit's bed. Quickly she set it up against the trapdoor leading to the roof. Then she opened the wardrobe, removed half of the floor and shimmied through into the tunnel. Pulling the floor back, so the tunnel entrance was hidden again, she crawled down the tunnel as fast as she could. When she stood up in the underbrush and trees, she watched the house and barn for Fowler. When he finally returned near sunset, he went inside, then in a few minutes ran out. He looked around, then ran to the barn, to see if the other horse was there. It was.

Finally, scratching his head, he went inside again. *Now* she'd take the other horse and skedaddle.

As she stood up, a hand clamped over her mouth, while a brawny arm pulled her backward into the bushes and laid her out flat on the ground. Brit knelt over her, and she looked up into his beloved gray eyes.

He lifted his hand from her mouth. "Sorry, but I didn't have time to warn you I was there. Are you all right?" He watched the house.

"I'm fine now that you're here." She sat up and gave him a big kiss on his cheek.

"Thanks, sweetheart." He did a double take. "The hell you're fine," he growled in a voice she'd never heard before. Tenderly he touched the purple bruise that was spreading up from her chin. "What else did the bastard do?"

"Nothing. He didn't dare touch me! I told him your Apache relatives would come after him." She rose on her knees and hugged him.

He glanced at the house, keeping it under surveillance. "And he believed you?" He wrapped his arm around her and kept her nestled against his side.

"You better believe it. How did you know where to look?"

"I asked myself where a scared smuggler, carting around a woman who was ten times smarter than he was and who was probably quietly sabotaging him at every turn, would go. Where would he think he was safe? And I came here."

He swept her against his side and kissed her. "Cally, I was worried about you," he admitted softly.

"I was worried about *you*." She feathered a trail of kisses along the purple bruise that started on his cheek and disappeared into his thick, coffee black hair.

She glanced around. "Are you alone?"

"Uh-huh. Your father sent patrols out in each direction looking for you. But I wanted it to be alone— just him and me."

A shot rang out, and Brit watched the house tensely. No other shots followed.

"That shot came from the house. Stay here. I'm going to investigate." He carried his rifle and moved cautiously away. Then she lost sight of him.

He returned in a few minutes. "Fowler's dead. He went up on the roof, and either fell or jumped off and broke his neck. That was his rifle going off when it hit the ground."

"He slept in your bed."

"I'll burn it when I get back." She had said *your* bed, not *our* bed. Did that mean anything?

She'd heard Fowler accuse her father of being a fellow smuggler. Had she believed him? With only Warwick left alive, he would be court-martialed as an example to everyone else thinking of doing the same thing. What would she do?

He brushed a light kiss across her temple as they walked arm in arm toward his horse.

"Let's go back to Fort Bowie."

He wanted to add, *my love*, but didn't.

Callista was heartsick. Brit had still not said he loved her. In fact, he hadn't talked about any future. Was there none with him? None at all?

When they returned to Fort Bowie, riders were forming columns on the parade ground, and other troopers were loading pack mules with supplies. Knowing her father would be in the thick of things, Callista stopped at headquarters with Brit.

"Hi, Sargeant Mac," she said as they walked in. The door to her father's office was open and she saw that he wasn't there. "Where's my father?"

The sergeant stood up. "He's—" He looked at Brit. "Sir, I should talk to you."

Callista backed up a step as a cold premonition went through her. "What happened? Is my father dead?"

"No, ma'am, but your father was wounded and—"

"Badly?" Callista whispered, reaching for Brit's hand.

"He'll live, ma'am, no fear on that account." His gaze met Brit's again.

"But—?" Brit said, squeezing her hand in support.

"The bullet hit him in the back, ma'am. He doesn't

have any feeling in his legs." Sergeant Mac's blue
eyes were full of sympathy.

"Oh, my God," Callista murmured. Brit wrapped
his arm around her shoulders as she blindly put out
her other hand, reaching for his strength. "Where is
he?"

"At home, ma'am."

"I've got to go to him." Callista felt as if she were
fighting her way through a thick fog that was clinging
to her, slowing every movement she made, even as
her brain raced like a runaway train.

Within minutes, she was hurrying up the steps to
her father's house. Brit strode along beside her, his
hand on her elbow.

Josephina opened the door as if she'd been watching for them and pointed toward her father's study.
Callista stopped then, and held Brit's hand to absorb
his strength, for she knew she'd need it. Finally, she
raised her head. "Wait for me," she whispered.
"Please."

He nodded. "I'll be in the parlor."

Brit watched her pause at the door before she
opened it and went in.

He'd been prepared for Callista's anger at her father's court-martial when he testified against him. But
it was something he'd known was coming, something
that he had to meet head-on if he had any respect for
himself—or for Callista. And it was something he
could fight.

But her father's paralysis was entirely different. He
could have fought against Callista's anger, but there
was no anger here—only pain and sorrow. And he
had no way of fighting them.

He'd lost Callista the second that her father had
been shot, he realized. He'd known all along that

he'd lose her, but he hadn't known how, hadn't known that it would be something he couldn't even fight.

Josephina brought him a tray with a pot of coffee.

Over the hours, he lost track of the cups of coffee and was reduced to reading Dickens, whom he hated. The sun went down, and still she didn't come. He was standing at the window, staring into the darkness and nursing another of the endless cups of coffee, when he caught a whiff of her scent. He turned as she walked into the room. ·

Her shoulders were straight, and she seemed all right, but her eyes were too bright when she stopped in front of him. Silently he held out his half-drunk coffee, and she drank it as if it were whiskey.

"Things are coming along fine, Brit, just fine."

Her voice was a shade too high, too confident. She had a brittle look, as if she'd shatter if he touched her. He took the coffee cup from her fingers and put it down on the table, then gently drew her against him.

He closed his arms around her and stroked her back and rubbed his chin against her hair. "It'll be all right, Callista," he soothed.

She straightened away from him. "No," she said in a dead tone that frightened him. "It won't be all right. It will never be all right again."

Callista picked up the empty coffee cup and turned it around and around in her hands. "It's because of Wickwar that we're here, you know," she said in the same despairing voice.

"Nonsense. R.C. Wickwar doesn't have anything to do with your father." Her head was bowed with despair, and he wanted to sweep her into his arms and make everything be all right.

"Yes, he does. Papa told me months ago that if it hadn't been for Wickwar, we wouldn't have left Washington."

Brit clasped her shoulders and pulled her against himself. "Callista, your father is an adult. He made his own choices. You did the right thing by exposing the fraud. You had no reason to believe it involved your father, and you still don't. Only an offhand comment by your father makes you wonder."

She stayed board-stiff. "It's okay, you can lean against me," he whispered, brushing his cheek over her hair.

She shook her head and pushed him away. "No. I can't." She closed her eyes for a long second, as if drawing on her inner strength. "Don't you see, I can't. If I lean now, I'll never stop leaning. And I have to be the strong one now."

He took the coffee cup from her hands before she dropped it. "I understand. But you can't always be the strong one." He started to hold out his hand to her, then stopped and slowly dropped it. "I'm here for you. You have to know that, my Cally."

She nodded. Moving to the other window, she wrapped her arms tightly around herself, as if to hold in her emotions, and stared out at the darkness. "I can't leave my father in this condition."

"I expected that. After all, you love him."

Brit watched her reflection in the window. A single tear rolled down her cheek. "I want you to forget me, Brit, and go on with your life."

"Nonsense. I realize that you're under a terrible strain. You don't have to make any decisions. I wouldn't want you to, anyway. Just know that I'm here, and I'll wait for you no matter how long it takes."

"No!" She whirled and her face was stark white.

"Don't wait for me! It could be months, years." She lifted her hands, palms up, in a helpless gesture. "I don't know how long. Please, go on with your life."

She was telling him that they had no chance of a future. No chance at all. Anguish knifed through him. His grip tightened on the cup. The Wedgwood shattered in his hand.

He looked down at the white pieces, broken into shards, just like their future.

Callista knelt to pick them up. He knelt, too, trying to think how he could reason with her. "Callista, I—" She looked up at him with eyes dark with despair, and he knew he couldn't get through to her.

"Callista, I won't leave you." He held out his hand for the broken china.

"You have to! Don't you understand that if I know you're waiting for me, I'll be torn apart every minute of every day all those years? I want you to find happiness, not to wait for me." She dropped the broken pieces into his hand, then gently closed them around the china. "Please, Brit."

"I'll be at the ranch. Just send word when you need me. When, Callista—not if."

She nodded and stood up, afraid to look at him, afraid she'd cry out her love for him. "Go," she finally got out.

He walked out on the veranda, and she followed him. Brit didn't look back as he strode to his horse— he didn't dare. He paused, looking down at the china he still held. He could glue the pieces of a coffee cup back together again, but he couldn't glue their future back together.

He threw the broken bits down, mounted, and rode off as fast as he could.

Men didn't cry. Not even when they lost their love.

* * *

Callista watched him go with tears streaming down her face. "Good-bye, my love," she whispered.

She walked to where he'd thrown the broken china down and carefully picked up the pieces. They were the last thing he'd touched before he rode out of her life.

Then she straightened her shoulders, turned, and walked back into the house. The house where all her father's dreams had died. And now hers had, too.

They returned to Galena, to the two-story house on the corner where Callista had been born and where they'd lived periodically through the years. But this time it was forever.

Callista and her mother opened up the big house, and whisked the sheets off the furniture and began a dusting and cleaning like the old house hadn't seen in years.

Callista's father was ensconced in the parlor, so he was in the thick of things. He was always in pain, and with his pain came irritability. The worse things got, the more Callista knew she couldn't leave her mother alone to tend to her father.

Every day, her hopes for a rancher and ranch in Arizona grew less, while her pain and her memories remained. More nights then not, she cried herself to sleep, weeping for the future that she would never have.

The days became weeks, the weeks became months, and she tried not to think of the years that stretched ahead. She had to stay, had to take care of her father, for she could not have lived with herself if she had followed her heart and left her family.

Even if it meant she lost the man she loved.

Chapter 23

Brit mounted Red and went home. Home to an empty house on an empty ranch owned by a rancher with an empty heart.

He told himself he'd shared his life with her for only a few golden weeks. He told himself he'd just grown accustomed to feeling her softness curled against him in the night, to listening to her laughter, to smelling her lilac scent.

Soon, he reassured himself, he'd grow accustomed to reaching for her in the night and finding her gone, to hearing the wind instead of her laughter, to smelling sagebrush instead of lilacs.

But he didn't.

Brit took care of his small herd of cattle and built fences and cut firewood for winter and stacked adobe bricks one upon the next. And ten times a day, he looked up from the slowly rising adobe walls of the ranch house he was building on the canyon rim for his bride.

Only now she'd never see it.

It was December, and an icy wind blew down from the high country, and gray clouds heavy with snow scudded across the sky. He worked until last light, finishing the roof of his new adobe home, making it weathertight for winter's chill.

But the chill in his heart went deeper than winter.

He opened the door of his ranch house and walked across the dark room, to the table where he'd left the lantern. Halfway across the room, he thought he caught a whiff of lilacs and froze.

"Callista?"

No one answered him. He heard only his own breathing.

Striking a match, he fumbled with the lantern and lit it. Holding it up, he turned a slow circle. But he was the only one in the room. He and memories of the woman he loved.

"Smelling lilacs, were you, Brit? Must have been your imagination," he chided himself as disappointment slashed through him.

Gathering an armful of firewood from the stack on the porch, he brought it in and laid it in the stone fireplace. But before he lit it, he stopped and stared off into the darkness.

The scent of lilacs had left his heart longing for Callista. She'd broken through his armor and become part of him. As breath was part of him. As his heart was part of him. His life was gray without her sunshine.

He slammed his fist down on the table. "Dammit, I need you, Callista. And I'm not letting you go without a fight."

Walking into the bedroom, he quickly threw clothes into his saddlebags. Then he walked out to the corral and saddled Red.

Brit rode into Fort Bowie two days later and went directly to the commandant's house. When he knocked, the door was opened by a brown-haired woman he'd never seen before.

"I'm looking for Callista Warwick," he said, sweeping his hat off.

"She's gone. She and her mother returned to the East with Colonel Warwick."

"Gone? Where? How long ago?" Of course they'd gone. He should have realized they'd leave.

"They left months ago. I'm sorry, I don't know where."

"Thank you, ma'am." Brit replaced his hat and walked down the steps.

He had that pain-in-his-side can't-take-a-deep-breath feeling that he'd had when he was shot. She was gone. He'd waited too long, and now he'd lost her.

She'd never see the home he'd built for her. Their babies would never rock in the cradle he'd made for them. His heart would never be whole again.

He swung up on his horse and turned him toward the cantina.

But before he got there, he reined Red in. Callista had talked about the town they always went back to. It was in Illinois and . . . had something to do with U.S. Grant. Where was Grant from?

Galena! That was it!

Had she gone back there this time, too? It was worth a try. Anything was better than losing her without fighting for her. Forever was a long time.

A week later he boarded the eastbound train in Flagstaff, Arizona. He changed trains in Chicago, and finally, he stepped off the train at the redbrick station in Galena, Illinois.

A Christmas tree glowed prettily with all its candles in the town square across from the station.

There was already a light dusting of snow as he went into the stationmaster's office and made inquiries about the Warwick family. It began to snow harder as he strode along the redbrick streets. Big elm trees arched winter-naked limbs high overhead. The two-story houses glowed with cheery yellow light.

A buggy went by, the bells on the horse's harness jingling merrily in the cold night.

Finally, he came to the house he was looking for. A two-story gray-blue with white trim, it stood on a large corner lot. Every window on the first floor shed a welcoming glow of golden light.

He walked up the stone steps, then turned the bell handle in the middle of the wide door and heard it chime inside.

Callista finished packing her suitcase and looked around her bedroom. In the weeks since Papa had died, she'd thought about Brit almost continuously.

She had found the man she'd love for the rest of her life and almost lost him. She'd tasted both grief and glory with him.

He had never mentioned marriage, or even love for that matter, but she didn't think the fireworks that happened when they made love could have happened if he didn't love her. Their loving in that little jewel of a valley had been extraordinary. It had been like the spectacular explosions of the grand finale every Fourth of July.

In the weeks since she'd seen him, she'd hungered for his voice and touch and kiss. She'd gone to sleep with his name on her lips and in her heart, and awakened the same way.

And she'd come to realize that no matter how few days they had together, Brit was worth it. If they had a year or ten or forty, she would love him with all her heart.

She picked up her suitcase, opened her bedroom door, and walked to the top of the stairs.

What would he say when she appeared on his doorstep?

"Letty, I'll be in Arizona at—"

The doorbell chimed, and Letty rushed to answer it.

He heard voices, one of which sounded like Callista's, but he didn't dare hope. Not after the phantom lilacs in his ranch house.

A maid opened the door. "Yes?"

"I'm looking for Callista Warwick."

"Who shall I tell her is calling?"

"Her future husband."

"I'll take care of this, Letty." Callista's voice was too cool and too calm.

Brit looked up to find her near the top of a curved staircase, watching him as she descended. She was wearing mourning black and her hair was pulled back in one of those prissy tight knots he hated and she looked wonderful and he wanted to sweep her into his arms and kiss her.

His mouth went dry with love and longing for her. After that first clash of eyes, she didn't meet his gaze.

"Why don't we go in here?" She opened the sliding doors to a parlor and walked stiffly all the way across the room before she turned to face him.

Brit studied her composed features. She stood behind the hunter green sofa, resting her hands on its back. He realized she was putting it between them as a barrier.

"Why don't you have a seat?" She nodded at a wing chair close to him.

"Callista, I—" Lord, he wanted her in his arms. "Why are you in mourning?"

"My father died three weeks ago."

"I'm very sorry."

"Thank you."

They were speaking meaningless formalities when she should be in his arms.

"Callista, I came here because I—" He was holding his hat by the brim, and the snow on it melted and slid off with a plop. He looked down at the puddles forming around his boots. "Callista, I need you." He looked up and caught the sheen of tears in her eyes. "What is it?" he asked, stepping toward her.

She shook her head. "Nothing."

"Callista, I followed you to Galena because I love you and I want you and I want you to come home with me."

"W-would you say that again?" she whispered.

"I love you. You know that." Why did she still look so unhappy? "And I know you love me," he continued, "because you told me so."

"Yes. I love you." Her lower lip quivered, and she turned away, to stare out the window at the snow-flakes swirling into white clouds.

He crossed the room on cat's feet, and clasped her shoulders with his big hands. "We love each other. So let's get married." *What was wrong*?

"Brit, do you think you could give up being a hero?" she asked in an unsteady voice. She rubbed her cheek against his hand.

"I have told you over and over again: I'm not a hero."

She shook her head. "It's your deeds that count, not your words."

"Deeds, huh?" He pointed to the sofa. "Sit down there, lady, and listen," he ordered.

"W-what?"

"Sit down," he snapped. "There."

She sat down at the very edge of the cushions, ready to bounce up and flee.

He leaned an elbow on the mantel above the fireplace and pinned her with a narrowed gaze. "Picture this: a wilderness full of Apaches who don't like White-eyes. Would you agree that someone who could flee but stays to help a wounded buddy in such a situation is a hero?"

Her brow furrowed. "Yes, of course. That's the definition of a hero: someone who helps at great risk to themselves, even when they don't have to."

"Good. That makes you a hero."

She bounced up. "Me? Are you crazy? I'm a devout coward."

He pinned her with his hard-eyed glare and slowly walked toward her.

She backed around the sofa, watching him.

"Did you get the bullet out of me when I was shot?" He kept coming.

"Yes." She kept backing until she came up against the wall.

"Did you take a horse and get out of Apache country like I told you to?" He rested a hand against the wall beside her head.

"No."

"Did you abandon me when you saw Apaches had found our camp?" He rested his other hand against the wall on the other side of her head.

"Of course not!"

"I rest my case. You, Callista Warwick, are a hero. You are *my* hero."

"No." She gave him a wide-eyed look of astonishment. "I'm not a hero. I was scared to death in all those situations. That first day, when I was huddled behind boulders, so frightened I couldn't move or speak, I saw you ride your horse into the Apaches and rout them.

"That was when I understood the real difference between people like me and people like David and you. Fear frightens me."

His eyes narrowed. "Let me get this straight: heroes don't feel fear like normal people do?"

"Yes."

"You should have felt the way my heart was pounding, Callista. I was damn scared when I rode Red into the Apaches. Everyone feels fear! You're a hero because you do what has to be done in spite of the fear."

"I'm not a hero."

"Sorry, but you're wrong. You're a hero." He sniffed behind her ear and smelled lilacs—and Cally. "However, even though you are a hero, I'm willing to marry you." He nuzzled her throat. "I'll get three for one: you, a hero, and R.C. Wickwar."

She smiled, even as she pushed him away. "Don't be ridiculous. I'm just me."

"And that is exactly how I feel when you call me a hero: I'm just me." He studied her for several heartbeats. "A man who loves you, very much."

"I never thought about it that way, Brit." She focused on the lapels of his jacket, smoothing her hands over them. "So you're saying that if I think it's absurd when you call me a hero, you find it just as silly when I call you a hero."

"Whatever you say," he murmured as he showered kisses across her lips. "I'm trying to get you to realize how baseless your fears are."

"Wait." She put up her hand to stop him. "Brit, I can't think when you do that."

"Good." He rained kisses across her cheeks. "I'm planning on being around for many, many years, Cally."

"Do you think you could be home for dinner every night?" Her hands slid inside his jacket and moved over the thick muscles on his chest with tantalizing pressure.

"I can't promise that I would be home every night, but I can promise that I would try to be. Especially if you were waiting for me. *Now* will you marry me?"

She walked past him into the hall and called, "Letty, would you bring my suitcase down?"

The maid brought it in, curtsied, and withdrew.

"What's that for?" Wasn't she ever going to answer his question? A man could die waiting for an answer.

She pulled a piece of paper out of her pocket and waved it at him. "This is my ticket to Arizona. I was coming to you."

"You were?" Stunned, he raked his fingers through his hair. "Does that mean . . . ?"

"Yes." She laughed and opened her arms to him. "A thousand times, yes."

He swept her into his arms.

Chapter 24

Dispatch to the *Times/Tribune* Newspapers

I know, dear readers, that you are impatient to find out what has happened since my last dispatch.

Our hero, Lieutenant Britton Chance, and this reporter were involved in the capture of the persons responsible for selling weapons to the Apaches. Without a supply of guns, many renegades have now stopped their raiding and returned to the reservation.

Mr. Chance is returning to civilian life. There is much to do at his ranch, as well as interceding for the Apaches in various capacities, which he wishes to do. This will be my last dispatch from Fort Bowie, Arizona Territory.

You see, tomorrow I am marrying Mr. Chance. When next I report to you, I will be Callista Warwick Chance, reporting about ranch life in the wilderness of Arizona.

Until we meet again, dear readers, this is Callista Warwick signing off. Farewell. Godspeed.

They were married in the chapel at Fort Bowie. Callista wore a white-lace dress and Brit his dress uniform.

Daisy and Jack came, and Ethan and Aurora Win-

369

throp brought Pincus Jones. Ethan was his brother's best man. Afterward, they walked out of the chapel under the raised swords of all the officers at Fort Bowie.

They had to pause on the top step while Pincus Jones took their picture. His flash explosion startled the horses near the chapel, and three ran away with Callista's ex-students in hot pursuit, yelling and waving their arms, terrorizing the poor animals even more.

After everything quieted down, Callista shook her head. "I hope that isn't a harbinger of what our marriage is going to be like."

"I hope it *is* a harbinger of what our marriage is going to be like," Brit said. "Full of chaos and surprises and laughter and life. What more could you ask for?"

Callista wrapped her arms around his arm and leaned against him. "How did you get to be so wise?"

"I fell in love with a wonderful woman."

They honeymooned in the new house Brit had built on the rim above their valley. The outer walls were up, and the roof was in place. Inside, only the bedroom had walls.

And they were half walls. "So we can see out," Brit said as he carried her over the dirt where the threshold would be.

He carried her into their new bedroom and set her down near their brand-new bed. Callista walked to the hole where the window would be. "But we're so far away from the stream for bathing."

"Not quite." Brit came up behind her and wrapped his arms around her. "Did you see that windmill I put in? I also put in a water pipeline. The windmill will pump the water up to a pool outside our bedroom door."

"Oh, Brit, how did I get so lucky?" She clasped her hands over his.

"If you want to get comfortable and take off your formal clothes, I'll start a fire in our bedroom fireplace." He smiled at her. "I like the sound of that. Our ranch. Our house. Our fireplace."

"I do, too. But it's getting toward sunset. Shouldn't we feed the horses? Then you won't have to go out again later."

He gave her a smile that would have melted an iceberg. "Are you planning on seducing me, Mrs. Chance?"

"Maybe, Mr. Chance." Her smile was sunshine and love, beckoning to him.

They drove the buckboard down to the finished barn. He gripped Callista's waist and swung her down.

"Why don't you get the hay, and I'll do the oats," she said.

"Fine by me. We'll get done in half the time."

Inside, Brit had just thrown hay in the manger in the first stall when Callista asked, "Brit, have you ever had a dog?

He paused and smiled over his shoulder at her. "Once. A long time ago." He turned at the sound of a high-pitched squeaking. "What's that?"

"I'll go look. You keep feeding."

In a few moments, Callista tapped him on the shoulder. When he turned around, she held a fluffy black-and-white border collie puppy in her arms. "I haven't given you your wedding present yet," she said with a shy smile.

"Hi, guy," he said softly, taking him from her arms. "What's his name?"

"Whatever you name him." She was willing to bet she knew what it would be.

He held the dog up nose to nose, and the puppy licked him with a bright pink tongue. "I think we'll call you Dog." He raised an eyebrow at her. "If that's all right with you?"

"I think Dog is a perfect name."

Something in her voice made him look, really look, at her. "You know about Dog, don't you?"

She nodded. And tried not to cry for that little boy Brit had been.

He rested his arm over her shoulders. "I'm not alone anymore. I have you. Come on, Dog." He put him down. "Let's see how you do while I feed." And he walked off with the puppy running and tumbling at his heels.

"Finished?" she called as she put the last measure of oats in a manger in the last stall.

"Meet me at the door." The puppy rode in the crook of his arm, looking quite contented. "He's too young to leave down here among the horses," he explained.

"I know. That's why Jack is sitting up on that hill, waiting for me to signal him to come get Dog. He and Daisy will keep him until we've got a safe place for him."

"Jack and Daisy were in on this?"

"How do you think he got in the barn?"

He laughed. "You are amazing, woman." He pulled her close with his other arm and kissed her soundly. "Hey, Jack," he yelled loud enough to be heard in the next county. "Meet us up at the house and have a drink before you leave."

After Jack and Dog left, Brit stretched out his long legs, laced his fingers behind his head, and contemplated Callista, who was sitting in the rocking chair Daisy and Jack had given them. "I haven't given you your wedding present yet."

"You've made me happy. What more could I want?"

"How about this?" In her lap, he laid a certificate good for twenty-five lilac bushes in the spring.

"Oh, Brit, what a wonderful idea." She pulled him down and kissed him. "In a few years our whole home will be perfumed by the lilacs in May."

"And this." He took a small, blue-velvet box off the fireplace mantel and brought it to her. "I hope you like it."

She opened the box and found an amethyst necklace. "Brit, it's lovely," she whispered. "Put it on me, please." She stood up and turned her back and lifted her long, flowing hair up, out of the way.

Brit fastened the necklace carefully. Then turned her around. "You are beautiful, with or without the amethysts."

"And I love you, with or without the amethysts," she murmured against his throat. "I would have loved it as much if you'd bought cows for our ranch."

"Uh-uh. I can't see myself kissing a girl with a necklace of cows." He dropped a tiny kiss on the tip of her nose. "Somehow, it doesn't have the same feel."

Callista giggled and kissed him back. "That's one of the things I love about you—laughing with you."

"Good." He kissed the shoulder hollow on each side of her throat, then he sniffed her satin-soft skin. "You smell of lilacs and sunshine and life and babies-to-be."

"Hmmm . . . I'll be back in a few minutes."

In the bedroom, Callista changed into the negligee she'd bought as a surprise for Brit. It was a delicate purple of the finest, most transparent silk she'd ever seen. It covered, but didn't hide. The V–front went to the waist and was laced with deep purple velvet ribbons. She tightened them and tied them at her waist.

Then she went to the doorway. He was staring into the fire.

"Brit," she said softly.

He turned and, slow as honey in December, looked her up and down. She began to blush.

"Callista," he rumbled, but there was a note of awe in his voice. "I can see your blush through the gown."

He rose and came to her. With one shaking finger he traced the swells of her breasts, then touched the lacing. "This looks rather complicated."

"I'm sure you'll be able to figure it out," she said, already beginning to feel breathless.

He swiftly stripped off his clothes, and in moments was naked and aroused. His eyes alight with silver fire, he closed his arms around her.

The breath thickened in her throat as she felt the springy curls on his chest. His arousal pressed against her belly. A wave of primitive exhilaration swept over her, making her blood run hot and fast.

This was where she was meant to be—in Brit's arms. They had all the tomorrows in the world, in each other's arms.

He traced the ribbon and lacing over her breasts, then he untied it and slowly slid it out of the eyelets, letting the velvet caress her body. The V spread wider and wider.

He brushed away the silk and filled his hands with

her breasts. "Put your arms around my neck and kiss me," he murmured.

And she did. Her bones began to melt as his thumbs brushed her nipples, and she gave a tiny sigh as his hands moved over her.

"My God, Callista, you're satin and silk and fire," he murmured.

Just when she knew her legs would no longer hold her, he swung her up in his arms and carried her to the bed.

He came to her in a rush of need and passion and wanting. She was ready, longing for him, and he moved in and out, going faster and faster as she arched up to take all of him.

Callista climbed higher and higher on that spiral of throbbing tension. He slipped one hand between them and ran his finger over the throne of her passion, and she shattered.

"B-Brit!" She gasped as waves of pleasure shimmered through her.

"Cally!" He felt her contractions closing around him, and he soared with her.

She was laughing and gasping and crying at once. "How can it keep getting better and better?"

"Because I love you more and more, every moment of every day. You are my sunshine, my laughter, my life." He separated the words with tender kisses. "You, Callista Warwick Chance, are my lady."

Dear Reader,

Whether you love contemporary romance or historical romance, Avon can satisfy your need for unforgettable love stories.

First, there's *The Maiden Bride* by Linda Needham. When widowed Lady Eleanor arrives at the castle of the husband she'd never met, she's shocked to find the place deserted. But then a mesmerizing intruder tells her to leave. The man is Lord Nicholas, back from the Crusades, and shocked to find the bride he thought he'd lost is now very much alive . . .

If you love contemporary romance don't miss *One Summer's Night* by Mary Alice Kruesi. Laurel has always done everything for everyone else, but now she has the opportunity of a lifetime to leave all that behind—so she grabs it, and along the way meets enigmatic Dane. Their passion grows, and she must choose between new-found love . . . and her former life.

If you can't get enough of rough-and-tumble men of the west, then *The Renegades: Nick* by Genell Dellin is just the book for you! He's a half-Cherokee outlaw on the run from the law. She's a determined young woman, trying to make a new life for herself. Together, Nick and Callie share a passion as wild as the west itself.

In *The Abduction of Julia* by Karen Hawkins, the fifth Viscount Hunterston elopes with the *wrong* woman. His plans for marriage are turned upside down . . . now that he's forced to wed do-gooder Julia Frant! Then Julia sets about to transform this rake into a respectable husband.

Happy reading!

Lucia Macro

Lucia Macro
Senior Editor

AEL 0300

Avon Romances—
the best in exceptional authors
and unforgettable novels!

THE DUKE'S RETURN   by Malia Martin
79898-0/ $5.99 US/ $7.99 Can

A KNIGHT'S VOW   by Gayle Callen
80494-8/ $5.99 US/ $7.99 Can

COURTING CLAIRE   by Linda O'Brien
80207-4/ $5.99 US/ $7.99 Can

MY LORD DESTINY   by Eve Byron
80365-8/ $5.99 US/ $7.99 Can

THE TAMING OF JESSI ROSE   by Beverly Jenkins
79865-4/ $5.99 US/ $7.99 Can

HIGHLAND LAIRDS TRILOGY:
THE MACLEAN GROOM   by Kathleen Harrington
80727-0/ $5.99 US/ $7.99 Can

THE SEDUCER   by Margaret Evans Porter
80772-6/ $5.99 US/ $7.99 Can

SCOUNDREL FOR HIRE   by Adrienne deWolfe
80527-8/ $5.99 US/ $7.99 Can

AN UNLIKELY OUTLAW   by Rebecca Wade
81021-2/ $5.99 US/ $7.99 Can

HIGHLAND BRIDES:
HIGHLAND HAWK   by Lois Greiman
80367-4/ $5.99 US/ $7.99 Can

MAIL-ORDER BRIDE   by Maureen McKade
80285-6/ $5.99 US/ $7.99 Can

Buy these books at your local bookstore or use this coupon for ordering:

Mail to: Avon Books/HarperCollins Publishers, P.O. Box 588, Scranton, PA 18512
Please send me the book(s) I have checked above.
❑ My check or money order—no cash or CODs please—for $_____ is enclosed (please add $1.50 per order to cover postage and handling—U.S. residents add applicable state sale tax, Canadian residents add 7% GST). U.S. and Canada residents make checks payable HarperCollins Publishers Inc.
❑ Charge my VISA/MC Acct#_____ Exp Date_____
Minimum credit card order is two books or $7.50 (please add postage and handling charge of $1.50 per order—U.S. residents add applicable state sales tax, Canadian residents add 7% GST). For faster service, call 1-800-331-3761. Prices and numbers are subject to change without notice. Please allow six to eight weeks for delivery.
Name_____
Address_____
City_____ State/Zip_____
Telephone No._____   ROM 129